# BENEATH THE FLOWERING FLAMBOYANTS

# BENEATH THE
# *Flowering*
# FLAMBOYANTS

## *Bev Clarke*

iUniverse, Inc.
Bloomington

# Beneath the Flowering Flamboyants

iUniverse books may be ordered through booksellers or by contacting:

iUniverse
1663 Liberty Drive
Bloomington, IN 47403
www.iuniverse.com
1-800-Authors (1-800-288-4677)

Because of the dynamic nature of the Internet, any Web addresses or links contained in this book may have changed since publication and may no longer be valid. The views expressed in this work are solely those of the author and do not necessarily reflect the views of the publisher, and the publisher hereby disclaims any responsibility for them.

ISBN: 978-1-4502-6286-6 (sc)
ISBN: 978-1-4502-6287-3 (ebk)

Printed in the United States of America

iUniverse rev. date: 12/06/2010

# 1

C lytie Prescott carefully adjusted her glasses to get a better look at the woman and the two little girls who were climbing the steps to the shop. Perspiration saturated their clothing and the sweat which had settled in beads on their foreheads now ran down the sides of their faces. She had never seen them before and wasn't sure what to think of the whole thing because white people on the island never entered the local shops. That was the duty of their servants.

"Howdy," said the woman taking a handkerchief from her pocket and drying her face.

"Howdy," replied Clytie looking from the woman to the girls. "What can I do for you?"

"Give me a pound of flour, a bottle of white rum and a pack of Trumpeter cigarettes," she said digging deeply into her pocket.

Clytie placed the items on the counter while still observing the threesome.

"Ma I want a polar lolly," said the little girl who looked about seven years old.

"If I buy one for you, then I got to buy one for your sister and I don't have no money for that."

1

"But Ma I'm thirsty," protested the child.

"When we pass by the standpipe, you can drink as much water as you want. Look at your sister Jackie. She don't beg for nothing and she is much younger than you. Why you don't learn to behave? How much I got for you?" she asked turning to Clytie.

"A dollar ten!"

The little girl whose name was Heather started to cry, all the while cleaning her face and nose on the sleeve of her dress, as her mother went about her business simply ignoring her. Clytie went to the fridge and returned with two polar lollies and handed one to each child who immediately ripped the paper off and proceeded to lick them.

"You tell the lady thanks?" shouted the mother.

"Thanks ma'am," they said almost in unison.

"I never seen you around here before," said Clytie.

"We live in the next village. Over there by the cliff!"

"We just moved out there," said the younger of the two children.

"She asked you that?" shouted the woman.

"That is a real long walk in this hot sun," said Clytie. "It isn't that I don't want you to come here but there got another shop closer to you. Right there by Austin corner."

"I know. I used to go in there, but they are real malicious. They are always asking a lot of questions," she said turning to leave.

"Alright, but you make haste and get home out of the hot midday sun," replied Clytie, taking a cue from what the woman said and not asking any more questions.

She watched them walk away; the children walking happily behind the woman and licking their lollies, as she quickened her pace with her parcels neatly tucked under her arm. The children's skins were red, their hair brown and straggly and tied into unruly pony tails which cascaded down their backs.

"The father must be a overseer because I never see them before," Clytie said aloud.

"Who was that?" asked Miss Una from behind the cash cage. "I didn't recognize the voices and I know every soul that come into this shop."

"I don't know them Ma. Never see them before. It was a young white woman with two little children. She could be 'bout twenty five or thirty years old. "

"Could be the children from the Henley plantation," said Miss Una.

"I don't think so Ma. The little girl say that they just move up here, and they calling the woman Ma. I don't think she is from here because she was talking with a little bit of a twang."

"Well we are going find out sooner or later. Nothing don't remain a secret around here for too long. I think that after I have my lunch, I am going to sit out back and rest my old body. I don't understand it. I just can't do as much as I used to."

"What you expect Ma? You are eighty five years old."

"My old mother pass away at ninety one and she was still carrying a bucket on the top of her head 'til just before she left this earth."

"You should lie down and get some rest after lunch and I would do the rest here by myself. Don't forget that Nora comes by every Tuesday afternoon to help out."

"You trying to get rid of me Clytie. What you up to?"

"What I up to Ma?"

"It is for me to know. Girl I ain't see Nellie nor Francis all this week. They like they forget we still live here Clytie."

"Ma you know Nellie got a lot to do. She is still looking after the school and now she running 'round on church business. Then sometimes she does look after Douglas to give Emily a break."

"If she is doing all that, tell me where she finding time for Francis? Francis is a good looking man, so she better be careful. It isn't good to neglect your husband."

"Ma I tell you already that Francois belong to all those organizations too and he really like looking after Douglas. But Ma he only got eyes for Nels."

"Yes but she got to find more time for Francis. You know that one o'them other women would only be too glad to snatch that good looking man from right under Nellie nose. I just don't trust half of them. A lot of them pretending to be Nellie friends now, but I know it is only because of Francis. By the way Clytie, you ain't hear nothing about Emily? It is about time she have that baby."

"That is true Ma. The baby is almost due, but don't worry. It isn't going to be like the last time. Emily got her husband with her and there isn't a thing Sarah could do this time."

"I hope this baby don't have the same problems that Douglas had."

"But everything turn out alright Ma. Alastair is a good man and he isn't going to let nothing upset Emily."

The phone rang and it was Ursy returning Clytie's call from earlier that day.

"I only want to know how things going with Emily," said Clytie.

"Emily alright. It is almost time for her to deliver, but Miss Bottomsley like she going off," she said dropping her voice to a whisper.

"What you mean going off?"

"In the head Clytie! Girl I hear that that woman let out

a scream last night that send everybody running to see what happen."

"Why she hollering out like that?"

"We don't know. All she keep saying was, he was in here, he was in here."

"Who is he?"

"We don't have a clue. I hear she was white like a sheet and shaking."

"Nobody ain't ask what she mean?"

"Yes, but all she keep saying was, 'he was in here, he was in here.' Old Bottomsley give her a shot of rum to calm the nerves and she went back to bed."

"That is the last thing Emily want now in her state."

"Anyway I got to go. A new woman coming today because Emily say I can't do all this work by myself. She really put her mother to shame."

"You say a mouthful Ursy. I got to go too. We going to talk later child."

"Something happen?" asked Miss Una.

"Ursy say that Miss Sarah like she is heading for the madhouse."

"Well what a man sow, that shall he also reap. The good book say that, and Sarah harvest like it ripe and ready to reap."

"Ma sometimes you ain't got no heart."

"Where that woman is concerned, I really ain't got none. She do too many wrong things. It is now time for payback."

———

"My girl the mistress in?" shouted the hawker with the tray on her head.

Nellie stared at her for she was wearing a very pretty frock which reached down to her ankles. She then got up from her chair on the verandah and went to get Otty, who came out wiping her hands on her apron.

"She wants to know if the mistress is in," said Nellie. "Tell her that the mistress would like some fruit and you look to see what else she has in the tray."

Otty laughed and headed towards the gate.

"What you got there in the tray?" she asked.

The woman lifted the load from her head and placed in on the ground. There was an assortment of seasonings, fruits and spices. There were about six different kinds of mangoes, sugar apples and figs. Otty wondered how she managed to carry such a heavy load on her head through the village. She bought the fruit she knew that Francois and Nellie liked while she conversed with the woman.

"You new 'round here?" Otty asked.

"Yes I move out here a couple weeks back."

"So you don't know Miss Bertrand?"

"Miss Who?" asked the woman.

"That is Miss Bertrand in the verandah. She own this house and everything you see around here."

"You mean that woman sitting down there in the chair?" asked the surprised hawker.

"Yes, that is Miss Bertrand. So next time you see her don't ask her 'bout no mistress."

"I didn't know," said the woman who raised the tray back on her head, waving to Nellie as she walked away.

"I don't think she is from here," said Otty. "She was talking like somebody that come from one of the low islands. She had a lot of mangoes but I didn't buy none seeing you got all those mango trees out in the back. She had cashews, but I remember how they stain up Mr. Bertrand white shirts, so I didn't buy none.

I buy this funny-looking thing here. She say it is a pineapple, but I really don't know how you would eat that. And look what else I got Miss Bertrand. Something I ain't see for a lot of years."

She pulled the brown sticks out of the package and showed them to Nellie.

"Cocoa?" shouted Nellie. "I haven't seen this since I was a little girl."

"Then I will make some for you right now," said Otty.

Fifteen minutes later she returned with a cup and handed it to Nellie.

"Cocoa tea!" she exclaimed. "Lord this is good. You made enough so Francois can have some?"

It was obvious that Otty had learnt her place and was now getting along much better with Nellie. Every sip of cocoa was like a walk down memory lane. Memories that were painful and memories that were filled with joy! She thought of her mother Hilda who would put little dumplings in the cocoa and have the bay leaves floating on the top when she handed it to her and to her sister Nora. Back then she drank it from a tin cup, but today she was sipping it from English bone china. How she had longed for this kind of lifestyle and with Francois, it had all come to pass. She thought about Sarah Bottomsley who had always drunk her tea from bone china, but was still one of the unhappiest persons she had ever met. She thought of Miss Una whom she knew would love some of the cocoa tea, so she had Otty fill a flask and went to visit the old woman.

"Yoo hoo," Nellie said as she knocked on the door and turned the handle.

"Nellie that is you?" shouted the old woman.

"Yes Miss Una. I bring something for you. Something I know you like. Why you aren't in the shop?"

"I out here on the back step Nellie. Bring a chair and sit down next to me. I was feeling a little tired so Clytie put me out here and say I suppose to keep my old body quiet."

Nellie smiled, lifted the flask and poured some of the steaming contents into a cup.

"Be careful Miss Una. It is still real hot."

"Cocoa tea?" she said after the first sip. "I don't know the last day I taste this thing. Girl I thank you. You bring enough so Clytie could get some?"

"You know I would never forget Clytie. I left hers in the flask in the kitchen."

It suddenly seemed as if the cocoa had taken a stranglehold on the old woman.

"Lord I could see my old mother and Ella. The only thing missing is the tin cup. It used to taste real good from that tin cup."

It seemed as if all the memories started to flow back into her mind and she started to sing and clap her hands.

Dat Cocoa tea, is a pizun (poison) to me,

From de time I drink it, I don't know where I be,

If you want to find me, you gotta look for me.

'cause he got my head turn upside down,

Wid a cup o' dat Cocoa tea.

Nellie joined in with the old woman and they both had a good laugh when the song was over. Miss Una seemed to be in a very good mood in spite of the fact that she was tired and not her feisty self.

"Sit down Nellie. Tell a old lady all the news. You hear anything about Emily? When the baby coming?"

"It should be any day now and I am hoping for the best."

"You mean you hope the child ain't going to look like Douglas."

"Yes Miss Una. It would bring too many questions and too many problems."

"What the Lord do is well done Nellie. You must remember that. You ain't got nothing to worry 'bout. Mr Alastair is there with his wife and Sarah can't do a thing this time. Speaking o' Sarah, you hear what happen to the old devil?"

"What happen to Sarah?"

"It look like she losing she mental faculties. The other night I hear she was shouting out, 'he was in here, he was in here."

"Who is he?" asked Nellie.

"Who knows? Must be she sins coming out."

"But Miss Una, who you think she was talking about?"

"Don't worry Nellie. It is all in Sarah head. Soon she is going to be down at Jenkins."

"Emily would never put Sarah in the mad house."

"What if they can't handle the old harlot?"

"I know Emily would do the best she can."

"How my boy Francis?" asked the old lady gleefully.

"He is still working real hard Miss Una. You know that he is by himself now. Mr. Bantree went back to England and poor Francois got his hands full. Now everybody is showing up at his door. Even some of the people from up here are turning up at the house on Saturday mornings and he feels he has to help them, even though some of them don't have a penny to pay him."

"Nellie, the Lord send you a real good man. All you got to do is take real good care of him. He going to get his reward in heaven."

# 2

"I'm worried," said Alastair to Dr. Sims. "My wife should have had the baby by now."

"It won't be too long. There is nothing to worry about."

"I do worry. I don't want anything to happen to her."

"Emily will be alright. Besides this is not her first child. It should be a lot easier for her this time around."

"That bit of news makes me feel better, but there is something I would like to talk to you about," said Alastair. "Let's go to the verandah."

The doctor poured himself a drink and walked out behind Alastair.

"I think I know what you want to discuss with me. If it is what I think it is, I already know. I have been speaking with my father and he told me the story about John Bottomsley and the baby he took from one of the plantation workers."

"I was afraid you would think ill of my wife and I wanted to speak to you in case the same thing happens again when the child is born."

"It was really a surprise to me since I didn't know the story, but rest assured this phenomenon happens in one out a thousand cases. Two Caucasian people seldom ever bring a child into the world, which looks so different from them."

"Do you mean the chance of this child looking like Douglas did at birth is very slim?"

"That's what I mean. And look at Douglas today! He doesn't look like the same child. Each time I see him, he looks more and more like his grandfather with his blue eyes and blonde hair."

"Don't misunderstand me. I would love my child even if it were green. If he looked like Douglas at birth, Emily and I wouldn't care."

"That is the attitude Alastair and you owe no one an explanation. When I arrived here and witnessed the intrigue, my first thought was to return to England; but as time went on, I learnt to choose my friends carefully and to keep a low profile. My father told me the story about John Bottomsley because I wanted to know how such a thing could have happened. Then I decided to do some research and can share the details with you. Anyway, the baby will be here soon and Emily is not sick. She is only in the family way. Get her out of bed. Go for a little walk. I know she's feeling uncomfortable at the moment, but the more exercise she has, the easier the birth will be."

"Thank you Doctor. I know what you mean about this island. I had the same feelings when I first arrived here, but I couldn't desert Emily, so I decided to stay and give it a try. Francois Bertrand and his wife Nellie have made a great impact on our lives and so we decided to stick it out."

"Yes I have heard of the couple, but we've never met."

"When Emily has her baby, we should introduce you to them."

"Excuse me sir," said Ursy standing at the entrance to the verandah, "a woman is out there waiting to see you. She say she name Jennifer Appleby."

"I must be going Alastair. We'll talk again soon. Call me if there is anything out of the ordinary with Emily. Say goodbye to her for me."

"Morning sir," said the wiry-looking woman.

"Morning! You must be Jennifer!" said an astonished Alastair, for the woman was white.

"Yes sir."

He had never before seen the woman. She had long stringy hair which was tied back in a pony tail. Fire red skin perhaps from spending too much time in the tropical sun; lots of freckles which invaded the nose area and a pair of beady grey eyes. Together they all seemed to make her look slightly under nourished.

"I take it you're here about the job?"

"Yes sir."

"Have you done this kind of work before?" he asked.

"Yes sir."

"My wife is in the family way and will soon have the baby, and we haven't enough household help. Ursy is the only one here and she is cooking and cleaning and it's way too much for one person. If you are chosen for the job, your main duties will be to help with the baby when my wife asks and also to help Ursy with the other chores around the house."

"Yes sir."

"Is there anything that would prevent you from carrying out your duties if I give you this position?"

"No sir."

"Well Ursy knows how things are done around here. She has been with the family for a long time and you can ask her whatever you want to know."

"Yes sir."

"Does that mean you are interested in the job?"

"Yes sir."

"Don't you want to know how much it pays?"

"Yes sir."

Alastair found it rather strange that a white woman who showed no interest in the wages would be looking for a job in a plantation kitchen. He put it down to the fact that she really needed a job and since the household helpers all seemed so down trodden, she might have been afraid to ask about the wages. Finally everything was arranged. She would work from Monday to Friday thus lifting some of the weight from Ursy's shoulders and also from his. He couldn't wait for things to return to normal since he was responsible for both the plantation and the household now that his wife had difficulty getting around. Father Bottomsley did his best to help, but he was getting on in years and just wanted to be left in peace to play with his great grand-son.

———

"Miss Una?" Harriet called out. "Where are you?"

"I am out here in the back with Nellie."

"I didn't know my aunt was here."

Harriet joined the two women on the back step.

"My mother tell you that Toby is coming home for vacation?" she asked.

"When I passed by, I didn't see anyone in the shop, so I came straight here."

"Well Toby get married and he coming home and bringing his wife with him."

"That boy got gall," said Miss Una. "All these years he left here, and only send home ten pounds every now and then for his poor mother. If Nora was waiting on that good for nothing boy, she would be dead by now. Thank God for Nellie you see sitting here."

"But Ma don't let that bother her Miss Una," said Harriet.

"But she should. After we wash his backside and make a man out of him, he went to Ingalund and forget his family. Who he married to though?"

"A girl from England named Judy."

"You mean to tell me he couldn't find a nice girl from the Rock. When I think back to the ones we got here like Sarah and that girl Tumbric (Turmeric), the last thing he should bring to Nora is one of them. I still think he didn't look hard enough to find a good girl from this here rock."

"Tumbric?" asked Nellie.

"Yes. That girl with the yellow hair! You know the one that Sarah married the brother!"

"You mean Ginger," said Nellie almost falling off her chair with laughter.

"It was Ginger?" asked Miss Una as she too laughed loudly. "Ginger, Tumbric! Same thing!"

"Miss Una, you going to kill me one day," said Nellie. "I am going over to the shop. I want to have a word with my sister."

———

"Bless my eyesight," said Clytie as she saw her best friend. "You so busy these days that we don't get a chance to talk like we used to."

"Girl I didn't think that this helping out thing would be taking up so much of my time, but you know I always phone to see how things are going."

"How Francois?"

"Francois is good! Good but always busy!"

"Where is Nora? I thought she was here."

"She is out in the back weighing out sugar."

"I have to talk to her. I hear that Toby is coming home and bringing his English wife with him."

"Girl Nora ain't too happy about it, so be careful what you say to her."

Nellie found her sister in a back room surrounded by packages of sugar which she had weighed out in half pound and pound parcels.

"I understand there is a new addition to the family."

"You talking about Toby? Tschuuuuuuuuuuuuups!" said Nora sucking her teeth.

"You don't seem too happy about it Nora."

"You know the last time I hear from that boy? Christmas before last! And now he got the gall to tell me he get married and bringing home a wife. I wonder where the two of them going to stay?"

"After all Nora, he is still your son. What is Percy saying about all this?"

"You know Percy. If I say it is alright, then it is alright with him."

"It might be only for a couple of weeks, so smile and put up with it. She might be a nice girl."

"Nellie you should be the last to think that those people nice. Look at the hell Sarah put you through. Not to mention that man Hurley. Then look at the hell that Ginger put Sarah Bottomsley through. Toby couldn't find a Bajan girl over there?"

"Nora I understand what you're saying, but he is still your son. Ungrateful or not! I think you work too long with Miss Una. When Harriet was telling me about Toby, you should hear how she started to carry on."

"You know that Miss Una is a real bright woman. No education, but Lord she got more common sense than all o' we put together."

"She nearly killed me just now."

"How?"

"She was saying something about Ginger Hurley and called her Tumbric Hurley."

Nora almost collapsed over the parcels of sugar and tears streamed down her face.

"Tumbric?" she asked as cackled like a hen that had just laid an egg.

"Wait until she meets Toby's wife. Lord I wouldn't want to be in that girl's shoes."

"Toby wife?" asked Nora. "Wait till she clap her eyes on Toby!"

The two women joined Clytie in the front of the shop and caught up on all the things that had happened the previous week.

"Ursy tell me they got a new maid at the plantation," said Clytie.

"Ursy couldn't handle all that work by herself. I remember when Miss Ella and I use to work like two mules especially when they had the big parties," said Nellie.

"Things ain't like that no more Nels. It look like if Miss Emily like a quiet life."

"Who did they get to work? I hope it is somebody who would take good care of my two grandchildren."

"I think Ursy say she name Jennifer and she white."

"A white woman in the Bottomsley kitchen? I don't know any Jennifer who used to live in the village. And we didn't have no white people living down there."

"Must be somebody from another parish," said Clytie.

"I don't know, but Emily taking real long to have that baby."

"I think the doctor say that she should have it sometime this week."

"That is what Alastair said. Everybody is waiting and waiting! I think we all just a little bit frighten. Anyway it really doesn't matter to Alastair. He knows it is his baby when it comes. No matter what colour it is. I just wish that Sarah wasn't living there because I could go and stay with Emily until the little one came along."

"You frighten for Sarah?" asked Nora.

"No, but I don't feel too comfortable around her."

"You don't have to worry 'bout Sarah 'cause she going off she rocker. Ursy say she hear she did shouting out again early this morning. Father Bottomsley give her a rum to settle her down. I tell you the two o' them drink more rum than all the villagers put together," said Clytie.

"As Miss Ella used to say, Sarah ain't a happy woman. She does hardly crack a smile."

"Now if she had something to worry about, I could understand. She ain't got to wonder where the next meal coming from. She got a roof over her head that she ain't got to pay a cent for, and even though she know everything belong to Emily, she still trying to call the shots. I hear that just one look from Mr. Alastair and she does remember her place real fast," said Clytie.

"I still feel sorry for Sarah though," said Nellie. "How could anybody have everything in life and still be so unhappy?"

Customers started to wander into the shop so they had to end their discussion. However they were all happy to see Nellie. She did not recognize the woman and the two children who appeared at the counter.

"You back?" asked Clytie.

"Yes. I want a pack of Trumpeter cigarettes, a bottle of Bottomsley white rum, a tin of condensed milk, a package of Sunrise biscuits and two pints of rice."

"Don't forget the polar lollies," said one of the little girls.

"Bring along two polar lollies too, else I will never hear the end of this."

"We moving again," said the little girl to Clytie.

"You talk too much," said the woman, inquiring from Clytie how much she owed.

"That is two twenty," replied Clytie eager to know where they were going, since she knew they had just moved into the neighbourhood. "I forget your name. You tell me the last time, but I can't remember."

"I tell you my name the last time?" she asked.

"Yes."

"That is strange! I don't remember that. Anyway thanks," she said turning to leave without revealing her name.

The eyes of the three women followed them. They got into a black car with a man who wore a cap which was pulled down over his eyes. No matter how hard they looked, they couldn't see his face, but they knew that he was also white.

"She is a strange woman," said Nellie. "That man must be the children's father."

"Could be, but you right Nels. There is something real strange 'bout that woman. The last time she was in here, I tell her the shop at Austin corner was closer than this one, but she say that the people in that shop real malicious. They ask too many questions. You don't think she got a little bit of a twang?"

"It sounds so but I have never seen them around here and I have been here for as long as I can remember. Anyway I can't worry my head about things like that. I have to look after the school and I am trying to encourage Jonas to go to Teachers' college. He is a bright young man and should do something so he could better himself."

"He probably take after his mother," said Clytie laughing loudly. "But I don't know if he want to leave 'bout here, because it look like if he courting Nels."

"Who is he courting?"

"I don't know."

"So why you say that?" asked Nellie.

"I hardly see that boy on the weekend anymore. He come home late every Sunday evening just in time to correct the school books for Monday morning."

"And you've never seen him with anyone?"

"No, but he is a good son," replied Clytie.

"What I do to deserve the one I got?" asked Nora.

"Toby ain't that bad. You just vex 'cause he bringing home a English wife."

"That ain't it. He never even send a kerchief for Miss Una, and she look after that boy like she was the grandmother and now he talking about bringing home a wife. He better come home with his hands full of something for that old woman."

"You right," said Clytie. "Not because she is my mother, but that woman ain't got a forgiving bone in that little body."

# 3

Alastair Chambers stepped out of the car, and pulled a piece of sugar cane from the field. He looked at it, turned it around and fully inspected it, just like Nick Bellamy had shown him. He then pulled a pen knife from his pocket, peeled away the hard exterior and sucked the sweet juice from the white fibrous sugar cane. It was good. This year would bring another booming sugar crop. Just as he was about to get back into the Land Rover, he saw something which stopped him in his tracks; a mongoose with a brood of little mongooses all in single file, crossing the road into the sugar cane field on the other side. The mother stopped and sniffed the air, looked at Alastair and realizing there was no danger, continued with her babies through the hedgerow and disappeared into the green ocean of sugar cane. She was a good mongoose mother. He too was awaiting the arrival of his child. He knew that his wife would soon give birth and wanted to stay in very close proximity to his home. He remembered the horrors of Douglas' birth and how far away he was when Emily most needed him.

Farther along to the next field, the workers were taking a break from the afternoon heat and jumped up when they saw the

Land Rover approaching. Each one of them waved as Alastair slowly drove by, inspecting the crops of potatoes, eddoes and yams. He parked the car and walked towards them.

"Afternoon sir," said a young man.

"Afternoon Clyde. Any problems to report?"

"None at all sir! Everything real good! I think we will get a lot more harvest this year than last year."

"Don't forget you must give the workers some potatoes, yams, eddoes and vegetables. The lorry should be coming by tomorrow morning to pick up the rest. Make sure everyone knows they must be here early to load them."

"Yes sir," said the muscular young man.

"And Clyde," he said stopping and turning around, "I would like to speak to you about something important. Sometime next week we can sit down and talk."

"Yes sir. I ain't doing a good job sir?" asked the worried young man.

"Of course you are doing a good job. Don't worry. You will still have a job," said Alastair resting his hand on his shoulder.

He drove slowly along surveying the fields as he went. It was almost time for the harvesting of the sugar cane and he was happy with the way things had gone. Nicholas Bellamy had taught him well and he was proud of his accomplishments. Bottomsley was one of the plantations which was still productive because Alastair had followed the ex overseer's instructions carefully and he also treated the workers well, so they were happy to work for him. However dark clouds were forming over many of the other plantations and they were being forced to cut down on their work force. Labourers were now moving from parish to parish with their families in search of work, so no-one would bat an eyelash when new faces popped up here and there.

Henley plantation was on the verge of closure, and that meant that many of the villagers could be moving away, but some of them decided to stay because they had learnt other trades and didn't depend solely on the plantation work. It was indeed a blessing for those people of Plum Tree Village in St. Lucy who had sought to be independent through another occupation.

No one understood why it was called Plum Tree Village because there wasn't an abundance of plum trees. If it had been called Mango Tree Village, then one could understand because there were mango trees as far as the eye could see. However those villagers who no longer had jobs, learned to fish in the turbulent waters off the cliffs, or they collected the dried Sisal plants which they then dried and wove into baskets. They also learned the art of chair-caning. They acquired chair-caning material and moved from village to village repairing backs and bottoms of chairs or worked alongside the joiner doing cane work on the backs and seats of his mahogany chairs.

The hawkers, most of them with broad backsides, moved around the area with trays of fish on their heads, calling out to would-be buyers. Fish! Fish! Come and get your flying fish! A car loaded with fish would also drive by calling out to customers and this would bring great confusion, because the women who moved around on foot would blame the driver for trying to push them into financial ruin. It was no competition. The motorists could carry greater loads and therefore sell their fish at a cheaper price than the buxom hawker with her load on her head.

Sometimes it became extremely entertaining when arguments broke out between them. Everyone was cursing everyone's mother or wife or husband or children. At the end of it all, the villagers would have a good laugh when the car driver would openly offer sexual advances to the woman in exchange for staying off her territory. This would once more stir the fire when the woman who obviously had no interest in him would fire back.

"Why you don't go home and see who your wuffliss (worthless) wife got in your bed?"

Roars of laughter and joking around would follow, forcing the driver who thought he could make mockery of the hawker to make a quick escape. Wherever he showed up, he would be teased unmercifully. He would probably be given a nickname like Wuffliss; a name which he would grow accustomed to and which would stay with him until the day he died.

"How you doing Wuffliss?" would usually be his greeting.

And he would cheerfully answer.

"I am holding on here by the grace o' God."

Younger children would ask their parents why Mr. So and So was called Wuffliss.

"You too young to understand," would be the answer, "but don't let me hear you calling him Wuffliss. To you he is Mr. Jones. You and him ain't no company."

It seemed as if every villager had a nickname, some of which were strange and some quite self explanatory. There was Cow Pork, Slasher, Dinga, Yesterday Cakes, Fresh Eggs, Pa Laddie, Waxy, Pebbles, Shabu, Suffer the hog, Stomach biscuits, One Hand Horny, Bottleneck and the list went on and on. Such was an example of the day to day life in Plum TreeVillage.

Francois Bertrand climbed the steps to Una Prescott's home and gently knocked on the door. Harriet opened it and greeted him cheerfully.

"Afternoon Uncle Francois. How are you?"

"Very well Harriet. I just came by to see Miss Una. How is she and how are you?"

Harriet looked at him admiringly. Tall. Trim. Handsome. Well mannered and goodlooking. And most of all, very down to earth.

"I real good," she replied while her thoughts started to stray.

*One day somebody like my Uncle Francois will pass my way, she thought as she gazed at him. My aunt is the luckiest woman on this Rock.*

"Is that my Francis?" shouted the old woman from the back door.

"Yes," he replied. "I just came by to say hello and to see how you were doing."

"Come and let me touch the flesh," she replied. "I doing pretty good for a old woman."

Francois sat down and held the old woman's hand. He was paying her a visit but was also there to pick up his wife to take her to Bottomsley plantation. They talked about life in the village and Miss Una as usual dispersed her words of wisdom. Finally she told him about her sister who had left the island so many years before and had never returned.

"She was the only family I had Francis, and she promise me that when she reach Carlina and things get good, she would send for me. But that was the last thing I ever hear from Ida."

"Have you any idea what part of The Carolinas she went to?" he asked.

"Not a inkling Francis. For all I know she must be long dead although she was younger than me."

"Well I hope you get a chance to see her again. I don't have any other family Miss Una. Nellie is all I have and I cherish every moment with her."

"You is a real good man Francis. Why I didn't find nobody like you when I was young? I was quite something you know Francis. I could dance and I had a few young men after me, and I choose Clytie father but he wasn't no good. You come here to see me and I talking too much. Anyway if you going down to Bottomsley, you got to watch out for Sarah," the old woman said as he stood up to go. "I hear she ain't too good in the head these days."

"Thanks for the warning," he replied kissing her on the cheek.

"I am here to pick up a beautiful lady," Francois said looking around the shop for his wife.

"Where are we going?" she asked now speaking perfect English.

"I'm taking you to Bottomsley to see Emily."

"But Francois, I'm not dressed properly."

"You look wonderful. I spoke to Emily and she is expecting us."

"What about Alastair?"

"He wasn't there, but she said he should be there by the time we arrive."

"It would give you a bit of time to visit alone with Emily. Are you worried about something?"

"I just don't want to be around Sarah Bottomsley. She makes me very nervous."

"I'll be there. So will Emily, Old Bottomsley and so will Alastair."

As usual Sarah Bottomsley was sitting on the verandah reading a book when they drove up. She didn't seem to hear the car, but looked up when Francois closed the door. She hadn't yet seen Nellie and continued to observe him until he opened the door on the other side to let his wife out. As soon as she saw her ex housemaid, Sarah disappeared and took refuge in her bedroom.

"You won't have to worry about her," said Francois. "She's gone."

"I hope she stays away until we leave."

Hearing the closing of the car door, Alastair looked out and was overjoyed when he realized it was Nellie and Francois. He hugged them both and was about to go in to get his wife, when he turned his head and whispered.

"Sarah says she's feeling poorly and has retired to her room."

"Tell her we wish her all the best," said Francois.

"You didn't believe a word of that," said Nellie.

"Of course not, but we can play along with her little game."

Emily struggled from her room. She looked like a sack of potatoes tumbling towards them. Alastair helped her to her father's plantation chair where she slowly eased herself in. Just barely fitting! Nellie looked at her daughter and had great compassion for her. She knew exactly how she felt.

"You must be very uncomfortable," she said.

"How I am longing for this to be over," she said. "These hot days certainly don't help my situation."

"It will be over soon," Nellie replied remembering her own pregnancy.

"I'll get Ursy to bring in some refreshments," said Alastair. "What will you have Nellie?"

"A glass of lemonade, thank you."

"And my friend?" he said turning to Francois. "The usual?"

"Of course," Francois replied.

Alastair disappeared into the kitchen and quickly returned.

"I wanted to come for a visit because there is something I would very much like to discuss with you," said Francois.

"May I ask what it's all about?"

"We'll get together and talk about it later. It can wait."

"Afternoon. Excuse me," said a voice that was not Ursy's.

The new housemaid had come in with the refreshments. She placed a glass of lemonade beside Emily, one beside Nellie and then returned to the kitchen, turning around to glance at Nellie, whose face held a questioning look.

"Is something wrong?" asked Alastair.

"It's just that I have seen her somewhere before."

"She has only been here just over a week."

"What is her name?" asked Nellie.

"Jennifer!"

"Does she have children?" asked Nellie.

"I don't think so," said Alastair. "As a matter of fact, I don't really know. Why do you ask?"

"I'm sure I saw her in the shop a couple weeks ago with two little girls."

"Do you mean the shop in St. Lucy?"

"Yes."

"You must be mistaken Nels," said her husband. "If she lives in St. Lucy, why would she take a job such a long way from home?"

"I don't know," said Nellie, "but it's not that important. We came here to see how the two of you were getting along. Where is Father Bottomsley?"

"Grandpa went out with a couple of his friends," replied Emily. "They play cards together on Tuesday afternoons. It's good for him to get out. They aren't many of his friends left anymore."

# 4

A car door slammed and Clytie looked up just in time to see a young man spring quickly out of a taxi. There were more occupants inside the car, but she immediately recognized the young man who came running up the steps.

"Clytie how are you? I came by to see if Mama was here," he said with a very British accent.

"Toby, is that you?" she asked. "Boy you look like a million dollars. I thought you was bringing your wife with you."

"Judes is still sitting in the taxi. She is tired. It was a very long trip."

"Nora at home. You must bring by your wife to meet Ma."

"How is the dear old lady?" he asked with a hoity toity British accent.

"Ma doing real good for a old lady."

"And where is my Auntie (Awnty) Nellie? I heard she married a solicitor and has done well for herself."

"You going to see all o' them in due course. Go home and get some rest. I never travel so far but I remember when Nellie come back from Paris how tired she was."

"My Auntie (Awnty) Nellie was in Paris?"

"Oh yes, Nellie and Francois does travel a lot."

"I must meet that chap. He sounds like such an exciting person."

"You right. He is a real exciting person," said Clytie.

"Then cheerio! I must get Judes home and to bed. She is very tired."

"Cheerio," said Clytie half heartedly.

She stared into the taxi trying to get a good look. What she saw made no great impression on her, but as he said, the young lady was tired. She had to inform Nora that her son and daughter in law were already in Plum Tree Village.

"Nora, your son and his wife coming in a taxi," said Clytie.

"Put down the phone Clytie. I got to go and change my clothes. Percy," she said shouting to her husband, "your son and his wife just pass by the shop. Change your clothes quick."

No sooner had they put their Sunday clothes on, than the brakes of a car were heard outside the home. Toby and his wife had their feet firmly planted in Plum Tree Village in St. Lucy."

"She real white," said Percy standing and peering out the front door.

"Don't worry. She is soon going to get some sun on that body. I hear the sun don't shine too often in Inglund," said his wife.

The driver removed the valises from the car and the couple stepped out. Percy stepped aside and let them in.

"Papa," he said hugging Percy who was not used to the hugging thing, "this is my wife Judes."

"Pleased to make your acquaintance," replied his father looking at his new daughter in law.

"And this is my Mama," he said turning to Nora, who shook her hand.

"The two o' you must be real tired. I never went in a plane, but when Nellie come back from Paris, she was real tired. I fix something and after that the two o' you can get some rest," said Nora. "I make up your old room. It big enough for both o' you."

In spite of being upset with her son, a feast was laid out for the newly arrived couple.

"Flying fish! My goodness! I haven't had one of these since I left the island. My mama always made the best flying fish Judes."

The young woman was quiet and hardly said a word.

"So you like the island?" Percy asked her.

"From what I've seen on the way from the airport, it looks beautiful."

"She will love it Papa. Tomorrow when she gets up and has a nice sea bath and goes into our beautiful sunshine, I know she will love it. Right Judes?" he asked stroking her arm.

"Of course!" she said softly.

———

It was nine p.m. when the telephone in the Bertrand household started to ring. Francois picked it up and on the other end was his best friend Alastair Chambers. Emily was in labour and he thought a friendly face would help her through the ordeal. Without another word, Nellie and Francois were on their way back to Bottomsley. When they arrived, Father Bottomsley was waiting on the verandah.

"How is she?" asked Nellie.

"As can be expected," he replied. "Dr. Sims is with her now."

"And where is Alastair?" Francois asked.

"He's also in there. I'll let them know you're here."

Father Bottomsley knocked on the door and told them that Francois and Nellie had arrived. There was no sign of Sarah

Bottomsley. She was perhaps still cloistered in her bedroom afraid to face life. Ursy and the new housemaid Jennifer were running around getting this and getting that.

"I'll let you have a moment with her," said the doctor speaking directly to them both.

"Thank you," said Francois.

"I'm so glad you're here," said Emily. "The doctor was right. It is not as bad as it was with Douglas. He says in another hour or so, it will be all over."

"We'll be right here, and we are praying for a safe delivery. Are you afraid?" Nellie suddenly asked.

"Of course I'm afraid. Who isn't afraid of pain?"

"That's not what I mean Emily. I was thinking of Douglas' birth." "We are not afraid," said Alastair. "This is my child and I can't wait to see him, no matter what he looks like."

"Him?" asked Francois. "How do you know it's a boy?"

"I don't know why I said he. Perhaps it's because I think we're going to have another son."

"Well I'm hoping it's a little girl," said Emily as a labour pain brought a scream from the depths of her belly.

"I think it's time to go now," said Dr. Sims. "Alastair you can stay."

Father Bottomsley stretched himself out on the plantation chair, his feet almost touching the floor for he was a very tall man.

"I'm going to be a great grandfather again," he said nervously. "Would you like a drink?"

Nellie asked for a cup of tea, and Francois joined the old man in a drink. Ursy and Jennifer were asked to stay later that night due to the impending birth. There was a huge pot of water boiling on the stove and towels in a basket just awaiting the doctor's call. Jennifer brought in the tea and set it down on a table beside Nellie.

"If you want anything else, let me know," she said to the three of them.

"Thank you," said Father Bottomsley.

"I know I have seen her somewhere before," said Nellie.

"I had never laid eyes on her until she came to work here and I know just about everyone on this island," said Father Bottomsley. "She doesn't talk a lot, but she seems to know what she is doing."

Nellie had forgotten to speak to Clytie about the woman, but at this time with Emily in labour, it seemed unimportant. Ursy was summoned and she stood at the bedroom door with a kettle of water and a porcelain basin, and Jenny with the basket of towels which they placed before the door. Fifteen minutes later, a loud scream was heard and then the cries of a baby.

What would the baby look like? Fear! Confusion! Relief was written over the faces of the two men and Emily raised her upper body to have a look at the child. He was whiter than snow, with a pair of lungs that shook the very foundations of the home. Sarah Bottomsley had probably been waiting for that moment, because she opened her bedroom door and came out.

"Good evening," she said looking around. "Did I hear the baby cry?"

"Yes you did," said Grandpa Bottomsley.

"I want you to meet my son," said Alastair as he presented the child wrapped in a blanket.

Nellie sank into the nearest chair because her legs could no longer support her. She was relieved and she wept. Sarah seemed afraid to get too close, so her son in law walked over to her and pulled back the corner of the blanket. She seemed really afraid to look at the child.

"It's another grandson. Would you like to hold him?" he asked her.

"No, he may fall from my arms," she said.

"He looks like his grandfather," said Alastair.

Sarah peeped at the little face, broke into tears and left the room. There were tears of joy and relief. She wouldn't have to explain anything to anyone. Her daughter had brought a perfectly white child into the world.

"Let's go," said Francois to his wife. "We can come back another time to see Emily and get a better look at the baby. I'm sure he is the spitting image of you."

"You always know the right things to say to me to make me feel better," she said.


"Clytie, Emily had the baby," said Nellie.

"I know. Ursy call to tell me and Ma."

"Everything went well. Everything!" she said putting more emphasis on the word.

"What about Miss Sarah?"

"She only came out of her room when the baby started to cry and then she cried when she saw it, because it is just as white as she is."

"Ma is real happy to hear that everything went alright."

"Clytie I know who the new housemaid is. You aren't going to believe who she is."

"Who?"

"Do you remember that white woman with the two girls who came into the shop last week? I am not sure if she recognized me, but I recognized her from the moment I laid my eyes on her."

"That is real peculiar Nels. How did she get that job? I didn't know that white people do kitchen work."

"She must have asked Alastair for the job in order to get it."

"White people don't work in kitchens. Something just don't seem right."

"I don't know," said Nellie. "All I can tell you is that she is working in Bottomsley kitchen."

"You don't find she is behaving like if she belong to a secret order? I got to put Ursy on her to find out what she trying to hide. Hey Nels, I almost forget. Your nephew come home with his English wife. She look real spawgy, and he spitting out the Queen English like if he was born over there. He talking about Mama and Papa, and telling me about cheerio when he was leaving."

"It looks like if he has turned into a right idiot!"

"Girl, he want to know where his Awnty (Auntie) Nellie was and say he hear that you married a real exciting chap. I had to rub it in and tell him 'bout when you was in Paris. "My Awnty (Auntie) Nellie was in Paris?" Girl you are going to collapse when you hear him. I can't wait for him to start talking to Ma like that, because she will dump cold water on him and put out that fire that burning inside his mouth."

———

"What happen to you?" shouted Ursy when she saw the condition of her co-worker's face.

"Girl I got a real bad toof-ache," (toothache) said Jennifer.

"That is almost under your eye. That isn't a little too high for a toof-ache?"

"No," replied the woman. "The toof right below it hurting me."

Ursy went to the larder and retrieved the bottle of cloves. She then emptied three pods into the woman's hand.

"Chew them up a little bit and then put it next to the toof that hurting you."

She did as Ursy said and went about doing her chores. She was the first white woman Ursy had ever seen working in a plantation kitchen, and as Ursy thought, was probably taking the job that some poor black woman needed in order to support her children. However from the way she spoke, Ursy thought that she had very little education and although she tried as hard as possible to speak like a Barbadian, she knew she wasn't born on the Rock. Some of the words she used were not commonly used in Barbados and people who looked like her and were poor usually lived on the other side of the island among the poor whites. These people had settled in the parish of St. John and hardly ever mixed with the other local people. Ursy did not believe the excuse she gave about having a toothache, because it looked as if she had been punched in the face, and since it was none of her business, she was not going to meddle.

"Oh Lord! The baby crying," said Ursy. "Knock on the door and ask Miss Emily if she want any help."

When she opened the door, Emily couldn't help but notice the swelling in the woman's face.

"What happen to your face child?" Emily asked in Bajan dialect.

"Just a slight toof-ache," she replied.

"Then you better get to the dentist. You may have a gum boil."

"I alright. You want me to take the baby?"

"Yes I'm going to take a shower. I fed him already so you can put him in his bed when he falls asleep. Do you have children?" asked Emily.

"Yes, I have two daughters."

"I won't be long," said Emily hurrying out of the bedroom.

Jennifer looked at the little child admiringly and kept on looking at him as she walked to the kitchen.

"Babies real sweet, ain't they?" asked Ursy.

"He looks real innocent. He looks just like his mother."

"You are saying that because you didn't know the grandfather. He is the living image of Master Bottomsley. He did a real good man. Can't say the same thing about Sarah Bottomsley," she said dropping her voice to a whisper.

"There you are," said Emily. "I was looking for you."

"He is real sweet Miss Emily," said Ursy. "He reminds me so much of his grandfather. He got the same little nose and that Bottomsley smile. You know that you look like just like your grand-daddy, don't you?" asked Ursy playing with the child's face.

"What if he answer you?" asked Jennifer.

They all began to laugh at Jennifer's comment, while still admiring the child.

"By the way Ursy, what happened to that photo of Alastair, Douglas and me? It was sitting on the side table, but it isn't there anymore."

"Maybe Mrs. Bottomsley moved it. You didn't see it Jennifer?"

"I didn't know that it was missing. It was there up to a couple days back."

"I'll find it," said Emily taking the child from her.

"Miss Emily, what are you going to name him?"

"My husband and I haven't yet come to a decision. Maybe John or Alastair or Francois, just like his godfather!"

The tinkling of a bell was heard. Sarah Bottomsley and Old Bottomsley were waiting to have their breakfast served.

"You must be a happy woman Sarah," said Old Bottomsley.

"Why?"

"Because of your new grandson!" he replied.

"Isn't he precious John? He looks just like his grandfather."

"He *does* look like my son Sarah," said the old man.

The conversation stopped when Emily entered the room followed by Jennifer. Sarah couldn't help but gaze at the distortion to the woman's face.

"You've got a real shiner there," said Father Bottomsley.

"Just a toof-ache sir."

"Looks more like you were in a boxing match," he replied.

"Bring me a pot of tea," said Sarah interrupting them. "Ursy knows what I like for breakfast. Tell her that. Mr. Bottomsley will have the same."

"Why thank you Sarah," the old man said, his tone ringing with sarcasm.

"Mother did you remove the photo that was sitting over there on the table?"

"What photo? And why would I remove it?"

"Hmmm!" said Emily. "It seems to have just disappeared into thin air."

"*He* took it," whispered Sarah to Father Bottomsley.

"He?" the old man asked.

She leaned over and whispered in his ear, and the old man looked as if he had seen a ghost.

"Listen to me Sarah. That is not possible."

"But it is. He is always coming to my room."

"And what does he do when is there?"

"Why are you two whispering?" asked Emily.

"Sarah is sharing a secret with me. Anything wrong with that?" asked the old man.

"Not at all," replied his grand daughter.

# 5

An invitation had been extended. Toby and his wife Judy along with the rest of the friends and family were having Sunday lunch with Nellie and Francois. Toby and his wife surveyed the property from the moment they entered through the garden gate until they stepped onto the verandah. Upon seeing the interior, his wife's mouth dropped open but she said nothing.

"You have done extremely well for yourself Auntie," said Toby looking around Nellie's living room.

"Thanks," replied Nellie. "It looks as if you've done the same. This is my husband Francois."

"I've heard lots of good things about you," replied Toby in his Oxford accent. "It seems as if you've had a very positive effect on my Auntie."

"Thank you but I would say *she* had a very positive effect on me," said Francois.

"And you're humble too. My goodness, I forgot to introduce you to Judes. Her name is actually Judy, but I call her Judes," he said.

This was the first opportunity Miss Una had to meet the

newly wed couple and she waited patiently while Toby did his utmost trying to impress Francois.

"Ma, don't say nothing to upset nobody," said Clytie.

"I old enough to say what is on my mind and nobody ain't going to stop me. What he just tell Francis?"

"I didn't hear Ma."

"Don't lie to your old mother Clytie."

"So what do you do in London?" asked Francois.

"I am in Transportation and Communications and Judes is in dress designing. Is that Miss Una?" he asked interrupting the conversation and going over to the old lady.

"If your wife is designing clothes, she should talk to your sister Harriet. She is a first class needle worker and know how to do hair real good too. And yes, it is me Toby. You don't remember me?"

"Of course I do," he said plopping a kiss on the old lady's cheek.

"Only Francis can kiss me like that," said the old woman.

Everyone broke into nervous laughter. Miss Una was cranking up and no-one knew what would be the next thing to come out of her mouth. Luckily Otty came in in the nick of time, carrying a tray with beverages and fish cakes and put them on the coffee table. The topic now changed to food with everyone helping themselves.

"Do you think Toby would like something stronger?" Francois quietly asked Percy.

"I think his majesty *would* like something much stronger than lemonade," he replied as the two men smiled and exchanged glances.

"So Toby, what may I offer you to drink?" asked Francois.

"A scotch on the rocks would do nicely."

"Unfortunately we have no scotch. All I've got in the house is some good local Barbados rum."

"That will do," he replied. "I've gotten so used to drinking scotch that I forgot that all you people here drink is rum."

"Don't pay him no mind," whispered Percy. "My son come back here a first class idiot."

"Good afternoon everyone," said a voice behind them.

"Jonas old chap!" shouted Toby. "You look just the same as the day I left."

The two men slapped each other on the backs and laughed loudly.

"So what are you doing now old boy?" he asked Jonas.

"I'm still teaching at Miss Nellie's school."

"Still there?" he asked. "Nothing beats a little stability! I'm in Transportation and Communications myself."

"Exactly what are you doing in communications?" Jonas asked.

"Jonas got him," whispered Miss Una as she snapped the fingers on her right hand. "Watch him get out of that one."

Toby quickly changed the subject and introduced his wife to Jonas.

"What it is exactly that you doing in Ingalund Toby?" asked Miss Una.

"Nothing that you would understand Miss Una!"

"I old but I ain't foolish. You talking 'bout all this communication, but tell the truth Toby, you still working on them buses as a conductor in that there Ingalund?"

One could hear a pin drop. He had forgotten what an astute and straightforward woman he was dealing with. That remark forced Francois' quick departure into the kitchen with Percy hot on his heels, where Clytie and Nellie were giving Otty a hand with the lunch preparation.

"I tell you my son is a first class idiot! He think he could come back here to pompaset on the Bajans. He don't realize that we move further up the ladder than him."

Francois laughed and so did Otty, but she hid hers behind a kitchen towel.

"I hope you are not talking about my beloved nephew," said Nellie. "If I didn't know him, I would swear he wasn't my sister's son."

"We better get back in there before Miss Una crucify him," said Percy.

It was a lovely afternoon and Toby seemed to settle down a little, especially since he realized that his life was no better than the people he had left on the island. He was a bus conductor in London and his friends had moved on to bigger and better things.

"Auntie," he said cornering Nellie in the kitchen. "You've got all this and no one to pass it on to. Tell me, who is going to get it all?"

Nellie could hardly believe her ears. It was obvious he knew nothing about Emily so she mustered up enough courage to put him in his place.

"You got a lot o' nerve boy. It isn't any of your business who I am leaving all this to. Have you ever sent me a handkerchief from London? Anyway a Will is a private matter, so you make sure you know who you are giving yours to."

"No offence meant Auntie."

"Are you sure?" Nellie shouted as her sister opened the kitchen door and entered.

"What happening in here?"

"Nothing," said Nellie leaving her alone in the kitchen with Toby.

"What you say to Nellie?" Nora asked.

"We can talk about it later Ma. It was really nothing."

"Don't give me that. I know my sister and she don't get vex unless she got a real good reason."

"I'll tell you about it later."

It was obvious Nellie was no longer in a good mood and Nora sensing it, decided they should leave. Francois took Nora, Percy and the newly weds home, leaving Nellie with her best friend Clytie, Miss Una, Harriet and Jonas.

"Nellie, I know you too long," said Miss Una. "You ain't behaving like your old self."

"I am alright Miss Una. Tomorrow I'll ask Francois to drop me off by the shop on his way to work and we can talk."

"Come Ma," said Clytie. "Francois get back."

They all clambered into the car for the short drive home with Miss Una sitting in the front with Francois.

"Francis what happen to Nellie?" she asked. "I know that child longer than I can remember. I seen her happy, I seen her sad, but never seen Nellie vex. Something make her real vex."

"I don't know Miss Una, but I'll talk to her as soon as I return home."

———

"I'm going to bed," said Nellie. "I am tired."

"Before you go Nels, you and I must have a little talk."

"Can't it wait until tomorrow Francois? I'm really tired."

"It won't take long Nels. Come and sit next to me."

"Alright," she said.

"I know that something is bothering you and I want you to tell me what it is. And please do not say that you are alright. Even Miss Una asked me about it."

"Well it's Toby."

"What about Toby? What could he have done to upset you like this?"

"He was demanding to know who I was leaving everything to since I have no children."

"Then I presume Nora never told him anything about Emily."

"No she didn't! Miss Una knows, Clytie, Nora and you. No one else knows and I must talk to Nora before she tells him anything."

"I wouldn't worry Nels. If she hasn't told him anything yet, she never will. Not even Percy knows. I'm sure his life in England is not all he says it is. Why do you think he would you ask a question like that? He thinks that perhaps there is something in your Will for him."

"How can you be so sure that Percy doesn't know?"

"Just by the way he talks when we go fishing together."

"I know I can trust Clytie and Nora. But what if Toby finds out?" Nellie asked.

"He won't, but we'll cross that bridge if and when we get to it. There is something else I want to discuss with you."

"What?" she asked.

"You can see that Miss Una is getting on in years. That lovely old lady! I want to do something for her."

"Something like what?"

"I would like to go to South Carolina to try to find her sister."

Nellie laid her head on his shoulder and soon she was crying.

"If I had known it would make you so unhappy, I never would have decided to do it."

"I am not unhappy Francois. It's just that you are such a

good man. I would like Miss Una to see her sister too before she passes on. Can you imagine what would happen if Ida showed up here?"

"I don't know if I will find her, so you shouldn't say anything about it."

"Are you taking me with you?"

"Nels," he said looking into her face, "it is not a good idea. South Carolina wouldn't be kind to you and I cannot bear the thought of anyone ill treating you."

"I don't understand what you mean?"

"Many of the plantation owners in South Carolina went there from here."

"Don't worry about me Francois. I can handle myself."

"You don't understand Nellie. There are laws there that keep the races divided. We couldn't stay in the same hotel, nor go to the same restaurants and I certainly wouldn't want to be kept away from you."

"When are you leaving and how long do you intend staying?"

"Hopefully in two weeks, but I will stay only as long as I have to."

"Won't they treat you the same way they would treat me?"

"They don't know that I am not white. By the way, when is the baby going to be christened? I can't be out of the island. I am going to be the godfather."

# 6

Nora paced back and forth waiting for Toby to get up. He was usually the first one up standing barebacked and gazing into the ocean, but after having consumed too much of Francois' rum, he probably had a hangover.

"Good morning," said Judes as she saw Nora in the kitchen.

"Morning! You want a cup o' tea?" Nora asked.

"I can get that myself," she said running over to grab the teapot. "I'm going over to Harriet's this morning. She wants to show me how to style hair."

"Why you want to do that?" Nora asked.

"Well I've got to find something to do."

"But you are only here on a short vacation! Why you don't try and enjoy your self?"

Judes turned as white as a sheet and said she had to get something from the bedroom.

"I am going over to see Harriet," said Percy. "Judy say she want to walk with me. You see her Nora?"

"She went to get something from the bedroom."

Nora watched as her husband and her newly acquired daughter in law started the short trek on foot to Harriet's. Her son had still not put in an appearance and she was anxious to talk to him. She knocked on the bedroom door and she could hear him snoring from outside.

"Toby get up. We have to talk."

He stumbled out of bed and made his way to the kitchen table.

"You mean to say that you ain't going to wipe the yampie out of your eye before you sit down in front of me? And stop picking that bugaboo out of your nose," his mother shouted.

"I got yampie in my eye?" he asked lapsing into Bajan dialect and cleaning his eyes with his forefinger. "Where is Judes?"

"She went off to see your sister. Tell me what the hell you was asking Nellie yesterday."

"All I asked was who she was going to leave all her precious belongings to seeing that she has no children of her own."

"What she is going to do with her precious belongings ain't none of your damn business. Because of Nellie we had a good life. You take off for Inglund and never once think you could send Nellie a Pound note, and now you coming back here asking questions that don't concern you. Who the hell you think you is?"

"Listen Ma, my aunt Nellie isn't poor. She didn't want nothing!"

"That ain't the point! You just don't understand that you are a real ungrateful boy."

"Stop calling me boy," he said standing up and looking out the back door.

"I can call you whatever I want. I bring you in this world and I can take you out."

"Now you're getting carried away Mama. All I did was to ask Nellie one simple question."

"You ain't got Aunt Nellie in your mouth? And that is

maliciousness. As long as you staying here I don't want you asking my sister no questions, you hear me?"

"Why is everybody around here so touchous? (overly-sensitive) Everybody wants to protect Nellie. Why? What is the big secret?"

"You old enough to know right from wrong so don't talk to me about being touchous."

"Alright Mama. Whatever you say! I will not ask Aunt Nellie anymore questions. I won't even go there again."

"Do whatever you want. This is Buhbayduss. This ain't Inglund! So just you mind your manners."

"You just don't understand Ma. You just don't understand!"

"What I don't understand?"

"Everybody thinks that life in England is a bed of roses, but it isn't. You don't understand the long hours and the rotten conditions I work under just to make ends meet. You don't understand the names we get called on the buses; people are afraid that my skin colour will rub off on them, so they drop the money into my hand and sometimes, it would fall on the floor and I have to bend down and pick it up. It did real hard Ma."

This seemed to soften Nora's heart and she sat down to listen to her son. The pompous young man, who had appeared at her door one week earlier, had now been reduced to a pitiful little boy.

"If things was so hard, why you didn't come back home? We down hearing 'bout Nelson statue and Trafalgar Square, them big upstairs red buses and the Houses o' Parliament. We did thinking those places just like ours, only bigger. Everybody here think that they got Pound notes floating 'bout in the air and people there all talking like their mouths full o'something or other. We thought that all the boys down there having a good time. I didn't know that you down there in the big place suffering. We ain't rich but we got a roof above our heads and there is always something to eat. I know Francois would find something for you to do. Nellie would see to that. What I don't understand is why you was behaving so when you come back last week. Everybody thought you did Mr. Riches. You did buying drinks for everybody and behaving like if you did come back with a trunk full o' money."

"I couldn't let everybody know that I didn't have anything."

"So what little you had, you spend it buying rum and showing off?"

"I had to do it Ma. I had to do it. Everybody around here seem to be better off than me."

"So what you plan to do now?"

"Judes and I will go back to England. She is a good seamstress and what ever she takes in helps to pay the bills."

"She don't say too much. She don't like it here?"

"Judes is real shy Ma, but she is a real nice person. She really helped me out during the hard times. I know people here are wondering why I marry Judes. They thought I should find a girl from the Rock to marry, but she was good to me."

"Your father and me, we ain't got much, but you can stay here and find something to do. I hear it real cold in Inglund and they only heat one room and everybody have to sit in that room. That is true?"

Toby started to laugh.

"They didn't tell you that we also have to put money in a machine in order to get the heat?"

"What you telling me boy? You live under them conditions all these years?"

He smiled again but did not answer.

"What 'bout the rest o' the boys that left here with you?"

"What about them?"

"It was hard for them too?"

"Some of them had it tough. Real tough! Probably tougher tham me Ma."

⁓

"I'm sure I put a fifty dollar bill in my wallet yesterday," said Alastair.

"Maybe you're mistaken," his wife said.

"When I was leaving the fields yesterday, Clyde gave me that bill because he had sold some ground provisions. Jennifer had already left by the time I got home and Ursy would never take money from my wallet. I always leave it there on the console and nothing has ever been taken."

"Do you think Grandpa or Mother took it?"

"I don't know what to believe. I do know it was in there when I put the wallet on the console."

"Mother is behaving quite strangely. Could it be that she has taken it, just like she took the photo and just can't remember?"

"What photo?" asked Alastair.

"The photo with Douglas, you and me, that was on the side table over there."

"I didn't realize it was missing."

"I've asked everyone and no one has seen it."

"Oh well, I'm sure it will turn up somewhere in the house."

"Don't forget to call Francois. I want to invite them over on Sunday so we can discuss the preparations for the christening."

"And what about her?" asked Alastair pointing to her mother's bedroom.

"I have also told her about it, but I'm not sure if she will leave her room."

"Why don't we go to Francois' instead?"

"We must think of ourselves. This is also our home and we shouldn't allow her to make us feel guilty about those we choose to invite here."

"Nellie doesn't feel comfortable around Sarah, so think about her. Besides you must get out and let the children have a bit of fresh country air."

"I guess you're right. Grandpa will probably stay with her. So we have settled for John Alastair for our son. I hope Francois won't be disappointed."

"I think he will understand. It is your father's name and my name. Maybe we can add Francois to that also."

"John Alastair Francois Chambers! Too many names for such a little fellow," she said laughing.

"Morning Miss Emily. Morning Mr. Chambers," said Ursy.

"Good morning Ursy. By the way Ursy, did you see anyone with my wallet last night?" he asked.

"No sir. Why are you asking?"

"Fifty dollars is missing from it."

"I was the last to leave here last night and it was right over there where you always put it and I didn't see anybody with it."

"Thank you Ursy."

"Is Jennifer there yet?" asked Emily.

"Yes, but I don't think she had nothing to do with it. And she isn't feeling too good today Miss Emily."

"I'm asking because John will be up soon and I want to take a shower. What is wrong with her?"

"She say she got toof-ache again, but she forget that last week, it was the other side o' the face."

"You mean her face swell up again?" asked Emily lapsing into Barbadian dialect as she did from time to time.

"It real big Miss Emily. This time it gone all cross the jaw bone. And to tell you the truth Miss Emily," she said dropping her voice to a whisper, "I think somebody cuff her in her face."

"Ask her to come in to see me."

The young woman came in trying to hide the swollen side of her face.

"Morning Miss Chambers."

"Good morning Jennifer. Do you want to tell me what happened to your face?"

"I got toof-ache ma'am."

"Is it the same tooth as last week?"

"Yes ma'am."

"Jennifer the other side was swollen last week, not this side. Now are you going to tell me the truth?"

"It is just a toof-ache ma'am," she said as Old Bottomsley walked into the room.

"Another shiner this week Jennifer? You should call the Police for whoever is doing that to you."

"It is a bad toof sir."

"That's no damned bad tooth Jennifer. I'm an old man who's been around the world and I know a shiner when I see one."

"It's alright Grandpa," said Emily as Jennifer once more disappeared into the kitchen. "Tell me something Grandpa, did you notice anyone with Alastair's wallet last night?"

"Not at all. Why do you ask?"

"There's money missing from it."

"Sorry my dear, I haven't got an answer for you. Have you asked Sarah? Last night I thought I heard someone moving around in the dead of night. It was probably just my imagination."

Needless to say Sarah was terribly upset when asked if she knew anything about the money. She immediately blamed the household help, whom she deemed as thieves who couldn't be trusted, and also blamed her daughter and son in law for being too kind and friendly to them.

"That one has never called me Miss Sarah," she said as Ursy came through the kitchen door.

Ursy pretended she hadn't heard the remark and turned around and left.

"Sarah Bottomsley is on the warpath," she said to Jennifer. "You have to be careful around that woman."

"Tell me something Sarah," said Old Bottomsley.

"What?"

"You know you can trust me. Have you seen him lately?"

"Him?" she asked running the knife through her poached egg.

"You know? You told me he comes to your room at night."

"As a matter of fact he was here last night," she said in a whisper. "He must be the one who stole Alastair's money."

"Pull yourself together. Listen to me Sarah. It is all in your imagination."

"You think I am crazy too?" she asked.

"Not at all Sarah!"

*"I can see it on their faces,"* she thought. *"They're all saying that Sarah's going off the deep end."*

# 7

Mother Nature was in a punishing mood. It seemed to be the hottest day of the year. Stillness! Heat! Suffocation! Not a leaf stirred on any of the trees and the heat was sucking every drop of moisture out of the air. The unfortunate field hands in their broad rimmed straw hats and long sleeved garments, which prevented them from being slashed to death by the sugar cane blades, did their best to stay cool by drinking as much water as possible and hiding under the very blades that sought to destroy them. The hungry blackbirds and sparrows that had been waiting around to see what delicate morsels the labourers would overturn, also headed for the shade of the nearest tree.

Alastair wiped his brow with his handkerchief and put it back into his pocket. He had never felt heat like that before. Not even when he was in Africa! He drove past the giant mahogany trees and to the fields where everything sprang to life as soon as he appeared. He picked up his water bottle and splashed a bit on his face for temporary relief.

"Hello Clyde," he said. "Quite a warm day!"

"Yes sir. I would more say hot than warm."

"I think you should send the workers home," said Alastair.

"It is up to you sir, but we accustom to the heat," said the young man who was only too happy to hear that bit of news.

"A man can die of heat stroke in temperatures like this. It is two thirty. Send everyone home. I wouldn't want to work under these conditions and I can't expect anyone else to do it. After you've let them go, come back and see me," Alastair said.

"Yes sir," replied the young man.

Half an hour later the two men were shaking hands. Clyde had been promoted to the position of overseer at the plantation and that meant there was now a little more money at his disposal to feed his family.

Otty brought a large pitcher with lemonade and placed it next to Nellie on the verandah.

"It real hot today Miss Bertrand, so I make some lemonade to help cool you off."

"Thanks Otty. My husband says he is coming home soon. He says it is too hot to work downtown. Save some lemonade for him and make sure you drink some too."

"Yes ma'am. You know Miss Bertrand, the last time we had heat like this was when we had that storm Millie. I remember it was real hard to catch your breath."

"Did you hear anything about bad weather on the radio?"

"No but I will keep listening."

Nellie's thoughts turned to Hurricane Millie. That was twenty seven years ago, the same year she had given birth to Emily. She remembered how John Bottomsley had come by to see his daughter and of the ten shillings he had given her. So much time had gone by. She was so deep in thought that she didn't hear the main gate open and see Francois park the car and make his way to the verandah. His shirts sleeves were rolled up to his elbows and his shirt collar was open with his tie loosely thrown over his shoulder.

"Mrs. Bertrand, have you one of those cool glasses of lemonade for me?"

"Francois I didn't hear you come in. Where did you park the car," she asked looking around the corner.

"First I need a cool drink and then I will answer all of your questions. I just can't remember it ever being this hot. I hope we're not going to have a hurricane."

"That's what Otty just said."

"If it comes we'll just have to deal with it," he replied.

*My husband, thought Nellie. He doesn't know the word panic! He is always so easy going! Lord I thank you for sending me this wonderful man.*

"I got a letter today from South Carolina," he continued.

"It had something to do with Miss Una?"

"It certainly did and it says that they found an Ida Prescott in the register, but she is no longer at the old address. It looks as if we are right back where we started, but at least we know she is somewhere in that area."

"Maybe she is dead."

"I don't think so Nels. The first thing I did was check the death register. I know she is alive, so I've sent a couple more inquiries out so that by the time I get there, I wouldn't have to spend anymore time than is necessary."

"What do you plan to do when you find her?"

"Bring her back here."

"What if she doesn't want to come?"

"She will. I am sure she would want to see her sister again."

"Do you want Otty to bring you some lunch?"

"I'm not really hungry. Just thirsty," he said. "And I've got a gift for you."

"What is it?" she asked as she poured him another glass of lemonade which he quickly drank.

He went to the car and returned with a box. Inside was a darling little puppy, its tongue hanging out and panting from the dreadful heat. Francois poured a little water into his hand and fed it to the animal, who licked his fingers dry.

"Where did you get it?" she asked showing little enthusiasm.

"One of my clients said she had a litter of puppies that she had no idea what to do with. I know you like cats, but I thought a little puppy would be a good change for you. It's a Terrier."

"Is that his name?"

"No. That is the breed."

"I've never had a dog Francois."

"I once had a puppy and his name was Long John. We could call him Long John."

"You have to build a house for him in the back."

"I thought he could be a house dog Nels. He could sleep in the house and be a pet. I'll wash him, take him for walks and make sure he is clean."

"I don't know," she said. "I've never seen a dog living inside the house."

"I'll take care of him. He is already house broken and all you'll have to do is play with him. Can you see Douglas' face when he meets him?"

"What do you mean by house broken?"

"He won't mess inside the house."

"And if he does?"

"He won't. You'll see."

And so Long John slept inside the Bertrand home much to

Otty's displeasure because she too thought that the dog should've been kept outside, but it was not her decision to make. The other family members laughed when Nellie told them that Long John was eating and sleeping inside the home.

"Dogs ain't got no right inside a house. We is humans and them is dogs," said the outspoken Miss Una.

"I thought so too Miss Una, but I've grown used to having him beside me. Long John is a sweet little puppy. I will bring him down here one day so you could see him."

"It ain't going to make one bit of difference. A dog belong in the yard where you can pelt a bone at it, and it is there to make sure that the people don't come by to teef your belongings."

"You don't want to hurt Francois' feelings," Nellie said.

"It ain't got nothing to do with Francis. That is just the way I feel."

"But you used to like Hurley Miss Una."

"You trying to confuse a old woman Nellie? Hurley was a cat, not a dog. And if one o' them talking ghosts ever come back, a dog can't help you. At least the cat would see it and start meowing."

Nellie felt a little uncomfortable. She had forgotten all about Thomas Hurley, and here was Miss Una bringing it all back to the forefront of her mind. He had met his untimely death and still hadn't found out whatever it was that he was looking for. However that was a long time ago and he was out of her life and also out of her daughter's.

Francois received the news he had been awaiting and early one Sunday morning, he boarded a flight which would take him to America. He was going to South Carolina to meet with Ida Prescott. They all heard he was going on a business trip and would be gone for at least one week, but Nellie kept the secret to herself. She was not used to being alone so she tried to keep herself busy during the evening hours. Long John followed her every step and even slept on the floor beside the bed. Whenever he heard anything, he wouldn't bark but would stand at the door wagging his tail, which would lash against the bedroom door. Nellie would talk to him and he would settle down again and fall asleep.

One evening just after she had gone to bed, Long John stood at the bedroom door and this time he started to bark. Nellie thought she heard someone gently sliding open a drawer. She listened while Long John continued to bark.

"Who's there?" she shouted.

There was silence but the dog continued to whine. She turned the light on and with the dog on her heels, stepped into the living room. There was no one there. She turned the corner to go to the kitchen and ran smack into the standing coat rack. Fear gripped her heart and her knees knocked uncontrollably against each other, while she held on to the hat rack to stable herself.

"Lord help me!" she whispered.

She thought of the Thomas Hurley episode and this made her even more fearful. Since she was no longer in the protective walls of her bedroom, she bit the bullet and opened the kitchen door. She looked inside. No one! She felt relieved. All the doors were closed but not locked as was customary, so she checked each lock and latch and secured everything from the inside. She returned to her bedroom with Long John and locked the door behind her.

The morning sun was creeping up from behind the clouds bringing the heat along with it and she was still asleep. Suddenly she was awakened by someone pounding at the door. With Long John close on her heels, she unlocked the bedroom door and realized the knocking was coming from outside the kitchen. Otty had been locked out.

"Why you lock the door Miss Bertrand? I couldn't get in."

"I heard someone in the house last night, so I locked all the doors."

"You hear somebody in the house last night?" Otty asked.

"I'm not sure. I didn't see anyone, but Long John was barking and I thought I heard someone open a drawer."

"We got a lot of strange people 'round here now and you don't know who you can trust no more. Once upon a time it was not a problem, but soul you have to be real careful these days. Just when Mr. Bertrand left something like this would happen."

"Maybe I was just dreaming Otty."

"You want the fish cakes I make yesterday for breakfast?" the woman asked.

"Yes Otty. What is the time?" she asked.

"Half past eight," replied her helper.

"Otty I think I need some strong tea this morning. My nerves are gone."

"By the time you shower and dress, I will have your breakfast ready."

Otty opened the fridge and just kept looking inside. Then she turned around and looked around the kitchen. The yellow platter with the fish cakes was nowhere to be found.

*I am sure I put them in the fridge before I left, she said. If Long John get in the fridge and eat them, what happen to the platter?*

The woman was totally perplexed. Maybe someone *was* in the house as Nellie had said, but no one would rob a house for food. They would look for money or gold or something they could sell. She decided to make something else for Nellie's breakfast.

"Come Long John, you must be hungry," she said as the little dog trotted alongside her.

Nellie looked at the breakfast on the table, expecting to see her favourite fish cakes, but instead there was only toast with guava jam and tea.

"What happened to the fish cakes Otty?" she asked opening the kitchen door.

"You sure you didn't have them for supper last night ma'am?" the woman asked.

"Of course I know what I had for supper. You brought it to me on the verandah and then you picked up the dishes."

"Miss Bertrand I can't find the fishcakes."

"What do you mean by you can't find the fishcakes?" asked Nellie laughing.

"I know I put them in the fridge before I left. I put them on the yellow plate with the big B in the middle and now I can't find the fish cakes nor the plate."

Nellie was now afraid because she realized that the woman was indeed serious about the missing fish cakes, and it was possible that there had been someone roaming around the house the previous evening.

"Miss Bertrand we better lock the kitchen doors at night. I think somebody come in and eat all the fishcakes. What I don't understand is what they do with the plate."

"When Long John started to bark, it surprised whoever it was and perhaps they ran with the plate."

"I don't know Miss Bertrand, but it got me real confuse."

# 8

It was early evening when Francois Bertrand arrived at his hotel in Charleston, South Carolina. He felt like an imposter as he followed closely behind the hotel employee along the hallway which led to his room.

"Thank you sir," said the man accepting the tip Francois handed him.

Because of the history of South Carolina, he had expected a black porter to be carrying his bags, but this one was white. It was a hotel for whites only. He felt terribly uneasy and was glad he hadn't brought Nellie along. It would've been like suicide. The room was pleasant, clean and comfortable. It looked just like some of the colonial hotels he had seen in Barbados. A four poster bed with a canopy, a morris chair and a standing mirror in the corner. In the bathroom were the miniature soaps, rose water and other toiletries. He hung his clothing on the broad wooden hangers that were in the wardrobe and took a cool shower. Then he looked down from his window onto the street. There wasn't a lot going on, but everyone he saw was well attired. He wanted to stay in his room but hunger forced him downstairs where the half full dining room was alive with chatter and the clanging of dishes.

Escorted to his table by someone who was better dressed than most of the patrons and with exquisite manners, he sat down. An opened menu was gently placed in his hands and a napkin carefully placed on his lap. He ordered a bourbon and soda and drank while observing the people around him. Some of the patrons, mainly men, had heavy accents and spoke just like they did back in Barbados. From their conversations, most of them seemed to be wealthy, and the more they drank, the louder they became. He had no desire to be there, but he kept on observing them until a slightly uncomfortable feeling engulfed him and he decided to head for the sanctity of his room. He wondered what life was like for the black people living there. He knew conditions there were worse than they were in Barbados. There were laws which kept the races behind their dividing lines. At least in Barbados, they had freedom and could go wherever they wanted; to a certain extent. What was it like for Ida Prescott, a woman who had endured the hardships of a colonial island, only to be replanted into another colonial world, where conditions were much harsher?

Safely back in the confines of his room, he re-read the correspondence which he had received on Ida Prescott. He looked at the map of Charleston. From what he saw, it seemed that she probably didn't live too far away from the centre of the city. He ordered a taxi for six thirty the following morning when he would set out to find Una Prescott's sister. Stretching out in this strange hotel bed, he looked around the room. There were pictures of some of the colonial structures in the area. Had he been in his bed beside Nellie, he would have thought he was looking at pictures of St. Nicholas Abbey or Farley Hill, but he was in South Carolina where they spoke like Barbadians and behaved like Barbadians. Even some of the food reminded him of Barbados.

He slept soundly until the ringing of his telephone told him it was time to go on the mission that had brought him to this strange land. There was no time for breakfast so he quickly dressed and jumped into the back seat of the waiting taxi and handed a piece of paper with the address to the taxi driver, who turned quickly to look at him.

"That is the coloured part of town," he said with the same Barbadian-like accent he had heard the night before.

"Yes I know. I must go there," said Francois.

"It could be quite dangerous. Only the Coons live in this area and we try whenever possible not to venture out into those parts."

"So will you take me there or should I find another taxi?" asked Francois wanting to reach out and strangle him.

"I'll take you, but you must be quick. I can't hang around there for too long. That could mean trouble for you and for me if we are caught in the coloured part of town."

"Is it that dangerous?" asked Francois.

"Not in this part where these people live, but the fellas in the white sheets won't want to see you or me there. We could share the same fate as the coloureds."

Francois knew exactly what he was talking about and an uneasiness crept over him. It would be a faster trip he thought, if he no longer communicated with the driver. He watched as the taxi left the well constructed roads of Charleston and delved deep into the countryside which was approximately eight miles from the city centre. The terrible condition of the roads did not detract from the beauty that was South Carolina. Spagnum moss resembling old mens' beards dangled from handsome old trees which were no less than one hundred years old.

*If only those trees had tongues, he thought.*

Babbling brooks disturbed the stillness of the morning and hilly grasslands dotted the landscape. High up on the hills were mansions just barely visible through the morning mist. Francois hoped it was not too early to be visiting Ida Prescott, for nothing was stirring but the taxi and the two men inside it.

"We're almost there," said the driver. "Don't be long."

A few old shacks dotted the landscape. It was still beautiful for there were bearded trees everywhere. Francois stepped out and looked around him. He wanted to say something to the driver, but when he turned around the man could no longer be seen. He was either very cowardly or very tired, because he was lying on the seat. It was peaceful around the old shack but he knew someone was there because through the half opened window, he saw the parted curtain fall. He knocked. No reply. Knocked again and finally he called her name. An old woman opened the door. He knew immediately that it was Ida Prescott for she looked just like her sister Una Prescott, only lighter in complexion.

"Good morning Miss Prescott."

"Who you looking for?" asked the old woman nervously.

"I'm looking for Ida Prescott?"

"I used to be Ida Prescott, but my name now is Ida Franklin."

"I'm here on behalf of your sister Una Prescott in Barbados."

"You mean to tell me that my sister Una still living sir?" she asked finding support on the side of the wooden shack.

"Yes and she would love to see you. She is eighty five years old and not so healthy anymore."

"You mean Una sick sir?"

"Not sick. Just getting on in years!"

"You didn't tell me your name sir."

"Francois Bertrand," he said extending his hand.

The old woman stared at it as if afraid to take it, then lifted hers in a half-hearted shake.

"My sister send you sir?" she asked in that strong Barbadian accent.

"No, she doesn't know that I'm here."

"Then why you come to find me sir?" she asked eyeing him suspiciously.

"It is a long story which you will learn more about if you return with me to Barbados."

"Sir, I forget your name."

"Francois Bertrand."

"Sir, I don't have no money to go to Barbados. That precious little Rock," she said as her mind started to wander.

"Hurry!" shouted the taxi driver.

Suddenly the old woman became very nervous. Not only was he there, but he had brought another white man with him. Nervousness took hold of her fragile body.

"Don't worry. He is only the taxi driver who brought me here. Would you like to see your sister again? I know she would love to see you."

"You look like a good man sir," she said. "And I would like to see my sister again before the good Lord call me home."

"So are you willing to meet me in Charleston and from there we will fly to Barbados?"

"I can't meet you anywhere sir. They would kill me and maybe you too, but I know what we can do."

"Have you any family Miss Prescott?"

"Never had no children and my poor husband pass away four years now, so I live here by myself sir."

The protests by the driver forced Francois to cut the conversation short, but Ida Franklin made arrangements to meet him at a given spot in Charleston.

"Have you got a birth certificate?" asked Francois as he was about to step into the taxi.

"Yes sir," said the old woman.

"Just a moment," said Francois stepping out again much to the driver's chagrin.

He took out his wallet and gave the old lady a sum of money.

"This will pay for your taxi ride to Charleston and don't forget to bring along your birth certificate. Pack your things and I'll see you in two days."

The old woman smiled for the first time, showing gaps where her front teeth used to be. She was still a little apprehensive, but to her Francois seemed like a good and kind person.

"Let's get out of here before anyone sees us," said the driver. "You're playing with your life and mine."

The morning sun had put in its appearance and the streets of Charleston were now a hive of activity. Francois went straight to the dining room and feasted on Buckwheat pancakes dripping with syrup, scrambled eggs and hot rich coffee. Back in his room, he set about making arrangements for an airline ticket for Ida Franklin. There were many hurdles to conquer, but he did it all in time for the departing flight. She had a Barbadian birth certificate. That was one problem solved. Everything had gone according to plan and he would soon be home again with Nellie. That night he dreamt about her. They were in Paris in the same hotel where they had previously stayed. They were looking down down on Champs D'Elysees from the Eiffel Tower and suddenly below he could see Sarah Bottomsley arm in arm with her departed husband John Bottomsley. He wondered what they were doing in Paris at the same time they were there. It was only a dream. Thank God! He wouldn't tell Nellie about the dream. It would only make her worry.

Two days later in the centre of Charleston, Ida Franklin was waiting for him at the arranged place. Her dress although clean and tidy had seen better days. She was still very nervous and smiled when she saw him although she didn't return his greeting when he waved to her. She walked back and forth until he was by her side. Passing eyes gazed upon the two but most thought them to be a wealthy man and his servant.

"I hope you haven't changed your mind," he said.

"No sir, but you should not be too friendly to me," she replied. "You ain't from here and you don't understand."

"I think I do Mrs. Franklin. We're leaving today for Barbados. Is this all your luggage?" he asked looking at the plastic bag which she carried.

"Yes this is all I have sir."

"We must be going then. We must be at the airport in an hour."

The old woman looked dumbfounded and did not move from the spot.

"Is something wrong?"

"I have to get a different taxi," she said.

Francois was angry and at the same time felt sorry for Ida Franklin. She had to find her way to the airport in a taxi just for people who looked like her and they would meet there. As angry as he was at the injustice meted out to Ida Franklin and people who looked like her, he knew it would be foolhardy trying to go up against the establishment because it could put both their lives in danger.

Of course Ida Franklin thought it prudent to walk behind Francois. He could see the level-headedness of Miss Una in her sister. He handled all the formalities, and in spite of the stares he was receiving, they were soon seated on the aircraft on their way to Barbados. Ida hardly ate anything, not because of her teeth, but because she was afraid. After an uneventful flight with her keeping vigil out the window, they eventually landed in Barbados.

"You're home again," said Francois.

"This is Barbados sir?" she asked still peering out the window.

"Yes."

"It look a lot different from when I left all those years back."

"Yes there have been many changes."

He picked up his valise and after a quick call to Nellie to tell her he was home and to meet him by Clytie's house, he got a taxi for the ride to St. Lucy. Ida waited in the background too afraid to move.

"We can travel together here on the island," he said reading her thoughts.

She seemed to loosen up and started to talk. She inquired about the length of the journey and asked several questions about her sister. She watched as the taxi sped by the fields of sugar cane and seeing this brought back many memories and tears to her eyes.

"I remember that big tree over there with the big brown fruits in it. They didn't have that in Carlina. What is the name again sir?"

"That is a Mammy Apple tree."

"Yes," she said staring at the fruit. "I remember how sweet they used to be. "I eat a lot of those when I was a little girl. Now I don't have teeth no more."

"They're still very sweet Miss Franklin. I'm sure my wife or your niece can get some for you."

"You have a wife sir?"

"Oh yes. I'm sure you must know her."

"I don't know no white people," said Ida Franklin.

Francois smiled but said nothing.

The taxi stopped in front of the Prescott home and Clytie looked out the front window. She saw Francois help an old woman from the car and wondered who she was.

"Nels it is your husband with a old woman," she said.

Nellie also looked out the window and her expression said it all. She was happy to have her husband back.

"This is where Una live sir?" she asked.

"Yes this is your sister's home."

Clytie opened the door and they stepped inside. She greeted her and stared at Francois.

"Clytie this is your aunt," he said.

"My aunt?" she asked.

"This is Ida Franklin, your mother's sister."

"My Aunt Ida?" asked Clytie as the tears started to flow. "I got to get Ma. She just went in to lie down."

"Miss Clytie?" asked the old woman. "My niece Clytie? Girl you prettier than a white rose on a moonlight night. You grow into a real pretty woman."

"Why you didn't write Aunt Ida? Ma thought you was dead."

"Where is my sister?"

"Ma somebody here to see you."

Miss Una made her way into the living room from the bedroom.

"Who?" asked the half blind old woman.

"It is your sister Ida," said Nellie."

"Stop skylarking around a old woman. My sister Ida up in Carlina and for all I know she long dead."

"Ma it is Aunt Ida."

Miss Una fixed her glasses and went closer to the stranger.

"Ida? It is really you?"

"Yes ma'am," said the old lady embracing her sister.

It was a day that would live long in everyones' memory. No one had ever seen Una Prescott cry and today the tears she shed were for all the years she had bottled them up inside.

"Why you didn't write Ida? You was the only family I had left beside Clytie and I didn't know if you was living or dead. How you get back here?"

"This nice gentleman here come looking for me."

"You mean Francis? You do that for my sister? Lord you didn't send only Nellie to help the poor, but you send Francis too. Let me touch you Francis. You is a good man."

Ida Franklin could remember Hilda Peterkin, but she didn't know Nellie. Happiness showed in the old lady's face as she started to acquaint herself with her long lost family. Francois watched from beside the entrance door with his arm draped across Nellie's shoulder. Ida Franklin looked at them in dismay. She felt a little uncomfortable seeing the two of them being so familiar with each other in the open.

"Aunt Ida, this is Nellie husband."

"You mean this is the wife you was telling me about?" she asked.

"Things aren't always rosy here on the island," said Francois, "but a lot has certainly changed."

The old lady started to weep. A bucket for each teardrop.

"Stop it Ida," said Miss Una. "This is a happy occasion. Enough crying! I am just real happy to see you Ida, and the Lord bless you Francis."

"Let's go Nels," whispered Francois. "I want to know what has been happening while I was gone."

"Everything went alright in Carolina?" asked Nellie.

"I had some uncomfortable moments, but when I saw myself in the mirror, I knew I had nothing to worry about."

"I am very happy to have you back," she said kissing him on the cheek.

# 9

"We'll just change all the locks," said Francois. "Otty are you sure you didn't take the plate home with you?"

"I am real sure sir. I don't take home no dishes from the kitchen."

"We will get the locksmith in to change all the locks and put additional latches on the windows."

"Who do you think it could be?" Nellie asked.

"I have no idea."

"I hope it had nothing to do with that nephew of mine."

"If you're talking about Toby, I don't think he would be roaming around our house in the middle of the night."

"He is my nephew, but I just don't have a good feeling about him. After all he was trying to find out about my Will."

"Maybe so, but I don't think he would do a thing like that."

"You don't do it so," said Harriet returning to find her sister in law trying to use a hot curling iron on one of her client's hair.

"Sorry Harriet," she said looking closely to see how her sister in law was maneuvering the instrument.

"If my hair drop out Harriet, it going be me and you," said the woman frowning.

"Nothing isn't going to happen to your hair. She don't really know how to work with black people hair yet."

"That is what I mean," whispered the woman.

"Everything is going to be alright," replied Harriet. "See how good your hair look now. She ain't do a good job?"

"Yes, it look real good. Thanks," said the woman smiling at Judes and Harriet as she went out the door.

"Don't mind her," said Harriet. "She like to think she real special with she obzocky looking self, but I got to be nice to her 'cause she was coming to my shop from the first day I opened it. But tell me something, why you want to learn to do black people hair?" asked Harriet.

"What was that word you just used?" asked Judes.

"You mean obzocky?" said Harriet laughing. "That only mean that she don't look right. She got a big fat behind and two sparrow bird feet."

"You make me laugh Harriet. You have your own English here on the island and it is so funny."

"But why you want to learn to do black people hair? We don't have good hair like yours. We got to do a lot of things to make ours look good."

The young woman suddenly seemed shy and did not want to answer Harriet's question.

"What is wrong with you?" asked Harriet.

"You must promise not to tell Toby," she said.

"Tell Toby what?"

"When we came here, we had no intentions of ever going back to England."

"What?"

"My mother know about this?"

"I'm not sure."

"If that is the case, why he isn't doing like you and looking for something to do, instead of spending what money he got at the rum shop?"

"Please do not tell him I told you that."

"Tell me something Judes," said Harriet, "how did you meet my brother?"

She laughed and then told Harriet the story. She was on a bus one day and saw him. He was the conductor and was having a very hard time with an abusive old woman.

"What kind o' hard time an old woman can give him?"

"Well she had never seen a black man before and instead of handing him her fare, she threw it at him."

"What?" asked an astonished Harriet.

"Yes, it is true. The young men from the West Indies who went to my country to work didn't have an easy life. Some of them couldn't find accommodation and they worked long hard hours. They were insulted at every turn. Darkie they called them. I just don't know how they endured life in England. They were also not used to the cold and the damp, and were usually covered up to their eyes when they went out. That's the way Toby looked when I first saw him. On the bus, working as a conductor and buttoned up to his eyeballs," she said with a smile.

"I felt really sorry for him and helped him to pick up the coins which the woman had thrown at him. Of course she then proceeded to swear at me. When I handed him the money, he pulled his scarf down from his face and said, Thank you Miss. I smiled and we began to talk and that's how I found out about Barbados. I had never heard about the island before that. Then he invited me to see a film that everyone was talking about. I remember it was called

African Queen. Toby thought it was a film about an African Queen and had lots to do with Africans. He was really excited about seeing the movie, because he said Miss Una had always talked about Africa. I think he probably borrowed the money to take me to see that film. He was disappointed because there was hardly anything about Africa in it. You should've seen the faces of the English people when we walked out together. If looks could've killed, we would both have been dead. Anyway our relationship started on the bus and two years ago, we were married."

"Two years?" asked Harriet. "I thought you got married just before you came here."

"This Christmas will be two and a half years since we were married."

"So you came here planning never to go back? Why you agree to come here to trick my family?"

"It was not my intention to trick anyone. I thought Toby would've told his parents by now."

"What about your parents? Did they like Toby?"

Judes fell silent for a moment and then she spoke.

"You must understand that they were not used to seeing people who looked like Toby. My father hasn't spoken to me since the day I decided I would marry him."

"And your mother?"

"She doesn't have a mind of her own. My father makes all the decisions. Two or three times we met secretly, but she was a nervous wreck."

"So they really don't like us over there in England?"

"You can't blame them Harriet. It is ignorance. These people have had no exposure to the outside world and are very narrow in their way of thinking. That's one of the reasons why we decided not to return there. I'm sorry if he hasn't said anything to your parents."

"Well he didn't tell my mother nothing and I think she has a right to know."

"Let me look after this lady," said Judes as another client walked in the door.

"I have to watch you, because you really can't handle it by yourself yet, but you doing a good job."

"Thanks Harriet."

Harriet liked her and reached the conclusion that her brother was taking advantage of his wife. In spite of what Judes had said, she needed to inform her mother of her brother's intentions. While Judes washed the client's hair, Harriet went next door to the shop to call her mother. The telephone rang and rang, and there was no answer, but when she returned to the salon, her mother was walking in the door.

"Hello Ma," said Judes to Nora.

"How you doing Judes?" Nora asked not waiting for a reply.

Harriet beckoned her mother with her finger and they both disappeared into the back room.

"Where is Toby?" Harriet asked.

"I think he went fishing with his father. Why you asking?"

"Judes just tell me that they ain't going back to Inglund."

"That no good brute," said Nora. "This morning he pretend that he was pouring out his heart to me, and I was feeling so sorry for him that I tell him he didn't have to go back to Inglund if he was so unhappy back there. And all this time he was deceiving me. He better take that wife of his and find somewhere else to live."

"She alright Ma. He is the one giving trouble. She was telling me how she meet Toby and Ma she was real nice to him."

"Well he isn't nice to her now, so she better open her eyes."

"She isn't stupid Ma."

"I just come from Miss Una," said Nora changing the subject.

" Her sister Ida from Carlina just come in. It look like if Francois went up there and bring her back."

"He is a nice man nuh! You would think that his head would be real big because he is so good looking, but Lord what a good man! I still hoping something good would come my way and I ain't settling for less than what Aunt Nellie got."

"Tell me something Harriet. You think it was your brother who was in Nellie house last week?"

"Ma I don't know what to think. You can't trust him, and poor Judes," said Harriet peeping around the corner, "she don't know that he running around here in everything that wearing a skirt. He ain't got nothing to offer them except the sweet words coming out of his mouth, and that piece of thing that dangling between his legs and all o' them like they real impress by that. It don't matter to them that he bring home a wife."

"Child I just don't know where I went wrong. Anyway he better not let me find out that he was the one searching Nellie papers and eating her fish cakes."

———

"She's gone Grandpa," said Emily. "You stay here on the verandah and I will search her room."

Emily searched her mother's bureau drawers, lifted the mattress, checked the hatboxes, but none of the missing items was found in the room. She opened an envelope and found some photos of her father. She sat on the bed and examined each one carefully. A very handsome man she thought. How she missed him. There was one photo there that she liked, so she took it. A couple more photos of her as a little girl, but nothing of her late and last husband Thomas Hurley.

"Found anything?" asked the old man peeping in the door.

"Nothing yet," replied Emily.

"I just don't know what to say," he said. "This one has me really baffled."

"Absolutely nothing was there," she said staring onto the horizon.

"Miss Emily, I make some snacks for you and Mr. Bottomsley," said Ursy.

"Thanks Ursy. Put them outside. Grandpa and I can sit outside on the verandah and enjoy the fresh air," she replied.

Ursy brought in a tray with a pitcher of lemonade and two glasses. Then she returned a little later with a platter and set it down on the table. Emily and her grandfather sat in silence while they feasted on Ursy's snacks.

"Did you bring this with you Grandpa?" Emily asked looking at the empty platter.

"No."

"It must belong to the plantation. There is a B in the middle of it."

"I've never seen it before. I wonder where Ursy found it."

She picked the plate up and turned it over. There was an inscription in French on the back. She couldn't understand it and dismissed it from her mind.

"Grandpa, we are going to Nellie and Francois on Sunday. Would you like to come with us?" she asked as she moved the plate around in her hands.

"I can't leave your mother alone."

"Well if you change your mind, you can come along. The fresh salty air in St. Lucy always seems to do me good; and it always allows me to sleep peacefully at night."

"I'll consider it Emily."

"Clytie, I can't make it down there. Jennifer father pass away and Miss Emily give her two days off for the funeral," said Ursy.

"Where he did live?"

"Somewhere down in St. John."

"Oh she come from under the hill by St. John church?"

"It look so. She never mention a thing about a father. Come to think about it, she never mention nothing 'bout nobody."

"Poor soul," said Clytie. "If anything happen to Ma, I don't know what I would do."

"Child we don't have no say in the matter. When the good Lord say come, we won't even have time to pack a valise."

"How things over there though Ursy?"

"Everything alright! Miss Emily going to Miss Bertrand next Sunday, so I think she might stop by so you all could see the baby. He real sweet Clytie, and he does smile a lot."

"He too young Ursy. That is all in your head. How is Miss Sarah?"

"She is still there mad as a cat."

"She still hollering out at night?"

"I don't think so. She still hate me, but it don't bother me because Mr. Alastair and Miss Emily are real good people to work for. Last week when it was so hot, Mr. Alastair send home all the plantation workers early. He figure if it was too hot for him, it would be too hot for the poor people working in that hot broiling sun."

"I got to run Ursy," said Clytie as customers started to stream in the shop door.

"Alright we going to talk later."

"Ursy, keep your eyes on Jennifer. I just got the feeling that something ain't right with her."

"It real hard to get close to her, 'cause she don't talk a lot."

# 10

"So what happen when you get to Carlina Ida?" asked Miss Una.

"Girl things was bad. First thing is that it was real cold and the little shack they give me to sleep in didn't have no heat. Many a night I thought I was going to meet my maker, but we had to make the best of the bad situation. I learn to put old newspapers in my clothes to keep warm and I had a bucket that I used to light a fire in."

"And we down here with all this heat and you didn't have none?"

"I used to remember how hot it was down here and how we used to complain, but girl when you was in that cold, all you could think of was them hot days back on the Rock. I always used to say that if I had enough money I would come back but things was hard. When we get on a bus, the black people had to crowd together in the back although they had seats up in the front."

"So why you didn't go and sit down?"

"Una they got laws that say we didn't suppose to mix. If you did real thirsty, you just couldn't walk in a shop to get something to drink. They would pelt you out or call the Police. So before you went in you had to look to see if it was a coloured shop or a white shop."

"I never hear such foolishness in all my born days. I know that the ones here foolish, but we could go wherever we want. It like it did a real hard life Ida."

"That wasn't the worst Una. They had some men who used to dress up in white sheets and run 'round at night looking for coloured people and when they catch one, all we could do was pray."

"Why?" asked Miss Una squinting at her sister.

"They would find the nearest tree and hing him from it. Nobody could help him because we did all too frighten. Then 'round foreday morning we would cut him down and give him a decent place in the burying ground set aside for the coloured folk."

"What he do though? He did teef (steal) something?"

"You don't understand Una. They just hate you because you is coloured."

"And how you use to get money to eat Ida, seeing you had no children to help you?"

"Well at the beginning, I used to work in the kitchen, but when I got too old it was too rough for me. When I was able, I used to pick cotton and sometimes the neighbour would send by something by one o' the children."

"And you live through that Ida? Lord have mercy! What we do to deserve all these things we get? Ella and me, you remember Ella?"

"Sure I remember Ella. She was the red skin woman who used to work in the Bottomsley kitchen."

"Ella used to say that on this Rock, we did worse off than slaves, but after listening to you, I know we didn't have it that bad."

"You want a drink of lemonade?" asked Ida getting up to go to the kitchen.

"A big one Ida."

Miss Una's dress was just a tad too big and too long for the old woman, but she was happy and she showed it whenever possible with her toothless grin. She returned with two glasses of lemonade and handed one to her sister.

"Things like they was pretty good for you Una. You still got your teef." (teeth)

"These ain't mine Ida. Nellie carry me to the teef man (dentist), and he put these in. You should get some too. It real easy to eat potatoes and dumplings with them."

"Whatever happen to that man Kennif?" Ida asked.

"He must be down there fighting with Lucifer," said Miss Una.

"When he pass 'way?"

"Clytie was only four, but even before that he never give my child a thing."

"So how you manage?"

"By the grace o' God and what little Ella get from the kitchen. Times did real hard but we didn't have nothing like what you had."

---

"How everything went?" Ursy asked Jennifer.

"He didn't have a big turnout, but everything was alright."

"But how you feel? It ain't no easy thing when you ain't got a father no more."

"We wasn't so close," said Jennifer.

"It don't matter. He was still your father. Lift up the table so I could put these pans o' water under the feet," said Ursy bending over.

The young woman raised her shirt and spread her legs in order to lift the table and what Ursy saw caused her drop the pan of water.

"Girl who do that to you?" she asked seeing all the black and blue marks on her upper legs and thighs.

"It ain't nothing," said the young woman.

"What you mean it ain't nothing?"

"I think you got to leave that man before he kill you. If you don't want to join your father down there in St. John burying ground, you better pack up and leave."

"I don't have nowhere to go," said the woman on the point of tears.

"Look, I live by myself, and you could stay by me until you find a place."

"I got two children. I can't leave them there with him."

"Bring the two children and come. My place isn't big, but there is room enough room for you and them. Don't wait too long because he like he is a real brute. Come 'long with me this evening and I will show you where I live."

Tears ran down the woman's cheeks and she dried them on her apron.

"Alright! You don't want to upset the children by crying, so dry your face and go in and get the baby."

"Thanks Ursy."

She closed the kitchen door, then immediately turned around.

"I am looking for a good solicitor. You know anybody?"

"Mr. Chambers is one but I don't know if he got the time. So is Miss Emily, but the best one I could think of is Mr. Bertrand."

"Who is Mr. Bertrand?"

"You don't remember that tall good looking fellow who was here last week with his wife?"

"I didn't know he was a solicitor."

"And a good one too. He does help a lot of poor people. I

could talk to Clytie because she know the wife real good. But why you want a solicitor?"

"My father left some property on another island and since I am the only living family, I think it belong to me."

"Girl you might be real rich. Don't forget your old friends when you come into all that money," Ursy said laughing and pushing her out of the kitchen.

"Jennifer," shouted Douglas, "Grandpa can't find his teeth."

The woman started to laugh. She had never heard of anyone losing their teeth.

"You hide them?" she asked.

"No. Grandpa put them in the glass last night and now he can't find them."

"Douglas," shouted Emily, "you mustn't tell Grandpa's secrets. How are you Jennifer? How was the funeral?"

"Real quiet ma'am. He wasn't from here so he didn't know too many people."

"Where did he come from?"

"One of the low islands ma'am."

"Did you take the children with you?"

"Yes ma'am. They were real frighten because their grandfather was the first duppy they ever see."

"I remember when my father died. I was very young. It was very hard for me because I really loved my father, and I'm sure it was the same with you."

"Yes ma'am."

"I have already bathed John and he fell asleep again. He seemed very tired and miserable. I thought it might have been a little too warm for him. Please keep an eye on the children because I must go out for a couple hours. Have to find Grandpa a new set of teeth," she whispered.

"I want to tell Miss Nellie and Uncle Francois about Grandpa's teeth," said Douglas.

"What if Grandpa doesn't want anyone to know?"

"Can I tell Grandma then?"

"Yes. Knock on her door and tell her," she said hoping to get rid of him. "Keep your eyes on the children Jennifer. I coming back real soon."

"Yes ma'am."

Sarah heard the instructions her daughter had given to the young woman and she cringed.

"Must she always drop to their level?" she asked aloud. "She hangs around with Nellie and Una, sits down at a table with them and now she is even speaking just like them. I sent her to England to be a lady and she is now behaving just like a scallywag."

"Grandma the tooth fairy stole Grandpa's teeth," said Douglas.

"How do you know that?" she asked.

"He put them in a glass of water last night and the tooth fairy took them."

"Why do you think it was the tooth fairy?" asked Sarah smiling.

"I think he was thirsty and swallowed Grandpa's teeth by mistake, but Mummy is taking Grandpa to get new ones."

Sarah was confused. Why would anyone want to steal false teeth? Someone had stolen a few things before. Money! A family photo! But false teeth? What Sarah knew she had to keep to herself. If she said what she suspected, they would all think she was crazy. Since she was lost in her own world the little child left the room and went in search of Jennifer. He found her in the kitchen feeding his brother John.

"He's small," said the child.

"You used to be small too," said Ursy.

"I was never so small," he said taking his index finger and running them along the child's eyelashes.

"Don't do that," said Ursy. "If you do that to your brother, the blackbird will pick out your eye."

He covered his eyes with his hands, all the while peering through his fingers at Ursy.

"You going to visit Miss Nellie on Sunday."

"Yes, and John too," he said running his hands along the child's hand. "Miss Nellie has a dog and I will play with him."

"True?"asked Jennifer.

"Yes. She said I could play with Long John."

The tinkling of a bell sounded and the child ran from the kitchen. Sarah Bottomsley sat at the dining room table waiting for her breakfast.

"Yes Miss Bottomsley," said Ursy pouring her a cup of tea, "what you want for breakfast?"

"Two slices of toast with Guava Jam and one boiled egg. Let what's her name serve it," she said.

"Whatever you say Miss Bottomsley," said Ursy.

"She wants you to serve the breakfast," said Ursy. "She pretending she don't remember your name, so don't tell her what it is unless she ask. She is a real idiot. She don't realise that her days of ordering servants around long gone."

"Why you didn't tell her I was feeding the baby?"

"Think that would make any difference?"

"Alright, let me belch him and then I will put him down. Morning ma'am," she said on her way to put the baby down.

No sooner was he placed in his bed, than he started to scream.

"Alright! Alright!" she said putting him on her shoulder and going back to the kitchen.

"I will hold him. You take in the breakfast," said Ursy.

"I heard your father died," said Sarah as Jennifer put the plate in front of her.

"Yes ma'am."

"That meant you needed money for the funeral."

"He had some money save up and we use it to bury him ma'am."

"Who is we?"

"Me and my friend," Jennifer replied.

"Where did you work before you came here?" asked Sarah.

"I only work a couple weeks with a lady in one of the low islands."

"What was her name?" asked Sarah.

"I don't remember. Why you asking me these questions ma'am?"

"Because I'm trying to find out who is stealing around here. I don't think it's the other one in the kitchen. She's been around here for a long time and we've never missed anything."

"You calling me a teef?" (thief) asked Jennifer.

"I never said that. I am just trying to figure it out."

"I talk to Miss Emily already and she know I didn't have nothing to do with it."

Ursy could hear the raised voices and put her ear to the door. She couldn't believe that Sarah Bottomsley was again trying to accuse another employee of theft. Sarah was heartless. How could she do this to the poor woman just after her father's death? Luckily she could hear other voices and she knew that Emily and her grandfather had returned.

"Grandpa," said Douglas. "You have more teeth."

"Yes son," the old man replied, "and I'm going to keep these locked up at night."

"Morning Mother," said Emily.

"Good morning," replied Sarah, who immediately knew that she had overstepped her boundary.

"What's going on here?" asked Emily after looking into Jennifer's face.

The woman broke into tears.

"Go back to your work Jennifer," said Emily. "Mother, are you going to tell me what's going on here?"

"All I asked her was if she had stolen the missing items."

"Mother! How dare you?" shouted Emily. "I have already spoken to Jennifer and I am satisfied she knew nothing about them."

Emily was very annoyed with Sarah. She took John with her and sat at the piano and played as if her life depended upon it.

"It is a real long time that somebody play that piano," said Ursy.

"Miss Emily could play real good," said Jennifer who was no longer sulking.

"I remember when she was little and Clytie and me would peep into the room just to see that little face sitting there and pounding on that piano. She tell us that piece she is playing name Bramms."

Jennifer started to laugh.

"What you laughing at?" asked Ursy.

"It ain't name Bramms. It is Brahms Lullaby."

"How you know that?" asked an astonished Ursy.

"Back in St. Lucia, we had a gramophone and my father used to play things like that every Sunday evening. We used to sit down on the porch and listen to them."

"And you remember that piece Miss Emily playing?"

"Oh yes. Miss Sarah don't know how to play?"

"Sure she know. She was the one who learn Emily how to play."

"Well she do one good thing in this life," said the young woman.

# 11

Clytie was busy preparing lunch on Sunday afternoon when the black Vauxhall pulled up in front of the house. She had already laid out the tray with three glasses and rushed out to get the lemonade.

"Miss Emily," she said opening the door and running down the steps to bring Douglas up. "You getting real big Mr. Douglas."

"How is Miss Una?" asked Alastair. "We brought the new addition to the family to see you."

"Ma, Miss Emily and Mr. Alastair out here with the baby."

Miss Una came in accompanied by her sister. Miss Una's forehead was wrapped with a piece of cloth and one could see green leaves peering out from behind the white bandana.

"I think I got pressure (high blood pressure)," said the old woman. "I got this funny feeling in the head!"

"Have you seen a doctor?" asked Emily.

"No those doctors does charge too much and what is he going to tell me? Una, you have pressure. Enough talk about me! Let me see the little one."

Emily brought the baby to her while she struggled to put her glasses on.

"He is the living image of his grandfather," she said. "What a sweet child!"

"Sit down," said Clytie to the family members. "I make a cool drink of lemonade because today is real hot."

"Miss Emily, I almost forget," said the old woman, "this is my sister Ida from Carlina. Say howdy Ida."

The old woman smiled and Douglas saw that she had no front teeth.

"Mama she is just like Grandpa. The tooth fairy swallowed her teeth."

"I'm sorry," said Alastair. "His great grandfather lost his teeth."

"He is just a little one," said Ida reaching into her pocket and retrieving a little box.

She opened it and put a pinch of the contents on the back of her hand and inhaled deeply. Douglas side stepped her making his way to Miss Una, but all the while looking quizzically at the woman.

"It name snuff Douglas. The people from Carlina like their snuff. Sometimes she does frighten me when she start to sneeze."

Ida said nothing. It was obvious she was feeling very uncomfortable in the presence of the white family.

"These is good people Ida. You don't have to worry 'bout them. What you all name that sweet little child?"

"Alastair after his father, and John after my father."

"Oh yes! John Bottomsley," replied Miss Una.

"We can't stay too long. Nellie and Francois are expecting us for lunch."

"Give them my best and tell Francis thanks for bringing back my sister to me."

"I'll do that for you," said Emily.

Ida looked out the window and watched as the car disappeared. She was still standing there when her sister called out to her.

"Una, there is something about that lady that I can't put my finger on."

"What you mean Ida?"

"She always had a easy life Una? Something tell me she should pray a lot."

"Everybody 'round here does pray Ida. Every single soul!"

⁓

Alastair handed the platter which was covered to Nellie, who in turn handed it to Otty. They fussed over the baby and did not realize that Douglas had disappeared. He was in search of Long John. The child hadn't forgotten that his Uncle Francois had promised that he could play with the puppy.

"Miss Bertrand, I could see you in the kitchen for just a minute?" asked Otty.

The woman seemed beside herself.

"What's wrong?" asked Nellie.

"Look at this," she said pointing to the platter. "This is the same platter I put the fish cakes on. This is the platter we was searching for."

"Are you sure?"

"I'm as sure 'bout that as my name is Otty."

"How could it end up at Bottomsley plantation? Are you sure we had only one?"

"As long as I was working with Mr. Bertrand, I was seeing that plate. He only had one of them."

Nellie was shaken and totally mystified about the whole thing. How could the platter have ended up at Bottomsley plantation?

Before there was anymore time to ponder, the kitchen door flew open and Douglas ran in with Long John hot on his heels. They had found each other. Although it was a wonderful afternoon, the case of the mysterious platter still rested heavily on Nellie's mind. She was enthralled with her new grandson and Francois behaved like the doting grandfather. Memories of Douglas' birth and the first year of his life flashed through her mind. He was now four years old and it was almost time to go to school.

"I don't want to go to school," he said. "I want to stay at home and play with Grandpa."

"Come here," said Francois. "You must learn to read and write. That's important. Who will look after the plantation if you don't learn to read and write?"

"John can do it."

"But he is only a little boy."

"May I go back and look for Long John?" he asked.

"He was tired and went to bed."

"I can sleep with him," said the child.

"Just leave him alone for a little while," said his father. "Come and sit with me and we can talk to Miss Nellie and Uncle Francois."

"I want to see Otty," he said disappearing into the kitchen.

Otty had saved a couple sugar apples for the child and she placed them on a plate and sat him down at the table. In no time, his little face was covered with the white flesh of the delicious fruit.

"You have to spit out the seeds," said Otty holding out her hand. "You forget how to do it?"

"I'll get the tea," said Nellie leaving Otty with the child.

"Let me help you," said her daughter.

"Emily there is something I want to ask you."

"What is it?" she asked looking a little concerned.

"You brought this platter here today. Where did you get it?"

"Oh I don't know. Ursy gave it to me. I thought it belonged to us since it had the B in the middle. Why do you ask?"

"A couple weeks ago, a strange thing happened. I was already in bed when I thought I heard someone moving around outside in the drawing room. I heard a couple drawers open and close, and that's when Long John started to bark."

"Oh Nellie, that must have been frightening. Where was Francois?"

"He was in South Carolina looking for Miss Una's sister."

"So what did you do?"

"I came out and looked around, but there was no one. I locked all the doors and latched all the windows and took Long John in with me and locked the bedroom door."

"But what has all that got to do with the platter?"

"That same day Otty had made some fish cakes and had left some in the fridge. The following day, since I hadn't eaten any breakfast by the time she had arrived, I decided to have them, but the fish cakes along with the platter had disappeared."

"How would it make its way to my home?" Emily asked.

"That is the mystery. Poor Otty was beside herself today when she pulled it out of the bag."

"The only thing left to do is speak with Ursy and Jennifer to find out how it got into the plantation kitchen."

Later that evening Nellie spoke to Francois and he too was just as mystified. He however decided that they would pay special attention to closing up the home at night. He felt that something wasn't right and knew they shouldn't be taking any chances. They allowed Otty to leave early telling her she could do the cleaning up the following morning and they retired early after a strenuous day.

The Chambers too had put their children to bed and turned out the lights. It had been a long day for them and their bodies were crying out for a good night's rest. After the last light was turned off they all fell asleep. Shortly after, the door to Sarah Bottomley's bedroom creaked and slowly opened. The intruder entered and clasped his hand over her mouth.

"Don't say a word. If you do, I will kill your grand children," he whispered in a hoarse voice.

He removed his hand and tore open her negligee and proceeded to fondle her.

"Please don't," she begged but to no avail.

"You'll like it. I know you will."

After slumping on top of her, he demanded to have some money. In the darkness she found her handbag and emptied the contents of the wallet into the stranger's hands.

"Don't think of changing the locks. If you do, you will get up and open the door for me. I will be back soon to bring you a bit more happiness. And don't forget! One word out of you and I will take your grandchildren. But then no-one will believe you even if you did say anything," he said with a laugh. "They will think you have gone completely mad."

Sarah whimpered and buried her head underneath her pillow and wept.

Jennifer had awakened her children and they were heading out the door. Everything was well planned and this is the night she had chosen to make her escape. The children were confused after being awakened from their slumber, but she hurried them along and hid behind a tree just as the headlights of a car came into view. They walked and walked until they reached Ursy's home where she gently knocked on the door.

"Come in quick," said Ursy who had been expecting them.

"Thanks Ursy. I will not forget this. Say good evening to Ursy," she told the girls.

"I only have one bedroom as I tell you, but that ain't a problem. You really need help. You have to tell the children to be careful and stay inside if we ain't here. Everybody around here know everybody else business and the minute they see you or one of the children, everything is going to be out on the street. News don't lack a carrier 'round here."

"I am going to talk to them before I go to work tomorrow."

"You got to be careful with that too. Your husband know where you working?"

"Yes, but he ain't my husband."

"Lord have mercy. I thought you was married to that man. Anyway I am going to show you the back way to get in the kitchen without anybody seeing you. He might be waiting for you outside the plantation house. Get some rest! It is past midnight and we got to get up early."

Ursy gave the woman a pillow and a couple sheets and the family lay on her floor to settle in for the night.

"Jennifer," whispered Ursy, "I ask Clytie about talking to Mr. Bertrand and he say you could come up Saturday morning to see him."

"Thanks," whispered Jennifer as she snuggled close to her children.

It was early on Monday morning when the two women awoke to get ready for work. The two girls Jackie and Heather were given strict instructions not to venture outside and not to answer the door in case their mother's partner should show up, although the women very much doubted that he would come to Ursy's door.

"Morning," said Ursy as she opened the kitchen door and saw everyone sitting in the drawing room.

The usually even-tempered Emily hardly looked in her direction.

"Where is Jennifer?" asked Alastair.

"In the kitchen sir."

"Ask her to come in. I want to speak to both of you."

"Which one of you put that photo there?" asked Alastair pointing to the photo which had been missing for a while.

"I didn't sir," said Jennifer.

"Nor me," replied Ursy. "It was not there when I left Saturday forenoon."

"And another thing, where did you get this platter?" he asked holding up the yellow piece of porcelain.

"From the kitchen sir," replied Ursy.

"I bring it here with something for Ursy sir."

"And where did you get it?"

"From my house sir."

"Do you see the letter in the middle? Does anyone in your family have a name beginning with a B?"

"Yes sir."

"Are you telling me the truth?" asked Alastair.

"Yes sir."

"Do you live alone Jennifer?"

"No sir. I used to live with my two daughters and a man, but I move out and Ursy letting me stay with her."

"What is his name?"

"Why you want to know that sir?"

"Just tell me his name."

"Brandon Harvey sir."

"I presume he is the father of your children?"

"No sir."

"Then how long have you known him?"

"About nine years sir."

"Thank you. That will be all," he said.

Sarah Bottomsley sat on the plantation chair while her son in law questioned the servants, and never once did she open her eyes. She thought that the intruder might have had something to do with the photo but she preferred to let the servants take the blame instead of allowing them to think that she was insane. But the grand children! What about them? Was she willing to put their lives in danger for her own selfish reasons?

"You think the man you used to live with steal that plate Jennifer?" asked Ursy when they were alone in the kitchen.

"From where?" the bewildered woman asked.

"Wait a minute," said Ursy. "I give them that plate Sunday with some little eats on it to carry to Miss Bertrand. You think the plate belong to them?"

"I really don't know. I find it in my kitchen and I put the salt fish pie on it to bring for you. I didn't even remember nothing about the plate."

"Something just ain't right! Something just ain't right," Ursy repeated.

———

"Long John kept me awake all night," said Nellie sitting up in bed and yawning.

"He did seem a little unsettled," said her husband. "He was probably missing Douglas. Anyway my dear wife, I must get up. I've got lots of appointments today."

"So do I."

"Don't let that Transport Commissioner walk all over you. Just tell him there were too may promises which were never kept and it is time something concrete happened. The people of Plum Tree Village have been walking with their heavy bags for much too long. It is time to get that bus running through the village. Tell him he doesn't want to face your husband."

"Sometimes you make me laugh Francois. I am not going to let him walk over me. Don't you worry!"

"I have something for you," he said enveloping her in his arms.

"What?"

"It's a secret! Just tell them to hurry up and get that bus running through the village. And tonight, when I come we must discuss the school and my secret."

"What is the secret?" asked Nellie. "I think I know. We're going back to Paris."

"Nothing of the sort," he replied.

# 12

"Miss Bertrand, I find this envelope on the back step," said Otty.

"It's addressed to me," she said quickly opening it.

She sat down and looked at it. Then she turned it over and read it again and again.

> *NELI,*
> *WE GOT A SECRET. YOU WANT IT STAY LIKE THAT? PUT*
> *FIVE HUNDERD DOLLARS IN THIS SAME ENVVELOPE*
> *AND LEAVE IT IN THE CRACK IN THE BIG MOHOGANY*
> *TREE BY THE CHURCH THIS EVENIN.*
> *P.S. DOAN SAY NOTHIN TO YOUR HUSBAN.*

She couldn't believe it. After all these years of holding onto her secret, someone was now actually trying to blackmail her. How did they find out? She folded the piece of paper and put it into her handbag. She didn't have five hundred dollars in the house and couldn't ask Francois for it. Five hundred dollars was a lot of money and he would certainly ask what she was going to do with it. Clytie! She would ask her and repay her at a later date. She pulled the letter out and read it again. She was not sure what to make of it. There were spelling and grammatical mistakes but these were perhaps intentional. None of the villagers could have written a note that well, so it was definitely not one of them. She however needed the money urgently before Francois returned home.

⎯⎯⎯

Nora was in a foul mood. Her son had not slept at home for three nights. His wife pretended she didn't care, but Nora knew she was hurting inside. His mother patiently awaited his return and when he did, she did not mix her words. His bags were packed and sitting behind a chair in the drawing room.

"Boy you ever see your father get on like that? Ever since you come back here, your pants crotch catch afire and you can't seem to put it out. You bring Judes here and tell everybody that she is your wife. Why you don't behave like a husband should behave? We ain't bring you up so."

"I'm not a boy any longer. I am a man," replied Toby.

"Well every man should be under his own roof, so I pack your bags for you. Do the thing a man should do and leave. You can pick them up on the way out. And don't think you going to my sister with no sad story."

"Where is Pa?" he asked.

"Gone fishing! You know where to find him. Don't even try telling him no sad story neither, because it ain't going to change nothing."

"Alright. I will pick up the bags when I come back. But what do you expect Judes to do?"

"Why you didn't think 'bout Judes before you start gallivanting 'round here? Anyway I ain't putting Judes out. Judes is a decent girl and she can stay here until she decide what she want to do with her life."

A forlorn Toby walked along the cliffs toward the beach. His mother watched as he stood in the middle of the way, unzipped his trousers and urinated next to the pathway. She could only shake her head and watch as he continued down to the beach where he saw his father throwing his fishing line out to sea. He went over and sat beside him.

"Ma throw me out," he said.

"Can't say I blame your mother," he replied.

"Nobody's on my side."

"You left this Rock and went away to better yourself, but you come back here behaving like the parish ram. Your wife behaving herself more like a daughter than you like a son. She call me Pa and she call Nora Ma. Even Nellie is Miss Nellie. She stay in that shop with Clytie and work until the last light out. What you doing to help? Nothing boy! I am sure if you went to Francois and Nellie they would find something for you to do."

"Why does everyone bow down to Nellie? It is always Nellie this and Nellie that."

"Don't let me hear you talking nothing bad about Nellie. Without Nellie, we wouldn't have the life we have today. Your mother never beg her sister for one thing, but Nellie make sure that everybody was looked after."

"That don't mean that you must be thankful until the day you dead," he said lapsing into Barbadian dialect.

"You is a real ungrateful boy," said the father hauling in his fishing line and picking up his catch of the day, leaving his son staring out to sea.

Toby stood up and put his hands in his pockets. He didn't have a penny. He decided to go to his wife to borrow some money. After all she had a job. Harriet must be paying her something for helping out in the hair salon.

Nellie was still contemplating where she would get the money to pay the blackmailer. Her best bet was Clytie who was now running the shop, 'Nellie's Bar and Grocery.' She was desperate. If Clytie had the money, she knew she could count on her.

"Morning Clytie," she said.

"Nels how you? Ma was asking 'bout you."

"Tell Miss Una I coming down today to see her. How Ida getting along?"

"She is doing alright. Judes and Harriet got her looking like a princess. They get a couple pieces of cloth from the Coolie man and she got some new dresses. The only thing missing is the teef (teeth). Yesterday Douglas say that she look just like his Grandpa because she didn't have no teeth."

Nellie forced a little laugh.

"You alright Nels? You don't sound like yourself."

"I have a favour to ask you," Nellie replied.

"You know you can ask me anything Nels."

"You have five hundred dollars that I can borrow?"

"Five hundred dollars?" asked an astonished Clytie. "Yes I have it, but why you want to borrow so much money? That is a lot of money."

"Does that mean you will lend it to me?"

"It isn't none of my business, but you and Francois running out of money?"

"Nothing like that Clytie. Somebody is trying to blackmail me. I think they want to tell the world that Emily is my daughter."

"What? Who would do a thing like that?"

"I don't know Clytie."

"What Francois say?"

"He doesn't know. The letter said I should not tell him."

"I still think you should tell him Nels. After all he would know what to do."

"And what if they expose my business to all the people on this Rock? Oh my poor Emily!"

"Alright Nels, we can talk later. I will have the money waiting here for you, but I still say that you should trust Francois and tell him what is going on. After all he is a solicitor and know 'bout these things."

Clytie had to hurry. She had left Harriet in the shop and Judes was alone in the hairdressing shop. After meeting, she and Nellie walked as fast as they could, and while she stood watch, Nellie was able to hide the money in the wide crack of the mahogany tree.

"You tell Nora?" Clytie asked.

"I didn't have time to tell her anything. All I could think about was getting the money."

"But Nels, what if they want more money?"

"Five hundred dollars is a lot of money and will last a life time," replied Nellie.

"Huh! I hope so," said Clytie.

"This is the worst time for something like this to happen to me. I was on my way to meet the Transport Board Committee because they are taking too long to get a bus running through the village."

"Try to forget about it Nels. I ain't in no hurry for the money. You go down there and you do your best for these poor people."

"Don't say a word about this to Francois!" she said.

"We should come back later and wait to see who going to pick it up," said Clytie.

"No Clytie. I am just too frightened to do that. I just don't want my business scattered all over the place. Not only my business, but my daughter's business and her children's business."

"Nels think about it. You can't handle this by yourself. You got to tell Francois."

"You will get back your money real soon Clytie. Don't worry."

"I'm not worried about the money Nels. You is the best friend I ever had. You was real good to my mother and my son and I don't want nothing to happen to you."

"Nothing is going to happen as long as they get the money Clytie."

"Alright I got to run. Harriet is in the hair shop all by herself."

"We will talk later Clytie."

When Toby showed up at the hairdressing shop, his wife was not there but his sister was. He was carrying his two valises and seemed a little out of sorts.

"Where you going with those two bags?" his sister asked.

"Ma put me out," he replied.

"You don't have nothing to worry about," said Harriet. "You can go back to the same place you spend the last three nights."

"You don't understand."

"I don't?" asked Harriet.

"I need a small loan."

"How much is a small loan?"

"About a hundred! I got to find somewhere to live, or can I stay with you for a short while?"

Harriett went to the back room and returned with seventy five dollars.

"This is all I have," she said. "How you going to pay me back? You don't work."

He had not expected the loan. He would've preferred to stay with his sister but she was having none of it. She didn't like his lifestyle and couldn't face her mother if she had allowed him to stay with her. Besides she had grown quite fond of his wife and didn't want him hanging around while she was there. Before he had a chance to leave, Judes showed up.

"Good morning," she said.

"Good morning Judes. How are you?"

"Very well," she replied continuing on her way to the back of the shop.

"Judes," he said following her much to his sister's disapproval, "would you talk to Ma for me? She threw me out of the house."

"She did?" his wife asked.

"Yes. I know she likes you and one word from you would make her change her mind."

"I am not getting involved Toby. Since we came here you have not treated me with any kind of respect. You probably think me stupid, but I'm not. I see how you play with the young girls around here, and worst of all I haven't seen you for three nights. Where did you sleep Toby? How could you ask me for any kind of help?"

She marched out and left him nearly knocking Harriet over. She had been listening in on their conversation and was proud of her sister in law. She also knew that Jonas had become Judes' confidant. She found him to be a good listener and an intelligent one too. Whenever she was feeling low, she always turned to him. He would invite her to the beach and once as far as they knew, he took her once to see a movie. He had even spoken to Toby about his philandering ways, but nothing had changed and Jonas could see that he was slowly losing his wife. Sometimes Jonas would call her from the school to invite her to the pictures, but she seemed afraid of getting too close to him. After all he and her husband were like brothers and she had learnt that in these parts, news never lacked a carrier.

# 13

Nellie returned home to find Long John throwing up all over the verandah. In spite of the discomfort, the animal was still happy to see a familiar face and wagged his little tail when he saw her. Otty seemed very concerned because she too had grown to love Long John.

"I don't know what happen to him," she said. "He was running around outside and then he start to throw up. And he making some real funny noises."

Nellie had no idea what she should do. This was her first dog and she loved him dearly. He was a good companion especially when she was alone. A quick call was made to Francois and Clarence accompanied Otty to the Vet with the animal, while Nellie continued on her way to meet the Transport Board Committee members.

Nellie walked into the room where there was just one man standing and gazing out the window. She was about to introduce herself, when he approached her.

"Can't say that we've met! Smoky Archer," said the man offering his hand to Nellie.

"Nellie Bertrand!" she said as the man held on to her hand.

"I was somehow expecting someone else," he said looking at her lecherously. "So you're the one fighting to get a bus through Plum Tree Village. I'll be damned. We could get this worked out between us."

"What could we work out?" asked Nellie pulling her hand away.

"You are a smart woman and I know you understand what I mean. One word from me and you could consider this done."

"I still don't understand what you mean Mr.?"

"Call me Smoky. Everyone calls me that."

"Well Smoky, explain what you mean, because I really don't understand," she said as his stale body odour mixed with pipe tobacco penetrated her nostrils.

"So pretty!" he said staring at Nellie. "So pretty!"

"Look Mr. Smoky, I don't know what you want from me, but I certainly don't want anything from you."

"Come! Come! We could have this over by this morning," he said drawing closer to her.

"There is no way I would let you touch me. We will vote this morning and I know we will be successful, so keep your advances for someone else. I have a husband and a handsome one at that," she said looking at the digusted fat man.

The conversation came to an end when two more committee members entered the room followed closely by the rest of the group. Nellie was still annoyed when the meeting was called to order. She had brought some notes which Francois had given her and she went about defending her case with venom and vigour and ignoring Smoky's gaze. After the minutes were read, the group took a break before they took a vote. A vote that would affect the lives of the people of Plum Tree Village.

Victory! Victory for the people who had struggled all their lives. Six to five in their favour! Nellie was elated. The victory was not hers, but all the residents of Plum Tree Village.

On returning home, Otty was still not there, so she called the Vet's office. Otty was still standing with Long John in her arms when she entered the waiting area where three other white people sat waiting their turn. They played with their animals, treating them more like little children than animals. She walked up to the reception and was abruptly told she should wait. Embarrassed, she stood and waited, then finally sat down. More owners entered with their animals and were immediately looked after. After this happened for the third time, she got up and spoke to the receptionist.

"You didn't have an appointment, so you will have to wait," she was told.

"My husband called and made an appointment. Check your books for the name Francois Bertrand! You kept my housekeeper standing here for almost two hours."

The woman grudgingly looked into the appointment schedule and told Nellie to follow her, much to the displeasure of the white woman who had been called and then asked to sit again. The receptionist was unapologetic although she realized she had made a mistake.

"Good Morning," said Nellie.

"Mrs. Bertrand?" asked the Vet looking at the file the woman had given to him. "What seems to be the problem with the little one?"

"He is throwing up."

"Let's have a look. What is his name?"

"Long John."

"I once had a little one called Long John. Isn't that a coincidence?"

"My husband named him Long John because he had a dog with the same name when he was a boy."

Long John was dehydrated and was given some medicine which perked him up and that made Nellie happy. There was nothing seriously wrong with the animal. She decided she wouldn't tell Francois about her encounter with the receptionist. It was time that she started fighting her own battles just as she had done with Smoky Archer.

"How is my Long John?" asked Francois as the dog met him at the door.

"He is just fine. The Vet gave him some tablets and something like life water because he said he was dehydrated," said Nellie.

"What happened at the Transport Board Committee meeting?" he asked.

"Everything went well. They said they are looking at the middle of the year for the first bus to start running through the village."

"I'm so proud of you," he said. "After one year of battling with that bunch of stubborn people, you have finally succeeded in getting the villagers a bus to save them travelling with those heavy loads on their heads. I'm sure they will all be grateful to you."

"It was tough, but I managed. In the end the vote was six to five in our favour."

"Now there's only the school left to discuss."

"I wish you wouldn't ask me to close it Francois."

"If there was no alternative I wouldn't ask you to do it, but since the government is offering free education in the new school, I'm sure the parents would prefer to send their children there rather than having to pay you."

"What about Jonas and the other teachers?"

"They are all qualified. Jonas is a very good teacher and they know it. Because he doesn't have a teaching certificate doesn't mean that they won't hire him. Look at the number of children he taught who all have gone on to high school. They should take that into consideration."

"Just too many changes all at once," said Nellie with a sigh. "Things as we know them are just slipping away."

"Don't worry so much Nellie. Think of all the free time you will have that we can spend together. What's good for dinner?" he asked.

"Otty made your favourite. Baked chicken with stuffing, mashed potatoes and string beans!"

"Mmm! I can't wait. I'll change my clothes and be right back."

"What is the surprise you have for me?" she asked.

He smiled, winked at her and made his way towards the bedroom.

*I wonder what it could be, wondered Nellie. Probably another trip to Paris!*

―――

"Prepare ye the way of the Lord," the woman's voice echoed disturbing the early morning peace.

Clytie got up and looked out the window. The short, barefooted, light skinned woman with the Bible under one arm preached as she went along. She looked from house to house as she spoke. Clytie cringed. Mrs. Hoyte was like the messenger of death. Wherever and whenever she appeared, it usually meant that someone in the village would soon be called home to rest. She could see the last of the stars disappearing into their celestial home and the last drops of dew still glistening on the grass. Why had Mrs. Hoyte chosen such a beautiful morning to bring her message? And of all the places, why Plum Tree Village? The woman's voice could still be heard even though she was out of sight. Finally the distance silenced her.

Jennifer was up at the crack of dawn and with two bus changes made her way to St. Lucy. She arrived at the Bertrand residence just before ten and waited outside the gate until she was ushered in by Otty.

"Morning sir," she said as Francois called her into his office beside the verandah.

"Good morning. Clytie told me you have a problem concerning some property on another island."

"Yes sir."

"Have a seat and tell me all about it. First tell me your name," he said picking up a pen and a note pad.

"Jennifer Appleby," said the woman.

Francois did not raise his head. It seemed as if he had been turned into stone. Finally he spoke.

"Tell me Miss Appleby, which island are you referring to?"

"St. Lucia sir."

He stared at the young woman for a couple of seconds.

"Are you Jennifer Applewhite? Is your father Teddy Applewhite or rather Appleby?"

"Yes sir."

"Miss Appleby, do you mind if I brought my wife in here with us?"

"No sir."

He got up and left the room. He paused outside the door, then went in search of Nellie.

"Do you remember my wife?" he asked the young woman.

"Yes sir," she said smiling at Nellie.

"I understand your father has passed away."

"Yes sir."

"And your sister? What happened to her?"

"She pass away too."

"How did that happen?"

Tears flowed as Jennifer told her tale of woe. She was cooking dinner one evening when her baby started to cry. Her father called out to her to pick up the child, but her sister Rose had already picked the baby up and was sitting outside when a man appeared from nowhere looking for Ted Applewhite. After speaking with the stranger for a couple minutes, her father told them to dress warmly and he would be back in about an hour. She had never seen the man and wondered what it was all about. They did as they were told and the two sisters had dinner and waited. Her father returned with another man and the whole family headed off to a deserted beach with just a few personal belongings. It was dark and the sisters were afraid, but their father said everything would be alright. They climbed into a fishing boat with an outboard motor and drove away from the island. Suddenly the engine died and they started to drift. It got darker and darker and the sea became very rough. The waves were high and they were in danger of being swept out into the open sea, but they hung on as hard as they could. With one arm she held the baby close to her chest and with the other she clung to the boat. Suddenly a great wave washed her father and sister overboard. He was a good swimmer but Rose perished among the waves. They searched for a little while with a torch light, but finally gave up and continued their journey. Her father was was afraid that if they weren't rescued soon, they would run out of food and water, and two days later they were picked up by a fishing boat which was on its way to Barbados. The skipper of the boat deposited them on a beach near the north coast and there they lived for seven years.

"Did your father report your sister's death?"

"No sir. I don't think so sir. He couldn't even talk about it. He was not a real good father, but when Rose pass on, it almost break his heart. He was a very sad man. He only went out to do some shopping or to get the child some clothes."

"Have mercy dear Lord!" said Nellie as she listened to the young woman whose tears now flowed like a river.

"Who is the child's father?" asked Francois.

The young woman hesitated before she answered.

"My father!"

"Dear God!" said Nellie holding onto the woman's hand.

"Are you telling me that you lived on this island for more than seven years and no one knew of your existence?" asked Francois.

"Yes sir!" she said through sobs.

"So has Ted Applewhite really died?" he asked her waiting for confirmation.

"Yes sir. He pass away about six weeks back."

"Now I remember something about your going to a funeral in St. John," said Nellie.

"But I thought you lived in St. Lucy," said Francois.

"We used to live in St. Peters, and then I meet a man down there and we move to St. Lucy. My father liked him at first, but then he didn't like him no more because of the way he started to treat me. So somebody told my father about a place in St. John that was safe and he pack up and moved down there."

Francois realized that Ted Appleby or Applewhite had chosen to live in St. John because once there he could hide among the poor whites. After all, he was still a man on the run.

"Are you still with this man?" asked Francois.

"No sir."

"Where is he?"

"Living close to Bottomsley plantation."

"What is his name?"

"Brandon Harvey sir."

"Is he British?"

"Yes sir."

"And where did you meet him Jennifer?"

"One night when we was still in St. Peters and I had just had my second child, we hear something hit 'longside the door. When my father open it, a man was lying down on the ground. We pull him in and see that he was in a bad way. He had a big gash on his forehead. We look after him and he stay with us till he was in good shape again. After he live with us for 'bout three months, he tell my father that I was a nice girl and he like me and my father say it was alright. But when my father see all the black and blue marks on my body, he say he was going to kill him. Then one day when my father went out, he moved me and the children to St. Lucy. He didn't want the children, but I couldn't leave them behind with my father. I didn't trust him. Anyway it almost break my father heart and he move away to St. John. My father say I was foolish and that he didn't want nothing more to do with me. A couple months after we move to St. Lucy, Brandon see something in the newspaper that say the owners of Bottomsley plantation was looking for somebody to work in the kitchen. I went down there and apply for the job and I get it. Then we all move down there."

"Does your friend work Jennifer?"

"No sir."

"Francois she needs a break. Let me take her to Otty so she can get something to eat and catch her breath," said Nellie.

Francois watched the two women walk away and turned to look out the window. Something wasn't adding up. He believed her story however there seemed to be a missing link. Why hadn't the man sought some kind of employment in a country where he was sure to get something important to do? After all he was white and British.

"You look puzzled," said Nellie looking at her husband.

"Why did he move all the way down there to have her find employment in the Bottomsley kitchen?"

"I guess they had to find a way to feed the children."

"No Nels, I don't think that was the reason."

"Then what do you think it is?"

"I don't know. Send her back here as soon as she is finished."

Jennifer returned and finished her story. She needed to get the inheritance left by her father so she could support herself and her two children. She had brought along a copy of his Will which she had found among his belongings naming her the sole inheritor of the properties stipulated on the list. Francois said it would take a while since her father had passed away and nothing had been done about the properties in St. Lucia since his sudden departure from the island.

"It also says here that your father owned some property in England."

"Yes sir."

"Do you remember your mother?"

"No sir. I was real small when we went to St. Lucia."

"Where are your children now?"

"They at home sir."

"Does he know where they are?"

"I don't think so. He don't know where Ursy lives."

"We are going to visit Bottomsley today and you can ride back with us. Otty will let you know when we are ready to go."

"How much is it going to cost sir?" the young woman asked.

"It is a lot of work and will take quite some time but I'll see what I can do for you."

"Thank you sir."

"Do the children go to school?"

"No sir. I am frighten to send them to school."

"Why don't you move back to St. Lucy and bring the children with you?" Nellie asked.

"I have to work to support them, and I like Miss Chambers. She is a real nice lady. I like the children too. If I left now Douglas would miss me."

The last statement cut through Nellie's heart like a knife through butter. Little did Jennifer know that she was referring to Nellie's child and her grandchildren.

# 14

Long John whimpered and was restless throughout the night. Francois slept like a log but Nellie only tossed and turned. She kept thinking of Jennifer and the hardships of her life. Her life had been difficult but it was certainly nothing compared to Jennifer's. She had a family that loved her and a husband who adored her. She was happy when morning came and darkness was no longer the eternal foe. Francois was up on the crack of dawn, showered, had a light breakfast and was on his way to work. When Nellie came out to feed Long John, she realized her husband had left a box of files by the door. She immediately called his office, but he had not yet arrived.

"Morning Miss Bertrand," said Otty. "This is for you."

Nellie looked at the envelope and her heart sank. Was the blackmailer requesting more money from her? She went to her bedroom and opened the letter.

*NELLIE, YOU HELP ME OUT THE LAST TIME! I NEED MORE MONEY. JESS LIKE BEFORE. FIVE HUNDRED. PUT IT IN THE SAME SPOT. NOT A WORD TO YOUR HUSBAND. REMEMBER IT IS OUR LITTLE SECRET*

The telephone rang and she ran to the living room to answer it.

"Nels," said a voice on the other end, "come over as quick. Something like it happen to Ma."

Nellie dropped the letter beside the telephone, called out to Otty, who in turn got in touch with Clarence the driver, and she was off to Clytie's home. Five minutes later, Francois returned home to pick up his box of files which he had forgotten.

"Where is my wife?" he asked Otty.

"Clytie call and she left in a real hurry."

He spotted the envelope with Nellie's name on the front and he opened it and looked inside. Shock registered all over his face and he immediately made a call to Clytie's home.

"Is Nels there?" he asked a devastated Clytie.

There was no response from Clytie. That was unusual because she was always very friendly to him.

"Clytie?" he asked.

"No it is Nellie," said his wife.

"Is something wrong Nellie?"

"Miss Una is gone."

"Gone where?" asked Francois.

"She died in her sleep last night."

"Dear Lord!" he exclaimed. "I'll be there in a minute."

"Hurry," she replied.

It was extremely quiet when he arrived at the house. Ida, Clytie, Harriet and Judes were quietly sitting in the drawing room while Nellie paced back and forth.

"I'm so glad you're here," she said as he entered the house.

"Was she sick? Did you call the doctor?" he asked.

"I make the breakfast this morning and call them like I always do. Aunt Ida come out and say she couldn't wake up Ma. When

I went into the room, Ma was cold like ice," Clytie said breaking into hysterics.

"Lord I wasn't able to spend a little more time with my sister," said Ida. "My only sister! But I know this was going to happen. What I am going to do now without my sister?"

"Don't worry Aunt Ida. You always got a home here with me and Jonas," said her niece.

"Would you like any help with the funeral arrangements?" asked Francois.

"Oh yes Francois. I can't handle this by myself," said Clytie.

"Let me get these files to the office and I will start making arrangements," said Francois.

"Don't stay away too long," said Nellie her eyes filled with tears.

"Would you like to come with me?" he asked.

"No I must stay here with Clytie and the others. They need me."

The family had lost its matriarch. The no-nonsense Una Clarissa Prescott had breathed her last breath. The villagers who had known her started to gather in the living room of the home to pay their respects. No one could believe that Miss Una was really gone. Just like that! Nora and Percy arrived and so did Jonas when he heard the news. It was one of the saddest days in Plum Tree Village. In respect for her mother's passing, Clytie decided to keep the grocery store closed for the day, and Harriet did the same with the hair salon. Nellie's school was also closed and the children were happy to have a day away from books and studying.

"I forgot to tell Emily," said a distraught Nellie.

Emily too was devastated. She had grown to love the old lady; the old lady who had helped her through her most difficult moments. Alastair had just left the house and as she ran after him to impart the bad news, she saw the back end of the vehicle disappear through the gate. As Alastair drove out, Francois was driving in and the two men drove back to Bottomsley Great House. Francois told him about Miss Una's death while the two men climbed the steps together. Then they sat down on the verandah.

"I know this is a bad time but I want to tell you something," said Francois. "I think Nellie is in some kind of trouble."

"What kind of trouble?" asked Alastair.

Francois pulled the blackmail note from his pocket and showed it to him. Alastair studied the note and handed it back to him.

"Definitely not one of the native people," he said.

"That's exactly what I thought. The wording is definitely not from a local person."

"Any idea who it could be?"

"None at all!"

"And what does Nellie have to say about it?"

"She doesn't know I have the letter. She was called away because of Miss Una's death and forgot and left it next to the telephone."

"We will certainly miss Miss Una. What really happened to her? When did it happen?"

"She died in her sleep lastnight."

"And where is Nellie right now?"

"She's with Clytie and her aunt at their home."

"Poor Nellie! Perhaps we should wait until Miss Una's funeral is over before we tackle this thing."

"I'm so afraid for her Alastair!"

"Don't be afraid," said Emily. "We can handle this together. Miss Una was always kind to me and we must see to it that she has a proper burial."

The two men breathed a collective sigh of relief. They thought that Emily had overheard their discussion about the blackmail note.

"When is the funeral?" Alastair asked.

"No plans have been made. I promised Nellie I would return as soon as possible to help out."

"You know you can count on us for any kind of assistance," said Alastair.

"What about all the workers from around here who would like to attend the funeral?" asked Emily. "I'm sure those who knew Miss Una would like to pay their respects."

"Well we should let them have the day off, because it would take quite a while for them to travel from here to St. Lucy."

"What about the van we have here?" asked Emily. "It holds twenty people and we could ask Clyde to drive them to St.Lucy."

"I am sure Clytie would be happy to see some familiar faces," said Francois. "Anyway I should be getting back to Nellie. She's not in a very good way."

Alastair walked with him to the car and the two men shook hands.

"After the funeral, we'll tackle that problem. From the way the note is written, it seems that she has given money to the blackmailer before. What do you think they are holding over her head?"

Francois stared at Alastair. No words were necessary. They both reached the conclusion that whatever it was, Emily was somehow involved.

# 15

C lytie's home was filled with strangers. Strangers who were singing loudly and totally out of tune. Doh re me fa soh la ti doh! They had consumed too much Bottomsley white rum, and as they drank, they cried. In their drunken stupour, they still knew they were mourning the loss of Una Prescott whose body lay in the room where she had slept for the last ten years. Her sister Ida Franklin sat on a chair close to the bedroom door not saying a word. Bereaved over her sister's death, she just kept dipping her fingers into her snuff tin and sneezing until her eyes watered and tears rolled down her cheeks. None of the strangers spoke to her because they hardly knew her.

Clytie had laid out a spread for the visitors. There were sardines, corned beef and biscuits, fish cakes and a couple bottles of rum on the table from which they helped themselves. The rest of the family and friends sat around deep in sorrow, but occasionally they would all have a good laugh when one of the mourners who had consumed too much alcohol would fall to floor and be unable to stand again.

Una Prescott looked as if she were asleep as she lay in the mahogany coffin in the drawing room of the home she had shared with her daughter and grandson. All the mourners filed by to pay their last respects, stopping to get a good look at the woman who had changed the lives of so many.

"You go along 'til I come," someone would say.

"She look real peaceful," said another.

"Clytie put her way real good," still another said.

That meant that Clytie did well in providing a casket fit to bury her mother in. Not just any cheap old box, but something befitting the status of the departed. Nellie, Francois and Clytie had seen to it that the old lady was given a beautiful farewell. Now running short of time, Francois and Nellie decided to go straight to the church instead of going back to Clytie's home.

Outside the home mourners had gathered for the procession to the church. The villagers from Bottomsley plantation and those from Plum Tree Village had all lined up outside the home, two by two. The women were all dressed in white and walked ahead of the procession; then the men in their heavy suits, quite unsuitable for the hot weather followed. A brass band with trumpets, drummers and tambourine shakers went before the car which took the family to the church. Then the carriage with the limping horse and its driver who was called Bottleneck because of his elongated neck, struggled along with Miss Una's body. A nail had been inserted between the horse's shoe and his hoof causing pain, thus giving the impression that the horse too was bowing to show respect to the departed.

It was indeed a sad day. There was a lot of sniffling, moaning and groaning. Francois' arm fit snugly around his wife's waist and remained there throughout the service. Alastair and Emily along with Ursy sat behind them. Clytie was helped along by Nora on one side and Judes on the other. Harriet had a firm grip on Ida Franklin who struggled through her grief at the loss of her sister.

She seemed to falter and a quick whiff of smelling salts from Harriet's pocket had her firmly on her feet again.

The service lasted for forty minutes with Francois bestowing a eulogy which brought just about everyone to tears. The casket was then carried out with Jonas at the head, then Alastair and Francois side by side, followed by Toby and Percy and five more men from Bottomsley plantation and Plum Tree Village. Clytie sobbed loudly, such was her grief. Arm in arm with Nellie who was also grief-stricken, they walked behind the casket of Una Prescott. At the graveside they were joined by Emily and Ursy as the priest said the final farewell. Slowly Miss Una's body was lowered into the earth, just a few feet away from her friend Ella Burnett. After the first handful of earth was thrown onto the casket, Clytie broke down and had to be escorted away from the graveside. A couple of minutes later, Ida too had to be taken away. She had completely lost her composure and was asking to be buried along with her sister. Irreverent as it may seem, it did bring muted laughter from many of the onlookers.

The final shovel of earth was thrown upon the mound, and those who had brought flowers with them, gently placed them on the grave. The old men from the village, still under the influence of alcohol continued singing their out-of-tune dirges. Were it not for the death of a woman like Una Prescott, it could've been considered a comedy. In spite of the severity of the situation, Francois found himself glancing around the churchyard in search of the big mahogany tree. Nellie's problem was resting heavily on his mind.

The Chambers along with Ursy were eager to get back to Bottomsley plantation since the children were left with Jennifer and Grandpa Bottomsley. Sarah was still busy twirling her locks and reading a book when they pulled into the driveway. John's pram was pushed to the side and Jennifer was busy playing ball with the children as Grandpa Bottomsley, glass in hand was observing it all from up above.

"How are the children?" asked Emily.

"They doing real fine Miss Emily," Jennifer replied.

"Let's take them upstairs," she said as Ursy picked up the younger child, who had no desire to go inside.

"I want to play with Jennifer," he said kicking and thrashing his arms.

"Jennifer has chores to do and you have played enough. Grandpa will read a book to you," said his father.

This seemed to satisfy the child and they all went upstairs.

"How was the funeral?" Grandpa Bottomsley asked.

"What can I say? It was a funeral. Sad! Very sad! Especially for Clytie and her Aunt Ida!"

"I never knew that Clytie had an aunt."

"She used to live in South Carolina Grandpa. Nellie's husband found her and brought her back about six months ago."

No one seemed to notice Sarah Bottomsley flinch at the mention of Nellie's name.

"What did you say was the name of Una's sister?" asked the old man.

"Ida!" replied his granddaughter. "Why do you ask?"

"No reason," said the old man.

"How are you Mother?"

"As well as can be! You must tell her not to take the children into the sun."

"I don't see anything wrong with that. It's good for them. They'll get a little colour on their skins."

"The last thing they need, especially Douglas, is more colour on their skins."

"What do you mean by that Mother?"

"I'm just thinking of the children's welfare," she said.

"I see no harm in allowing them to get as much fresh air as they can."

Grandpa Bottomsley followed the family into the house leaving Sarah alone on the verandah.

"What's with her?" Emily asked.

"I don't know. She seems to be absolutely worried about the children. There was nothing I could say to her to put her mind at rest."

"There is no need to worry. Jennifer is quite capable and so is Ursy."

"Something seems to be bothering her. Although she doesn't really take the children in her arms, I still think she loves them."

"Well she has nothing to worry about. Tell her that."

<hr>

"I think I should stay here overnight," said Nellie.

"Where will you sleep? The house is full," said Francois. "You could come back early tomorrow morning."

"I want to be sure everything will be alright with Clytie and Miss Ida."

"Don't worry about them," said Judes. "I'll stay here with them tonight and I think Harriet intends to do the same."

"Alright. You can always call me if you need me."

"Yes Miss Nellie. I will make sure they are alright," said Judes.

"Nice girl," said Francois. "I wonder what she saw in your nephew."

"Toby isn't a bad child. He just got a little too big for his boots."

"I just don't know. The only one who was able to put him in his place is now lying under the earth," said Nellie bursting into tears.

"Come Nels. I know it is difficult for you, but Miss Una wouldn't want to see you crying over her."

"She knows that I will miss her. It was just like when ......."

He knew what she was about to say and did not push her to continue. She was thinking of John Bottomsley's death. Long John was elated when they entered the house. He was obviously hungry and walked closely behind them. Francois set about feeding him while Nellie reclined on the sofa deep in thought. She suddenly got up and started to search the drawer.

"Where did I put it?" she whispered.

"What are you looking for?" asked her husband as he entered the room.

"Just a piece of paper I left here."

"Is it something important?" he asked.

"Yes."

"Is this what you're looking for?" he asked pulling two pieces of paper from his briefcase.

Her heart started to race. How could she have been so careless? She was afraid for Francois. The letter specifically stated that she shouldn't tell her husband.

"Where did you find them?"

"Exactly where you left them! Come over here," he said taking her hand and leading her to the sofa.

Tears ran down Nellie's face. All the fears and the tears overflowed like a volcanic eruption.

"Come, come Nels. It's not so bad."

"Yes it is!"

"You know that you can come to me with anything. Whatever

affects your life, also affects mine. I wish you had told me about this when it happened."

"I didn't know what to do. The note said I shouldn't say anything to you."

"This isn't something you can handle alone. Whoever this is has found a source for money and will keep coming back again and again. How much did you give them the last time?"

"Five hundred," she replied.

"Five hundred? That's a lot of money Nellie. Now they want five hundred again. Have you any idea who this could be?"

"I thought of one person, but I don't think he would do this to me."

"Who?"

"I don't want you to be angry."

"Who do you think is doing this to you Nellie?"

"Toby."

"Your nephew? Why do you think Toby would do a thing like that?"

"He has no money and is constantly borrowing from his sister."

"He knows nothing about Emily."

"What else could it be? I don't have any other secrets."

"Let me think about this."

"Do you really think he would do this to me? I am his aunt."

"I don't know Nels, but we must find out before whoever it is sends us to the poor house."

Francois put the two notes side by side on the drawing room table as Nellie carefully studied his face. He gritted his teeth which caused the veins in his temples to beat like a throbbing heart.

"Look at this Nellie. I think someone is really trying to confuse us."

"Why do you say that?"

"Look at the way your name is spelt in the first note. Now look at the second one."

"They didn't spell it right!" she proclaimed.

"Now look at the first note. Hardly any punctuation! I don't think it is Toby. When I compare the two notes, I know whoever it is, is trying to confuse you and put doubts in your mind."

"What kind of doubts?"

"I think the mistakes in both notes were made intentionally. First I think the person forgot how they had spelled your name. The local people never use words like 'crack' or 'spot'. Don't you think they would say things like 'the hole in the tree instead of the crack in the tree'?"

"I guess so," she said with doubt etched across her forehead.

"Then the word hundred is also written incorrectly. Another intentional mistake! And somehow in spite of the mistakes, they were able to construct two notes which could be understood. It could be Toby, but somehow I don't believe that he is the culprit. Let's go to bed. I'll show them to Alastair tomorrow and find out what he thinks."

"Don't do that Francois."

"Don't you want to find out who's behind this?"

"Yes but I don't want Emily to worry about it."

"No need to tell her. It will be just between Alastair and me. In the meantime Nels, I want you to keep every door locked. No matter what time of the day it is. Also keep Long John inside the house if you get busy. I'll have a word with Otty about this also."

"Now I'm beginning to get really frightened," said Nellie.

"You've just got to be careful, that's all."

# 16

"You hear anything from Mr. Francois?" Ursy asked Jennifer.

"No but he say it was going to take a little time, and he would let me know when he had any news."

"I don't understand why it is taking so long. You say he left it in the Will for you."

"But a long time pass since we left St. Lucia."

"That don't mean nothing. What is yours is yours."

"Well I have to wait until Mr. Bertrand call me. Isn't a thing I can do about it until then."

"You got two daughters and you have to get something for them. What about that man you used to live with? You ain't see nor hear nothing from him?"

"Not a thing! I find it real strange! He isn't the type to let go things so easy especially since he don't have no money. Sometimes I feel real frighten for my two girls."

"You can't expect them to stay in the house all the time. They are children and might want to go outside to play with the other children."

"Well I warn Heather that they ain't to go outside."

"You got to send them to school Jennifer."

"I know, but I don't want him to carry them 'way from me."

"You should talk to Clytie. Those girls need to get away from around here. What he going to do with two little girls anyway if he carry them 'way. He can't even support himself."

"I don't understand what you mean by getting them 'way from 'round here," said Jennifer.

"See if you can send them to St. Lucy. Clytie son Jonas is a teacher at Miss Nellie school."

"I didn't know Miss Nellie had a school too."

"Yes and she used to work in this very kitchen just like you and me. And look at her today. A lady just like Miss Emily!"

"So you think I should try and get them back to St. Lucy?"

"I really think so. Girl this is a strange world."

"They real quiet," said Jennifer.

"We should be quiet too because we got to get up early tomorrow morning."

And so Ursy blew the kerosene lamp out and they settled in for the night.

―――

Sarah Bottomsley jumped and sat up in bed because someone had just opened her bedroom door. She was afraid but knew the intruder wouldn't harm her because he was dependant upon her for his upkeep.

"Sarah, were you waiting for me?" the husky voice asked.

She did not answer but kept staring at the silhouette which was approaching her out of the darkness.

"I know you are waiting for me," he said easing himself onto her bed.

She clenched her jaw and remained as stiff as a board.

"Remember the grandchildren Sarah," he said as he started to fondle her.

She allowed him to have his way with her until he eventually was satisfied. Then he stretched out beside her on the bed.

"That's more like it Sarah. You look forward to my visits. I know that. I am a little short on cash and thought you could help me out."

"Take it all from my purse," she whispered.

He stood up, moved in the darkness until he found her purse, removed the contents and put it into his pocket.

"Goodbye Sarah. I'll be back to visit you soon," he whispered putting his face close to hers.

She turned away from him, but he only laughed. Then he slowly opened the bedroom door and closed it behind him. Only the sound of her weeping bade him goodbye.

The moonlight was shining directly into the drawing room as the intruder headed towards the door. Then he turned around, picked up the photo of the Chambers family and left. Sarah Bottomsley could only keep on weeping. She had found herself in a situation from which there seemed to be no escape. She must do something! But what? This man had a stranglehold on her life. Not only on her life, but his presence threatened the very lives of her grandchildren.

———

"Dear Lord!" said Emily. "Not again!"

"What is wrong dear?" her husband asked.

"That photo is missing again."

"What photo?"

"Our family photo! I picked it up last night before I went to bed. I was thinking of what Mother had said and I was looking at the children. I know I put it back there before I turned in and this morning it's gone again."

"There must be some plausible explanation. Have you asked Ursy or Jennifer?"

"No I haven't, but I am beginning to feel terribly uneasy. If it isn't the photo, it's money or it's Grandpa's teeth."

"I just don't know what to say," replied Alastair as he settled down to the mountain of papers on the table.

The sound of a car engine brought him onto the verandah as Francois Bertrand was stepping out of his car.

"Aren't you a little late this morning?" asked Alastair.

"There were some loose ends that needed tying up, and then there was that matter with Nellie."

"Oh yes! Come in. Emily and the children are still having breakfast."

"Well I don't want to disturb you."

"No disturbance my friend! Come in. She'll be very glad to see you."

"Who is it dear?" asked his wife.

"A dear friend," was his reply.

"Francois! It is so good to see you. How's Nellie?"

"She's alright."

"I guess she is still a little under the weather because of Miss Una."

"She is!"

"Is something wrong? You don't seem like yourself this morning,"said Emily.

"Well I promised Nellie I wouldn't tell you anything about this," he said quickly looking around, "but I am sure this must have something to do with you."

"What is it Francois?"

"Someone is blackmailing Nellie," he replied pulling the notes from his briefcase.

Emily placed the notes next to each other and studied them.

"This is terrible. I'm sure it is not a worker. It has to be an educated person who is doing this, and deliberately making mistakes to confuse you. Look at the way hundred is spelt. Look at the way Nellie is spelt. What are you going to do?"

"You do have the mind of a solicitor. That's exactly what I told Nellie. It's someone who is trying to confuse us."

"What are you going to do?" she asked again.

"That's why I'm here. I wanted to see if we could put our heads together and come up with some sort of solution."

"We could fill the envelope with paper and wait to see who picks it up," said Alastair.

"This note is more than a week old. That means waiting every night to see who the scamp is," said Francois.

"What I propose is that we wait until another note is delivered. Nellie has already paid them five hundred dollars and they know she will deliver."

"She has already paid them money?" asked a shocked Emily.

"She did without informing me," said Francois.

"She should've called me or Alastair. She should never have paid them one penny."

"She was afraid and didn't know what else to do, so I can't reprimand her for what she has done."

"There is also something awfully strange going on around here," said Emily. "Items are being taken from this house. And very strange things! Like Grandpa's teeth for example."

"What's with my teeth?" asked the old man as he entered the dining room.

"Good morning sir," said Francois standing to greet him.

"We were discussing Miss Una's sister," said Emily quickly changing the subject.

"Oh yes! Ida! What has that got to do with my teeth?"

"Ida has no front teeth and Douglas said that she looked just like you without her teeth" said his grand daughter. "Do you know Miss Ida Grandpa?"

"Ida who?" asked the old man.

"Miss Una's sister!"

"How would I know her? You said she lived in South Carolina."

The discussion had to be brought to a close because of Grandpa Bottomsley and Emily knew that her mother would be coming out at any moment, so Alastair accompanied Francois to his car, giving him words of encouragement as they went.

"Nellie must be careful. And please let us know when the next note arrives. We'll handle this together," said Alastair slapping Francois on the back

# 17

Just before they were about to leave that evening, Jennifer left the kitchen and hurried to the outdoor toilet. Ursy had unexpectedly walked into the kitchen earlier that day, and the moment Jennifer saw her, she quickly hid a piece of paper in her bag and this aroused Ursy's curiosity. No sooner was she out the door than Ursy decided she wanted to know what was in the note she had hidden. She was about to read it when Emily entered the kitchen, forcing her to hide it behind her back. After giving her some instructions, Emily returned to the living room and Ursy continued to read the note. It seemed as if she was in shock by what she had read. So engrossed was she by what she had learnt, that she did not notice Jennifer open the kitchen door and enter. Ursy turned to her with the note in her hand, but said nothing. When Jennifer left the room again, she tried to put it back into her bag but there was only enough time to shove it on the top. She was certain the young woman would know that she had read it. Now ready to leave for the evening, Jennifer pulled her bag from under the table and stared at the note which sat on the top. She knew she hadn't left it there, but said nothing as she threw the bag over her shoulder and left the kitchen.

"The plantation is slipping away from us Emily," said Alastair. "Our profits this year amount to just over eighty per cent of last year's total."

"What do you suggest we do?"

"The only solution is to lay off some of the workers. If we continue like this, we won't be able to make ends meet. I just hate the thought of making their lives any harder Emily."

"Maybe we could reduce their working hours. That way they will still have some form of income."

"There's an idea I had in my head for a while," he said. "I could return to work as a solicitor. That would mean more income for us. Clyde is quite capable of handling the plantation by himself."

"Where would you find work as a solicitor?"

"With Francois," he replied. "He asked me once before and since his partner returned to England he seems really over burdened with all the work he has to do."

"I don't know what to say."

"Think about it Emily. That way he would be able to spend more time with Nellie and I can concentrate on renewing my skills as a solicitor. I must say that I have really missed it."

"So have I."

"Douglas is seven years old and John is three. Why don't you go back into law practice when he turns four and is off to school?"

"I would love to practise Law again, but I don't want to leave my children alone. Not just yet. I remember my lonely life as a child, when I longed to have my mother there for me and she wasn't."

"I didn't think about that but we are by no means destitute. There is still a great deal of money in the bank but if we keep on as we're going, that means we will have to use the profits to keep us ahead of the game, and I don't think that's a very wise thing to do."

"Of course you're right, but the workers have been with us for a long time and we must still think of them when we make our decisions."

"We should consider my returning Law. Not only because of the money, but I have studied long and hard and invested a great deal of money into my profession," said Alastair.

"You are really not into the plantation lifestyle," said Emily smiling. "I know you've done it because of me and I love you for it. Go ahead and speak to Francois. And I want you to know that I don't blame you for falling profits. It seems to be the trend nowadays. Look at the number of plantations that have had to close their doors."

"Thank you for understanding Emily. You know I would never leave you in the lurch."

"I know that. I think I'll drive by today and see how Clytie is getting along. It must be very hard for her at this time."

"Say hello to her and the rest of the family."

"Grandpa," shouted Emily, "I'm going for a drive to the country. Would you like to come along?"

"Wouldn't mind if I do! I could do with some fresh country air," he said slapping his palms on his chest.

"Where is Mother? I haven't seen her at all this morning."

"She was out last night," whispered the old man. "Perhaps she has a boy friend."

"Mother and a boyfriend?" asked Emily. "Oh Grandpa! I'll be ready to go in five minutes."

She went to the kitchen to inform Ursy that she was going out and found her alone.

"Where's Jennifer?"

"She went to the toilet ma'am."

"We're going to St. Lucy and should be back in the early afternoon."

"Yes Miss Emily."

They drove along the plantation fields where the workers stopped whatever they were doing and waved to them. Alastair was a good employer and treated the workers well, and they in turn treated the family with the greatest respect. Emily slowed the car down and waved back.

"My son would be happy to see how things have progressed," said Grandpa Bottomsley.

"I'm sure he would. Don't you think Alastair has a done a good job Grandpa?"

"He certainly has my dear, considering he knew nothing about sugar when he arrived on the island."

"Grandpa, we haven't been as profitable this year as last year."

"That happens sometimes my child. One year it is up and the next it is down."

"But Grandpa many plantations have had to close their doors and if it keeps on like this, we will be next. Alastair is thinking about going back into law practice."

"Are things that desperate Emily?"

"No Grandpa. We are getting ourselves prepared just in case. I'm also thinking of returning to law practice one day. If John were a little older, I would start right away, but I can't think of leaving my children alone at such a tender age."

"That's right. Children need at least one parent who will be there for them. Servants can never take the place of parents. Although when I think about you and Clytie, I know how much she cared for you and just about gave up her life to see that you were loved and cared for."

"And I loved her more than I loved Sarah! Maybe things would have turned out differently if Papa hadn't died at such a young age."

"Yes my son did die much too early. Ah the smell of the ocean!" said the old man inhaling deeply.

"I'm going to stop by Clytie to see how she is getting along."

"Una's death must have caused her great distress. I'm sure about that. I won't mind going up to say hello to her."

"She would like that Grandpa."

"Come in Miss Emily," said Clytie. "You remember my Aunt Ida?"

"Of course I do. How are things with you?"

"So, so!" she replied.

"I know how hard it must be for you."

"I still can't believe that Ma is gone. Excuse me sir. The head isn't working these days," she said to Old Bottomsley. "Sit down. I am going to get some lemonade."

"Got anything stronger?" asked the old man.

"Yes sir," she said placing a bottle and a glass in front of him.

She went to the kitchen leaving her Aunt Ida with the two visitors.

"Are you alright Miss Ida?" asked Emily.

"I just make it back in time to see my poor sister. We was getting along real good, when just like that she up and left me and Clytie."

"I know how you feel. I remember when I lost my father. It was a feeling I can't describe. What about you Grandpa?"

"He was my only son. I never expected him to go before I did, but it happened," he said throwing back his head and swallowing the grog.

"You are Bottomsley the plantation owner father?"

"Yes Ida. You remember me?"

"I used to see you when you come by with your son at the plantation where I used to work," she said with a toothless grin.

"Whatever happened to the Fielding family?"

"I only stay with them for about six months. Then I went to work for another family and didn't hear nothing more about them."

Clytie returned with the lemonade and they continued to converse about old times.

"I had a real strange dream last night," Clytie said. "Ma was in it and she say that she went to a picnic. It was somewhere like Bathsheba and she see Master Bottomsley and Miss Ella. Then she say something that was real strange."

"What did she say?"

"She say she look everywhere for Thomas Hurley and couldn't find him."

"But she hardly knew him Clytie."

"That was what I find so strange. She say that nobody there know him nor ever hear 'bout him. Even Master Bottomsley say he didn't know him."

"But my father knew him Clytie."

"Well I am happy to say that he can't spoil nothing, because he isn't up there with them. He got to be down there with Lucifer."

"I'm sure of that," said the old man still looking at Ida.

"Miss Emily, I have to tell you something about Thomas Hurley," said Clytie.

"What?" asked the old man suddenly turning his attention to Clytie.

"When he was treating Miss Sarah real bad, I decide that I had to help her."

"What did you do? Put castor oil in his food?" asked the old man slapping his thigh and laughing loudly.

"No sir. Worse than that! I never tell this to nobody except Ma. I went to the obeah man for him and one week after that he disappear."

"I didn't know you believed in such things Clytie," said Emily.

"I don't believe in nothing so. I had to help Miss Sarah. She wasn't happy at all. Anyway the obeah man say to bring certain pieces of Hurley nasty clothes and some of his hair. Miss Emily, I was never so frighten in my life. When he disappear I didn't know what to do. I thought the police would find out and they would put me in Glendairy prison. Ma say it didn't have nothing to do with me, but I still think that the potion Dootie put on him was too strong."

Everyone listened in silence as Clytie told her tale.

"I take it then that you never told Mother about this."

"No Miss Emily. I didn't expect him to disappear. I thought he would get sick or his teeth would fall out. He was a real bad man. And when his sister Ginger start to run the household, it was hell for Ursy and me. We had to buy the very plums off the tree and when we cook, she only give us three pieces of chicken. One piece for each of them. Many a night me and Ursy left that house hungry."

"Why did Mother allow all this to happen?"

"She was frighten for them Miss Emily."

"Did you know about this Grandpa?"

"A bit of it. Millie confronted Clytie in the kitchen one day."

"Well I'm sure his disappearance had nothing to do with you. He probably got what he deserved," said Emily.

"It was real nice of you to come by Miss Emily and you Mr. Bottomsley. If you going by to see Nellie, I know she is home," said Clytie as Emily and her grandfather bade them goodbye.

"Clytie I worry about that lady," said Ida after they had left. "It look like if she got a rain cloud over her head, but I ain't sure if the rain going to come."

"You talking about Miss Emily Aunt Ida?"

"Yes. I just can't put my finger on what it is," said the old lady.

# 18

"That was quite a story," said Grandpa Bottomsley to his granddaughter.

"Not only did she care for me Grandpa, but she also cared for my mother. Such a shame Sarah isn't interested in no one else but Sarah," she replied.

"Do you think she is really that selfish?"

"I don't know Grandpa. After all these years, she still remains a mystery to me."

"I think that deep inside, Sarah is a very unhappy woman. My son gave her everything she needed. She never had to work one day of her life and yet I don't think she really loved him."

"I have always known that Grandpa. Without Clytie our lives would have been a shamble," she said as they reached Nellie's house.

Long John and Otty ran on to the verandah followed by Nellie.

"Where are the children?" asked Nellie.

"We needed a break, so we left them at home."

"You know how much I like to see them."

"I know, but Grandpa and I both deserved a little break."

"That's true Nellie. A diversion is what we both needed. We stopped by Clytie and Ida on the way here."

"I've only seen them a couple times since the funeral because I have been very busy."

"Got anything for a thirsty old man to drink Nellie?" asked Old Bottomsley.

"Of course! I am certainly forgetting my manners. What would you like?"

"A strong one and straight up!" he replied.

Nellie put a decanter of rum on the table with a glass. The old man poured himself a double, threw his head back and swallowed. He squeezed his eyes shut and shook his head as the alcohol burned his throat on the way down.

"Good old Bottomsley rum," he said as he poured another. "My son would be proud."

Otty came in with Long John on her heels. She had baked a cake and had made a pot of tea. She placed them on the table and returned to the kitchen while Long John sniffed the air, as the lovely aroma of the cake worked its way down to him.

"Come Long John," she said when she realized he was not in the kitchen with her.

The old man had another drink and then he walked outside. He looked around and seemed to be pleased with what he saw.

"How are things Nellie?" asked Emily.

"Not so good. I really miss Miss Una's voice. Sometimes I find myself calling over there and expecting her to pick up the phone, when it suddenly hits me that she's no longer with us."

"It's sad but there's nothing we can do about it Nellie. How are you really Nellie?"

"I'm happy Emily. As long as I've got Francois on my side, I will be a happy woman."

"Francois told us about the notes you have been receiving," she said looking around to see where her grandfather was.

"He promised he wouldn't get you involved."

"That's true but Alastair thinks that I am somehow involved and thought I should know about it also. I don't know if Francois told you, but some strange things have also been happening at Bottomsley."

"What strange things?"

"Items have been missing and then showing up again. Someone even stole Grandpa's teeth."

At that point, Nellie started to laugh.

"What would anyone want with his teeth?"

"That's what I don't understand Nellie. Very strange things have been happening. Do you remember the platter with the B in the middle that we all thought belonged to Bottomsley plantation, but later found out it really belonged to Francois' family? No one knows how it made its from your house to our house. Jennifer told us that she had brought it from her home with something for Ursy. She also didn't know how it got to her home."

"Now that is a strange thing," said Nellie.

"Well Nellie, it looks as if someone is trying to confuse us both."

"Francois had all the locks changed on the doors and extra latches put on the windows. We keep the entire house like a prison even during the day."

"Have you any idea who it could be?"

"None at all."

"Where did Grandpa go?"

"Seems as if he is looking around the grounds," said Nellie. "He's probably bird watching."

The two women went to the verandah but the old man was nowhere in sight.

"Clytie told us that she had a dream about Miss Una, Miss Ella and Papa."

"Really?"

"She said that Miss Una was looking for Thomas Hurley, but couldn't find him. Even Papa said he didn't know him."

The name Thomas Hurley still made Nellie's hair stand on end.

"But Miss Una hardly knew him."

"Dreams are strange things, aren't they?"

"Nellie," shouted the old man. "You'll have to do something about your postman. Just found this letter with your name on it under the Flamboyant tree."

Nellie looked at the envelope and fear crept through her body. She took it and placed it on the table beside the teapot. Emily sensed that something was wrong because Nellie's face had taken on a very strange expression.

"Do you want me to open it?" she asked.

"Yes," she answered just barely above a whisper.

"Has Grandpa gone outside again?"

"He is sitting on the verandah."

Emily carefully opened the note and then slowly sat down.

*"Nellie you didn't bring the money. I know it was because of the funeral, but I need it by tonight. You know the time and place. Don't disappoint me."*

This time there were no intentional errors and they knew for sure that it was someone with a high level of education.

"Nellie I don't think anyone knows about us. I believe they are just bluffing. If they had known, they wouldn't have kept it a secret for such a long time. This person believes there is a secret because you've already given them money, and so they will keep on asking for more and more."

"I should call Francois."

"And I should try to find Alastair. He said something about meeting with Clyde the overseer today."

The Constable was called in and a plot was hatched. Francois and Alastair would take Nellie to the tree with an envelope stuffed with paper and the constable would send two policemen to wait to make the arrest. Suspense hung heavily in the air. The two men paced back and forth waiting for word.

The two policemen had parked their bicycles behind the church in the Sweet Lime hedge and settled in to patiently await the blackmailer.

"Want a swig?" asked the owner of the bottle.

One of them had brought a small bottle of white rum and they passed it back and forth while they waited. It became dark. Pitch black, and the men tested their torch lights to be sure they were still working. They fingered their clubs which they thought they would use on the blackmailer when he showed up. After a two hour wait, they both became bored, tired and a little tipsy.

"I getting real sleepy," said one to the other. "I got to shut my eyes for a minute. Wake me up if you see something."

"Alright man, but don't snore. He might hear you."

The other policeman had another shot of the white rum and he too stretched out on the grass. An occasional flicker from the street light in the distance! An intake of air! Then absolute silence! A lonely figure shrouded by the darkness made its way to the tree, snatched the envelope and was gone. Then a snort caused one of them to stir.

"Wake up man," said one policeman to the other.

"What happen? You see somebody?"

"No."

"You drop to sleep too?" asked the other, his voice filled with annoyance. "Man you is a real joke. How you could do something like that? You shouldda wake me up so I could keep watch."

"What we going to do now?"

Francois and Alastair got tired of waiting and returned to the churchyard just in time to see the two men pedalling away on their bicycles.

"Did you see him?" asked Alastair.

"No. I am sure it was a duppy," said one of them.

"What are you talking about?" asked Francois.

"You see sir, we sit there and wait and wait, and when we get up and went to the tree, the envelope was gone. So we say only a duppy could do something like that."

"That's nonsense," shouted Francois. "You both fell asleep and I can smell alcohol. You've been drinking."

"No sir. When my partner here was getting a little shut eye, I keep my eyes open and I watch. And we wasn't drinking sir."

"You both fell asleep," said Alastair. "Now he will never return and we will never know who it was."

"We can come back tomorrow," one of them said.

"Forget it!" said Alastair driving off and leaving them in a cloud of dust.

# 19

"Did you get him?" asked a worried Nellie.

"No but the envelope was gone. At least there was no money in it this time," said Francois.

"I think we ought to call the constable and let him know what happened."

"What will you tell him? That a duppy took the money?" asked Alastair.

"What duppy?" asked Nellie.

In spite of the seriousness of the situation, they all began to laugh.

"Did they really say that?" Nellie asked.

"The two bumbling idiots fell asleep and then had the nerve to say that a duppy took the envelope."

After a hearty laugh, Francois did call the Constable but was told he couldn't be there until the following morning. He wondered what the Constable's reaction would be to the duppy story.

Sarah Bottomsley turned over in bed and saw that the moon was casting long shadows through her bedroom window. On moonlight nights, she liked to sleep with the curtains open. She was about to close her eyes again when the hinges on the bedroom door creaked. She sat up in bed and watched as someone entered her room.

"I see you're waiting for me," said the intruder.

Sarah did not answer.

"I said you are waiting patiently for me," he repeated.

Still Sarah did not reply.

"You spoilt stubborn old witch," he said slapping her across the face.

"Please do not hurt me," she whispered.

"Then answer me and give me what I want," he said.

"My purse is on the night stand. Take the money and go."

"You know that's not all I want. Take your clothes off Sarah. Take them off!" he commanded.

Sarah lay in bed stiff as a log and when it was all over, he placed his hands around her throat and tightened them.

"One word about what happened here tonight to anyone, and I will really get rid of those two grand children. Do you hear me Sarah?" he asked in a loud whisper, as he eased the grip around her neck.

"Yes! Yes!" she whispered between coughs.

Sarah didn't understand it. Why was he being so cruel? After all he always got his way, always took her money and she had never told anyone about him.

Emily could not believe the story her husband had just related about the duppy.

"What are you going to do now?" she asked.

"We'll just have to wait until he makes contact again. At least he didn't see those two idiots. My God I hope he didn't."

"I believe that whoever it is, knows nothing about Nellie. Since she already paid them five hundred dollars, they think it is easy to obtain money from her, and so they will try and try again."

"And what about the paper that was stuffed into the envelope?" asked Alastair.

"I wish I had an answer for you, but I don't. If they are so determined to spill Nellie's secret, this would be the time to do it."

"Francois has decided to stay at home and work from there today. At least Nellie should feel a bit more secure."

"Mother, what is the matter with your face?" asked Emily noticing the black and blue mark under her left eye as Sarah emerged from her bedroom.

"I tripped and fell against the door," she replied.

"You ought to see Dr. Sims. That doesn't look good. I'll go with you."

"That's not necessary. It will go away in a couple of days."

"You should try to be a little more careful Mother. I still think you should see Dr. Sims in case something is broken."

"It looks worse than it is Emily. It doesn't hurt."

"Sarah you should have it looked after," said Alastair. "It does look painful."

"Dear God woman!" said Grandpa Bottomsley walking into the dining room. "What the hell has happened to your face?"

"She fell and knocked it against the door Grandpa."

"Better get it looked after Sarah. Might be something broken there," said the old man.

"I wish you would all stop harassing me at every turn. I said it doesn't hurt."

"Whatever you say Sarah!" said the old man. "What's good for breakfast Jennifer?"

"Ursy make some bakes and she also got frizzle salt fish for you."

"Bless that Ursy. She knows what I like."

"Yes sir," Jennifer replied looking at Sarah Bottomsley's face. "You want a cold towel ma'am?"

"All I want is my breakfast and some peace," replied the agitated Sarah.

"She was just trying to be helpful Mother."

"I can do without her help."

"I must be going," said Alastair standing up and kissing his wife. "I've got business to discuss with Francois today."

Emily got up and walked her husband to the door.

"Keep your eyes open today dear and watch out for the children. I have such an uneasy feeling. Do you really think Sarah fell and knocked her face against the door?"

"What else could've happened?"

"Perhaps a duppy did it?" he asked laughing.

"On your way," she said with a smile.

# 20

"That can't be true Aunt Ida," said Clytie.

"Why not?" asked the old woman. "He is a man and that is how men does behave."

"But Old Bottomsley?"

"Yes old Bottomsley. He did real hot Clytie. Nobody didn't know nothing about it 'cause I used to work on another plantation. Girl that man used to come in the kitchen and creep up behind you, and he had real roaming hands. When you hear the shout, you yourself did too hot to even say no. And even if you want to say no, you remember that extra money that you would get."

"But Aunt Ida where you went with him? You couldn't let him do what he want right there in the kitchen."

"Why not? Right there in the kitchen! But he did love a cane piece. He wasn't no better than we men. The cane blades never seem to bother him, but I couldn't take it at all. I used to have little cuts everywhere especially on my behind."

"Aunt Ida!" said Clytie.

"I am telling you the truth Clytie."

"And what about his wife?"

"I forget the name. She did in the drawing room carrying

on like a princess and he did in the kitchen trying to see what he could get from me."

"That was Millie. We used to call her Princess Millie when I was down at Bottomsley. She wasn't too bad in the end. She turn out to be real nice after the son pass away."

"I think the son did know what his father used to do, but he used to turn a blind eye, because the mother was a confuse woman."

"I can't believe that he remember you after all these years."

"Girl when you sweet, you sweet," said the old woman. "How he could forget Ida?"

Clytie was feeling a little embarrassed because she had never had such conversations with Miss Una, furthermore with an aunt she hardly knew. However, having Ida around did ease the pain of losing her mother. Ida was shy at first, but after a while, she opened up and was great fun to have around. Her only fear was being in the presence of white people. Living in South Carolina had taken its toll on her.

"Talking 'bout sweet Clytie, I thought Judes was married to Nora son."

"Yes they married in name only. Toby isn't no good."

"Clytie girl, I think she and Jonas got something going on."

"You just like Ma. You seeing something where there isn't a thing."

"Mark my words Clytie. The two of them does look at one another with real sweet eyes, and if you ain't careful, you going to be a grandmother real soon. Tell me something else. Harriet ain't got no boy friend?"

"All Harriet interested in is work and money Aunt Ida. That girl like money and more money. She does work every single day of the week."

"She too young for that. She should be going out and enjoying life."

"You tell her that Aunt Ida. But getting back to Carlina. Why you left the Estwick family?"

"I didn't leave them Miss Clytie. They get rid o' me."

"Why?"

"When I left here, I was in the family way but I didn't know. Only after I get up there I start to show and they let me go. They say I was more trouble than profit."

"And what you do then?"

"There was another family who was looking for a cook and because I could cook real sweet, they give me a job."

"So what happen to the child Aunt Ida?"

"Girl he barely see the light o' day and then he left this world. Those half-caste children ain't so strong. He did a pretty little fellow though."

"You tell the father about it?"

"Why I would want to do something like that? The child was dead."

"Aunt Ida, Old Bottomsley was the father?"

"How you could put two and two together so fast Clytie? I just tell you one or two little things and right away you know he was the father. But that is between me and you."

"You never tell him Aunt Ida?"

"What for? It wouldn't serve no purpose Clytie."

"That child was my cousin."

"Nobody would believe that. That child was white, white, white!"

———

The sun had already disappeared behind the horizon when Jonas Prescott appeared in the doorway of Harriett's salon.

"I know you didn't come to see me," said Harriet.

"Don't I always come by to say hello Harriet?"

"You smelling too sweet and you got a strange look on your face."

"Is Judes here?" he mustered up enough courage to ask.

"Why didn't you say that from the beginning boy?"

"I love you sis," he said throwing his arms around her.

"Judes coming back soon. She just went into the back to get something."

"You finish for the day already?"

"Yes and I am going over to Ma. I am real tired. Let me see what Judes doing. She taking real long. Judes," shouted Harriet, "somebody out here to see you."

She was pleased to see Jonas and he invited her to go for a walk down to the beach. She changed into a pair of shorts, a little top and a pair of sandals. She no longer looked like the young woman whom Clytie had described as spawgy. She now had a beautiful bronze complexion and the sun had bleached her hair to a very light blonde honey colour. It was a beautiful night. The moonlight twinkled across her hair as she walked beside Jonas.

"It's a beautiful night, isn't it!" he said.

"I don't think I have ever seen such a big beautiful moon. Back in England it always seemed to be so much farther away. Even the stars seem closer. I am sure if I had a book with me, I would be able to read it by the light of the moon."

"That's what we used to do when I was a young boy living close to Bottomsley plantation with my mother and grandmother. We would sit outside and read by the moonlight."

"It seemed like such a wonderful life," said Judes.

"It wasn't that wonderful. It was really hard for my mother and grandmother. My grandmother worked in the fields from sunrise until sunset and my my mother worked in the plantation kitchen for long hours so that I could get an education. Thanks to the plantation owner, a school was opened for the children of the village."

"And did you go to school there?"

"Oh yes. I went to school there and I absorbed everything that the teacher Miss Hurley told us. I even taught some of the adults in the area to read and write."

"I bet Miss Clytie was proud of you."

"She still is," he said shaking his head. "My mother's best friend Miss Nellie really pushed me to always do better. She said I had to make something out of my life."

"And what happened to Toby?"

"I don't know Judes. He was my best friend until he left for England. I got about two letters from him and never heard from him again until he showed up here two years ago. I'm glad he came back Judes."

"Why? He hasn't done anything with his life since his return."

"He brought you here and I am really happy for that."

"Don't tease me Jonas."

"I'm not teasing you Judes. I'm serious. His misfortune was my good fortune. I'm glad I met you," he said intertwining his arm in hers.

She didn't reply. They just kept walking until they were a few yards away from the beach. She was far from the damp and cold of London. A beautiful moon! Stars by the handful! A cool tropical breeze and a handsome young man beside her! He turned to face her and she kissed him. He kissed her back. The fire was lit and soon the embers started to glow.

"Is Harriet coming back tonight?" he asked her.

"She usually spends Tuesday nights with her parents."

"Then can we go back to the beauty shop?" he asked now unable to put out the fire which was burning out of control.

"Yes, yes," she whispered in his ear.

They were both out of breath from hurrying. It was dark inside the hair salon. She unlatched the door and they stumbled in. In the darkness, they caressed each other. His long fingers gently eased their way through her silky hair. He had never touched a white person's hair. Didn't feel at all like anything he was used to. He touched it over and over again as he stood in front of her; her back against the wall.

*This is what they call good hair, he thought. Smooth and silky.*

"Are you sure Harriet isn't in there?" he whispered in her air.

"I'll have a look."

She returned with the news that they were alone. He guided her to the backroom and they fell onto one of the single beds. He had lost all self control and his hands were everywhere. He was like an octopus.

"I want you Judes," he whispered.

They were devouring each others' bodies, when Judes climbed onto him and kissed him. More devouring! Tongues touched creating a series of mini explosions which numbed their senses. Fire crackers exploded all around them. The fireworks display created a colourful painting that hovered close to the ceiling above their heads. His hands wandered through the smoothness of her hair and his thighs held her head in a vize-like grip, such was the sweetness of the moment. Toby Peterkin was a stupid man he thought. He allowed this woman to slip through his fingers. Why was he thinking of Toby at that moment?

"Lordy! Lordy," he suddenly shouted. "I never feel anything like this. Nobody ever do this to me!"

He returned the pleasure and without knowing it, Jonas Prescott had joined Napoleon and his band of sixty million Frenchmen. More touching! More fondling! Fires were raging which when extinguished, started all over again. It was two o'clock in the morning, before they eventually fell asleep. It seemed as if he had only slept for fifteen minutes when suddenly Judes was shaking him and whispering. The beautiful dream was over.

"Wake up Jonas," she whispered. "It's six thirty and Harriet should be here pretty soon."

He quickly dressed and she followed him to the door. He stepped inside again and kissed her full on the lips. Then making sure the coast was clear, he dashed out and up the steps to his home.

"Had a nice time with Jonas last night?" asked Harriet.

"Yes I did. He is a nice young man and funny too."

"Girl I am happy for you. He isn't a thing like my no-good brother."

"Toby has his good sides Harriet. He wasn't always like that."

"Don't feel sorry for him Judes. He is right there where he wants to be. Right there in the guts of Bridgetown with his own kind."

---

Three months had passed since Nellie received one of her blackmail notes, but everyone was still on the lookout for any suspicious characters who might be hanging around places like the churchyard and the Bertrand home. Nellie was her old self again and still missed Miss Una, but was growing closer to her sister Ida.

Items were still being taken from the Chambers household, but they weren't anything of great worth. Emily and Alastair were still worried, but decided it wasn't worth calling the Constable in.

⁓

Everyone in the city had grown used to the sign Bantree & Bertrand which was proudly displayed on the front of the building. They were the most prominent solicitors in the town and even though Mr. Bantree had returned to England, his name still took a place of prominence on the building in Swan Street, in Bridgetown. Today however, Bantree was removed and another name stood in its place. Chambers! It was renamed Bertrand & Chambers. Both wives were delighted because their husbands would now have a little more time to spend at home with them and with their families.

Two months after the union, a registered letter arrived, addressed to Francois. It was from another solicitor in England whom he had contacted in the case of Jennifer Appleby.

"Hmm! This is something you should see," said Francois.

"Is this the same Jennifer who works with us?"

"It certainly is."

"Does she know that she owns all this property?"

"She does, but she has no idea how much it is worth."

"A wealthy woman toiling away in the Bottomsley kitchen!" said Alastair. "I always thought there was something unusual about her."

"Don't you know who she is?" asked Francois.

"Is there something else I should know?"

"Her father owned two properties in St. Lucia and Nellie bought the vacation home from him."

"Teddy Applewhite the alcoholic! Is she the same little girl Jennifer he would bring to the house?"

"That's her!"

"But there were two girls as far as I can remember."

"The other sister Rose died at sea while they were trying to escape from St. Lucia."

"Good Lord! But how did she end up here in Barbados?"

Francois told his partner the sad story of Jennifer Appleby and the death of her sister. He also explained that Thomas Appleby had hidden out among the poor whites in St. John for more than eight years.

"And what happened to the man who appeared at their door that night in St. Peter?" Alastair asked.

"I don't know. She was apparently still living with him until earlier this year."

"That explains it. A couple of times she showed up at work with bruises on her face. I understand she moved in with the cook a couple months ago."

"And where are the children? Are they still with him?"

"I don't think so. Emily would know what happened to them."

"Are you willing to handle this one?" asked Francois. "It may mean a bit of travelling if it gets too complicated."

"That means the father of those two little girls was also their grandfather."

"I think we should try to keep the father-daughter relationship between us, especially since not many people know about it."

"We must fight to get her everything he owned. She certainly deserves it."

A meeting was called by Alastair Chambers, and it had to be at a location away from Bottomsley Great House because there was a very pressing matter to be discussed. The seaside café where Emily and her father went many years before for private discussions was the venue. Jennifer was worried. What had she done to be summoned to such an important meeting? She hadn't stolen anything, which would have been the reason for dismissal. She was always punctual and the children loved her. They each ordered a lemonade and Alastair waited for the waiter to leave.

"Jennifer, you are probably wondering why my wife and I brought you here," said Alastair.

"Yes sir. But I didn't do nothing."

"Of course you didn't. You no doubt realize that I have gone back into my profession as a solicitor and am working with Francois Bertrand."

"Yes sir."

"Mr. Bertrand has passed your case over to me and I want to know if you have anything against that."

"When I was looking for a solicitor, Ursy say you didn't do that kind of work no more."

"That's true. So she told you about Mr. Bertrand?"

"Yes sir."

"So will you allow me to handle your case?"

"Yes sir."

"Do you remember us at all Jennifer?"

"Yes. I remember seeing you in St. Lucia a few years back."

"So you do remember?"

"Yes sir."

"Mr. Bertrand received a letter yesterday from a solicitor in England and I want you to know that your father's property there will make you a very wealthy woman. Of course it will take some time before you can lay your hands on the money, but once that's out of the way, you will have a much better life."

"What about the two houses in St. Lucia?"

"We haven't heard anything about them yet, but I will let you know as soon as we have received word about them."

"We have one very important question to ask you. Where are your children?"

"They are living with me at Ursy house."

"What about school?" asked Emily.

"They don't go to school. I don't want nobody to frighten them nor do nothing bad to them."

"They should be in school Jennifer. They must learn to read and write."

"I teach them at night but most of the time I am too tired to help them."

"So they sit in the house all day? Why are you so afraid?"

"We run away from the man I used to live with and I don't want them to have nothing to do with him."

"That was the man you mentioned before. What is his name?"

"Brandon Harvey sir!"

"Well you just can't keep the children shut up all day like caged animals. They need freedom and education."

"I don't know what to do sir."

"Let me speak to Nellie," said Emily. "You must move away from here and take the children with you."

"I don't want to do that ma'am."

"Why not? You must think of the hardship those girls have already suffered. It is time to make their lives and yours easier."

"I don't have any money for that ma'am and I don't want to leave Bottomsley and the children. Douglas would miss me."

Emily thought of her life and Clytie. That was the same situation Clytie had found herself in. Not wanting to leave Bottomsley, because she loved her too much.

"Dear Lord!" Emily whispered.

"There is a new school opening in Plum Tree Village and I'm sure it would be good for them."

"That is Miss Nellie school?"

"Mrs. Bertrand's school will be closing and this new one will take its place."

"Let me talk to Nellie," said Emily. "I'm sure we can sort something out."

"Jennifer, how did you find out about the position at Bottomsley?" asked Alastair.

"Mr. Harvey see it in the newspaper sir."

"Did he tell you to apply for it or did you do it yourself."

"He say we need the money and he bring me down there to get the job."

"Where does he work?"

"He don't work sir."

"So how does he live?"

"We used to use my pay, but I don't know about now sir."

"When was the last time you saw him?"

"About three months back."

"Did he ever ask you any questions about the plantation or the family?"

Emily was now totally confused. She knew that this Brandon Harvey seemed to be a freeloader but had no idea where her husband's questioning was leading.

"He used to ask about Miss Sarah and Miss Chambers, but nothing 'bout you sir."

"We should be getting back home," he suddenly said. "Grandpa and Ursy are alone with the children."

# 21

"You said you had a surprise for me Francois. I have been waiting and waiting, but I think you forgot all about it," Nellie said patting Long John's head.

"Have I ever forgotten anything when it comes to my wife?" he asked.

"Well you haven't said anything else, so I thought you had forgotten."

"There was so much going on that I decided to put it aside for a while."

"What was going on?"

"There was Miss Una's death and then there was our case with the police and now this partnership with Alastair."

"It is a funny thing," said Nellie. "Since that evening with those policemen I haven't received anymore blackmail letters."

Francois started to laugh.

"Do you mean the episode with the duppy?" he asked.

"Those two fools! It is funny now but it wasn't funny back then."

"Let's not get too complacent Nels. Whoever he is, he must be out there just waiting for the next opportunity. I forgot to tell you that we got a letter from the solicitor in England about Jennifer's property."

"And?"

"She will be very well off when this is all over."

"Does she know?"

"Alastair should've told her by now. I handed the case over to him yesterday."

"She deserves it. That poor girl! Misused and abused at every turn," said Nellie.

Their conversation was interrupted by the ringing of the telephone and by the way Nellie responded to the caller, he knew it must've been Emily. She wanted to come by the next day to discuss something important. Suddenly Long John ran to the drawing room door. He didn't bark, but continued to sniff at the bottom of the door.

Francois turned on the verandah light and looked out, but no one was there.

"Probably just a stray cat," said Nellie as Long John headed for the kitchen door.

"Who's there?" asked Francois as he turned the light on in the backyard.

After checking the doors and windows, they decided to go to bed with Long John following closely behind them. Although he had seen no one, Francois was still a little concerned because he was sure there was someone prowling around the premises.

Midday found Emily in St. Lucy sitting on the porch with Nellie. Otty came in with refreshments and also had a little something for Long John in her apron pocket.

"This is the second time we've seen each other this week and you haven't brought the children," Nellie said.

"Douglas is at school and John was taking a nap when I left."

"What do you want to discuss with me?"

"It has to do with Jennifer. Her children are locked up all day long in the house and they don't have a chance to go to school."

"Why would she do something like that?"

"She is afraid of the man who used to be her common law husband."

"What do you want me to do?"

"She doesn't want to leave Bottomsley because of my children, and I was wondering if you knew of anyone up here who would look after her children, so that they can get a good education and be out of harm's way."

"I can ask my sister. I know she has one spare bedroom since Toby moved out."

"Do you think she would do it for Jennifer?"

"I don't know but I can talk to her."

"What about Toby's wife? Judes is her name, isn't it?"

"I don't think they will get back together. She stays in the room at the back of Harriet's shop. Miss Ida thinks Clytie's son has his eyes on her."

"Nellie, my husband seems to think he knows who has been blackmailing you."

"Is it Toby?"

"I don't think so, but I can't tell you just in case the person he suspects is really not the culprit."

"Francois said he also didn't think it was Toby."

"Alastair says he will discuss it with Francois and then they will see where it goes from there."

"Now you are scaring me. Francois thinks there was someone walking around the house last night."

"Well we have also decided to get the locksmith in and change all the locks and bolts on the doors and windows. We haven't lost anything of great value, but just the thought of someone prowling around our home is frightening, especially with the children around. And speaking of children, I must pick up Douglas by three o'clock, so I should make a start."

"Would you drop me off at Clytie's house? I want to see how they are doing."

"Of course. I would like to say hello to them too."

Nellie informed Otty where she was going and asked her to keep Long John inside the house. The little dog followed them out the door and ran to the back of the house, before any of them had the chance to grab him.

"Come Long John," said Nellie. "We don't want you outside."

The dog returned and it was licking its lips.

"What you find to eat?" asked Otty. "Sometimes you real lickrish."

———

"Come in Miss Emily. Come in Nels. We real glad to see you," said Clytie. "You just in time. Aunt Ida just cook something name Frogmore soup. She say they eat it in Carlina."

"Sorry Miss Ida. I don't eat frogs," said Emily.

"There ain't got no frogs in it. I don't know why they name it so. It got crabs that I get from Percy. It got corn and potatoes but I had to use some salt meat because I didn't have no sausage. It taste good. Sit down and try it."

The old woman was staring straight at Emily, who thought it would've been insulting not to try the soup, so the four of them sat down to Ida's Frogmore soup.

"Miss Ida, are you sure there aren't any frogs in this soup?" asked Nellie.

"No ma'am," the old lady replied.

One sip! It was so delicious that Emily found herself having a second helping, and so did Nellie.

"I am going to make some more food like this for you. Just tell me when you can come by," said the old woman to Emily. "I like you."

"Let me get that," said Clytie getting up and going to the phone.

"It is Otty," she said to Nellie.

"Yes Otty?"

"What? I'll be home soon."

"What's wrong?" asked Emily.

"Something is wrong with Long John. Otty says he is just lying there and doing nothing. He was fine when we left about an hour ago."

"Give it some Nux Vomica," said Ida.

"What's that?" asked Nellie.

"Whatever he eat will come back up," said the old woman.

"Miss Ida, we don't know what is wrong, so we should take it to the Vet."

"I'll take you back Nellie, but after that I'll have to head for home."

It was obvious that the animal was suffering and needed medical care. Emily called Alastair and he decided to pick up Douglas from school, and Francois decided to meet them at the Vet's clinic. It was not busy when they arrived but they were forced to wait for a couple minutes. The lifeless animal just stared at Nellie as if asking for help.

"How much longer do we have to wait?" Emily asked the receptionist.

"Just a few more minutes Mrs. Bertrand. I also need the booklet we gave you from the last visit."

"I'm not Mrs. Bertrand," said Emily. "Where is the booklet?" she asked turning to Nellie.

"It is still at home."

"Do you live far from here?" asked the receptionist.

"No," replied Emily.

"Send your girl to get it for you then."

"What girl?" shouted Emily. "That is my..... See here! We can bring the booklet another time!"

The raised voices brought the doctor on to the scene who tried to calm the situation. He had remembered Nellie and went straight to her.

"It's Long John, isn't it? What seems to be the trouble?" he asked taking the animal into his arms.

"We don't know," said Nellie as Emily followed them to the room.

"Let's have a look. Do you have any poisons lying around the home?" he asked.

"No."

"He is showing signs of poisoning," the Vet said as he continued his examination.

"Mr. Bertrand is here," said the impertinent nurse. "Should I show him in?"

"Certainly," said the mild mannered man.

Francois entered the room and looked at Long John who in spite of being ill, started to wag his little tail.

"What do you think is wrong?" he asked.

"Looks like poisoning," the Vet said to him.

"We don't have such things lying around the house. Is it possible it could be something else?"

"Not a chance!"

"What are we going to do?"

"Whatever he has ingested, we will have to get it out of his system. We must act quickly before he starts to bleed internally. You'll have to leave him here and we'll get to work on him right away. Give me a call tomorrow morning and by then I hope I'll have good news for you."

The three of them said their goodbyes and Emily started on her way home.

"This was done intentionally,"said Francois.

"I know. Last night he was very irritable. Do you remember? He just kept running from one door to the other."

"I think someone has tried to kill him."

"When we were leaving this morning, he ran out the door with Otty behind him. When he came back he was eating something and I remember Otty telling him what a greedy little thing he was."

"I think I should call the Constable again. There seems to be no end to this. Nels I think this is in revenge for filling the envelope with paper and getting the police involved. There is one thing we know for sure."

"What?"

"They know nothing about you or Emily. If they had, they would've spread it across the air waves by now. The five hundred dollars you gave to them made you an easy target."

"I was afraid Francois. All I could think about was Emily and me of course."

"Tomorrow morning I will go by and speak to the Constable face to face."

The next morning, Francois sat at the dining table looking at a mountain of documents while Nellie stepped gingerly around him. They were waiting until nine o'clock to call the Vet.

"Thank you sir," said Francois. "That will make my wife very happy."

"What did he say?"

"Long John is not out of danger, but he is showing signs of improvement."

"The poor little thing! I would like to see him?"

"I don't see why not!"

In her rush to see her dog, Nellie was the first to enter the office.

"You don't have an appointment," said the receptionist. "People like you don't know what to do with animals and shouldn't have any."

"Were you speaking to my wife like that?" asked Francois hearing the onslaught on Nellie.

She had really overstepped her boundary and now had no idea what she should do.

"Are you here to see the little one?" asked the Vet as he came by to collect some papers from the receptionist. "Come this way. He'll be happy to see you."

"How much longer will he have to stay here?" asked Francois.

"I cannot give you an answer now. It's just too early."

"Have you got a moment sir?" asked Francois. "I would like to speak to you on a very delicate matter. It won't take too long."

Nellie took a seat in the waiting room among the other clients and their animals while the receptionist hardly raised her head. Five minutes later the two men walked out and the Vet stopped and shook Francois' hand and also took another little patient back to the examining room.

"Has she ever treated you like that before?" asked Francois.

"Yes but I thought I could handle it. Yesterday Emily had to chastise her because of her behaviour."

"Why do you keep these things from me? You know I would never allow these kinds of things to be done to you. You must trust me more Nellie."

"I don't want to come to you with every little thing Francois."

"I don't consider such behaviour little things. You must trust me Nellie. Really trust me!"

# 22

"Morning," Nora said as she entered the house.
"Morning," said Otty.

"Where is my sister?"

"She went to the Vet."

"Something happen to Long John?"

"Somebody try to kill him."

The sound of her sister's voice sent Nora running to the verandah.

"What is this I hear about somebody trying to kill Long John?"

"It certainly looks like it Nora. The vet thinks he ate poison."

"Who would want to do that to a sweet little puppy?"

Nellie looked to see where Otty was before she spoke.

"Nora someone has been blackmailing me."

"What you mean blackmailing you?"

"They were asking for money to keep my secret."

"What secret?"

"About Emily and me."

"Tschuuuuuuuups!' said Nora. "And you fall for that? Not a soul don't know nothing. You, me, Miss Una, Emily, Sarah and

Clytie know. Now which one would tell that to anybody? It ain't
Miss Una. The dead don't talk Nellie. You know that. It ain't you.
It ain't Emily, and it certainly ain't me nor Clytie."

"What about Sarah Bottomsley?"

"Don't be foolish Nellie. If there is one thing that woman
would want to keep a secret, it is that."

"I was so frightened I didn't have time to think about it the
way you just did. Francois said something just like that."

"You panic too quick Nellie. I hope you didn't give them any
money."

"I gave them five hundred dollars."

"Five hundred dollars?" shouted Nora. "My sister gone
mad!"

"Shhhh! Otty doesn't know anything about it."

"So how Long John get into all this?"

"Nora I have a story to tell you that is going to make you
laugh."

"Tell me. You know I like nothing better than a good
laugh."

"About three months ago, the same day Miss Una passed away,
Otty found a letter on the back step and they were asking for five
hundred dollars. The telephone started to ring and it was Clytie, so
I put the letter next to the telephone and forgot about it."

"You trying to tell me, that Francois didn't know nothing
'bout this?"

"Nothing, but he saw the note and went to the Constable.
They filled an envelope with paper and had two policemen waiting
to catch the blackmailer, but those two idiots fell asleep. Not only
did they fall asleep, but they told Alastair and Francois that it was
a duppy who carried away the envelope."

"A what?"

"A duppy!"

"I hear what you say, but I just find it a real joke that they could open their mouths and say something like that."

"Anyway we have never heard from the blackmailer again, but two nights ago, we were sure that somebody was walking around the house because Long John ran from door to door sniffing. We think that the same person put poison down for the dog."

"But Nellie why you didn't call me? I would give them the same thing I give Thomas Hurley."

"Don't call that name Nora. I can't even bear to hear that name."

"You tell me you want to talk to me."

"Yes. It is a request from Emily."

"You know that I would say yes to anything from my niece. What does she want?"

"Do you remember that white girl who came into the shop with the two little white children?"

"How could I forget? There ain't too many white people walking into shops around here."

"That was the same little girl Jennifer from St. Lucia."

"You mean the one the father used to sleep with?"

"Yes. She is now working in the kitchen at Bottomsley."

"I know that. We hear that a long time ago from Ursy. But you sure she is the same little girl from St. Lucia?"

"Now this is just between you and me. The father died sometime this year and everything that he owned now belongs to her. A bariffla of money!"

"He shoudda dead a long time ago. He was a nasty old man. What happen to the other sister?"

"She drowned when they were trying to escape from St. Lucia. Anyway Francois is now looking after her affairs and if everything work out the way they think it will, she will soon be a very rich woman."

"That girl had some real hard knocks and she white to boot!"

"Anyway she was living with a man who used to beat her, so she is now staying in Ursy's little house with the children. She is afraid to send the children to school because she doesn't want them running into him."

"I getting the picture now. She want to move up here and don't have nowhere to stay."

"Not quite Nora. She doesn't want to leave Emily's children especially Douglas. I suggested that she send the children up here where they can go to school and where there will be somebody to look after them. She will pay you for it and only God knows what will happen to you and Percy once she gets her fortune. I know you have Toby's empty bedroom and all the others down there in Plum Tree Village who would keep an eye on them."

"We ain't had it that bad after all Nels. Every man she come across does treat her real bad. Even her own father!"

"Does that mean you will do it?"

"Well I have to talk to Percy first. I really won't mind having some young people in the house again."

"What about Toby?"

"I haven't clapped my eyes on that boy in months. It look like he latch onto some poor woman somewhere down in Bridgetown and forget all about St. Lucy."

"I understand that Jonas has his eyes on Judes."

"She is a good girl and Jonas is a son to be proud of. It won't bother me if they get together. And you know what Nels? They can help the two girls with their schooling."

"You still have to ask Percy."

"Nels I think I can say yes, but I will call you after I tell him."

"Get back to me today Nora."

"Alright, but I was sitting down here for nearly two hours and ain't even get a little drink. Otty don't know she should bring out the refreshments?"

"I think she realized we were talking about something important and didn't want to interfere."

"The two of you like two peas in a pod, and now you making excuses for that woman."

"She has changed a lot Nora."

"So when they going to send home Long John?"

"We don't know yet."

———

Nellie was busy running back and forth between the kitchen and the dining room when Francois slipped an envelope under her plate. He put a bottle of red wine on the table and sat down.

"What are we having for dinner this evening?" he asked.

"Nothing special," she replied.

"Are you trying to tell me that I bought this lovely bottle of wine for nothing?"

"I know it must be something special. It is not my birthday."

"So don't you want to know why I have a special bottle of wine on the table?"

"You always do something special for me. Sometimes flowers, sometimes......."

"Nellie, aren't you going to ask?"

"The Vet is sending Long John home."

"Not yet and since you won't ask, there is an envelope under your plate."

Nellie eagerly pulled it out and saw her name on it. Her heart missed a beat because anything with her name on the outside seemed to spell bad news.

"Open it."

"London?" she asked, her voice filled with surprise.

"Read on Nellie."

"Accra? Where is that?"

"It's in Africa."

"Are you trying to say that we are going to Africa Francois?"

"First we will go to London for a few days. Then it's on to Ghana in West Africa. You don't seem very pleased. Would you prefer to go back to Paris?"

"I am just surprised, that's all. What kind of clothes do I need? Wait until I tell Miss Una…….. I guess I can't do that! She always talked about Africa and the stories her grandmother had told her about Africa."

"So you're happy?" he asked.

"I am! I am Francois! What about Long John? I can't go to Africa and leave him at the Vet."

"If you look at the tickets, you will notice that we aren't leaving for another three months. That will give us enough time to be vaccinated and to make sure all our travel documents are in order."

"Vaccinated against what?" she asked.

"Things like malaria. I'm not sure what we need but we will go to Doctor Norton and perhaps Emily can tell us which vaccinations she had to take."

"Africa! We're going to Africa Francois," she said squeezing his cheek.

"I guess you forgot all about Paris."

"No, but I would like to see where we came from. I'll get it," she said as the telephone started to ring."

"He said yes? Percy is a good man. We're going to London and then to Africa Nora."

"Why you want to go there?" asked her sister.

"London?"

"No Nellie. I mean Africa."

"Francois thinks it is good to see where we came from."

"I don't know Nels, but you can tell me about it when you come back. When you leaving?" she asked with very little enthusiasm.

"Not just yet Nora. Francois has a few things to straighten out before we can leave and we must bring Long John home from the hospital."

Francois smiled. He listened to his wife and knew she was happy.

Saturday morning found Jennifer and the two children preparing for the journey to St. Lucy. Suddenly a voice rang out in the still of the morning.

"Prepare ye the way of the Lord," Ursy heard Mrs. Hoyte say.

"Who's that?" asked Jennifer.

"I hate it when she come around the village. That is Miss Hoyte. We call her the messenger of death. She is the woman who always come to preach when somebody in the village going to pass away. You smell real good girl. Just like Sarah," said Ursy.

"This is some perfume that Brandon Harvey give me for my birthday last year. It is called Lady of the Night," she said looking at the bottle.

"Whatever it is, it smell real good."

Jennifer placed her opened handbag on the table and returned to the bedroom to get the children's valise. Ursy noticed that one of the big keys which hung on the keyboard at the plantation house with the big Bottomsley logo on it was in her bag. She returned just in time to see Ursy staring at it.

"You looking at the key Ursy? I forget to put it back on the keyboard."

"But why you got it?" she asked. "That key isn't even one that they use at Bottomsley."

"I went to open the cold room downstairs and pick it up by mistake, and forget to put it back.

"You all have a good journey," said Ursy happy to change the subject since she didn't believe Jennifer's explanation.

The mother and her two daughters could now take a bus directly from the city to St. Lucy. It was much easier now that Nellie had fought the Transport commission to give the people on the northern part of the island, a better way to get around. Jennifer promised the girls they would have a freer life and she would be back every weekend to visit them. She also warned her older daughter not to talk to strangers nor to give too much information about themselves. She wanted them to be polite and respect Mr. Percy and Miss Nora. And most of all, they were to stay out of the way of Brandon Harvey. They should hide if they ever saw him because she knew he kept himself abreast of everything that went on. But why didn't he ever show up at Ursy's house? That was a mystery. She was sure he had found out where she was staying. She hadn't told the children anything about the money she had inherited, because she wanted it to remain a secret; a secret from Brandon Harvey.

"Which room you all want?" asked Nora
"This one," said the older daughter Heather.
"Why you want this one?" asked Nora.

"Because we can see the sea from this window," said Jackie.

"Good because the other room belongs to my daughter Harriet. Although she sleeps in the back room at the beauty shop sometimes, this one still belongs to her."

The two girls went to the window and gazed out at the ocean.

"Don't worry about them," said Nora as she noticed the tears in the mother's eyes. "They are going to be real safe here and we going to make sure they do their homework."

"Can we go fishing too?" asked the younger child.

"Percy, that is my husband, he likes to go fishing. So when he and Mr. Bertrand go on Saturday morning, I know they won't mind if you go along with them."

"I can stay with them tonight?" asked Jennifer.

"There isn't nowhere else for you to stay, so I expect you to stay here."

"Thanks Miss Nora. Thanks."

"Now I expect you to do things with them on the weekends. Percy and me going to make sure that everything go alright in the week, but as the Mother, we expect you up here on the weekends to look after them."

"Oh yes Miss Nora. If Miss Emily ask me to work on the weekend, it would be alright with you?"

"Not too often Jennifer. Percy and me ain't too young no more, and we try to take life easy."

The children were tired and so was Jennifer and they settled in to spend their first night in Nora's home. It was nine thirty when the last flicker of light went out.

———

The full moon was rising like a one-eyed man trying to focus on everything in sight and all the children went out to enjoy the beautiful moonlight. Ursy looked out her window and smiled as she saw them playing the same games she had played as a child. Gazing at the twinkling stars, she felt as if she should've been out there with the children. She was feeling a little lonely. She had grown used to Jennifer's company and she was spending the night in St. Lucy getting her children used to their new surroundings. Then an unfamiliar sight in the village! A car drove by! Black or navy blue! No one in the village owned a car and no-one knew anyone personally who owned a car. The children stopped their play and Ursy watched as the vehicle slowly drove along the road and out of sight.

"Wonder who that is?" she asked aloud.

Already forgotten, the children soon started to play again.

*Huvana, Buvana baby sneeze,*

*Host, toast, sugar and tea.*

*Potato roast and English toast,*

*Out goes he!*

The children were scrambling around when it started to rain. Ursy blew her kerosene lamp out and crawled into bed. She had to be on time for work because the Chambers family would be going to church early the next morning. She could hear voices, the voices of some of her neighbours who were still enjoying the moonlight. She drifted off to sleep.

# 23

The following morning, everyone was bright eyed and bushy tailed except Jennifer.

"You didn't sleep good last night?" asked Nora.

"Not so good," she replied. "The sound of the waves keep me awake most of the night. I ain't used to it."

"Well you could get a good sleep on the bus back to Bridgetown. An hour and a half rest better than nothing," Nora replied looking at the black marks which covered her neck and upper arms.

"You looking at these marks?" she asked when she realized where Nora was looking. "That always happen when I get too tired."

"Thank God my skin black, so I don't have those problems," Nora said laughing.

It was chaotic at Bottomsley Great house. It was Sunday morning. That was not unusual. The Bottomsley family was getting ready for church. When they went to the dining room expecting to see their breakfast on the table, there was none and there was also no sign of Ursy. They couldn't leave the children with Sarah because she was not capable of looking after the two active youngsters, and besides she was probably also going to church. They decided to wait a while, while Emily fixed a little breakfast for the family. Nine o'clock came and went and Ursy still hadn't shown up, forcing Alastair to go to her home. He knocked on the door and called out her name, but there was no reply. Seeing the car parked there, the villagers who had not gone to church assembled in front of Ursy's home. One of them who worked at the plantation volunteered to go inside the house. Suddenly there was a loud scream and Alastair ran into the home. Ursy lay on her bed, stiff as a log. There was no blood or any signs of violence, except that the bedding at the bottom of the bed, seemed in disarray; but Ursy was dead.

"Let's get out of here," said Alastair. "I've got to call the Constable."

A horrified Alastair Chambers called the Constable and then had to relate the sad story to his wife who broke down and cried. He then drove back to Ursy's home to await the Constable's arrival.

"She was as strong as a horse," said Grandpa Bottomsley. "It must've been her heart!"

"It doesn't matter Grandpa. Ursy is gone. What are we going to do? She had no family."

"What about Jennifer? She was staying with Ursy."

"My God!" said Emily. "She and the children went to St. Lucy."

"What are they doing up there?"

"She took the girls up there to go to school. She was afraid of leaving them alone for such long periods of time."

"Good morning," said Sarah coming from her bedroom.

"Morning Mother. I've got bad some bad news. It looks as if Ursy died in her sleep last night."

"What did the coroner say?"

"We don't know yet. The Constable should be there by now."

"That means I'll have to get my own breakfast. Where is the other one?" she asked.

"I don't believe you Mother. You will never change. Besides you know that Jennifer never works on the weekend," said Emily grabbing John and heading for the verandah.

"Sarah you must be careful with your words," said Old Bottomsley.

"What did I say?"

"How could you be thinking of breakfast at a time like this? Ursy was good to us."

"John, she wasn't good to us. My daughter paid her for her work."

"It is useless," said the old man also heading towards the verandah.

"Don't get yourself all worked up over her," he said to his grand daughter. "Sarah has always been selfish and will probably remain that way."

Emily did not reply. She just stared into the distance.


"We have a catastrophe on our hands," Emily said to Nellie. "Ursy is dead."

"What do you mean dead?"

"We were waiting to go to church, but she never showed up. Alastair went to get her and found her dead in her bed."

"What happened to her?"

"We don't know. Alastair went back there to meet the Constable."

"She was a strong woman Emily. Maybe she had a heart problem that we didn't know about."

"We'll just have to wait until Alastair returns before we know anything."

All the villagers had now gathered in front of Ursy's home. Some still in their church clothes mingled with the others who were there from the beginning, and all of them shocked by the untimely death of one of their own. The Constable, the Coroner, two policemen and Alastair all gathered inside the house.

"I must take you back to the station with me, since you're the one who found the body," said the Constable to Alastair.

While the Coroner examined Ursy's body, the constable and a policeman walked around the house searching for any clues that may have led to the woman's death. One of the policemen walked to the back door and pushed the upper window portion of it open. He then propped it open in that position with a stick which was beside the door. He looked out.

"Sir," he shouted to the Constable, "there is something you should see."

Alastair hurried along behind the Constable and the three men stood at the door and looked into Ursy's backyard where they saw her three footed pot still sitting on three stones. That was where she did her cooking.

"See those footprints sir?" the policeman asked.

"Were you out here at all Mr. Chambers?" asked the Constable.

"No. One of the women who works at the plantation and I entered the house from the front."

"Step aside please," said the Constable looking down to the floor.

Dried muddy footprints in one direction made their way around the table but were partially hidden by the oil cloth which Ursy used as a table cloth. Another set of footprints, barely visible were seen going in the opposite direction towards the backyard. The Coroner came out of the bedroom clutching his bag and asked the Constable if he could speak with him. Alastair and the policemen could only watch as the Constable kept nodding his head. Alastair now knew that Ursy's death was not from natural causes. The photographer was summoned and photos were taken of the crime scene.

"Where is the lady who entered the premises with you? Is she still out there?" the Constable asked.

"I'll have a look," said Alastair.

The woman was identified and also taken to the station.

After a lengthy questioning, Alastair and the woman were both free to go.

"How did she die?" Alastair asked him before leaving.

"Strangulation!" said the Constable. "Keep your eyes open Mr. Chambers. If you hear or see anything unusual, please report it to me immediately."

Nellie called her sister and told her the bad news. This threw Jennifer and her children into hysterics. She couldn't believe the woman who had been so kind to her and to her children was dead. She had to get back to Bottomsley. They would probably need her there. Nora called Clytie who wailed and wailed upon hearing the news.

"He did it," whispered Heather to her sister.

"Who did it?" asked Nora overhearing the child's comment.

The little girl just stood there and said nothing more, but Nora called Nellie and repeated it to her.

"Who is he?" asked Nellie.

"I don't know."

"We're going to Bottomsley and we can take Jennifer with us if she wants to go along. Tell her to meet us by Clytie's home."

And so Jennifer set out to meet Nellie and Francois leaving her two frantic children behind with Nora.

"Jackie! Heather!" shouted Nora. "You hungry?"

"No ma'am," they said in unison as tears rolled down their faces.

"Sit down," said Nora. "Don't cry so much. I want you to tell me what you mean when you say 'he' did it."

The two girls looked at each other.

"I am waiting on you," said Nora.

"Brandon Harvey," said the smaller child timidly.

"Who is Brandon Harvey?" asked Nora.

"My father!" she replied.

"I thought your father was dead," said Nora realizing she had just made a big mistake.

"No my father lives close by Miss Ursy's house."

Nora realized the children had no idea that their father was the man who had passed away and whose funeral they had attended. He was their grandfather as well as their father. Whoever this Brandon Harvey was, it was certainly not their father. Nora decided that that piece of information had to be passed on to the police.

"Ursy was strangled," said Alastair to his wife.

"Who the hell would want to do a thing like that?" asked Old Bottomsley. "She was a nice enough young woman."

"Well there seems to be a murderer in our midst so we must be on our toes," Emily said.

"I just don't like it," said Alastair deep in thought.

"Luckily we have changed all the locks and added bolts to the doors," said his wife.

"And I intend to personally do an inspection every night

before I turn in. There are just too many strange things going on around here."

"It's like the Phantom," said the old man. "First he stole my teeth, then he stole your money and that photo………My God! It's there again."

"Alright! Let's all sit and talk about this," said Alastair.

Sarah and Old Bottomsley sat on a sofa. Emily gathered up the children and they all took seats in the living room, while Jennifer stood by the kitchen door.

"Now I want to know who put that photo there again, and I want the truth."

"Of course, you know I had nothing to do with it," said Emily. "Did you move the photo Douglas or did you see anyone move it?"

"No Mama."

"How about you Grandpa?" Alastair asked.

"You certainly don't think I would steal my own teeth, do you?"

"Forgive me sir. I'm just trying to cover everything. What about you Sarah?"

"What would I do with his teeth and why should I remove the photo?"

"From tonight on, I will be locking the doors and keeping the keys. Then and only then, will we be able to understand what's going on around here. That means no one will be able to open the door from the inside. Does anyone have any objections?"

"I just don't understand why we should all be held prisoner in this house," said Sarah.

"Think of your safety and the safety of your grandchildren."

"As long as you put it that way," she said grudgingly, "but I have always lived in and ran this household and it was never necessary to lock the doors."

# 24

There had always been tales about the Heart Man or the Steel Donkey, who would steal childrens' hearts or destroy people's property, but no one really believed them and looked on them as old folklore. It was different now. Someone had taken Ursy's life and no one knew who had done it. The children were no longer allowed to play in the street like they were accustomed doing and the grownups latched and nailed their doors shut before going to bed. The villagers could be seen peeping out the corner of the windows before daring to step into the road. Fear was in everyone's heart.

"What do you think happened to her Francois?" Nellie asked.

"I really don't know, but my suspicions tell me it had something to do with Jennifer."

"Why do you think that?"

"Didn't Ursy allow her to move in with her to save her from her daily beatings?"

"Yes, but why would he want to hurt Ursy?"

"I guess it was revenge."

Before Nellie could ask what he meant, the phone started to ring. It was a call from the Vet.

"Yes! I understand. We'll come over," he said putting the receiver back in its place.

"Are we going to pick up Long John?"

"Long John is no more," said Francois slumping into the nearest chair.

"What do you mean?" Nellie asked.

"Long John didn't make it. The poison had infiltrated his system and there was too much internal bleeding."

Nellie cried as if her heart would break.

"We'll get him and bury him in the back yard," said Francois.

"I can't take too much more of this," she said. "What's going to happen next?"

———

"Miss Chambers, can I sleep in the servant quarters in the back?" Jennifer asked.

"No one has slept there for years. The windows need opening and the bed needs airing," she replied.

"I can't go back to Ursy tonight. I am real frightened ma'am."

"Go ahead and do what you have to do. Ursy will get you some…..I'm sorry," she said putting her face into her hands.

"That is alright ma'am. I will get some sheets and a pillow."

After opening the windows and dragging the bed into the backyard, Jennifer cleaned the room and returned to her chores.

"Ma'am you looking for someone to take Ursy place?"

"For the moment, I will do all that I can to help out, but I think I will wait a little while longer."

"She was the only friend I ever had ma'am. She take in me and the children when we didn't have nowhere else to go."

"It is so sad Jennifer. I can't imagine why someone would do a thing like that."

"I don't understand it ma'am."

"You moved in with Ursy a couple months ago. Why?"

"I was frightened for my children ma'am. I wanted them to have a good life."

"Was he threatening them?"

"Not really ma'am. I just didn't want them to get mix up in the quarrels we used to have."

"Then it would be better if you did stay here. Are the children with Mrs. Bertrand's sister?"

"Yes and I know they are safe up there."

"What you want for dinner ma'am?"

"I'm really not hungry. Make something for the children and the others."

"What she want for dinner?" asked the timid Jennifer.

"Whatever you make for the others, she can also have. Are you afraid of her Jennifer?"

"Not really ma'am, but she is real fussy."

"Don't worry about my mother. I'll see to it that she doesn't bother you. Is there a lock on the door to your room?"

"I don't know ma'am."

"Go down and have a look so that I can let my husband know before he leaves Bridgetown."

There was indeed a lock on the door, which was double locked when the little clip on the inside was pushed down. There she would be safe. Ursy's death was weighing heavily on everyone's mind. The police had not yet spoken to Jennifer but since she had left the village early on Saturday morning and had not returned until after Ursy's death, they thought it could wait. Nora found them on her door step and her heart missed a beat. Ever since the untimely demise of Thomas Hurley, she had stayed well away from the police.

"What can I do for you?" she asked.

"I've just a couple of questions," said the Constable.

"Go ahead," she replied.

"Are those two girls Jennifer Appleby's children?"

"Yes sir."

"When did they come to your home?"

"Round eleven o'clock on Saturday morning."

"Was the mother with them?"

"Why you asking me all these questions?" Nora asked.

"We just need to know where the mother was on Saturday night."

"She was right here with me, my husband and the two girls."

"Where is your husband?"

"Before I call my husband, I want to tell you something that one of the little girls say."

"What was that?"

"She say that 'he' did it."

"Who is he?" asked the Constable.

"After the mother left, I asked them who they were talking about and they said somebody named Brandon Harvey."

"Who is Brandon Harvey?" asked the policeman.

Nora peeped around the corner before she said anything else, then she proceeded to tell the constable everything she knew about Brandon Harvey. Satisfied that Jennifer Appleby had spent the night in St. Lucy with Percy and Nora Trotman, along with the bit of information from Nora, they left.

Emily heard the brakes of a car and she looked over the verandah and saw the constable and his assistant step out.

"Mrs. Chambers," he said removing his hat, "is Miss Appleby here today?"

"Yes. Do you want to speak to her?"

Jennifer was trembling as the two policemen met her at the kitchen door. Realising she was afraid, Emily also followed them to hear what they wanted.

"We understand you spent Saturday night in St. Lucy."

"Yes sir.

"We also understand you have been living with the deceased for a couple months."

"Yes sir."

"Did you know her for a long time?"

"No sir."

"So how did you end up living with her?"

"She took me in to help me out, because I had nowhere to go with my children. I wasn't getting along good with the man I used to live with."

"Was that man Brandon Harvey?"

"How you know that sir?"

"I'm a policeman. It is my job to know everything that goes on around here. When was the last time you saw this Brandon Harvey?"

"A couple months back sir."

"Did he say anything to you?"

"He didn't see me sir."

"I understand you used to live in St. Lucy before you moved here and applied for this job."

"Yes sir."

"Did Brandon Harvey tell you to apply for the job?"

"Yes sir."

Emily listened carefully. She knew where the questioning was leading.

"Did you tell anyone you were going to St. Lucy on Saturday morning?"

"No sir."

"Are you sure you didn't tell anyone?"

"Yes sir."

"Who do you think killed Ursy?"

"I don't know sir."

"Don't you think this Brandon Harvey killed her?"

"No sir. And if he killed Ursy it was a mistake."

"What do you mean?"

"If he did it sir, I don't think it was Ursy he wanted to kill, he thought it was me."

The two officers seemed shocked at her answer and with that the young woman broke down and wept.

"Do you think you can come back another time?" asked Emily. "It seems to be too much for her right now."

"You think I can I get my clothes from the house?" asked Jennifer. "I was wearing this dress since Saturday."

"As soon as we have finished our search of the home, we will inform you and you can go by to pick up your clothes. Where are you staying now?" he asked.

"She has taken up residence on these premises," said Emily.

"Just make sure you're safely locked in at night," he said before he left.

Sarah Bottomsley was sitting on the verandah staring out on the horizon.

"Ma'am," said the Constable raising his hat as he passed by.

Sarah showed no hint of recognition and just kept staring ahead.

# 25

Old Bottomsley sat on the verandah, his favourite drink in his hand. He threw his head back and swallowed. Gulp! The rum burned his throat on the way down causing him to shake his head and close his eyes tightly. He coughed. Then he coughed a second time. Staring out on to the horizon at the beautiful Caribbean Sea, he noticed a freighter was sailing slowly towards Bridgetown. Black smoke rose skywards from its funnels mingling with the snow white clouds which were floating by.

"There you are," said Sarah Bottomsley sitting next to him. "Where is what's her name?"

"Who?" asked the old man.

"Jennifer. I want her to help me with my valise."

"Well I saw here go out with Emily about ten minutes ago. And Sarah you could be a little nicer to her. She has gone through a lot in the past couple of weeks."

"It must be her own doing," she replied.

"Anyway were you also looking for me?" the old man asked.

"I wanted to speak to you about a very disturbing matter."

"What is it Sarah?"

"I don't know about you, but this Ursy matter has scared me out of my wits. Who do you think killed her?"

"I wish I knew," said the old man. "If I knew, then we could all rest easier around here."

"They said she died of strangulation."

"That's what the police said. What about you Sarah? Have you any thoughts on who could've killed the poor woman?"

"None at all Father Bottomsley."

"What about him?"

"Him?"

"You are always saying that *he* visited you. Could *he* also have been Ursy's murderer?"

"Oh Father Bottomsley! Did you believe that?" asked Sarah.

"I just don't know what to believe anymore. If Millie were still alive, I'm sure she would have an opinion on all this."

"I'm sure she would."

"Yes she would! I'm getting another drink. Would you like one?"

"No thank you. I'm going out for a short while."

"I think you've got a boyfriend Sarah, you sly old thing," said the old man.

"Father Bottomsley, I'm just going to take some clothes to the parish church, and the rest I am selling to a friend. I promised the Reverend I would come over this afternoon to deliver some things for the poor."

"Are you alright Sarah?"

"Whatever do you mean?" she asked getting up from the chair.

"You have never been the charitable type. Now suddenly you're giving some of your clothes to the poor? Where are they going to wear them? When they go to weed the hedgerows?"

Sarah was incensed by the remark. She went to her bedroom and returned with a valise which seemed heavy, but she managed to lift it to the verandah.

"I'll help you Sarah," said the old man picking up the case which he quickly allowed to fall to the floor. "What have you got in here? Rocks?"

"Probably my old shoes and pocket books have made it heavy. Don't worry. I can manage it," she said picking up the heavy valise and walking down the stairs.

Old Bottomsley had never seen Sarah lift a plate. He had no idea the woman had such strength. She had always behaved like a very fragile and helpless person. He watched as she opened the trunk, lifted the heavy case into it, closed the door and drove off.

~

The trap was set to catch Brandon Harvey. It was difficult because no one on the island knew a Brandon Harvey. About fifty five years old, six feet tall, shaven head, a dark moustache and a long scar on his forehead just over his right eye! Would you call him handsome? Yes one could say he is a handsome man. He drives a dark blue Morris Minor with the number E 758.

The Constable summoned the woman who along with Alastair had found Ursy's body.

"Have you ever seen a blue Morris Minor driving through your village?" he asked.

"No sir, but come to think of it, the night before Ursy pass away, a car was driving through the village real slow."

"Was it a Morris Minor?"

"I don't know what that is sir."

He brought out some pictures of cars and showed them to the woman. First car he showed her the Morris Minor.

"I ain't too sure sir."

He then showed her more pictures none of which she identified as the car which she had seen on that fateful Saturday night. The Constable was now totally confused. There weren't that many cars on the island and why wasn't the woman able to identify the Morris Minor?

"What was the colour of the car?"

"I think it was black sir."

"Are you sure it wasn't dark blue?"

"Now that you put it that way, it could be."

"Did you see the driver?"

"It was dark at that time sir, although the moon was shining. Maybe it went behind a cloud, so I didn't see who was driving."

"You're quite sure?"

"Yes sir, but one thing I remember is that when it went by, I smell something like a flower."

"What kind of flower?"

"Lady of the Night," said the woman.

"But those flowers grow everywhere."

"We don't have none in our village sir, although we was trying for the longest time to get some."

"Lady of the Night," said the Constable. "Thank you. I'll get back to you if I need more information."

"Hurry and catch the person sir. Even the little children don't want to go out to play no more."


Everyone was hoping for a quick resolution because there was a murderer in their midst and they were afraid. The Constable didn't know a Brandon Harvey and he knew all his British peers. The Reverend had also never heard of him, the Cricket clubs had never heard of him and his name couldn't be found anywhere on any registers on the island. He had to pay another visit to Jennifer Appleby. She held the key to the capture of this man.

Night after night, the police waited and watched the house where he and Jennifer had lived together, but there was not a trace of the man and more confusing was the fact that the car wasn't spotted anywhere. He was really a phantom. The Constable thought he should return to St. Lucy and talk to the two girls. If they were sharp enough to finger him as the murderer, they must know something else that would lead them to him

The two policemen walked into Clytie's shop and ordered two red Ju-c's.

"That is all you want?" she asked. "I got some hot fishcakes that just come out of the oil."

They ordered two fish cutters and drank the sweet drinks straight from the bottles. Clytie heard a low belch come from one of them.

*Probably didn't have time for breakfast, she thought.*

She wondered what they were doing in the area.

"You looking for somebody around here?" she asked.

"No ma'am. We're just driving around. You never know what you will find when you drive around. Things aren't what they used to be."

"When you all going to find the person who kill my friend?" Clytie asked.

"You're talking about the woman who was killed a few weeks back?" one of them asked. "Did you know the deceased?"

"Yes we used to work together in the kitchen at Bottomsley plantation."

"It is real hard when you lose a good friend, especially under the circumstances."

"Yes sir. It certainly is. Ursy was one of the best friends I ever had."

"Did she have any enemies?"

"Ursy? None that I can think of sir!"

"We hope we can find him before he murders someone else."

"I hope so too."

"We didn't get too much from her," one policeman said to the other. "Let's pay a visit to Nora Trotman. I would like to talk to the two girls."

"The children in school," said Nora. "They got a lot of catching up to do. Those girls ain't see a school door for nearly four months."

"And why was that?"

"The mother say she was frighten to let them out of the house. She was hiding them from the man she used to live with."

"Brandon Harvey?"

"I believe so. You can come back later or tomorrow evening. Don't come too late. I like to make sure they do their homework and go in their bed early."

"Yes ma'am," said the Constable. "And by the way, you haven't learnt anything else from them?"

"Anything like what?"

"Why he would want to murder their mother's friend or where he often went and where we may possibly find him?"

"No I didn't talk to them about nothing so. They is just children and they had a real hard life already. I want them to enjoy their childhood. You can understand that sir."

"Yes I do, but if they should say anything that would put us on the right path, be sure and let me know."

"I intend to do that," Nora replied.

Ursy had a couple of relatives who were all very poor, so a simple funeral was paid for by the Chambers and she was laid to rest in the same cemetery as John Bottomsley and his mother Millie Bottomsley, just farther to the back. Emily found herself by her father's grave. She wiped away the dust from his headstone. 'John Bottomsley, London, England' was all that was written there. She smiled a feint smile, laid some flowers on his grave and walked away. The villagers mourned the loss of one of their own; a kind-hearted woman who had never done a bad deed.

# 26

Nellie was not her cheerful self. The events of the past few months had taken their toll on her. However not one to sit around and feel sorry for herself, she decided to visit Clytie, but Clytie was in the same situation and tried to stay busy by working day in and day out in the shop. Ida had taken the place of Miss Una at the cash cage receiving and paying out money. She was beginning to recognize the faces that came into the shop and they began to talk more freely with her especially after they found out she was Miss Una's sister.

"Miss Nellie, you don't look happy," she said as Nellie walked into the shop.

"I've got too many things on my mind Miss Ida. Just too many things!"

"As they used to say in Carlina, it ain't going to help if you let these things drive you mad. You pray to God Miss Nellie?"

"Yes Miss Ida. I always thank God for his mercies."

"I know my sister look on you as a daughter. If you want to talk, Ida will listen."

"Where is Clytie?"

"I promise to do the cooking today, so she went home to put out the things, but she coming back soon. How is Mr. Francis?"

"Francois is good, but he is real busy."

"I thought his name was Francis. Una tell me so."

"His name is Francois Miss Ida. He is from one of the French islands."

"Well you got yourself a good man. When the Lord put his hand on your shoulder Miss Nellie, he left it there for a real long time. Me? He only left it there for a few seconds. When I think that Francis come all the way up to Carlina to find me, just to make my sister happy, I say to myself, Ida, there got some good white people in this world, and he is one of them."

"Francois isn't white Miss Ida."

"You could fool me. He look white to me."

Two customers entered the shop and interrupted the conversation. Ida slowly walked out from behind the cash cage and it was obvious the dress she was wearing wasn't hers. It was one of Miss Una's. Since she was not as tall as her sister, the dress was just about one inch above the floor. She was quite a sight in her long dress with her toothless grin. The customers were served and they went on their way. Then Ida held onto Nellie's hand.

"You got a good life on this here Rock. Back in Carlina, we didn't have no say in nothing. Sometimes you did too frighten to even look at the white people in case they say you say something or do something to them. Life was real hard Miss Nellie. No school for the children and sometimes I had to stand up in the back of the bus, even though they had a lot o' seats up front. And you know Miss Nellie, the feet was hurting because I was standing up since six o' clock that morning and I was in the family way."

"I didn't know that you had children Miss Ida."

"Don't have none Miss Nellie. It didn't live and I know God was looking ahead, while I was only seeing what was going on right there and then. He could see that child would have a hard life, so he make that decision not to put him through that misery. So Miss Nellie, put whatever it is that is bothering you in God hands. You got to say to yourself that God know best and he give you somebody that love you and that you can talk to. Ain't too many o' we coloured women who can say a thing like that."

Ida's little talk seemed to put things in perspective for Nellie and she started to talk to the old woman just as she had talked to her sister Una.

"I really miss Miss Una," said Nellie. "She was the best friend I ever had, even though she was so much older than I was."

"Una was always like that Miss Nellie. She was always a good sister and I tell her when I went up to Carlina, that I hope she could come up and join me, but Miss Nellie things did bad and I didn't want to bring my sister to all that suffering, so it was better that she stay here. And you see what I mean, Una and you get to be good friends and you care for Una. But Miss Nellie, you got to pray and pray a lot."

"She was good to me too, real good," said Nellie as Clytie walked in.

"I didn't know you was here Nels."

"Yes and while I was waiting for you, Miss Ida and I had a good conversation."

"You know they ain't catch that man yet who kill Ursy."

"Everything does happen in good time," said Ida. "Nobody ain't really know if he really killed the poor woman, but every finger pointing at him."

"Know what they say 'bout who the cap fit Aunt Ida? Let him wear it."

"I still say they should wait to see if he really do it," said Ida.

"Anymore letters come asking for money?" asked Clytie.

"None at all."

"Who you think it was Nels?"

"I really don't know Clytie."

"Somebody begging you for money Miss Nellie?" asked Ida.
Clytie and Nellie looked at each other.

"You can tell her Clytie."

"Somebody was trying to blackmail Nellie. They was leaving
letters asking for money."

"I hope you ain't give them none," said the toothless old
woman. "Give them one time and they going to keep coming.
When you ain't got nothing to hide, you don't have to worry about
these people. And I know you live a straight life and ain't got no
bones rattling around your closet."

"Huh?" asked Clytie because she had no idea what Ida was
referring to.

"I just mean she don't have nothing to hide."

"Oh!" said Clytie looking at Nellie.

It was obvious there was one secret the old woman knew
nothing about. She hadn't been told anything about Nellie and
Emily. Miss Una had taken the secret to her grave. The old woman
however liked Nellie just as much as her sister did.

"I am leaving the two of you to talk. I going over and start
to cook," Ida said.

They watched as the petite woman dressed in her sister's
clothes ambled down the steps and went to the adjoining house.

"She is just like Miss Una," said Nellie.

"I am so glad Francois bring her back here. Now that Ma is
gone, it is real comforting to have Aunt Ida around."

"You have to get her some teeth Clytie. She is younger than
Miss Una, but she looks older and it seems like if she really had
a tough life."

"Nels, you is my good friend and I know I can tell you."

"What?"

"It look like if she and Old Bottomsley had something going on before she left the Rock."

"Ida and Old Bottomsley? Where did you hear that?"

"He come by with Emily and recognize Aunt Ida. When he left, she say that Old Bottomsley used to interfere with her in the Fielding kitchen."

"What?"

"And Nels, she had a child by him."

"The child that died?" asked Nellie.

"How you know about that Nels?"

"She was telling me about her life and the hardships in South Carolina."

"She didn't tell you Old Bottomsley was the child father?"

"No."

"Anyway that is between you and me. You going by to see Nora?"

"I didn't plan to but I should. I haven't seen much of her since she became a mother again."

"She is really looking after those two children like if they belong to her."

At one o'clock Nellie helped Clytie to close the shop for the lunch hour and together they walked over to Clytie's home.

"Aunt Ida Cou Cou should be finish by now," said Clytie.

"Is that what we're having for lunch? I got up this morning thinking that was exactly what I wanted."

"You in the family way Nels?" asked Clytie laughing.

"For that my friend, I'm much too old."

"We here Aunt Ida," shouted Clytie after she closed the door.

"Come in the kitchen. I almost finish."

Clytie and Nellie walked into the kitchen expecting Cou Cou with crab sauce, and were surprised by what Ida had prepared.

"But I thought you was making Cou Cou Aunt Ida."

"I had a longing for some good Carlina food and I know you will like it too."

"This look like Okra Slosh. And you make so much of it. What is it?" asked Clytie.

"It name Seafood Gumbo Clytie. It is Creole cooking from Carlina."

"And what is this?"

"That name Corn Bread. They don't go together, but since I had the corn meal, I decide to make it."

"But we did looking forward to Cou Cou Aunt Ida."

Nellie gave her friend a glance which she immediately understood. She did not want the old woman to feel offended.

"I'm sure it tastes good," said Nellie sitting down at the table.

"You like it?" asked the old woman looking at her as she raised the spoon to her mouth.

"This is really good Miss Ida. Did you say the Creoles eat this?"

"Yes."

"Then I'm sure Francois would love some of this. He would eat anything that has crab in it."

Clytie took the plunge and was surprised how good it was.

"It real good Aunt Ida. Why you never cook this before?"

"Don't forget to put aside some for my Francois," Nellie said.

After Nellie left, Ida spoke to her neice.

"That Nellie is a real lady. When she down here with us,

she does fit in real good. But you notice when she talking to her husband, she does speak real sweet? Just like them hifaluting English people. And when she with us, she is a real downright Bajan."

"Nellie is a good person Aunt Ida. She ain't forget where she come from."

# 27

"I've just received a letter from Jennifer Appleby's solicitor in St. Lucia," Alastair Chambers said to his partner.

"And what did he have to say?"

"He didn't foresee a problem with her inheriting everything, but he needed the Death Certifcate of the sister Rose Appleby."

"That does throw a wrench into things, but we should have expected it."

"That means I'll have to speak to Jennifer and open those old wounds once again."

"You know there will be a mountain of questions about her sister's death, because the matter was never reported to the police."

"Luckily for Old Appleby, they can't question him."

"How would you say you are getting along here Alastair?"

"It's actually not as difficult as I had expected, but just like England, there is certainly a lot of bureaucracy."

"You'll get used to it," said Francois. "There is something I want to ask you."

"Go ahead. You know you can ask me anything."

"I know there has been a lot going on, and you also know I

had planned to take Nellie away on vacation. Do you think you
are ready to be left alone?"

"Of course I can handle things. If I am uncertain about
anything, I'll ask Miss Weatherby. She knows everything that
goes on around here."

"Does that mean I'm free to take my wife on holiday?"

"Of course! I think Nellie needs to get away for a while, and
so do you. She has gone through a lot in the past few months. I
know she still misses Long John."

"She does. He was like a little child running around the
house. Do you think you will get another dog?"

"I don't think so Alastair. Losing him was heart breaking and
I don't want to put Nellie through that again."

"Have you told Douglas yet?"

"No I haven't. There was so much going on with Jennifer and
all this stuff around the house that I really forgot to tell him."

Nellie was not as elated as he thought she would be when
she heard the good news. They would be leaving in four weeks
for London and then for Ghana, Africa. She had always heard
Miss Una speak of Africa and also remembered the stories which
her mother and grandparents had told her about the continent,
but the happenings of the past few moths had tempered her
excitement.

"You will feel better about it in a couple of days," said Francois.

"Maybe I will."

"Do you remember how happy you were when I told you we
were going to Paris?"

"Of course I remember, but things weren't so complicated
back then. This is what I have been longing for, but now I know
that having a bit of money can be a blessing as well as a curse."

"Nellie I am worried about you. You were always on top of things. Nothing really ever made you feel so low."

"It's not just one thing Francois. Look at the number of things that have happened around here in the past three months."

"I know. Getting away from here will give you a chance to rejuvenate. New surroundings and new faces will really make a difference. You'll see. Do you remember the show we saw in Paris?"

"Yes."

"When we get to London, I'll take you to the West End where there are lots of theatres and shows just like those we saw in Paris."

"Give me a little time to shake these feelings off. I guess the worst of it was losing Miss Una and poor Long John."

"Would you like to have another cat just like Hurley?"

Nellie cringed. After all those years the very name of Hurley was enough to scare her out of her wits.

"And I missed him when he disappeared," she said with tears in her eyes.

"Why don't you call Nora and we can go over for a visit? We can see how the girls are getting along, and I can make my Saturday appointment with Percy to go fishing."

"Yes, let's get out for a while," she said.

"By the ways Nels, the children know nothing of their mother's wealth. Alastair received a letter today from the solicitor in St. Lucia."

"Will she get that money too?"

"I believe so, but they need a copy of her sister's death certificate."

"Is that a problem?"

"Well old Appleby never did report his daughter missing. He couldn't report it because he was a man on the run."

"So what is she going to do?"

"Right now I don't know. We've never had to deal with anything like it."

"Jennifer was a child then. She could explain herself to the authorities."

"That's what she'll probably have to do."

"What are we having for dinner tonight?" he suddenly asked.

"Miss Ida made something and I brought you some of it, but you must close your eyes when I bring it in."

Nellie went to the kitchen and a few minutes later, she shouted to her husband to close his eyes.

"And don't open them until I tell you."

She placed the bowl in front of him, raised the spoon and asked him to open his mouth, which he did.

"Seafood Gumbo," he said looking into the bowl. "I didn't know Ida could cook Gumbo."

"Well Clytie and I were upset because we went over expecting Cou Cou and this is what we got. I didn't like the look of it, but it really is delicious."

"When are you bringing her over to cook us some good Creole food?" he asked.

"Don't you like our food?" asked Nellie.

"Of course I do, but this brings back memories of my childhood," he said as tears settled in his eyes.

Percy was sitting outside smoking a pipe when the Bertrands arrived. Francois greeted Nora and then joined his friend.

"How's the fishing these days?"

"Didn't catch much! A couple ning-nings, one old wife, a barber, some chubs and a baby shark."

"I'll come out on Saturday morning and we'll see if our luck changes."

"We got to get some crabs too. Ida is out there cooking up a storm and keep asking for crabs. She is always making something like okra slosh and putting crab meat in it. It did taste good but nothing don't beat a little bit of good Bajan food."

"I had some of it too," said Francois. "That's what we used to eat when I was a child."

Nora came out with a pitcher of Mauby and two glasses and put it on the work bench in front of the two men. Francois filled the glasses and they looked out onto the deep blue waters of the Atlantic Ocean.

"How are the girls?" Francois asked.

"To tell the truth, I really didn't want them here, but Nora is very happy to have them around. Maybe it is because we don't have any grandchildren of our own."

"Heard anything from Toby recently?"

"Not a word. He will come by when he runs out of money to harass his sister, but she don't skylark. She does call a spade a spade."

"It runs in the family Percy."

"Evening," said a little voice.

"Heather, say good evening to Mr. Francois."

The little girl did as she was told and settled down at the workbench with a book and pencil.

"Homework?" asked Francois.

"Yes sir."

"What is it?"

"Arithmetic but I can't do it."

"Would you like my help?" he asked.

"Yes sir."

The little girl listened as Francois explained the Maths problem to her.

"It is easy the way you explain it, but the teacher makes it seem really hard."

Percy winked at Francois.

"I am real glad you come by because they always confusing me with these things and I ain't got a clue 'bout arithmetic."

"But you are a carpenter Percy. How do you make cabinets and such things without knowing a little arithmetic?"

"Common sense Francois. That is what my mother used to say, without a little commonsense, you ain't nothing but a damn fool. And that is how I live to this day. With common sense!"

"Maybe you should get Jonas to give them some extra lessons."

Percy looked behind him before he spoke, and then said to Heather.

"Let me see that book child. Ain't nothing but spotters and skinners you got here. Go and bring the rubber."

As soon as she was out of sight, Percy continued.

"Jonas courting strong. He holding onto Judes."

The two men laughed while puffing away on their pipes and the little girl returned with an eraser and proceeded to rewrite everything she had written.

On their way home, Nellie and Francois stopped by Clytie's to see how they were getting along. She and Ida were still in the shop, but were getting ready to close. Before leaving, Clytie told her friend she wanted to ask for her help in a serious matter and asked her to come by the following day.

# 28

"Morning Miss Nellie," said Ida. "I was just making some tea. You want a cup?"

"Thanks Miss Ida. Where is Clytie?"

She run over to the shop to get something. She coming back soon."

Nellie looked out the window, then turned around and was on her way to the kitchen when Ida returned with a teapot. The fragile little woman seemed hardly able to carry the pot, but looks were really deceptive. Nellie stopped just outside the bedroom door and her whole body seemed to shudder. Ida stared at her and quickly put the teapot on the table.

"You feel it too?" she asked Nellie.

"Feel what?"

"Everytime I pass that spot, a cold feeling does pass over my whole body. You know if anything bad ever happen in this house?" she asked.

"I used to live here and I can't remember anything out of the ordinary happening," she replied.

Nellie knew it was the exact spot where Nora had struck Thomas Hurley and where he had fallen. She was afraid, not only of the past, but because Ida seemed to have a sixth sense.

"I know you feel it too. I see it when you stop so sudden."

"Yes it was a really strange feeling; something I've never felt before and I have lived in this house for a very long time."

"Sometimes you have to pray. I know it ain't Una. Somebody else soul just isn't resting."

Nellie was glad when Clytie returned and brought the uncomfortable conversation to an end. The two women laughed and talked for a few minutes before Clytie took Nellie to the bedroom leaving Ida drinking her tea and perhaps still wondering what sinister thing could have happened inside the house. Clytie reached under her bed and brought out two rather large square biscuit tins.

"You used to run the shop before Nels. I want you to tell me how you put away the money."

Clytie opened the first biscuit tin and Nellie's eyes popped opened wide. The tin was packed full with money. When she opened the second tin, it was also full. She then emptied it all onto the bed and a piece of cloth along with its contents also fell from the tin. Clytie opened it and then she started to laugh. In the piece of cloth were the seeds of a Casuarina tree; seeds which she had picked up on the way to the obeah man so many years ago.

"If these seeds could talk!" she said.

"They're only Casuarina seeds," said Nellie.

"Yes but Nels behind these seeds is a story. These seeds I pick up on the way to Dootie, the obeah man. Remember how I was trying to help Miss Sarah to get away from Thomas Hurley?"

Nellie smiled a feint smile. She did not want to talk about Thomas Hurley and so she got back to the business at hand.

"All this is the money from the shop Clytie?"

"Yes. Every night I put it in here."

"Does anyone else know about this money?"

"No. Not even Jonas."

"You can't keep this money here. Suppose somebody steals it or suppose there is a fire?"

"Tell me what to do with it Nels."

"You must put it in the bank."

"You know I don't know nothing 'bout these things."

"Tomorrow morning when Francois is going to the office, get ready and we will go with him into Bridgetown and open an account. Do you know how much money you've got here in these tins?"

"Well I just ain't get around to counting it this week, but last week I had a little bit more than six thousand dollars."

"Dear Lord," said Nellie. "You can't sleep with this in the house tonight. You wouldn't know if anyone stole anything out of it."

"Nobody isn't going to teef nothing Nels, because they don't know that it is in here."

"This is almost two year's shop money in here Clytie. We have to put it in order and count it before we can take it to the bank. We will do it just like JB showed me."

"Nels you still remember JB a lot?"

"Not really Clytie. It would be like being unfaithful to Francois and I don't have any intention of doing that."

"He's a real nice fellow Nels. I know that nothing good is going to happen for me, 'cause I am a little too old now."

"Don't say that Clytie. All I can tell you is that when he comes along, you aren't supposed to show him this money."

The two women had a good laugh and Nellie advised her friend to find a safer place for the money that day. They counted it and reached the sum of seven thousand and one dollars and a few cents. They were wondering where they should hide it when Nellie remembered that underneath the bed was a loose floorboard. Carefully placing the cash in the calico bag and tying the top, they then hid it under the floorboard, leaving only the drawstring visible which they then covered with the empty biscuit tins. They left the bedroom and Nellie hurried past the doomed spot outside the bedroom door. Ida Franklin continued sipping her tea as she watched the two women who came out laughing. Just as Nellie was leaving for her home, her sister knocked on Clytie's door.

"I didn't know you was here Nels."

"Clytie wanted me to help her with a little problem, so I came down with Francois. How are the girls and Percy?"

"Everybody is doing alright. I wanted to get out of the house for a little bit because I can't get out like I used to with the two girls there."

"It won't be forever Nora. As soon as Jennifer gets her money, I'm sure they will move out."

"They are nice little girls. For children that went through so much, the mother do a real good job."

"Listen to me Nora. I think that Ida could see things."

"What you mean? What she seeing?"

"About half an hour ago, I stop on that spot right there," she said pointing to the entrance to Clytie's bedroom. "Suddenly a cold shiver went through my body and I stopped and shuddered. Ida noticed it and said it happens to her often on the same spot. Then she asked if anything strange ever happened in the house."

"What you tell her?"

"I said that I lived in this house for many years and I can't remember anything strange ever happening here."

"Remember we promised to go to the grave with that secret."

"Yes but Francois knows."

"Nellie you promised you would never tell it to anybody."

"I didn't have to tell him. He knew."

"You mean he is like Ida? He can see things too?"

"No, but he knew. I didn't have to say one word. Don't forget he is a solicitor and he can figure things out."

"You just make sure that nobody else figure out anything. I too old for Glendairy."

"The children ask anything about their mother?"

"Sometimes I let them call Bottomsley to talk to her. It make her feel good to know that they learning and they are in good hands. Girl they even calling Percy Papa."

"You skylarking?" asked Nellie.

"God is my judge. I am Miss Nora and Percy is Papa. You should see them together doing homework, and Percy ain't got a clue you know. When they ask something he don't understand, he always get up to get a drink hoping by the time he get back, they would forget about it. But that little one, she don't forget a thing."

"Anyway I'm expecting a phone call around midday, so I must get back home. Just be careful around Ida. That woman seems to know everything that's going on without you opening your mouth."

# 29

Life seemed to have returned to normal and the Bertrand's day of departure was fast approaching. Harriet and Judes were kept busy making light clothing for Nellie for the African part of the trip. She modeled everything for Francois. Some of the clothing he liked and some he didn't. And since all seemed quiet on the home front with no more blackmail notes, Nellie once again became her old jovial self.

Sarah Bottomsley too was breathing a sigh of relief for since her son-in-law had locked all the doors at night, she was no longer being accosted by the intruder and was able to use her money for beautifying herself again.

There was still no word about Ursy's killer and Brandon Harvey had completely disappeared, but the constable was still on the lookout for any sightings of the missing man. There was still one thing that worried the constable and it was the witness' words about the smell of the perfume, Lady of the Night. Since no such plants could be found growing in the village, was it possible there a woman with Brandon Harvey on the night Ursy was murdered? He still had a lot of work to do.

Nora and Percy at arrived at the Bertrand home the night before their departure to say goodbye, to find them both still packing their valises. Nellie's was bulging at the seams.

"There ain't no space left for the presents you bringing back," said her sister.

"I've told her that already," said her husband. "It's summertime in England and it's always summer in Ghana."

"I thought you were going to Africa," said Percy.

"Ghana is in Africa," said a proud Nellie. "Francois said it was the place where they kept the slaves until they put them on the ships to the Caribbean."

"But that don't happen no more," said Nora.

"That's true, but it's just like here. They are still living under a British colonial government. We can tell you all about it when we get back," said Nellie. "We will tell you about England too."

Before they went to bed that night, Nellie made a call to Emily and Alastair. Otty had agreed that if they were in need of help, she would be willing to pitch in to help the family.

———

Things were progressing for Jennifer Appleby. Under Alastair's instructions, she wrote a letter to the court explaining the circumstances of her sister's death. The death certificate was all that stood between her and the two homes and land in St. Lucia. The estate in England seemed to be almost finalised. One of Francois' missions while in London was to meet the solicitors face to face and have everything brought to a close.

It had been a while since the Chambers family had taken a holiday and they decided they would go to St. Lucia for an extended weekend. Sarah Bottomsley proclaimed she had no intention of sitting down with Nellie at the same table and therefore would not be going.

"Nellie won't be there Sarah," Grandpa Bottomsley explained. "She and her husband are at this very moment in London."

"What are they doing there?" she asked.

"They're on holiday. Something you should think of doing."

"I haven't that much money," she replied.

"Sarah you get an allowance every month and in addition, you had a handsome sum in the bank when my son died."

"It's just about gone Father Bottomsley."

"What?" asked the astonished old man. "You have a home, your meals are prepared here and you have been giving away your clothing because you have way too much."

"Well I don't have too much left."

"Would you like me to lend you some money Sarah?"

"No Father Bottomsley."

"So you won't come with us to St. Lucia? Emily says it's beautiful there. We are going to stay in Nellie's guest house right on the ocean."

"Then I really won't go. I wonder where she got that house?" the vindictive woman asked.

"Doesn't matter Sarah. I haven't left this Rock since I came here and I intend to enjoy myself with Emily and the children."

"I'll stay here and amuse myself," she said.

"That's up to you," said the old man.


"Grandpa I must speak to you about something," said Emily.

"You know you can ask anything of me my dear."

"I hope you won't be upset."

"What is it Emily?"

"It's almost six years since Grandma died and we haven't done anything with the house."

The old man's smile disappeared and he stared at his granddaughter.

"Do you intend selling the house Emily?"

"Maybe Grandpa, but if it bothers you, I won't. It has been sitting there since Grandma's death with all the furniture and her belongings in it. Don't you think it is time we did something about it?"

"Six years is a long time. We could get some income from the home. Wouldn't you think of renting it first and selling it later?"

"I know a great part of your life was spent in that home and you still feel attached to it. Maybe we should get rid of some of the contents and put it up for rent."

"That makes me feel better Emily. I know Millie would appreciate that."

"When we return from our trip to St. Lucia, we'll discuss it further. Have you spoken to Mother about the trip?"

"She won't be swayed Emily and intends to remain here. She says she wants nothing to do with Nellie or anything that belongs to her."

"After all these years Grandpa and she is still as stubborn as she always was. Then we will just go without her."

"Why don't you try persuading her to come with us? I think she is very lonely."

"Grandpa, Sarah has controlled my life for as long as I can remember. I will not allow this blackmail to continue any longer. She has forgotten that Nellie is my mother and that as my mother I will have feelings for her. I will not allow her to stand in my way."

"Then we can't take Jennifer with us."

"She can take the time to visit her children in St. Lucy."

"And Sarah?"

"What about her?"

"Who's going to look after her?"

"She can take care of herself. She was given a choice. Jennifer needs to see her children and now is her chance."

"You are just like your father."

"Is that a good thing Grandpa?"

"Yes you are strong headed but sensible. Shouldn't I stay here with Sarah?"

"No Grandpa. You are coming with us."


"Is everything packed Jennifer?" asked Emily.

"Yes ma'am. I've put the children's clothes in this bag and I've still got a bit of ironing to do for Mr. Chambers."

"We'll be leaving late this afternoon, so please have everything ready by the time he comes home," she said as she fussed around in the kitchen.

"Yes ma'am."

How Jennifer wished she too could've made the trip to St. Lucia with the family to see her old home, but her priority had to be her children.

"When are you leaving for St. Lucy?"

"On the first bus tomorrow morning ma'am."

"We'll be back on Monday evening. Can you return in time to prepare dinner?"

"Yes ma'am, but what about Miss Sarah?"

"What about her?"

"Who is going to look after her?"

"She'll manage Jennifer. Don't worry about my mother."

The Chambers family set off for their trip to St. Lucia, leaving a moping and sullen Sarah sitting on the verandah.

"Sarah, are you sure you won't join us?" asked Alastair.

"I've got an exciting book to read and I will spend the time perusing it," she said.

Jennifer cleaned up the house and was about to go when Sarah rang the bell.

"Bring me a drink. Rum on ice."

"Yes ma'am."

Jennifer brought the drink and asked if she needed anything else.

"That will be all," she replied.

Her dinner in hand, Jennifer hurriedly left the house in case Sarah should ring the bell again. She picked up her clothing from the clothesline and opened the door to her room. She jumped. Sitting on her bed was Brandon Harvey.

"What you doing here?" she asked.

"I need you," he said pushing her to the bed.

"Somebody will hear you," she said.

"No one will hear us. I saw them leave. The old woman is still there but she won't interfere."

"What do you want? Do you need money?"

"You know I don't have any. You also know I can't work because of this," he said pointing to the scar. "Yet you left me without thinking where I would get something to eat or a cigarette to smoke."

"Sorry," she replied.

"You're not," he said raising his hand.

"Not in my face," she said ducking from his extended hand.

He pushed her onto the bed and proceeded to slap and punch her. She did not beg for mercy nor did she cry. He stared into her face and she into his. He grabbed her long hair with his left hand and pressed her head to the bed, then with the other hand, unbuttoned her blouse and roughly grabbed her breasts causing her to gasp. He then hurriedly climbed on top of her, and her body rose to meet his. They both heaved and moaned and when it was all over, he kissed her over her face and body while she lay there seemingly satisfied.

"Why you kill Ursy?" she asked.

"I didn't kill her. I know they're looking for me, but I had nothing to do with her death."

"You didn't kill her?" she asked in a tone filled with surprise.

"I swear I know nothing about the woman. Forget about her. It has been a long time since I felt like this," he said running his hand over her breasts and once again conquering her.

"Do you want money?" she asked.

"Naturally I want money. How do you expect me to eat or to get a smoke?"

She handed him her purse and he opened it, took what he needed and threw it back at her.

"Where did you hide the girls?" he asked.

"I didn't hide them. I send them away."

"Where did you send them?"

"They went away to school."

"Come Jennifer, you don't have the means to do that. Where are they?"

"I tell you I send them off to school."

"Where?"

A bit of quick thinking saved the day.

"They went to England. To my father family."

"Where in England?"

"London!" she said.

"You're a liar. I will find out where you sent them."

She shared her dinner with him and once it was over, he

shoved her against the headboard and started to make love to her again. In his throes of ecstasy, he placed his hands around her neck and tightened them. She thrashed around, her arms flailed and her eyes bulged. Slowly he loosened his grip and she coughed and spluttered. He then gently kissed her all over her body until she was at the breaking point. After it was over, her thoughts immediately turned to Ursy. His brutality showed its ugly face only during lovemaking but no one had said anything about Ursy being raped. They spoke for a while and then lay quiet until she heard his breathing become shallow. He had fallen asleep.

When she awoke the following morning, he was gone and she breathed a sigh of relief, but her body with the exception of her face was covered in bruises. She wore a dress which hid most of the marks and set out for the long journey to St. Lucy.

# 30

"Clytie, I need your help?" said a rather sad voice on the phone.

"Who is this?" she asked not fully recognizing the voice.

"It's Sarah Bottomsley. Would you like to come by and help me?" she asked.

"Miss Sarah?" asked an astonished Clytie. "What is wrong?"

"Everyone has left and there is no one to help me. I haven't even had breakfast this morning."

"Where is Miss Emily? Where is Jennifer?"

"They have all deserted me Clytie. I wish you would come by and help me."

"Miss Sarah, I am running my own business and only my aunt is in the shop and she can't manage by herself."

"I thought I could count on you Clytie. You have let me down too."

"No Miss Sarah. I just can't.............

There was only dial tone. Sarah had put the receiver down.

"I don't know what she expect from me. I just can't drop everything and run when she call," said an irritated Clytie.

"The ways of the world," said Ida. "Who was that?" she asked.

"That was Miss Sarah from Bottomsley plantation. I used to work there in the kitchen."

"She want you to come back?"

"It look like if everybody else gone away and left her by herself."

"Why she didn't go?"

"I don't know Aunt Ida."

The public bus stopped in front of the shop and Jennifer climbed down from the running board and made her way towards the shop.

"Jennifer how you?" asked Clytie.

"I good," she replied.

"Why you leave Miss Sarah by herself with no breakfast?"

"Miss Chambers say that I could take the weekend off and spend it with my children because she and the rest of the family went to St. Lucia."

"Why they didn't take Miss Sarah?"

"She didn't want to go. I hear her telling the old man that she didn't want nothing to do with Miss Nellie."

"She say that? But Nellie isn't there. Nellie went on vacation."

"How you know she is there by herself Miss Clytie?"

"She just call and beg me to come down and help her."

"Miss Emily say I should cook and leave something for her for three days and I do that. She tell me not to worry about making breakfast that she could do it herself."

"It don't look like if Miss Sarah going to ever change. She was always selfish. Go and look for the children. Don't let Miss Sarah confuse your head."

Ida listened to the conversation but said nothing. She just kept staring at Jennifer. After she had left, she turned to her niece and asked a very strange question.

"Tell me something Clytie. Why is that girl working in a

kitchen? I never see white people on this island working in a kitchen. She look like somebody who got a lot of troubles. You see those blue marks in the back of her neck?"

"I didn't see no marks Aunt Ida."

"That girl in a lot of trouble. She isn't the girl who used to live with the woman that get kill?"

"Yes that is Jennifer. The two children who live by Nora belong to her."

"She got a lot of troubles. She got so much trouble 'round her neck that she just about drowning. She is going to get some money. A lot of money, but she got to be careful. That girl isn't as innocent as she look."

"You don't see a lot of money for me too Aunt Ida?"

"You don't need nothing child. The Lord is good to you. That girl look real quiet Clytie, but she isn't so quiet. She is a smart girl, but a smart girl who had a hard life. She got to watch that woman she working with too."

"You mean Miss Emily?"

"No the other one with the yellow hair who think she put on this earth to rule."

"You mean Miss Sarah Aunt Ida?"

"Yes that is the one. How you know she got yellow hair?"

"Girl there ain't a thing Ida Franklin don't know."

"Then tell me who kill Ursy."

"That I can't tell you, but my suspicion tell me it ain't the man with the red hair and the red moutsnatch."

"What man is that?"

"What the girl name again who was just here?"

"You mean Jennifer?"

"Yes, the man she was with got red hair and he also got a red moutsnatch."

"No Aunt Ida. He bald and he ain't got no moustache."

"Then I must have the wrong person," she said as she started to stack coins on top of each other.

Clytie stared at her and her thoughts began to spin around in her head. It seemed as if her Aunt Ida could see things nobody else could. Strangely enough she hadn't predicted the death of her sister. If she had known she had never said a word to anyone. Saturday mornings were busy since this was the time most customers chose to buy their foodstuff. The line just kept growing longer and longer, so Clytie went next door and asked Judes to lend her a hand.

"If it get too busy here, I want Judes to come back," said Harriet.

"Just shout and let me know," Clytie replied.

"Morning Miss Ida," said Judes.

"Morning," replied the old woman with her toothless grin. "You looking real rosy."

"Thanks Miss Ida."

Judes was busy attending to a customer when Ida made a hissing sound with her lips. Looking around Clytie realized she was trying to get her attention.

"You going to be a grandmother," she said.

"How you know that?"

"You can't tell?" she asked her niece.

"I don't know what you talking about Aunt Ida."

"I think that Judes is in the family way."

"You sure about that? I know she and Jonas real friendly, but she got more sense than to get herself into something like that."

"Sometimes you behave just like a country girl Clytie. Sense don't got nothing to do with it. When a man and woman get together and things get hot, sense don't play no part in it. You never had a man in your life?"

"Aunt Ida, sometimes you sound just like Ma."

"We was sisters Clytie. I just sorry that the good Lord ain't give me more time with her."

Lord have mercy," was all that Clytie could say.

———

The long weekend flew by and Jennifer had to leave to be back at Bottomsley for the arrival of the family. She took the three o' clock bus from the village and was satisfied that her daughters were getting along well and in good hands. She made it home with enough time to prepare dinner before the Chambers returned.

She saw Sarah sitting at the piano. She was playing a classical piece. The Blue Danube! She remembered it well. It was one of her father's favourites. When he was sober, he was a good man in spite of what he had been doing to her and her sister. Tears filled her eyes. She was thinking of her sister Rose. Opening the kitchen door a little, she listened. Sarah was a good pianist. She moved to the dining room to set the table, all the while still enjoying Sarah's music, and she continued playing, totally ignoring Jennifer's presence. She heard voices and she also heard the engine of a car. The family had returned.

"Jennifer, Jennifer," said Douglas. "I brought you something."

"What you bring for me?" she asked.

The little boy had brought her a box of sand. She took it and thanked him. Little did he know what joyful memories that box of sand had brought her! The very sand she had played on as a child back on the beaches of St. Lucia. It also brought her pain, because she now thought of her sister Rose whose body the sea had claimed. Everyone had a story to tell of their little trip away from home. Even John tried to talk which made everyone laugh, for no one could understand what he was trying to say.

"Sarah, I do say you missed quite a lovely weekend," said Old Bottomsley. "I forgot how wonderful it could be just walking barefoot on the beach with that beautiful water tingling between your toes."

"Oh Father Bottomsley," she said. "We've got all that here."

"It wasn't the same Sarah. We ate well. We drank well and we didn't have a care in the world. All except Alastair of course who insisted on mixing business with pleasure. My granddaughter and my great grandchildren, along with Grandpa had a beautiful time, didn't we Douglas?"

"We certainly did," said Emily. "How are you Mother?"

"Very well," she replied.

"It must've been a bit lonely. Here all by yourself."

"One gets used to such things Emily. I'm like an old shoe."

Emily and Alastair looked at each other and she thought the best place to be was in the kitchen with Jennifer.

"When dinner is over Jennifer, I would like to have a word with you," said Alastair.

She was worried. Why did he want to see her? Did he know that Brandon had spent one night on the premises? She was careful not to let the bruises show because Emily would certainly ask what had caused them. Luckily they were fading away and shouldn't be a cause for any questioning. After dinner she approached him and he took her into his study and closed the door.

"I hope he gets rid of her," said Sarah as she noticed them going behind closed doors.

"Yes sir," she said.

"Have a seat Jennifer. As you know we were in St. Lucia, quite close to one of your properties, which is beside Mrs. Bertrand's guest house."

"Yes sir?"

"The property is badly in need of repair. No one has been there since you left the island. Have you given any thought to what you would like to do with it?"

"Not really sir."

"Of course the land is worth quite a bit especially since it directly on the beach. The other property is not in much better condition, but the house is still full of furniture, some of which would bring a rather handsome price."

"Can you give me some advice sir?"

"Are you thinking of returning to St. Lucia?"

"No sir."

"Well my suggestion is to sell both properties and invest the money."

"You would have to help me with that sir."

"I'll do what I can."

"What about the house in England?" she asked.

"I do think you will get it, and we will have the final word when Mr. Bertrand returns. Of course the properties in St. Lucia are not quite ready. That will take another couple of months."

"Can you sell them for me? I need money for me and the children."

"Yes I can understand that. Tell me something Jennifer, when you get the money, what will you do?"

"I don't understand the question sir."

"Do you intend to stay on the island?"

"I didn't think about that."

"You should. It's your future and your children's future. Of course we will miss you but you should consider getting away from here and starting a new life."

"But I don't know where to go sir."

"As long as you are able to look after yourself financially, which you will be able to do, any country will accept you."

"Where you think I should go sir?"

"I don't know. You speak some French, don't you?"

"Yes. I learn it in St. Lucia. It isn't real French but I could still understand real French people."

"What about France? Or Martinique? Or Guadeloupe? French is spoken in all of those countries. Or perhaps you can go to England. The girls would get a good education there."

Alastair got up from his chair, went to the bookshelf and handed her a book on England.

"Have a look at this. It will give you an idea about British life."

"Thank you sir. A man come by two days ago and left that envelope over there for you."

"That must have been the bookkeeper," he said glancing at the big brown envelope.

Sarah Bottomsley seated in the plantation chair, heard the study door open and she looked up. Jennifer didn't seem unhappy, so she gathered she hadn't lost her job. She was at a loss to the reason why she and her son in law had spent more than half an hour behind closed doors.

Bottomsley Great House was as secure as a fortress just before battle. Alastair went around double-checking every window and door before he turned in. Meanwhile downstairs, Jennifer sat on the edge of her bed and looked at the book Alastair had lent her. Her profile, caught by the bright moonlight stood out on the wall of her room. Her thoughts were far away. In Paris, Martinique, London, Guadeloupe. Alastair was right. For the sake of her children she had to make a decision. She had no friends except the few she had met since starting to work at Bottomsley. She was twenty five years old and knew she had to make a start and soon. A gentle knock on her door made her jump. She was happy she had put the security lock on. She did not reply, but turned the light out and waited. After a short while, she threw her legs onto the bed, covered herself and was soon fast asleep.

# 31

What a beautiful day it was! The Plum Tree Villagers were at the beach with their children enjoying the beautiful sunshine. All the budding entrepreneurs had taken up their positions; the sugar cake woman, the mauby woman, the woman who picked and sold all the local fruit and even the barber with his calabash and straight razor had positioned himself under a coconut tree. Beside him several men were playing dominoes and arguing about everything possible. The more they argued, the more they emptied the bottles of Bottomsley white rum. Several little boys with gutter perks were trying to knock some blackbirds from a tree, much to the annoyance of the Dominoes' players. Nora and Percy had also taken the two girls to play with their friends. Nora watched as they ran into the water and back again. She was happy that the children who were once so timid and shy had come out of their shells and were enjoying themselves. Joining them on the beach were Harriet, Jonas and Judes. Nora was happy to see that her daughter had closed the shop and taken a day off. It was obvious to the onlooker that there was something going on between Judes and Jonas. He was very attentive and she seemed to laugh at everything he said. Nora knew that going to

Teachers' College was now out of the question for him, especially since Nellie had closed her school and the children were now attending the government owned elementary school. She had always known him to be a level headed boy since they had lived in the Bottomsley tenement, but he had now fallen in love. She was happy for the girl since her son didn't seem to have the slightest interest in her anymore. Judes got up, kicked her shoes off and strolled to the water's edge and his eyes followed her.

"Miss Nora," said Heather, "may I have a penny to buy some Fat Pork?"

Nora put her hand into her pocket and handed the child a penny. She scampered off and stood in front of a buxom woman whose legs were sprawled in front of a large tray. She handed her the penny and the woman filled her hands with the small red fruit. She gave some to her sister and then returned to Nora and offered her some.

"I don't like those things child. They does tie up my mouth. She didn't have no cashews? And be careful, that sea ain't got no back door," she shouted after her.

The child skipped happily away, perhaps glad that Nora hadn't taken any of the Fat Pork, because she could now have them all to herself. Percy, a man of few words quietly puffed away on his wife. Suddenly he turned to his wife and spoke to her.

"Nora, the last time I went fishing with Francois, he say that if you draw a straight line from here right across the sea, you would run straight into Africa."

"So?" asked his wife.

"It is just that if it wasn't so far away, we would be able to see Nellie and Francois."

"You like you getting sentimental in your old age Percy. You miss Nellie?"

"I miss Nellie and Francois. Things ain't the same without the two of them around here."

"Lord have mercy. They are coming back soon. It is now three weeks since they left. I will tell them that you was pining behind them."

"You talking foolishness woman. You miss them too but you just too shame to say so."

"Percy, who you think kill Ursy?"

"That is one question I can't answer. All I can say is I hope they catch the person real soon."

"You mean you don't think it is Jennifer man Harvey?"

"Like I tell you I just don't know. My question is if he do it, what reason he had to do it? They didn't know one another. You see those marks on Jennifer neck last week?"

"Not last week. The week before."

"It look like somebody was choking her. All around the neck was full o' nothing but black and blue marks."

"She probably didn't sleep good the night before. She say that always happen when she had a sleepless night."

"Or she telling you lies."

"Could be," said Nora.

The golden evening sun started to dip beyone the horizon and Nora called the children.

"Tomorrow is school and I didn't see the two o' you doing any homework."

"We did it already," said the younger sister eager to get back to what she was doing.

"Well I ain't see it and you got to show me."

Alastair Chambers called his wife into the study. In front of him lay a mountain of paperwork. The bookkeeper had brought the financial statements from Bottomsley plantation.

"How are we doing?" she asked.

"Could be better, but we are holding our own. Production has fallen but the Rum is certainly keeping us in business."

"That's good news."

"Clyde is doing a good job. I wasn't sure if we could've pulled it off this year, but he has proven to be a good leader. Well everyone's safe for now. We won't have to lay off any of the field hands."

"I was speaking to Grandpa about his home. It has been closed for more than six years and he seems ready to move on. I really thought that selling it would be the best thing to do, but for that, he wasn't ready."

"What are we going to do then?"

"He agreed we should put it up for rent. Do you think we should give him the money or should we put it into the Bottomsley account?"

"What would you have done with the money if you had sold the property?"

"I hadn't thought about it."

"Don't forget he now lives here and really has no expenses. You can increase what you give him every month."

"What are we going to do with the furniture? Papa had furnished the house with beautiful antique pieces."

"Let's see if there is anything we want to bring here and the rest we can rent along with the house."

"Let's go to bed," she said. "You look tired."

"I can hardly wait until Francois returns. It really is a lot of work for one person. I just don't know how he did it all alone."

"They'll be back at the end of next week. I hope they had a good time in London and in Africa."

"I'm sure they did. Francois makes everything seem interesting, even if it isn't."

"She's lucky and he is too of course."

"You're biased," said Alastair.

"I almost forgot," she said. "On Wednesday I promised to work at Douglas' school. That means that Jennifer must do all the housework alone."

"Didn't Nellie say that Otty would help out if we needed her?"

"That would be great if she could pitch in. I'll call her tomorrow to see if she can help."

⁓

"What was that?" asked Sarah Bottomsley as Otty returned to the kitchen after clearing the dining room table.

"What?" asked Old Bottomsley.

"Didn't you see it?" asked Sarah.

"See what?" asked the old man.

"A strange looking creature just picked up the dishes from table and disappeared into the kitchen."

"You mean Otty? That's Nellie's housekeeper."

"And what is she doing here?"

"My granddaughter had a lot to do today, so she is helping out with the cooking and such things."

"Nellie's housekeeper?" asked Sarah aloud.

"Now Sarah, what are you thinking?" asked the old man.

"Nothing. Let's have a drink Father Bottomsley."

"I know you Sarah, and I know you are up to something," he said placing the drink in her hand.

She rang the bell and Jennifer ran on to the verandah.

"Send the other one in," she said not looking at Jennifer.

Jennifer returned to the kitchen and gave Otty a couple words of caution.

"Ma'am?" asked Otty.

"Mr. Bottomsley and I would love to have some drinks. Do you know how to make drinks?"

"Yes ma'am."

"I'll have rum on ice and so would Mr. Bottomsley."

Otty looked at the two glasses on the table that had hardly been touched.

"Yes ma'am," she said.

She left and returned a couple minutes later with a tray and two glasses.

"What took you so long?" Sarah asked. "Do you keep Nellie waiting this long?"

"No ma'am," she replied. "Is that all ma'am?"

"You know Otty, that is your name, isn't it?"

"Yes ma'am."

"Do you know that your Nellie used to be my maid and serve my drinks just like you are doing?"

"No ma'am."

"Oh yes she did. Isn't that right Father Bottomsley?"

"Leave me out of this Sarah. You are asking for trouble."

"I'm just telling Otty the truth. Did I say something wrong?"

"Thank you Otty. Very nice drink, as usual," said Old Bottomsley.

Otty left the verandah and Sarah turned to the old man.

"That was fun, wasn't it?"

"What's going to happen if this gets back to Emily's ears? Or to Alastair's for that matter!"

Sarah realized that she had really gone too far, and so like Old Bottomsley, she sat and sipped her drink while gazing onto the horizon. A car pulled up and the police constable stepped out.

"What does he want?" asked Sarah.

"We will soon find out," replied the old man.

"Afternoon ma'am, sir," he said. "Do you mind if I sit?"

"Sit, sit," said the old man. "What brings you here? I hope you're here to tell us you've caught the rogue."

"Not quite sir. Lovely perfume," he said to Sarah.

"Thank you."

"What is it? The wife's birthday is approaching and I'm sure she would love that scent."

"Gardenia," said Sarah half-heartedly.

"Reminds me so much of "Lady of the Night," he replied.

"Not only are you into solving crimes, you seem to know your fragrances," she said getting up and leaving the verandah.

"Did I say something to offend her?" he asked.

"She's just a little touchy today. What brings you here?"

"I really wanted to speak with Miss Appleby. Is she here?"

"She's in the kitchen."

"Do you mind leaving us alone for a moment?" the Constable asked Otty.

Otty went down the back steps and in the direction of the orchard, leaving the two alone.

"I have some good news for you," the Constable said.

"Yes sir?"

"We've caught Brandon Harvey."

"When you catch him?"

"Two days ago. We decided to also watch you, hoping you would lead us to him and on Saturday morning, we thought we saw a shadowy figure leaving these premises. We followed him at a safe distance and saw him get into a blue Morris Minor. He drove to the home you shared and that's when we arrested him. I came by a couple times but you weren't here and the lady of the house refused to give me any information."

"I went to see my children."

"I thought you would inform us if you had seen him."

"I didn't have the time sir."

"Come Miss Appleby. You know there was enough time to inform the police."

She started to cry.

"I didn't know he was coming. He surprised me when I open the room door."

"Did he threaten you?"

"No sir but he say he didn't kill nobody."

"Then who could've done it?"

"I don't really know sir."

"Tell me, do you wear perfume?"

"No sir."

"Perhaps you should come down to the station and see him. Would you like to?"

"Yes sir."

# 32

When Emily arrived home, Old Bottomsley told her about the visit from the Constable and as far as he knew the suspect had not yet been apprehended, but he did not tell her of the interaction between Otty and Sarah Bottomsley.

"How is John? He is so quiet."

"He spent the whole day with Jennifer. Whenever he saw Sarah's face, he immediately started to cry."

"Children are very perceptive creatures Grandpa. He knows Sarah isn't really fond of children. Everything went well with Otty?"

"Oh yes, she is sharp and she is quick."

"So I wasn't missed. Douglas," she shouted, "where are you?"

Of course she found him in the kitchen with Jennifer and Otty. He was explaining to them what he had learnt in school that day. He was growing into a lovely young man. He reminded Emily very much of her father, not only in looks, but in his deportment and also his way of thinking. How she wished her father had been alive to see his offspring. He would've been a happy man.

"Grandpa, I was thinking that tomorrow you and I should go over to the house to see the condition it's in."

"Sorry my dear. I can't go with you tomorrow. It's my day to spend with the old chaps like myself."

"Tomorrow is Thursday. You've already spent time with them this week."

"Have I? Are you sure?"

"I thought today was Monday. Then of course we can go to see the house tomorrow."

"Good, then we will leave as early as possible because I want to spend some time with John."

"I wish you could've had the same kind of life when you were growing up Emily. You're such a good mother. If only Sarah….."

"Where is she Grandpa?"

"She went to her room when the Constable asked her about her perfume. Said he liked it and wanted to buy the same for his wife for her birthday."

"What was wrong with that?"

"Well she probably thought she and the Constable's wife were not in the same league and probably shouldn't be wearing the same perfume."

"She has always been that way and has no intention of changing. My goodness! I forgot all about Otty. There is no place for her to sleep tonight."

"Maybe Jennifer will allow her to sleep with her for the two nights."

It was all arranged. Emily didn't have to make the long drive to St. Lucy and back. Jennifer seemed to be happy to have the company of the older woman. It made her feel safe.

"You like Miss Bottomsley?" Otty asked Jennifer.

"I stay out of her way. She isn't a friendly woman."

"She was telling me about Miss Bertrand. Things she shouldn't be talking about."

"What she say to you?"

"How Miss Bertrand was a maid just like me and used to work in the kitchen just like me."

"You didn't know that?" asked Jennifer.

"Yes but she didn't have to tell me nothing 'bout it."

"Ursy didn't like her neither. We used to have a good laugh about her. She was always vex because Ursy never call her ma'am."

"What she used to call her?"

"Miss Bottomsley."

"That isn't her name?"

"Yes but she like it when you call her ma'am."

"Ohhhhhhhhhh!" said Otty. "I real glad Miss Bertrand isn't like that."

———

"So they've caught him," said Alastair to his wife.

"Him?"

"They caught this Brandon Harvey. The constable said he told it to Jennifer. Didn't she say anything?"

"She didn't."

"I wonder why she never mentioned it."

"You know how she is? She speaks only when she is spoken to, but seeing it has to do with Ursy, she should've said something. Where did they catch him?"

"At the home he had shared with her."

"Well I'm happy about that. I was always looking over my shoulder, now I won't have to."

"I still wonder why she didn't tell us. She knows she can talk to us. I'll speak to her tomorrow.

———

"Ma, can we go in the back room and talk?" asked Jonas sheepishly.

"Go ahead son. Tell your mother your troubles," she said laughing.

"Can we go into the back room?"

"This sounds real serious."

The mother and son went into the back room of the shop and closed the door.

"You noticed that Judes and I have been keeping company, haven't you?"

"I ain't blind Jonas. I see everything. What happen?"

"I know you will not be happy with what I'm going to tell you."

"She expecting a baby right?"

"How you know that Ma?"

"I didn't go to school Jonas, but I got common sense. Either you bring me back here to tell me that you want to get married, which I know isn't the case, because Judes is a married woman. So the only other thing it could be is that she in the family way."

"You were always a smart woman. Just like my grandmother."

"So what you want from me?" Clytie asked.

"Well you know that Judes sleeps in the backroom of Harriet's shop. I was wondering if she could move into the house with us."

"But we only got two bedrooms Jonas."

"I've thought about it Ma. We could bring one of the beds from Harriet's shop and put it in your bedroom and Aunt Ida could sleep on that."

"You like you got everything figured out," said Clytie.

"Well Ma?"

"Under the circumstances, I am going to say yes because Judes is a good girl and I like her, but I want to tell you something. You disappoint me. What are you going to tell Nellie when she come back? For a man with education, you do something real foolish. You didn't have no money to buy a frenchie?" (condom)

"You know how it is Ma. Sometimes these things happen."

"Don't let it happen again Jonas. I only had you and because of that we could eat real good. These ain't days to bring so many pickneys in this world. You got to feed them and you got to buy them clothes and send them to school. You understand what I am saying?"

"Yes Ma. I understand. So I can tell Judes she can move in?"

"Yes. It isn't a problem. Aunt Ida like her and I like her, but I want you to put something on that thing between your legs before you think about bringing another child in this world."

"Thanks Ma. I will let Judes know."

Ida and Clytie watched as he skipped down the steps to the house next door.

"He is real happy that he going to be a father," said Ida.

"I tell him after this, no more. Judes still married to Toby, although that don't mean nothing."

"You didn't believe me when I tell you that she look real rosy. The young people of today are different. The same thing happen to me, but I didn't have no education and that was a lot of years back."

"Aunt Ida, I was meaning to ask you if we could go to the dentist and get some teeth for you."

"I alright Clytie. I got Una teeth. I would wear them but they real uncomfortable. Those things give you labour pains."

"But Aunt Ida, you can't wear Ma teef. The dentist make them just for Ma."

"That is why they hurt so bad. I thought if I take the time and get used to them, I could wear them."

Clytie couldn't stop the laughter that poured from the depth of her bowels.

"Somebody having a lot of sport," said Nora walking into the shop. "I want to laugh too."

"Aunt Ida, tell Nora what you just tell me."

"You think I is a poppit? You tell her if you want her to know."

"Aunt Ida want to wear Ma false teef."

"No Miss Ida," said Nora. "You can't do that. Only Miss Una could wear those teef."

"Well where she is she can't use them no more and that is why I thought I could wear them."

"Believe me Miss Ida, those teef would give you nothing but trouble."

"Alright, I believe you."

"I got some news Nora. I don't know if you want to hear it," said Clytie.

"What news?"

"Judes in the family way."

"Girl I know that something like that would happen. The two of them always up under one another."

"So you ain't vex?"

"Why I should be vex?"

"Because she is married to Toby."

"Toby living his life and she got a right to go on with her own. The only thing is that the two of them should wait before they bring a pickney in this world."

"That is exactly what I tell Jonas. I let him know that if he didn't have money to buy a frenchie, he know he could come to me. But I don't think it got nothing to do with money. It is pure slackness. When they get too hot, they isn't no turning back."

"What is done is done and I wish them all the happiness in the world."

"I real glad Ma isn't here to see this. She must be rolling over in the grave."

"Miss Una would be vex at first, but she would get over it."

"Anyway he ask me if he could bring Judes to live with Aunt Ida and me, and I tell him yes."

"You can't throw him out in the street. Jonas is a good son. Nellie is going to be real disappointed because she say he should be going to the College of Teachers."

"You only bring them into the world, but you can't tell them what to do. You can only try to push them in a certain direction. Know what I mean?" asked Ida.

"You right Aunt Ida, there isn't a thing more that I can do."

"I am really looking forward to see Nellie again. The six weeks did feel like a year."

"She is coming home this Saturday morning right?"

"Yes and I hope the Lord bring my sister and her husband home safe."

When Emily awoke, Alastair had already left for work and Jennifer had already set the breakfast table for the rest of the family members. As usual, Douglas did not want to get out of bed, but with a bit of gentle persuasion, he was soon under the shower and was ready for school. Jennifer brought his cereal in and he ate slowly while looking around at every thing in the house. Old Bottomsley joined them and coaxed the child into eating his breakfast.

"Douglas please hurry up. Grandpa and I have things to do today."

"What are you going to do?" the child asked.

"We are going over to Grandpa's house."

"I would like to see Miss Nellie too and Uncle Francois," he said.

"They went away on vacation Douglas. Now hurry up or you will be late for school."

"When are we going to see Miss Nellie and Grandpa Francois?"

"Soon. We can talk about it later. Hurry or you'll be late for school."

She got up and disappeared into the kitchen. She hadn't had a chance to speak with Jennifer about the arrest of Brandon Harvey.

"I was trying to forget about it ma'am," was her reply.

"I understand they caught him at the house you shared together."

"That is what the policeman tell me ma'am."

"Grandpa and I are going to take Otty back to St. Lucy. Maybe you should come along with us so we can take John for a drive. While I talk to Clytie you can run over and have a visit with your daughters."

"Thank you ma'am, but they in school."

"It will be lunchtime by the time when we get there, so there is a chance you will see them. Make some breakfast for my mother and I will tell her she has to help herself."

"Thank you ma'am."

Sarah Bottomsley came out of her bedroom just as they were leaving the house. She looked at the table and sat down to breakfast.

"Are you going out also?" she asked Old Bottomsley.

"Oh yes. I feel so much better after I have breathed in some of that fresh country air."

Clytie was pleased to see Emily and so was Ida, who had now gotten used to seeing the Chambers family. She took John from Emily and the child screamed as if he had seen a ghost.

"He's not used to you," said Emily. "He's usually very well behaved."

"He's only a little one," said Ida. "Where is my friend? The other boy who say that the fairy carry 'way my teef?"

"Douglas is at school. He didn't want to go especially when he heard we were coming to St. Lucy. He thought he would see Nellie and Francois and Long John. I forgot to tell him that Long John had died."

"Children get over things real fast. The next time he visit he will forget all about the dog."

"I can't wait to see Nellie and Francois. It seems like years since they left to go on vacation," said Emily.

"Two more days and they are going to be home. I hope they liked Africa. I can't wait to see the two of them."

"This is just a short visit Clytie. We came up to take Otty home."

"I didn't even know she was at Bottomsley."

"With Ursy gone, it is just too much for Jennifer to handle alone. Nellie told us Otty said she would pitch in to help if we needed her. I hope Jennifer comes back soon. Grandpa and I have a little errand to run. Where is he anyway?"

"He is on the step talking to Ida."

Jennifer returned with her two children who were on their way back to school.

"Say good day to Miss Chambers and Mr. Bottomsley," she said to the girls.

"Good afternoon sir. Good afternoon ma'am. Hello Miss Ida," they said.

"What are your names?" Old Bottomsley asked.

"I'm Heather and this is my sister Jackie."

"Are you learning well at school?" Emily asked.

"Yes ma'am."

The children were more interested in John than talking to the adults.

"He is a sweet little baby," said Heather.

"Can't we stay and play with him?" asked Jackie.

"No, say goodbye and hurry to school. Don't be late. I am coming to see you soon again," said their mother.

The two girls hugged Jennifer and without even glancing back, joined a group of children who were also on their way back to school. Emily and her family wished Clytie and Ida goodbye and drove off. Jennifer sat in the back with John who also seemed to be enjoying the beauty that was St. Lucy. Emily and her grandfather spoke of the wonders of the countryside and how lucky the others were to be living there.

"One day I may just sell Bottomsley and move out into the wide open spaces," she said.

"It is yours to do with as you please my child, although my son may not be very happy about it."

"Papa, we won't have to worry about. It is Mama who may strongly object to it."

After half an hour of discussing the pros and cons of the country air, they arrived at Grandpa's house. It looked a bit dilapidated. The bush had grown through the divisions in the walkway and Millie's beautiful gardens looked like a forest.

"How could we have let this beautiful home fall into such disrepair Grandpa?"

"I wish I had an answer for you Emily. All I could think of was leaving it just the way Millie had arranged it. I guess I was a little selfish."

"Grandpa I forgot the key."

"We can still look through the flaps and see what it looks like on the inside."

Old Bottomsley led the way with Emily behind him. They reached the door and he pushed the flaps to open them and the door too opened.

"That's funny. I was sure the last time I came here I locked the door."

"Let's look around and decide what repairs are needed to bring it back to its old glory."

Everything was covered in white sheets except one chair, which looked as if someone had removed the cover and had forgotten to replace it. They walked around looking at the furniture when Old Bottomsley started to cry.

"What's the matter Grandpa?"

"I was thinking of the times Millie and I spent together here. They were good times although quite often, she would make me so angry that I would want to throw her out," he said managing a smile.

"That was Grandma. She always had her way and she was not always right, but she was a good Grandma. I remember when she threatened to throw the Hurleys out of the house."

"That was my Millie alright."

"What's this?" asked Emily picking up a writing pad from the bed.

She looked at it carefully but the imprint was not clear, so she took the pencil that was next to it and shaded the message.

"What does it say?" asked her grandfather looking closely at her.

"Dear Lord Grandpa!"

"What's wrong Emily? What does it say?"

"Sit down Grandpa. We never told you this but someone has been blackmailing Nellie and whoever it was wrote the notes right here in this room."

"Let me see it," he said.

*"Nellie you didn't bring the money. I know it was because of the funeral, but I need it by tonight. You know the time and place. Don't disappoint me."*

"Grandpa, who do you think wrote this?"

"As far as I can tell from the handwriting, it looks like your mother's."

"Sarah?" she asked. "It does look like her handwriting, but she wouldn't do a thing like that. Besides she has money of her own."

"Apparently not! She told me a couple days ago that it was all gone."

"What did she do with it? Don't answer that Grandpa. She must've given it all to Thomas Hurley."

"But she has the most to lose by blackmailing Nellie. She wouldn't want the people here on this island to know that she isn't really your mother."

"What are we going to do Grandpa?"

"Maybe we should ask her."

"Not yet. Let me think about this carefully."

She folded the sheet of paper and put it into her pocket, and they continued looking around the house. Old Bottomsley found himself in the second bedroom looking around when he noticed a valise propped against the wall next to the window. It looked like the same valise Sarah Bottomsley had struggled to take down the steps. He lifted it. It wasn't as heavy but it was not empty. He opened it to look at the contents. There was only mens' clothing there. Whose were they? He had seen to it that his son's clothing had been given away after his death. Could they be Thomas Hurley's? The old man lifted each item out and inspected them all. Some of them he recognized and others he didn't. Sarah had kept them all those years.

"Emily?" he went to the door and shouted.

"Yes Grandpa?"

"Look what I've found."

"Are they yours?" she asked.

"No, I think they were Thomas Hurley's."

"Thomas Hurley's? How did they get here?"

"Sarah."

"Are you sure?"

"I remember that day Emily. You had gone out with Jennifer and John and so she had to bring them out herself. I wanted to help her but it was too heavy. She told me she was taking them to the church for the poor. I had even remarked that she was beginning to show her charitable side."

"Oh Grandpa. What are we going to do?"

"Talk to Alastair first. Get his opinion and then you can speak to Sarah."

"That explains why the door wasn't locked. Someone with a key must have opened it."

They hadn't finished the task they had set out to do. Remaining in the house had brought about a very uncomfortable feeling. They closed the door as best they could and joined Jennifer and John outside.

# 33

Sarah Bottomsley was sitting in her usual position on the verandah reading a book when they returned. She never looked up when Jennifer passed by with John in her arms, but rudely accosted her daughter when she stepped onto the verandah.

"I raised you with dignity and taught you the way things should be done. Do you think it is right that you deserted this house this morning taking what's her name with you before she had served me my breakfast?"

Old Bottomsley knew and understood his granddaughter and hurried inside before Emily could respond.

"I had business that I needed to get out of the way. You are not an invalid Mother. Jennifer set the table before she left. I saw you come out of your room as we were leaving. All that was left to be done was to sit and enjoy your breakfast."

"And what if I wanted something else that was not on the table?"

"You lived in this house long enough. You know your way to the kitchen Sarah."

"No one has any respect for me. I am treated like an old shoe.

I used to run this house the way it should be run, but you have dropped to the level of the servants. You even find yourself in the kitchen alongside her doing the cooking."

"If you got up and lent a helping hand, then I wouldn't have to do that."

"Emily," she said in a beseeching voice, "couldn't we bring Bottomsley back to its former glory?"

"Those days are gone Mother. Besides I won't surround myself with hypocrites who are there when everything is going well, and the moment something goes awry, they turn their backs on you. You should know that."

"Yes but it's different with you. You are a solicitor. Alastair is also a solicitor. It is time to invite your friends over and have some civil parties like we used to have long ago."

Emily looked at Sarah Bottomsley long and hard and then walked into the house, leaving Sarah staring after her.

"It's the company she keeps. The likes of Nellie and Clytie," muttered Sarah under her breath

"What did you tell her?" asked Old Bottomsley in a low voice.

"Grandpa I don't know what to do with her. She seems to be lost in a world of her own making."

"Emily, I love you dearly and from what we have seen, I think you should be careful. Sarah is a devious woman. I'm really glad you aren't anything like her."

They lowered their voices since Jennifer was removing Sarah's breakfast dishes from the table and because they didn't want Sarah to know that they were privy to what they thought she had done. Emily picked up her son and walked down the steps. She filled the galvanized bath from the water hose and put her son in. He enjoyed splashing around in the cool water and she enjoyed watching him. Sarah could also see them from her vantage point.

"Appalling!" she said. "She insists on doing the work servants are paid to do."

"You should join them" said Old Bottomsley overhearing the comment she had made. "I'm going to."

He sat on the garden chair and watched as his great grandson enjoyed himself while his mother looked on. Millie Bottomsley had never seen any of her great grand children. It was indeed a pity. In spite of being a difficult woman, Millie kept the family close to her heart but never held back when she thought they needed to be told of an impropriety. Old John Bottomsley loved Emily even though she was the daughter of the kitchen help. He now looked beyond Nellie's past and looked at what she done and the lady she had become; one who he was inwardly proud to call the mother of his granddaughter. Emily sat next to her grandfather and he put his arm around her shoulders and kissed her on the cheek. He knew what she was going through.

"Papa! Papa!" shouted John as Alastair's car drove in.

"How is my little one?" he asked standing away from the tub for fear of having his suit ruined.

The child became more and more excited on seeing his father, so Emily took him from the tub, dried him in a towel and put him in his father's arms.

"How are you sir?" he asked Old Bottomsley.

"For an old man, still doing mighty well," he replied.

"Are the two of you having a family conference?" he asked.

"Something like that," replied his wife.

"Maybe I can offer some advice," he said. "So how much do you think we need to fix the house up? Is that the reason you both seem under the weather?"

The tears rolled down Emily's face and her grandfather did his best to console her.

"Let's go upstairs," he said handing John to Old Bottomsley.

Sarah watched as they walked past barely glancing at her. She shrugged her shoulders and continued reading. Once in the bedroom he closed the door and spoke to his wife.

"What's the matter Emily? I haven't seen you like this in a while."

After a few minutes of coaxing and consoling, she reached into her pocket and handed him the copy of the blackmail note.

"Do you know who is responsible for this?"

"I think so. I believe it is Sarah."

"Sarah? Why would she do a thing like this?"

"I don't know Alastair. Grandpa thinks she has no money left."

"What did she do with it?"

"Probably stolen from her a long time ago by Thomas Hurley," she replied.

"But why didn't she come to us?"

"She's a proud woman."

"A proud woman who it seems has broken the law," he responded. "All this time Francois and I have been trying to come up with an answer. We thought it might have been Nellie's nephew who came back from England."

"I forgot something," she said jumping up.

"What?"

She returned with a key.

"I wanted to see if the key to Grandpa's house was still in its place. The door to the pathway was open when we arrived there and we found this note on the bed. In the second bedroom was a valise with Thomas Hurley's belongings."

"How did it get there?"

"Sarah! Grandpa saw her struggling down the steps with that very valise and he said he thought she was a very strong woman to have managed to take it down the steps all by herself."

"But why Emily?"

"I just don't know. She is much more devious than we thought. What are we going to do?"

"I'll talk to her alone."

"I want to be there."

"No Emily. Trust me. It is better if I do it alone."

Alastair made his way towards the verandah, bumping into Jennifer on the way.

"I have some news for you," he said to her as he continued walking.

Looking down he saw his son and Old Bottomsley still having a whale of a time, sprinkling each other with water from the tub. This was his chance to speak to Sarah while everyone else was occupied.

"Sarah, may I see you for a moment?" he asked.

"Yes, what is it Alastair?"

"I want to speak to you in private," he said.

"We are alone."

"I don't want any interruptions Sarah, so I'll be in my study."

She opened the door and sat down with a sigh.

"What is so important? I was just reaching an exciting point in my book."

"This promises to be much more exciting, I promise you."

He stared at the note that lay in front of him, and then passed it over to Sarah Bottomsley.

"Tell me what you know about this and I want the truth."

"What is it?"

"Read it," he commanded.

There was silence in the room. She slowly read the note and then threw it back to him.

"So?" he asked.

"So what?" she asked.

"Don't you recognize the handwriting?" he asked throwing it again in front of her.

"Should I recognize it? Nellie is getting only what she deserves."

"Don't play games with me Sarah. I know what you are capable of."

"Are you trying to say that I wrote that?"

"If you didn't write it, then who?" he asked.

"I'm not a detective. Call up the constable. Ask him."

"Alright Sarah, I have another question. Who put the valise with your ex-husband's clothing in Grandpa's house?"

"I did. I wanted to get rid of them once and for all."

"So why didn't you give them to the church for the poor?"

"I don't know. That was the first idea that came to my head and that's where I put them."

"How did you get into the house?"

"I used the key of course."

"This is your handwriting Sarah. I know you wrote this."

"You'll just have to prove it," she said getting up and leaving the study.

Jennifer was busy setting the dinner table when Sarah dashed out of the study, almost knocking her over.

"Bring me a drink right now," she commanded.

"What you want?" asked Jennifer.

"You should know by now what I drink. Rum on ice!"

Sarah's absence was quite noticeable at dinner. Showing contempt for what she considered abominable questioning, she decided to stay in her room. Emily asked Jennifer to take her a tray, which she unceremoniously kicked through her bedroom door after she was finished.

"Strangely enough, I do believe she didn't write the note," Alastair said.

"It is her handwriting. If she didn't write it, then who did?" asked Old Bottomsley.

"I wish I knew. She didn't seem at all nervous when I showed it to her and she was quite forthcoming about the valise."

"What bothers me is how someone could've gotten into the house."

"Maybe Sarah had forgotten to lock the door," said Emily.

"Two solicitors both living under the same roof! We will find out soon enough," said Grandpa Bottomsley.

Alastair excused himself and went to the kitchen where Jennifer was busy washing the dishes.

"Yes sir?" she asked, unaccustomed to seeing him in the kitchen.

"I wanted you to know that you are now the proud owner of two properties in St. Lucia. You said you were no longer interested in maintaining them. Should I go ahead and put them up for sale?"

"Yes sir. Thank you sir."

"As soon as I have spoken to a realtor, I'll let you know if I consider it a reasonable price."

"Thank you sir."

"Jennifer I know that once the sale is over, you may want to leave immediately."

"I ain't going to leave Miss Chambers high and dry. I will wait until she find somebody to take my place."

"Thank you Jennifer. Goodnight."

"Goodnight sir."

⸺

The Boeing 707 circled the island and Nellie looking out the window, recognized the cliffs on the St. Lucy coastline. She and Francois were happy to be home even though they had had an enjoyable vacation. Since they did not make arrangements to be met, they took a taxi for the long ride to St. Lucy and in spite of their fatigue the familiar landmarks brought joy to their hearts. They passed within a two mile radius of Bottomsley plantation and both wondered how the family was.

"I'll call Alastair when we get in," said Francois.

"And I'll call Nora and Clytie because I know they'll be anxious to hear about Africa."

After fifteen minutes, exhaustion set in and they were both fast asleep in the back of the taxi. They were not aware that they were already in St. Lucy and had already driven past the shop which still bore Nellie's name.

"You're home," said the taxi driver who jumped out and started unloading the baggage.

They had left the island with two suitcases and returned with four. The driver struggled through the gate with two of them while Francois carried the smaller ones.

Otty heard the sound of the engine and came out of the renovated stable, which she called home. She was excited on seeing the two of them.

"You all had a good time?" she asked taking one of the valises from Francois.

"We certainly did Otty. Is everything in order around here?" he asked.

"Everything is ok."

Francois paid the driver who lifted his cap and proceeded on his way.

"You want me to help you unpack Miss Bertrand?" Otty asked.

"Not this evening," she replied. "I'm very tired. Tomorrow we can do that together. I brought something for you from Ghana."

"That was real nice of you to remember me ma'am."

"Did Mrs. Chambers ask you to help her?"

"Yes and she bring me back home day before yesterday."

"How are the little boys?"

"They are real sweet Miss Bertrand. Miss Emily nice too but I don't know if I should say this, but I didn't like the mother."

"You mean Sarah? Sarah is living in her own little world."

Francois called out to Nellie. He had the Chambers on the phone and they just wanted to say hello and make arrangements to visit them in St. Lucy which they planned to do the following Sunday. Nellie then called Clytie and Nora who were both overjoyed and they too planned to visit the following day.

"Goodnight Otty," said Francois. "I'm taking a shower and then it's off to bed."

"I will see you tomorrow then. Anything in particular you want for breakfast sir?"

"Something delicious," he said disappearing into the bedroom.

⁓

The smell of pig manure filled the air in Plum Tree Village. A solitary blackbird sitting on the overhead electrical wires, spied down on a flock of sparrows which had invaded the pasture below.

The blackbird moved its head from side to side, trying to see what delicious thing they had found. Then it suddenly swooped down sending the sparrows scattering in a hundred directions. A little boy in a pair of ragged trousers crossed the road with a sheep, which he staked out in the same pasture the blackbird was now investigating. Another boy with a home made roller manouevred it back and forth, barely looking up, so intent was he on what he was doing. Time for soccer! A group of boys was kicking around a pig's bladder which they had blown up by using a paw paw shank.

"Pass the ball," they kept on shouting at each other.

"Nigel, come and carry out the goat," a mother shouted. "If I got to tell you that again, it is going to be me and you."

"Coming," was his reply.

"I want to play 'til he come back," said the first boy who had tied out the sheep.

A man with a heavy package on his shoulder walked in the direction of Clytie's home.

"This is the leg o' pork you order and these pork chops belong to Miss Nellie," he said. "She say that she want to order them the next time I kill a pig."

The village butcher! Without a doubt, it was Saturday morning. That's when he delivered his meat after the animal was slaughtered.

"Where the feet and the ears for my puddin' and souse?" asked Clytie.

"I bringing it back directly," he replied.

"Send it by one o' the boys. I have to cook it before I go to the shop. Miss Nellie come back from vacation yesterday and I want to surprise her."

After being paid, the butcher went back to his home and

shortly after a little boy arrived on Clytie's step. Pig's ears! Pig's snout! Pig's feet! Maw! Tongue! Intestines! Clytie set about washing and cleaning the meat and placed it on the stove to cook.

"Aunt Ida," she shouted, "I have to open the shop. Keep your eyes on the souse on the stove. I clean the belly too. You only have to grater the potatoes and make the pickle for the souse."

"I can finish it Clytie. Lastnight I cut up all the seasoning, and I am ready to go," she said springing around the kitchen like a young girl.

"Go 'long and open the shop door Clytie. You leaving everything in good hands."

As the sun crept up from behind the cliffs, Otty was already in the kitchen and she was cooking up a storm. There was bacon, toast, eggs and something which she knew they would both enjoy. She had bought three sea eggs from the hawker. One she had for dinner and the other two she seasoned and baked for her employers. The table was laid, but the two of them were still fast asleep. When she could no longer bear it, she knocked on the bedroom door and two sleepy people emerged a couple of minutes later.

"What's that lovely aroma Otty?"

"Something delicious," was her reply. "Sit down and I will bring it in."

"A feast fit for a king," he said as he saw what she had prepared.

"What about a queen?" asked Nellie.

"Fit for a queen too of course."

Otty fussed around them pouring tea and making fresh toast when there wasn't any left on the table.

"So tell me what has been going on while we were gone Otty," Francois said.

"Well I spend two days with John and Douglas. I went to help Miss Chambers because you know that Jennifer working by herself now. They also hold the man they think kill Ursy."

"When did they catch him?"

"Day before yesterday," said Otty, "the policeman come in the kitchen and ask me to leave because he want to talk to Jennifer in private. Then I find out that was what he want to tell her."

"I guess we can all breathe a sigh of relief now that he is no longer a free man."

"What if he didn't do it?" Nellie suddenly asked.

"Who else?" asked her husband.

"Everything seems just too easy. They didn't suspect anyone else?"

"Not as far as I know."

"Well Otty, I guess we should start unpacking and sorting out the clothes."

While Francois gazed at the mountain of bills in front of him, the women unpacked the valises. Otty was anxious to hear about Africa, but she didn't want to be the first to broach the subject.

"That valise is full of dirty clothes," she said as Otty started to open it. "This is the one with the gifts. We should open that first."

"This cloth real pretty," said Otty.

"They call that Kente cloth. I brought a piece for everybody."

"I am getting a piece too?"

"Yes. Everybody is getting a piece."

"Morning Francois," said Nora and Clytie coming in the door.

"Girl I love your hair. Everytime you go away and come back, we got to change the hairstyle. They look just like the corn rows we got here, but something different about them. I hope you watch when they were doing it, so you could show Judes and Harriet. Now I want to hear all about Africa. It pretty? The people there just like the people here? They live in houses like ours?"

And the questions went on and on. They were surprised to hear about the beauty of Africa and the friendliness of the African people. They were also surprised to hear that Africans wore clothes and not a sheath held up by a string around their waists. They were pleased to hear of the Ashanti Kings who decked themselves out in gold and wore the beautiful Kente cloth.

"I know that we did come from some real good place," said Nora.

"So Nels, what kind o' clothes they wear?" asked Clytie.

"Let me show you. This is a Bou Bou. The men wear these. I think this is what Francois bought for Percy. You would like Ghana. The people are so nice. I mean the African people. The white people are just like those we have here. Real foolish! Anyway I didn't let that get to me. I enjoyed myself and so did my Franny."

"Now if the men wear these, what the women wear?" asked Nora. "And I hope you bring me one of them."

"That isn't all I brought for my dear sister. Look at this."

"A gold bracelet Nels?"

"Ghana has so much gold, they don't know what to do with it."

"This is real pretty," said Nora. "It got snakes on it."

"Yes and I have one for you too Clytie."

"We went to see where they used to keep the slaves. I couldn't stay too long because my heart went out to those poor people. They used to treat them worse than animals before they put them on the ships to bring them to the West Indies."

"I real sorry that Ma isn't here. She always used to talk 'bout Africa."

"They suffer a lot Nels?"

"Some of them didn't live long enough to make it as far as the West Indies."

"That is real sad Nels. Yet these people 'bout here behaving like Kings and we was really the Kings and Queens," said Nora.

"But Nels, what about England? You went there too."

"Girl I almost forgot about that. Francois and I went to London and to a place they called the Westend and we saw two plays. Something like what we used to do at the church, but much better. Everyone over there talks just like Sarah Bottomsley," she said mimicking them.

Francois looked up at his wife and the antics she was performing. He smiled. She was happy to be back with her friends and relatives.

"Where is Percy? Why didn't he come over?" he asked.

"Percy is sitting on the cliff with his pipe sticking out of his mouth," said Nora. "That man don't have a care in the world."

"I wish he had come over. I am stuck here with three women and no one to talk to."

"My poor Franny," said Nellie kissing him on the cheek.

"I got to get back soon. I left Judes in the shop by herself," said Clytie.

"How is Miss Ida?" asked Nellie.

"She still there prophesying. Ma used to say things but to me it was because Ma had a lot of commonsense, but Aunt Ida coming out with some things that I can't call it nothing else but prophecy. It look like she could see things and tell you before it happen."

"Like what?" asked Nellie.

"Like Judes being in the family way and a lot of other things. She say that Jennifer got a lot of clouds over her head, but they going to move away. She still say that she don't trust her."

"Wait a minute," said Nellie. "You said Judes is in the family way?"

"Yes and Jonas bringing her to live with Ida and me."

"What does Jonas have to do with it?"

"You went away too long. You don't know what is going on. Jonas and Judes got something going and she going to have his baby."

"Help me Lord," said Nellie. "And Ida saw that before they said anything?"

Francois looked up again. Although he pretended to be busy, he listened carefully to everything the women were discussing.

That evening the entire group of friends and family were at Clytie's house enjoying Pudding and Souse. All with the exception of Judes and Francois. She just couldn't bring herself to eat the parts of the pig which in her country were not fit for human consumption. She tried the pudding, but that had to be squeezed out of the pig's intestines before it was presented to her. Francois on the other hand ate only the pudding but it was not necessary to remove it from its casing. They were enjoying the tasty delicacy, grinding every bone into powder until only tiny mounds lay on their plates.

"They make anything like this in Africa?" asked Nora.

"I didn't see anything like it," said Nellie, "but I didn't like the food too much. They like to boil everything and what I found real strange is that they hardly use any spices."

"So where we learn to cook so good?" asked Nora.

"Not from the British," said Clytie. "Take Miss Sarah for instance, that woman only like a little bit o' salt and a bit o' pepper."

Nora nudged Clytie because she had forgotten about Judes sitting there with them.

"Sorry Judes," she said.

"I understand," said the young woman. "I like the food here but I can't eat the souse. I keep seeing the face of the poor pig."

Peals of laughter! Fancy her feeling sorry for a pig who had already given its life so that the families of Plum Tree Village wouldn't go hungry. People on the island never cared about such things. They had to feed their children and found the most economical way of doing it.

# 34

It was one of the hottest days of the year when the Chambers family descended upon the Bertrands. Nellie was happy to see her daughter and her grandchildren and couldn't wait to share the news about their trip to England and Ghana. Francois on the other hand had more serious matters to on his mind. High on the agenda was the arrest of Brandon Harvey and why he had killed Ursy. Then there was the matter of Jennifer Appleby's estate in London.

"Who is he really?" asked Francois. "I remember Jennifer said that he mysteriously appeared at their front door late one night."

"I have been searching everywhere and just can't find anything about anyone under that name. He is just a mystery. It doesn't make sense asking Jennifer anything, because it seems as if she knows as much as we do or less."

"Do you believe her?"

"I don't know what I should believe anymore. However, there is another pressing matter which I must discuss with you and it has to do with Nellie."

"My wife?" asked a surprised Francois.

"Yes. For quite a few months, Emily has been talking about

cleaning up her grand father's home. Earlier this week, the two of them set out to see how big a task it would be and this is what they found," he said pulling a sheet of paper from his pocket.

A look of horror registered across Francois' face.

"Who? Why?" he asked.

"It looks like Sarah's handwriting, but she said she had nothing to do with it, and Francois, I believed her. In one of the other bedrooms, they also found a valise packed with Thomas Hurley's clothing. Now Grandpa had seen her with the valise and had offered to help her with it, because she said she was taking her old clothing to the church for the poor. When I questioned her about that, she admitted taking the clothes there, because she didn't know what else to do with them."

"She is not familiar with St. Lucy. How would she know about the crack in the mahogany tree? Do you think she killed my dog?"

"I wish I had all the answers Francois."

"What about the envelope that we stuffed with paper? Wasn't that there also?"

"I haven't gone to the home, but maybe we should go together sometime. Emily had taken Jennifer and John with them, and didn't really have the time to search the property."

"Have you changed the locks?"

"Why?"

"Sarah knows you suspect her. Maybe there is more evidence there. It would be a shame if someone else had the chance to get rid of it before we found it."

Otty arrived on the verandah with a pitcher of cold lemonade and advised the two men that lunch would be ready in half an hour. Meanwhile Nellie and Emily spoke about the trip and their experiences in England and Ghana.

"Emily there is one thing I don't understand."

"What is that?"

"The English people speak really funny. Like if their mouths are full of something. I hope you won't tell Alastair I said that."

Emily laughed.

"I understand only too well Nellie. I remember when I first arrived there, I found it extremely difficult to understand what they were saying. I was only a child back then and I remember how they laughed at my accent in the boarding school."

"They did?" asked Nellie like a concerned mother.

"Yes but after a couple months there I was speaking just like the rest of them."

"Miss Bertrand," interrupted Otty. "Douglas is still in the backyard searching for Long John."

"I have already told him that Long John was sick and he died. You see Nellie, children have no concept of death. I remember when Papa died, I just couldn't believe that he had just gone away and left me alone with Sarah."

"I know what you mean."

"You loved him didn't you Nellie."

"Yes I did, but that is now all in the past. I love Francois. A very kind and thoughtful man," she said as tears welled up in her eyes.

"I'm sorry Nellie. I didn't mean to bring back all those memories."

"Otty, tell Douglas I will get another Long John soon," Nellie said. "Where is John?"

"He is running around behind his brother. If Douglas makes one step, he is right there with him."

"How is Mr. Bottomsley?" asked Nellie.

"Grandpa is still there. I offered to bring him with us today but he thinks he has to stay at home to keep Sarah's company."

"That's too bad. I know he loves the country air."

"He feels responsible for Sarah. I just don't understand why. She does not deserve his kindness."

"Don't say that Emily. After all…."

"You don't understand how horrible she is Nellie. I am thinking of finding her a little flat somewhere and moving into Grandpa's house with Alastair, Grandpa and the children."

"Are you thinking of selling Bottomsley?"

"Maybe. It is not making as much money as it used to. That's why Alastair decided to go into partnership with Francois. Of course you know that! Clyde the overseer is doing a very good job, but he can do only so much."

"What has Sarah got to say?"

"She knows nothing of our plans."

"I know that the plantation is yours and your father wanted you to have it, but you have a profession. A good one! The sugar industry isn't what it used to be. I think you should go back into your profession and hold your head high."

"We don't want to put so many people out of work. What will they do Nellie?"

"It might be hard at first, but they will survive Emily. I remember when I first moved to St. Lucy and there were so many people out of work or just barely making ends meet. I always let them have the foodstuff until they could pay me. Times were hard especially for those with children."

"I know why my father loved you Nellie. You are such a good person."

"So what did Sarah do to make you so angry?"

"I'm sure Alastair is telling Francois about it. He will tell you."

"It sounds very serious."

"It is Nellie. Otty has so much to do that she shouldn't be out there running after Douglas and John."

"We prepared most of the lunch earlier this morning, so we've just got to put it on the table."

"Are you having a good time Emily?" asked Francois on his way to fill up an ice bucket.

"You can't believe how much I missed the two of you. It seemed like years instead of weeks that you were gone."

"That's the same thing your husband said," he replied disappearing into the kitchen.

"I forgot to show you what I brought you from Ghana."

Nellie brought out a little box tied with string.

"Open it Emily," she coaxed.

"That is pretty Nellie," she said looking at the golden bracelet. "I did hear that there is a lot of gold in Ghana. This is just perfect."

"We have gifts for Alastair and the children too."

At that point the children came running in and John shouted to Otty.

"You got any o' them sweet apples Otty?"

The adults all started to laugh. The child had learnt to speak Bajan dialect and was using it whenever possible.

"John," said his mother, "what did you just say to Otty?"

"I ask if she had any o' the sweet apples."

"Ask her properly John," said his father.

The child started to laugh and stare at Otty.

"Come on John," coaxed his father, "you can do better than that."

"Do you have any of the sweet apples?" the child eventually asked.

"Yes I have some for you and your brother," said Otty.

In spite of the dark clouds hovering over their lives, the Chambers and the Bertrands had a lovely Sunday afternoon together. Nellie was pleased that her grand children could spend so much time with her and the children were pleased with the gifts she and Francois had bought them from Harrods in London. Alastair received a pen which had been beautifully engraved with his name. A belated gift to welcome him into the company! With the evening clouds gathering and night creeping in, the parents bundled the children together and set out for home.

"What did Sarah do?" asked Nellie.

"I don't understand what you mean."

"Emily said that she was sure Alastair would tell you and you could tell me the story."

"They think it was Sarah who was blackmailing you."

"Sarah is not a nice person, but she is not stupid. She would never tell anyone that Emily is not her daughter. She is too proud."

Francois smiled.

"Why are you smiling?" she asked seemingly a little annoyed.

"Because that was the same thing I said. Could it be that someone forced her to write those notes?"

"So who took my money?" she snapped.

"I'm on your side Nellie," said Francois seeing how irritable she had become.

"I'm sorry Francois. It is just that when I thought this was all over, it is right back here again."

"We have decided we won't go to the police with this piece of information. Alastair and I are going to go through Old Bottomsley's house with a fine tooth comb. We're sure that whoever it was must have unwittingly left a bit of evidence behind."

# 35

On Monday morning, Jennifer Appleby received the news she had been waiting for. Francois had brought it back from London. After a long battle with Wills, Deeds, Death and Birth Certificates, Legal Searches and claims, she was now the owner of all the properties her father had left behind, following both his quick escapes. Alastair advised her that once the money came through to the firm, he would be willing to hold it In Trust for her. The young woman had no idea what it meant so he took her to the study to explain about the handling of her money. A bell tinkled and she knew that Sarah Bottomsley was waiting to have her breakfast served. She jumped up on the last tinkle but Alastair told her to sit.

"My mother-in-law can wait for a few minutes," he said calmly.

Sarah was fit to be tied when Jennifer walked out of the study.

"Didn't you hear me calling you?" she asked.

Jennifer hurried into the kitchen without acknowledging Sarah's question and quickly returned with a pot of tea and the breakfast she had started to prepare before Alastair Chambers had summoned her to the study. Sarah stared at the breakfast and then slowly began to eat.

"Will that be all ma'am?" Jennifer asked.

Sarah waved her away and continued eating, but deep in her heart, she hated the young woman and wondered why she and Alastair were always in the study behind closed doors.

"Good morning Father Bottomsley," she said cheerfully.

"You're in a good mood this morning Sarah."

"Father Bottomsley I have a question. Why do you think that Alastair and what's her name in the kitchen are always sequestered in the study?"

"Do they do that Sarah? I have absolutely no idea."

"I intend to find out what it's all about."

"Leave well enough alone Sarah. You know how annoyed he becomes when anyone tries to meddle in his business."

"Don't you find it peculiar that they always seem to have something to discuss?"

Before the old man could answer, a car engine was heard. It was Francois Bertrand. He would normally get out of the car and come to the door, but the news he had received about the blackmail notes put a sour taste in his mouth and he had no desire to see Sarah Bottomsley's face. For Emily's sake he had always been polite to the woman, but now he had no desire to see her. Alastair left the house, got into his car and was followed by Francois. Upon reaching Grandpa Bottomsley's house, Francois could not help but admire the beautiful home. Yes there was a lot of work to be done, but it certainly had lots of potential. Alastair was reaching for the key, when he remembered that the door wasn't locked. They were going to make a thorough search of the house. They started by going through the drawers in the kitchen. Just Millie's cutlery, dish towels and a few odds and ends. Then it was on to the living room where everything was neatly hidden by dust covers.

"It's just as they left it," said Francois.

"We should've gotten rid of it a long time ago. Emily is sentimentally attached to it because of her father and her grandparents, so we thought renting the place out would be the best thing to do."

"It is a nice house. Just needs a coat of paint and a few repairs," said Francois making his way towards one of the bedrooms.

"This must be the valise with Hurley's clothing," Alastair said lifting the case.

They threw the contents on to the bed and searched each pocket, but there was nothing. All that they found was an expired British passport. Francois opened it and looked at the photo.

"He looks like a nice enough chap," said Alastair.

Moving to the bottom of the bed, one of his shoes made contact with something under the bed. He got to his knees and looked. A pair of shoes with mud-caked soles.

"They are not Grandpa's. Much too small for him. And from photos I've seen of Thomas Hurley, he was a rather large man and these would also be too small for him."

"Whose could they be?"

He placed the shoes at the door and they continued their search. They found the writing pad still lying on the bed where Emily had left it. They replicated what she had done in order to read the note, but they couldn't. There was no other evidence in the house to tie anyone to the blackmail notes.

"What are you going to do with the shoes?"

"I don't know yet."

"Just a moment Alastair. These shoes are much too small for a man. Could they be ladies' shoes?"

"Whose?"

"That I don't know my friend. That's something we'll just have to find out."

"Sarah? No. She never steps out on a rainy day especially since she has no reason to. Everyone there is at her beck and call and besides they are simply not her style. All of her shoes are quite dainty."

The two men left the house with Alastair in possession of the shoes and Hurley's expired passport.

Alastair Chambers arrived home earlier than usual. The mud encrusted shoes he carried was uppermost in his mind. He was met at the door by his wife and younger son.

"Is Grandpa here?" he asked.

"He just got up. He was having an afternoon nap. I guess that's because Mother wasn't on the verandah and he felt a little out of sorts. What's in the bag?" she asked.

"You're not going to believe this," he said removing the shoes.

"Where did you get those?" she asked laughing. "If you think I'm going to wear them you can forget it."

"These were under the bed in Grandpa's house."

"I didn't see them when I was there. Maybe Grandpa knows something about them."

The old man heard the chatter and joined them in the living room. Upon seeing the shoes, he became very annoyed.

"What are you doing with Millie's shoes?" he asked.

"These are Grandma's?" asked Emily.

"Why are they so dirty? Who has been wearing Millie's shoes? Millie wouldn't have been too happy to see her belongings being treated this way. I'll have a drink. What about you Alastair?"

"Don't mind if I do."

"Here comes Jennifer. She will make it for us, won't you Jennifer?"

"Yes sir. Sir," she said turning to Alastair, you have a minute for me sir?"

"Yes go ahead."

"Now that everybody is here ma'am, I want to tell you that I have decided to go away and take the children with me. I want to tell you early so that you could find somebody else to take over my job."

"Must you go?" asked the old man. "I will certainly miss you."

"I don't really want to go, but I have to think of my children."

"I understand," said Emily. "How soon do you think you will be leaving?"

"As soon as you find somebody else to look after the family," she replied.

"Then we should start looking right away," she said looking to her husband for confirmation.

"Thanks for letting us know," said Alastair. "I guess I have to work full steam ahead to get your affairs in order."

She then continued her household chores and set about making dinner.

"Sir," she said as Alastair walked by, "when you can sell the house in England, I would like to keep the money over there. You could get a bank account open for me?"

"I'll see what I can do. So have you decided to settle in England with the children?"

"For now sir. It looks as if the girls would get good schooling over there."

"Well I guess I can get that organized for you. What about the money you've got here?"

"I would like to take that with me too sir."

"All of it?"

"Yes sir."

"You shouldn't be walking around with that much money on your person," he said.

"I'll be careful sir. I ain't going to let it out of my sight."

"Then tomorrow I will get the ball rolling for you."

"Thank you sir."


"She wants the money in paper notes Emily."

"All of it?"

"That's what she said."

"She's probably old-fashioned and thinks that's the best way. Why didn't you talk her out of it?"

"I tried, but she said she will be very careful."

"Can't be too careful if you're carrying that much money around," said Emily.

"I'll warn her against that. Just yesterday I spoke to her about leaving, and she was in no hurry to leave. Strangely enough, today she is quite eager to go. I wonder why?"

"As she says, her children need a safe and stable environment and I couldn't agree with her more. She hardly sees them and Nora seems to have taken her place."

He looked at Grandpa Bottomsley who was now cleaning his dead wife's shoes. There was something about the shoes that still seemed to bother him.

"Someone wore Millie Bottomsley's shoes and I don't know why," he said to Emily.

"Whoever it is should steer clear of Grandpa. He's annoyed they left them in such a terrible state. I wouldn't worry too much anymore. We now know they were Grandma's shoes."

"But your Grandma didn't wear them Emily. The blackmail note and the shoes all found in Grandpa's house still disturbs me a bit. We also found this," he said pulling the passport from his pocket.

"Can't challenge Mother on that subject! She will only become more stubborn."

"Have you been in touch with Nellie?" Alastair asked.

"No. Christmas is fast approaching and I would love to do something with her and Francois. The children enjoy seeing them very much."

# 36

A handcuffed Brandon Harvey was escorted into the courtroom and advised of his rights.

"Have you anything to say in your defence?" he was asked.

"I am innocent your Honour. I didn't kill anyone nor have I ever killed anyone," he replied.

"Is your barrister present Mr. Harvey?"

"I haven't got a barrister sir."

"Can you afford one?"

"No sir."

"Then the court will appoint one for you."

After a brief court session, he was not taken back to the station, but to Her Majesty's prison to await trial. The Judge watched carefully as he was handcuffed and led from the courtroom. He stared after the man as if in a trance. Something about him was worrying. The next case was called and he put Brandon Harvey out of his mind.

The court appointed barrister Christopher Peacock entered the prison and waited for his client to be brought to him. They conversed for a short while and the barrister promised to have him out on bail. There was nothing that pointed to the man's guilt and he should not have been imprisoned. He was held only on suspicion of murder and would have to be freed immediately. There was much disappointment on the part of the local population because he was guilty as far as they were concerned. Sitting in jail waiting for his freedom, his appearance was making startling changes. Red hair had started to protrude on his bald head, and so was the case with his moustache. The prison officers thought it odd, but thought he was of a different persuasion since that was the only concept they had of a man with red hair. He seemed masculine enough but they weren't taking any chances. He was teased by other prisoners and sometimes by the guards, so he kept to himself and hardly left his cell, hoping this would lessen the confrontations.

Mary Sealy, a middle aged woman from the Bottomsley tenement had applied for Jennifer's position and was quickly learning the ropes. She had previously worked in another plantation house, so it was just getting used to the way things were done at her new place of employment. She impressed the household. She was no-nonsense and even Sarah Bottomsley learnt to show her some respect.

It was time for Jennifer Appleby to say goodbye. All her belongings she packed in one bag and after a tearful goodbye set off for St. Lucy. Alastair promised he would be there is she needed any help. Nora and Percy were not informed of her arrival. She had bought new dresses and coats for herself and the children, and with the birth certificates she had found in her father's possessions, she was able to obtain passports for all of them. Jennifer had done her homework. She knew that the weather in England at that time of the year could be quite unforgiving.

"What are you doing here at this time o' the day?" asked Nora.

"I didn't want the news to get out Miss Nora. I decide to leave and take the children."

"Where are you going?"

"I am going to England. The girls would get a good education over there."

"You mean to tell me you taking those children from me? Percy isn't going to like that."

"Sorry Miss Nora, but you know I just want to get away from Brandon Harvey."

"He is still in jail."

"I understand they might let him go because there ain't no evidence to say that he kill Ursy, so I thought I should leave as soon as possible."

"The children coming in from school soon. I know they ain't going to be happy neither. They got their friends here and they like the school."

"I wish I didn't have to do it, but you have to understand Miss Nora. You is a mother and you know that we only want the best for the children."

"I am real sorry to see them go. I am going to really miss the two o' them. One day you have to bring them back so I can see them."

"Yoo hoo," said a voice from outside.

"Miss Ida? What you doing here at this time o' the day?"

"You forget that Clytie does shut down the shop half days on Thursdays?"

"Miss Ida! I know why you come here. You look like sixteen with your new teef."

"They are giving me the tisic though. They are hurting the gums."

"Give them a chance. You will get used to them. This is Jennifer. You know her?"

"That is the mother o' those two little girls?" she asked gazing at the woman.

"Yes."

"Well I am going back home. Where is Percy?"

"Where else? Down by the fishing hole. He looking for crabs because everybody now want to eat Gumbo."

"Bless his heart," said the older man.

"Tell Clytie I am coming by to see her tomorrow."

"Alright, she replied. "Have a safe trip," she said turning to Jennifer.

Nora and Jennifer stared at each other. How did Ida know about the trip? So far the only ones who knew about it were The Chambers and Francois Bertrand, who hadn't yet had the chance to inform his wife of Jennifer's sudden impending departure. Needless to say the girls were happy to see their mother but their happiness was short-lived when they realized that they were leaving the island the following day. Of course they wanted to tell their friends, but the mother convinced them that if they sent letters, it would make the friends happier. Percy, also shocked to find that she was taking the children so suddenly and so far away from their home, tried to convince her to let them stay, but she was having none of it.

"Why are we always moving?" asked the older daughter.

"Sorry Heather. I will make it up to you."

With the girls snug in their beds, Jennifer asked Percy to join her and Nora at the table.

"You don't have no right to do that to those children," said an annoyed Percy. "Those girls need a stable life. You move them from pillar to post not giving one iota how you mashing up their lives."

"With Brandon Harvey getting out of prison, I thought it was the best thing to do Mr. Percy. I got their interest in my heart. I just want to say thanks for everything you do for the girls. I know that they were real happy here with you. I can't thank you enough for what you do for them. So I want to give you this to make up for all of that."

She handed Nora an envelope and said goodnight.

"When you get up tomorrow, the girls and me would be gone. The plane is leaving real early and I expect the taxi to come by at half past six."

"Well I am going to get up to make them some breakfast before you drag them off," said Nora with tears in her eyes.

"Thank you Mr. Percy and Miss Nora."

No sooner had she left the room, than Percy coaxed Nora into opening the envelope.

"Open the thing woman so we can see what she give you."

Nora's eyes almost fell out of her head when she saw the money.

"This is a lot o' money," she said.

"Let me count it," said Percy.

They turned off the light and went to their bedroom where they counted the money. Five thousand dollars!

"Have mercy Lord!" exclaimed Nora. "I hear she was going to get money, but she must have a real lot. Five thousand dollars! We could go to Africa Percy."

"Steady yourself Nora. This is a dream. When we get up tomorrow, we are going to see it was just a dream."

"Well just in case, I putting it right here underneath my pillow," said Nora.

Before the first fowl cock had a chance to crow, Nora got up and looked under the pillow. The envelope with the money was still there. She then left the bedroom and turned the light on. It was extremely still. Jennifer and the children were sound asleep. She thought she should wake them up. She knocked on the bedroom door and not receiving an answer, opened it to find the room empty.

"Percy they gone," she shouted.

"I tell you it was a dream," he said.

"I talking about Jennifer and the children."

"But she say the taxi was coming at half past six," he said looking at the clock on the mantel and scratching his head. "It is only half past five."

The couple sat at the dining room table and neither one of them knew what to say. They couldn't believe that they didn't have a chance to say goodbye to the children they had looked after in their home for the past six months. They were soon joined by Harriet who had spent the night in her parents' home.

"I don't like this," Percy finally said.

"What is it you don't like?" asked his daughter.

"We talking about Jennifer and the two girls'" said Nora.

"She say she was going to the airport at half past six. Why she sneak out of the house so early without a word?"

"I don't know what the two of you are talking about," said Harriet."

"Jennifer come by early yesterday afternoon and say she was leaving today with the children. She tell us she was leaving early this morning and we plan to get up to say goodbye to the girls, but when we get up she was gone," said Nora.

"I am going to miss those two girls. I am really going to miss them. They was good little girls. Lord I hope she settle down and let them have some friends in their life," said Percy.

"I hope she gone real far with those children so that the man they think kill Ursy can't do them nothing."

"What you mean think?" asked Percy. "Who else would do something like that?"

"I don't know," said Harriet.

"I ain't like it," Percy said again. "The money is still there?"

"Yes I see it this morning. It still right there under the pillow where I put it last night."

"What money?" asked Harriet.

"She give Percy and me five thousand dollars for taking care of those two girls," said her mother.

"Where did she get all that money?"

"She inherit it," said Nora."

"Call Nellie and find out if she really going to England. Nora you don't think she run off with that man?" asked Percy. "What man?"

"The man who used to beat her."

"He is still in jail Percy."

"You really think so?"

"She say they was going to let him out."

"Call Nellie and find out," said Percy.

"It too early. Aunt Nellie ain't get up yet," said Harriet.

"A strange thing happened yesterday," said Nora. "Ida come by when Jennifer was here. She tell me only five minutes before Ida arrive that she was going away, but when Ida was leaving, she tell Jennifer to have a good trip."

"You mean that Ida know something?"

"I don't know. Come Percy. We going to see Ida Franklin."

"Where you put the money Nora? Put it in your bosom and walk with it," said her husband.

Clytie was surprised to see them at that early hour and they sat down to tell her the sad story. Ida was still asleep but on hearing the voices, she too came out and joined them. She was a different Ida this morning. She was not wearing her false teeth.

"It is a sad morning," she said on entering the room.

"Why you say that Miss Ida?"

"She get the money and she gone with the two girls. That is what you come to say. I tell Clytie a while back that she had too many clouds above her head. Way too many! And dark ones too!"

"She gone by herself Miss Ida?"

"They isn't nobody else for her to go away with except the children."

"What about that man Brandon Aunt Ida."

"He is in jail. I don't think he know she is gone. He isn't going to see that woman again in this life."

"Why you don't like her Aunt Ida?"

"Ain't to be trusted. She ain't to be trusted," the old woman repeated going back to her bedroom.

Clytie picked up the telephone on the second ring.

"Morning Clytie," said Nellie. "I am looking for Nora. You see her yet this morning?"

"She and Percy here Nels. That Jennifer take off with the children without saying goodbye."

"Take off? What do you mean take off?"

"Let me put Nora on the phone."

"Morning Nellie."

"What is this I hear about Jennifer taking off without saying goodbye? Where did she go?"

"I think she went to off to England with the children. I was going to get Judes to talk to her about England, but this morning when we get up, she was long gone."

"She's gone Francois," Nellie said.

"I know she was eager to go, but isn't this a little rushed?"

# 37

Two weeks after the court appointed barrister Christopher Peacock fought the courts on his behalf, Brandon Harvey walked out of Glendairy prison a free man. There was no evidence that led them to believe he was the murderer. His first thought was to get to Jennifer as fast as he could, but since he had no transportation or money, his court appointed barrister who felt a little sorry for him, drove him to his home.

"You're not yet off the hook," he said to him. "They will be watching you. And another thing, do something about the hair, you may just find yourself attracting the wrong type of person."

He smiled, thanked him and went into his home. He stretched out across the bed and stared at the ceiling. He wanted to see Jennifer. He wanted to be with her. In a strange way he did love her. It had been quite a while since he had been with a woman and she was the woman he wanted to be with. Now that it was no longer necessary for him to hide, he hoped she would move back into the home with him. He fell into a deep sleep and dreamed. Pleasant dreams!

## MURDER SUSPECT RELEASED FROM PRISON

The newspapers carried the headlines that morning. Brandon Harvey had not yet seen it, but Francois was reading the article aloud, while his wife looked over his shoulder.

*Since there wasn't a shred of evidence to tie him to the murder, the courts had no other choice but to release Brandon Harvey and the case of the murdered woman remains open and unsolved.*

"That means he didn't do it?" asked Nellie.

"There's no evidence that points to him."

"There is still a murderer walking around between us," said Nellie.

"I'm sure he did it," said Francois. "Because there is no evidence to prove otherwise, doesn't mean he isn't guilty."

"But they've released him."

"I am sure they will be keeping an eye on him. One wrong move and they will arrest him again."

"What do we do in the meantime?"

"Be very careful. You must remind Otty to keep the doors locked during the day. If you're in the back, lock the front doors and same thing if you're in the front."

"Do you think he had anything to do with the blackmail letters?"

"I don't think he knows Sarah Bottomsley."

"Francois, didn't she say that Brandon Harvey sent her to Bottomsley to work after he had read about the job in the newspaper?"

"I have always wondered why they moved from St. Lucy to Bottomsley to find work. They could easily have found something around here or in St. Peter for that matter."

"She always said she liked going to Clytie's shop because they asked too many questions at the other shop by Austin Corner."

"Perhaps she didn't want her business thrown into the open. I wouldn't. Abused by your own father and bearing his children? No I wouldn't want anyone to know that."

"Well she has left and in a real hurry. Maybe she knew they were going to release him."

"Maybe they left together," said Francois.

"I don't know, but Percy and Nora are very upset with her."

―――――

The sun was setting and a hungry Brandon Harvey showered and dressed waiting to visit Jennifer. He got into his car and drove along the country roads hoping to kill time until he thought she was finished in the Bottomsley kitchen. After an hour, he parked his car in a discreet location and found his way at the entrance which led upstairs to the kitchen. Glancing around and seeing no one, he quickly opened the door to the servant's quarters and entered. The bed was unmade, but he paid little attention to it. He climbed into it and waited. It seemed like a rather long wait. He couldn't hear any activity above him in the kitchen. It was an eerie stillness. He waited another half hour and then decided to leave.

*Where could she be, he wondered.*

She must be at their secret meeting place. He drove there and tried to open the door but it was locked and it was pitch black inside the house. Could she be at Ursy's home? He parked the car outside the village and went on foot to the house. He met a few villagers on the way who were surprised to see a white man in their midst. He tried to enter the home through the back door, but it was locked. It was also very dark inside the house. Absolutely no sign of life! He returned to his home to find it just as he had left it. He was panic-stricken. Where could she be?

The following morning, the phone rang at the Bottomsley

home. Someone was asking for Jennifer Appleby. Mary Sealy the new housekeeper informed the caller that Jennifer was no longer working there. When asked where she could be found, the woman said she didn't know.

He had no money and had no idea what he should do. Maybe she was in St. Lucy. Why hadn't he thought about that earlier? Driving through Plum Tree Village, he felt like an animal being cornered. He was jittery and tried to keep out of sight. The best place to ask would be the shop which still carried the name Nellie's Bar and Grocery but he couldn't just walk in. Clytie would be sure to recognize him. He saw a little boy pushing his home-made roller along the street and asked him if he wanted to earn a penny. The little boy happily agreed and off he went to speak to Clytie.

"You know Jennifer?" she asked the little boy.

"No."

"Then why you asking after Jennifer? I don't know where Jennifer is. Who send you here?"

"Nobody," he answered.

"You are telling lies. I am going to tell your mother and you going to get a good licking."

As fast as the child had entered the door, he left. The man gave him a penny and drove away. The child was back in the shop to buy a polar lolly.

"Where did you get this penny?" Clytie asked.

"A man give it to me."

"The same man who want to know about Jennifer?"

"Yes ma'am," the child replied.

So Jennifer it seemed was still fraternizing with the man she claimed had always beaten her; the same man they were sure was responsible for Ursy's death. So Clytie thought! It looked as if

Ida was right about Jennifer. There were too many unanswered questions surrounding the young woman.

Lying in his bed, Brandon Harvey now had to plan his next move. He didn't have a job and his only source of income seemed to have vanished into thin air. He looked at himself in a little mirror which he used to shave. He was not happy with the face that looked back at him. He moved to the little kitchen and looked into the cupboard. There was hardly anything there. A can of sardines, a tin of milk, some Eclipse biscuits! He reached for a plate and something fell to the floor. He picked it up. An envelope with his name on the outside! Sardines and biscuits forgotten, he sat down and ripped the envelope open. A letter and one hundred dollars!

*Brandon, by the time you read this letter I will be far away. I think it is in the best interest for all concerned that I leave the island and take my children with me. I know you will be disappointed by my sudden departure but I can only say that I am truly sorry. I hope they realize that you are not capable of murdering anyone and that in time you will gain your freedom. Don't try to find me, because it will be useless.*

*Use this money to buy some food. I hope everything goes well for you.*

*Jennifer*

"That bitch!" he shouted jumping up from the table. "She left without a word. I'll fix her."

He sat down again and slowly re-read the note. Perfectly written! No one who knew her would believe she could write or speak so perfectly. She had played her part well and he could take credit for her creation. He had trained her to seduce and deceive other people. Now she had also deceived her teacher. But where did she get the money to pay for herself and also for her two children? He intended to find out. The sooner the better!

# 38

Little John Chambers cried and cried. He missed Jennifer and nothing Mary Sealy did helped or mattered. Emily was now spending more and more time with him to help him get over his loss. Grandpa Bottomsley also tried and he would be happy for a short time, but the moment he remembered Jennifer, he would once again be unhappy.

"He's now old enough to go to a private school," said Emily. "He will meet other boys to play with."

"You know that the first few days will be difficult," said Grandpa Bottomsley.

"I know. I know that only too well Grandpa."

"Maybe I will get him a puppy. That might help."

"Splendid idea!" said the old man. "Would Sarah like that though?"

"I'm interested in my son Grandpa. He comes first."

"I love you Emily," was all the old man said.

"Then I'll buy him a puppy. He used to play with Long John. It will teach him and his brother a bit of responsibility."

"Where do you think Jennifer went?" asked the old man.

"I thought you knew. She left for England two days ago."

"Strange thing Emily. The new housekeeper Mary said that someone called here yesterday asking for her."

"Was it a man?"

"I didn't ask," he replied.

"Well she should be there by now. It was not my favourite place Grandpa. I know you love England, but I found it too cold and damp and dreary. Can you imagine how I felt when Thomas Hurley and Sarah sent me there? I had never experienced such feelings. Loneliness and abandonment! I was lucky that Grandma and Grandpa were caring people, but in spite of that I wasn't happy until I went to school and found many friends."

"We had no say in that matter. You know that Millie and I would've fought them both, but Sarah had fallen under Hurley's spell."

"Do you ever wonder what really happened to him?"

"Too much Bottomsley rum. I'm sure in his drunken stupour, he fell over the cliff."

"I just don't understand why he would've chosen to go all the way to St. Lucy. It is so far away from Bottomsley."

"No one knew what was going on in his head or his sister's for that matter."

"Mother said she met an Englishman here on the island and returned to England with him."

"And I hope she stays there."

"Well I think I should give Mary a hand, although I don't think she wants me in the kitchen."

"She certainly knows what she is about. She doesn't mess around either."

"I like that Grandpa. Sarah certainly can't push her around like she did Jennifer."

On the kitchen table Emily found a handwritten note.

*Friday forenoon   Order meat from the butcher – It will come Saturday morning.*

*Thursday at 12     Order the foodstuff*

*Little Douglas like scramble eggs and Mr. Alastair like them fry on one side*

*Miss Emily and Grandpa Bottomsley like the same thing – Bakes or fishcakes*

*And don't forget the sanitary inspector come by the last Thursday every month to spray the cesspools. He always come by early morning.*

Emily looked at the note and smiled. Even this information she hadn't forgotten to pass onto Mary. She would miss Jennifer very much. That evening at dinner Emily told her husband about the note. She praised Jennifer and her loyalty to the family. She also spoke to her husband about the plans she had for Little John. If he didn't get a puppy, she would try to get him into a private school so he would have other children around his age to play with.

"He could go to school as well as get a puppy."

"I thought it would be too much for him. He is only four."

"That will keep him busy. Do you remember how fond he and Douglas were of Long John?"

"I think Nellie is getting another puppy so they could play together when we visit."

"They both really miss Long John."

"Where can we get a puppy?"

"Are we getting a puppy Mama?" asked Douglas overhearing the conversation.

"If we did get a puppy, it would be your responsibility. Yours and John's. You'll have to walk him, feed him and bathe him. Do you understand that?"

"It's not sanitary having dogs in the house," said Sarah. "Besides I'm allergic to them."

"You are allergic to cats Mother. Not dogs!"

"I still stay I don't like them in the house."

"Would you deprive your grandchildren the pleasure of having a lovable pet in the house Mother?"

"They will look after it for a while and then they will forget to bathe it."

"Then you can help them to look after it Mother."

Alastair did not speak. He watched his wife handle her mother in her own way.

"You have a servant. That's what servants are for."

"I'm here to look after the family," said Mary on hearing Sarah's remark. "I don't have nothing to do with dogs."

"Don't mess with her," said Emily laughing. "I'll show you that note. You'll find it rather amusing."

After dinner, Emily handed the note to Alastair. He took one look at it and agreed with his wife that she would certainly be missed at Bottomsley. After a couple nightcaps, the family with the exception of Alastair turned in for the evening. Something was bothering him. He went to his study, took the blackmail note out and had a long look at it. Then he compared it to the note Jennifer had written. He was right. The handwriting on both notes was the same and was also identical to Sarah's handwriting. Then there was the case of Millie Bottomsley's shoes. Did Jennifer wear them and why? She was a smart young woman. So why did she leave them in such a miserable state?

Alastair Chambers had a sleepless night. All kinds of thoughts were swirling around in his head. Ursy had been a faithful housekeeper whose death had thrown everything into chaos. What did Jennifer know about her death? The more he thought of it, the more convinced he was that she was in some way involved. A good heart to heart with Francois will make things clearer.

After a hearty breakfast, he collected Millie Bottomsley's shoes, which Old Bottomsley had already cleaned and the two notes and left for the office. Francois was already there and he entered his office and closed the door.

"A sleepless night?" asked his partner.

"It shows, doesn't it?"

"What's on your mind?"

Alastair handed the notes to Francois who gazed at them long and hard. He looked from one note to the other and then back to Alastair.

"So you are convinced that your mother in law is indeed the culprit."

"These were not written by Sarah, but by Jennifer."

"Jennifer Appleby? Your housekeeper? How did you reach that conclusion?"

"This note with the appointment times, she wrote to help out the new housekeeper. When Emily gave it to me last night, I immediately saw the similarity in the handwriting. It certainly looks like Sarah's handwriting, doesn't it?"

"So Emily realized it and showed it to you."

"No she doesn't know about my suspicions."

"Then why did she give you the second note?"

"Because she thought Jennifer was the ideal housekeeper and we were losing a great worker."

"So what are you going to do? You've got to tell the police."

Miss Weatherby the office secretary knocked on the door and turned the handle.

"Excuse me Mr. Chambers, there is someone here to see you."

"Who is it?"

"The constable," she replied.

"I wonder what he wants. Send him in."

The constable entered and after a few pleasantries, asked to speak to Alastair in private.

"I have some rather disturbing news," he said.

Alastair sat down and waited for the constable to continue.

"A very strange thing has happened."

"What is it?"

The Constable took a deep breath and sat down to tell him the news. Shortly after he began, Alastair seemed to realize where the story was heading and requested that Francois join them. Approximately forty five minutes later, the three men emerged from behind closed doors. Alastair and Francois seemed troubled.

"So on what grounds can you arrest him again?" asked Alastair.

"We'll think of something. We cannot allow him to escape from the island."

"Before you go," said Alastair, "there is another matter I would like to discuss with you. We found this piece of paper in my wife's grandfather's house, and yesterday we found out that our former housekeeper had written this one to assist her replacement."

"It's the same handwriting," the Constable said staring at them.

"At first we thought it was my mother in law's handwriting," said Alastair. "We even accused her of writing the note. And another thing sir, we found a pair of mud caked shoes in the same home under the bed and I think there is a link somewhere here."

"You spoke of your former housekeeper. Are you referring to Jennifer Appleby?"

"Yes."

"Where is she?"

"She left for England about three days ago."

"I wish she hadn't left the island," said the constable.

"She wasn't considered a suspect," said Alastair.

"She is now. I'll have to take these shoes with me," he said turning them over and looking at the soles.

"Don't forget she was in St. Lucy the night Ursy was murdered."

"That's true," he said getting up from his chair. "I'll get back to you when there's something to report."

Alastair walked the constable to the door and by the time he returned, Francois was ready to leave the office.

"I didn't know you had an out of office appointment today."

"I didn't. I must go home immediately. Nellie is alone today and I want to be sure she is alright."

"My children and my wife!" said Alastair suddenly.

"I don't think we have too much to worry about, but maybe you should make sure they are alright. If I called and told Nellie to lock the doors and windows, she would just start to panic," said Francois.

Alastair didn't understand Francois' urgency to see his wife, but he quickly dismissed it from his mind.

———

"What are you doing here at this time of the day?" Nellie asked.

"Can't I come home to visit my wife? Maybe I missed you."

"You left here two hours ago Francois."

"I know."

"So tell me the real reason why you've returned. Aren't you feeling well?"

"I'm fine Nellie. Sit down. There is something very confidential I must tell you."

"What is it?"

He stared at her and then reached out and held her hand.

"You'll soon be hearing it on the news, so I wanted you to know before that happened."

"I can handle it Francois. What is it?"

He told her what the Constable had said and she suddenly became a basket of nerves.

"Nellie," he said pulling her to him, "you cannot tell this to anyone. At least not yet! I wanted to tell you on the telephone, but I thought it better if I told you face to face."

"Are you going back to work?"

"Would you prefer it if I stayed with you?"

"Yes," she said as the tears rolled down her cheeks.

"I don't know Nellie, but it seems as though he had an accomplice."

"Was it Jennifer?"

"Yes they think she helped him."

"So that's the reason she left in such a hurry."

"Probably! I'll remain here for the rest of the day, but you must promise me that you will keep the doors locked especially when you're here alone. I want you to be careful. The Constable said Brandon Harvey could be re-arrested today. I hope they do it quickly."

"It is my fault. It is my fault for being so selfish," she said.

"What are you talking about Nellie?"

"I wish I hadn't let greed stand in my way. I should've taken Emily and left Bottomsley, but instead I sold my soul to the devil and this is my punishment."

"Nellie please listen to me," said Francois sternly. "You are not to blame for any of this. John Bottomsley made it impossible for you to say no. He knew you loved him and he used that to his advantage."

"But I should've loved Emily more."

"You told me you didn't want Emily to go through the same hardships you endured. You wanted to have a child you could be proud of."

"But she isn't my child Francois. She belongs to Sarah Bottomsley. She calls Sarah Mother and calls me Nellie. Do you know how hard that is Francois?"

"Emily loves you. I know she does and it would hurt her to see and hear you right now."

"Francois there is something I wanted to tell you a long time ago. I want to tell you what happened that night when Thomas Hurley disappeared. I need to get it out of my system, so I want you to listen."

"If it will make you feel better Nellie, I will listen to you."

And so for the first time Nellie was able to tell someone what had actually happened on the night that Thomas Hurley disappeared. When she was finished he held her close.

"I can only say that he got exactly what he deserved. I think he must have suspected something regarding Emily and so he hatched a plot to get the information he needed. What we need to do right now is to get out and have a change of scenery. Let's take a nice long drive. What do you say?"

"I don't know."

"Come on Nellie. Dry your eyes and change your dress and let me take you on a little excursion."

It was a long time since she had been on the east coast of the island. Francois parked the car on the top of a hill where they could get a good view of the rocks that dotted the Bathsheba coastline. It was beautiful. The turbulent Atlantic waves crashed against the shore bringing with them sea moss and jelly fish. They made their way on to the road below, where Francois encouraged her to remove her shoes and stroll along the beach. Hand in hand they walked, laughed and talked, temporarily forgetting their troubles. She collected bits of sea moss that lay strewn on the shoreline and he bits of bark which the tide had brought in. They then sat on the deserted beach and just stared into the water.

"Africa is over there," he said pointing straight ahead.

"I know," she murmured as she put her head on his shoulder.

"Hello Grandpa," said Alastair.

"A devil of a day it is!" the old man said.

"Where is Emily?"

"She's in the driveway with John. Do you want to speak with her?"

"Yes."

"Hello my love," she said. "I was having a bath. John has me soaked from head to foot."

"Well Grandpa says it's a rather warm day, so a bath will help to keep you cool. Do not repeat what I'm about to tell you. Is anyone close by?"

"No Grandpa is looking after John and Mother went out."

"I've got something very important to tell you," her husband said.

She listened to him and after he had finished, there was an eerie silence.

"Emily?"

"Yes, I'm still here."

"How did they find that out?"

"A good bit of detective work on the constable's part."

"What are we going to do?"

"Nothing right now. Hopefully he will be arrested again today."

"I've got to go Alastair. I've got to call the school in case anyone tries to pick Douglas up."

# 39

"A murderer, a thief and a blackmailer," said Alastair.
"Don't be too quick to jump to conclusions about Jennifer.
I'm sure there is an explanation to all this. Perhaps he forced her
to write the notes."

"And did he pull your grandmother's shoes on to her feet also?
She decided to leave the same evening I brought the shoes home.
She knew the noose was tightening and she had to make a quick
escape. I can't believe it was staring us in the face all the time and
we didn't see it."

"Don't blame yourself Alastair. We trusted her."

"Days such as this, I long to be back in England. So many
times I have considered just packing up and getting far away from
here. Have you ever considered returning to London?" he asked
his wife.

"Oh Alastair these things happen all over the world."

"Yes they do, but they happen just one thing at a time."

"What would we do with Grandpa if we returned to England?
I won't leave him alone here."

"Wherever you go my dear, I will follow you," said the old
man overhearing the last sentence.

"Thank you Grandpa."

"What about Sarah? She can't be left alone in this mire."

"I wish Mother was a nicer person," said Emily with a sigh.

"Oh what a tangled web we weave," said the old man with a sigh.

"My children," said Emily jumping up from the table and running to the bedroom.

The two boys were fast asleep. She turned around and walked back to the living room and collapsed onto the plantation chair. She felt close to her father at that moment and suddenly a great disgust for the home she had inherited from him.

Night after night, the police kept watch on Brandon Harvey's home and also on Ursy's home. They thought that at sometime, he would return to the scene of the crime. He had no money and he also didn't work. It was just a matter of time before he was caught.

Three and a half months had passed and Bridget Middleton along with her two daughters Victoria and Diana, stepped off the passenger ship in Perth Australia. It was a long and exhausting journey but she was relieved and happy. Happy to be in a country where no-one knew her. She was a clever woman and had eliminated all traces of her former existence. Everyone had a price and she had found someone who for a price was willing to find her new passports and new identities for her and her two children. Staying in London wasn't on her agenda, and she had had great difficulty obtaining her inheritance in cash. Week after week, she made arrangements to take as much as she could from the account which Alastair had set up in her name. Both she and the children had totally different appearances and day by day, they rehearsed their new names. She was quick to punish, when one of them made a mistake and used their old names. Finally with all the money neatly packed in a little case, and with new identities, they started their lives anew thousands of miles away from the tropical island of Barbados.

Brandon Harvey parked his car between two fields of sugar cane and crossed the road. Darkness! No one in sight! He quickened his pace and hurried in the direction of Ursy's home. There should be something there that would offer a clue to the whereabouts of Jennifer Appleby. He had already visited the servant's quarters at Bottomsley plantation, but the room was completely empty. This was his chance to find out if there was anything hidden at the housekeeper's home. He slithered along the galvanized paling of the home and seeing no-one, broke the door at the back of the house and entered. He turned his flashlight on and started to search the kitchen drawers. Nothing! He moved into the bedroom flashing his searchlight as he went. Suddenly another light shone in his face.

"Hands up," shouted someone. "What are you doing here?"

"I am just trying to find some information on the whereabouts of my wife," he replied.

"By breaking down the door? You are under arrest."

Brandon Harvey was handcuffed and shoved into the Doris which arrived fifteen minutes later. He was driven to the police station where the constable was waiting.

"Well Mr. Harvey! Returning to the scene of the crime?" the constable asked.

"Like I told the officer, I was just looking for any information that would lead to me to my wife."

"And must you do that in the middle of the night?"

"Well sir, everyone thinks I'm guilty of murder, but I can assure you that I'm not."

"Lock him up," the constable replied. "And Mr. Harvey, you should get in touch with your barrister as soon as possible."

## BRANDON HARVEY RE-ARRESTED

Everyone woke up to the headlines in the daily newspaper. No explanation was given for the arrest but everyone breathed a sigh of relief because in their minds he was guilty of murder.

"What it say?" asked Ida.

*Late yesterday evening Brandon Harvey was once again re-arrested. Speculation has it that evidence linking him to the crime was probably uncovered, but the prosecutor's office has not issued a statement to confirm this. The accused has been transferred directly to her Majesty's prison until such time as he is granted bail or until the trial begins.*

"He is a vagabond, but I still say he ain't responsible."

"Aunt Ida, why you keep saying that?"

"It is a feeling I got here in my heart. I don't like them people too much but right is right and wrong is wrong."

"Who you think do it Aunt Ida?"

"I don't know. All I can say is that I think they should look somewhere else. They putting all their eggs in the same basket and my old mother used to say that ain't a good thing to do. When the basket tumble over; bradderrax! Every egg gone."

"All he got to do is prove he ain't do it."

"They let him go the other day, and now they holding him again. That mean they ain't sure about something."

"I wonder what happen to Jennifer," said Clytie. "Nobody ain't hear a thing since she left."

"And you ain't going to hear neither. She gone for good. That is all the newspaper say?"

"Yes that is all."

~~~

The young man clad only in his underwear, stood with a cake of blue soap lathering his body at the standpipe. It was still early and a group of women were waiting with pads on their heads and their buckets beside them. They were patiently waiting until he was through with his morning ablutions, all the while laughing and discussing the latest bit of news. Sometimes they would flirt with him.

"Hurry up boy. I got to go home and make something for my children to eat," one woman said.

"If you in such a hurry, you could step down here and help me."

"Me? Touch you?" she asked as the raucous laughter of the other women filled the air.

"What you think o' this Harvey fella?" another asked.

"All I can say is Thank God he behind bars again. It ain't safe 'round this place no more."

In single file with their buckets balancing on their heads, their made their way back to their homes, just as the sun climbed from behind the cluster of mahogany trees.

~~~

At the Bertrand home Nellie and Francois sat together quietly drinking tea and staring at the newspaper.

"What do you think will happen to him?" asked Nellie.

"It depends on the charges."

"I hope this comes to an end real soon. I don't think my nerves can take much more of this," said Nellie.

"Why don't I take you down to Clytie's on my way to work and I will pick you up on the way back?"

"I don't know. I am very nervous."

"Remember, you aren't allowed to discuss what I told you with anyone."

"I know. We should be happy because Christmas is coming. Instead of joy, I have a heavy heart."

"The trial will be after Christmas, so let's try to concentrate on having a good time."

"I don't think I want to go to Clytie. I am sure they will realize that something is wrong. Not only that, Ida seems to know everything and I don't want to be around her right now."

Francois waved to Clytie as he drove past the shop. Noticing that she had run out of the shop, he reversed to talk to her.

"You think this time they will keep him lock up?" she asked.

"I don't know Clytie. We will just have to wait and see."

"How is Nels?"

"She's fine. Why don't you give her a call?"

"I thought she was coming down here with you this morning. She say so yesterday."

"Call her. She must have forgotten."

"I want to ask her if she would sell me the house we living in. I could pay for it."

"You'll have to speak to her," he said driving away.

"Why you think they pick up Brandon Harvey again Nels?" her sister asked.

"Maybe they found out something."

"Well I hope they keep him lock up this time because I don't have to sleep with one eye open no more."

Nellie started to laugh.

"You don't have one ounce of fear in your soul Nora. When you sleep, you sleep with both eyes closed and you snore. So if he came around, you wouldn't even know."

"Well be that as it may, I am still glad that he is behind bars this morning."

"Have you heard anything from Jennifer?"

"How long since she left? Over four months? I ain't hear a word from that girl."

"Well I don't think that after such a long time, you will hear anything."

"I want to know 'bout those two little girls and how they getting along in that cold, cold country."

"I used to get letters from Emily when she was over there, so there is nothing to prevent them from writing to you."

"Girl that is life. You see Judes lately? That girl is just about ready to deliver that baby."

"Does Toby know?"

"What you asking me 'bout Toby? That boy ain't show his face 'round here in months. Life must be good. Could be that he find somebody to leach off."

# 40

Christmas carols filled the air and the citizens of Plum Tree Village went about doing what they liked doing at that festive time of the year. Old men and women with their hoes were weeding out the grass from between the pebbles in front of their chattel houses, while others were busy applying varnish to the few pieces of mahogany furniture they owned. Men with flat sisal rope wrapped around their arms went from house to house in search of work. They were the repair men for any broken canework in the mahogany furniture. Harriet's sewing machine was working into the wee hours of the morning, since the villagers all wanted new white dresses to wear to church on Christmas morning and new white lace curtains to flutter in the wind.

The Coolie man was doing a profitable business. All the women waited patiently for him to put in an appearance and he knew what they wanted because his car was filled with white cloth. Some for curtains and some for clothing! This in turn also contributed to a booming business for Harriet.

In the shop Clytie and Nora parceled out sugar and flour into one pound packages and rice into one pint bags. Clytie was continuing the tradition which Nellie had started. All her customers would receive a gift of some food items and ten salted hams were ordered for the long standing customers with big families in return for their patronage. With Miss Una gone and Ida not knowing the usual customers, Clytie was forced to spend all her time in the shop during business hours to ensure that only her customers were given these food items. Although the name Nellie's Bar and Grocery had now been replaced with Clytie's name, it was still referred to as Miss Nellie's shop.

Clytie encouraged her Aunt Ida to accompany her to the Anglican Church where she sang in the choir. They were practising for their yearly Christmas recital. Although she wasn't a regular churchgoer, Clytie still held a place, not in the regular church choir, but the choir which provided live in maids and the likes with a bit of spirituality. Judes on the other hand, had never heard or seen anything like the little one-roofed high spirited churches and so she would sit in the last pew and enjoy the sermon, in spite of it being so different from what she was accustomed to. The members were all dressed in white and wore white head ties. Some members claimed to be taken over by the Holy Spirit and would throw themselves on the ground with arms flailing and thrashing and speaking in tongues until someone assisted them to their feet. She had never become a member but they had grown used to seeing her there. After it was obvious that she was in the family way, she was approached by the preacher who inquired about her husband. Having no husband and being in the family way meant that she was no longer allowed to take her place in the last pew. She was a sinner! She found herself back in the Anglican Church with all her friends and family.

Nellie was also very busy in the church and the priest relied on her for her generous offerings and support to the church.

"I would like to speak to you on a very delicate matter," Reverend Willoughby told her one day.

She had no idea what she or any member of her family had done, but she went to speak to him in private.

"Miss Nellie," he began, "you know that many plantations have closed their doors and many of our faithful members have returned to the mother country."

"I know that Reverend Willoughby."

"Well I was wondering if you would be interested in buying one of the pews for you and the family."

*Such an affront, she thought.*

Her memories took her back to her earlier years when she stood with her mother at the back of the church because all the seats were taken except the same seats in the first two rows of the church. Although those seats were empty, black people were forced to stand throughout the service. Those seats had been purchased by the British white church members who sat there only until they had taken communion and then took their leave.

"Well Reverend Willoughby," she said, "God has been seeing me and my family from the fifth row for the last fifteen years and I have been seeing him too, so I don't think I can get any closer to him by moving up to the front."

Although he was offended by her remark, he kept a stiff upper lip because he knew he could count on her generosity.

It was also the time of year for Christmas parties and it fell upon the partnership of Bertrand & Chambers to say thank you to their clients for their patronage and for a prosperous and fulfilling year. Nellie and Emily were the organizers of the affair which would be held on the twenty third of December.

Miss Weatherby was also called upon to assist since she had been with the company for a long time and knew all the clients. A guest list was sent out and the event was to be held at a hotel on the south coast of the island. Since her first unforgettable meeting with Miss Weatherby, Nellie never did get close to the secretary and she kept a respectable distance from her employer's wife. A local four piece steel band was hired for the entertainment and the menu was chosen. Even though her spirits were dampened by news she had received a week earlier, Nellie decided she was going to enjoy what was left of the Christmas season.

Two days before the event, her husband called her to the bedroom and in his hand he had a red elongated and battered box.

"I wanted to keep give this to give to my wife on a special occasion, but I've decided not to wait any longer. These belonged to my mother. During the early days of my parents' courtship, when things were wonderful, my father gave these items to my mother and I think it only fitting that as my wife, you should now wear them."

She stared at him and at the tattered box.

"Come on. Take it. I want to see how they look on you. There is a special piece which I hope you will wear to the Christmas party."

"They are beautiful," she said as she saw the items in the box.

"Let me help you. This emerald and diamond necklace was the first gift my mother received from my father. I think it had belonged to his mother. It looks beautiful on you."

"Are you sure you want to give them to me?" she asked.

"Who else should I give them to Nellie? There is also a matching bracelet somewhere in the box."

"This is really beautiful," she said admiring the jewellery in the mirror.

"Try the others. There are two more necklaces there. How about trying the pearls?"

Each piece of jewellery seemed to enhance her beauty. Sarah Bottomsley immediately sprang to mind.

"Now I'll have a difficult time choosing which one I'll wear."

"Have you decided on the outfit you will wear?"

"I thought I would wear one of the evening dresses I bought in Paris. Or do you think it is too old?"

"Parisian fashions rarely go out of style. No one else at the party will be able to hold a candle to you."

"You always say just the right things Francois. I thought I would wear the cream dress which I wore to the first show."

"Great choice! I've got to go to the office for an hour or so. Don't leave the box sitting around. I wouldn't want you to lose it."

Harriet appeared at the door in the early evening to style her aunt's hair. When Nellie faced Francois in the living room, he was speechless. He helped her with the clasp to the beautiful emerald and diamond necklace and that was all that was needed. She gazed into the mirror hardly recognizing the woman who was looking back at her.

"I have seen you beautifully dressed before, but tonight I haven't the words to describe how absolutely gorgeous you look."

It was a room filled with colonial splendour. Overhead ceiling fans were working overtime keeping the guests cool on a warm night. Mahogany trees had spilled their blood for the paneling in the room. Rich brown hues hid the concrete that lay beneath it. Decanters filled with scotch and gin and rum were lined off like soldiers behind the well-stocked bar. Young men with trays hanging around their necks walked around offering cigars and cigarettes to the guests. The men in their formal attire reminded Nellie of photos of birds she had seen somewhere in a magazine. Penguins! The women were all clad in evening dresses with big bows on the shoulders or roses in their hair. They were mainly colonials, who having exchanged the dampness of London for the tropical paradise, were busy toasting each other and usings phrases like 'old boy and old chap.'

Emily and Alastair were also spellbound by the beauty and sophistication of Nellie Bertrand. Of course an invitation had been extended to Sarah Bottomsley, but she had declined. It was their duty to welcome the guests and so the two couples stood at the entrance shakings hands and smiling wide smiles. The men were complimentary and the women, some of whom had never met Nellie, were amazed at her beauty. Some of the women flirted with Francois, promising to keep the last dance for him, but he had eyes only for Nellie. It was a beautiful evening and everything went according to plan. Every man in the room wanted to dance with Francois' glamourous and sophisticated wife, while their wives looked on in envy.

"You look like two sisters," said a man to Emily and Nellie.

"Yes," said Emily laughing. "She is actually my twin sister."

"Do you realize I had only one dance with my wife?" asked Francois on the way home.

"You were too busy with all the other wives," she responded.

"That's because my wife was too busy with all the other husbands in the room. Did you enjoy yourself?"

"I was a little scared at first, but when I realized how nice they were, I really let go and started to enjoy myself. And most of all, I was very happy because Sarah didn't show up."

"Can't go through life always side-stepping Sarah," he replied.

"I know," she said placing her hand on his knee.

―――――

The sweet smell of ham boiling in its salty water excited her nose as she opened the door to Clytie's home. It was indeed the Christmas season! In the kitchen she found Ida and Clytie creaming sugar and a mixture of New Zealand and Palm Tree butter together. It was time to get those Christmas cakes in the oven. Clytie was happy to see Nellie at that moment because Ida was too short to help her lift the oven onto the stove.

"You just in time Nels," she said. ""Help me to grease these cake pans."

Nellie sat down beside Ida, rubbed a piece of paper in the lard and greased the pans.

"You aren't going to ask me what happened last night?" she asked her friend.

"How I could forget that? Give me all the news Nels."

"Girl I danced my feet off last night."

"Francois must be real tired this morning."

"He is still sleeping, so I can't stay too long. Would you believe I only had one dance with him?"

"But I thought you say you dance off your feet."

"Yes girl. You wouldn't believe how these people behaved last night. They were real friendly and all the men wanted to dance with me."

"Poor Francois," said Clytie.

"He didn't mind at all. As a matter of fact, he was watching me and smiling."

"Didn't I tell you that the Lord keep his hand on your shoulder real long?" asked Ida.

"I know that Miss Ida, but I really didn't expect them to be so nice because this place is full of poppits."

"As long as you had a good time Nels. What 'bout Miss Sarah? What she say when she see you doll to death?"

"She didn't come."

"Just as well," said Ida. "Better that she stay home and do something with that yellow hair."

"So what bring you down here at this time o' the morning?"

"You know I had to tell you everything that went on."

"Francois give you a message from me?"

"No. Maybe he forgot. What did you tell him?"

"Well Nels, seeing that I am going to be a grandmother real soon, I was wondering if you would sell me the house. Judes going to have a baby anytime now."

"I'm real glad that you are going to look out for your grandchild. Let me have a word first with Francois about it. You know we have to make these decisions together. But knowing him, I'm sure he will say to sell it to you."

"What are you doing here today?" asked Nora coming through the back door. "Percy is out there with his paint brush and every chair is outside the house. He is varnishing and he is painting."

"That is a good man Miss Nora," said Ida.

"We went out last night and Francois is still sleeping."

"Oh yes, you went to the Christmas do? You had a good time?"

"I had a wonderful time," replied Nellie.

"In here smell real good," said Nora sticking her finger into the butter and sugar mixture Ida was creaming.

"Do that again and I will slap off your hand," said the old woman.

"You won't slap me Miss Ida," said Nora laughing. "I get up early to help with the cakes, but I see I'm too late."

"No you ain't," said the old woman. "Take this from me. My old shoulders ain't what they used to be. And keep your fingers out of it."

"Christmas is the best time o' the year. Turn up the Rediffusion so I can hear the carols," said the ever bubbly Nora.

*Oh the weather outside is frightful,*
*And the fire is so delightful.*
*And since we've no place to go,*
*Let it snow, Let it snow, Let it snow.*

"I wonder what snow really like? It look so white and pretty! I wonder if it get as cold up there as it get 'round here at Christmas time."

"You don't know what you asking for," said Ida. "When that wind start to blow and you start tumbling down in that snow, it ain't too nice."

"Yes but when you hear these carols, they make you feel real good and you want to see it for yourself."

"Well Miss Nora, if I never see another bit o' snow again, I would be a happy woman."

"It can't be that bad."

"Oh yes," said Ida. "And worse. You hear anything from that girl Jennifer?"

"Not a word."

"I was thinking that because Christmas coming, she would send a card or something."

"She gone and that man o' hers lock up in Glendairy. Thank the Lord," said Ida.

"Well I think I should get back home before Francois gets up," said Nellie suddenly.

"Where you going so fast?' asked her sister. "Wait 'till the cakes come out of the oven. Besides I got something to ask you."

"What?" asked Nellie.

"When Jennifer left, she give me some money and I want to surprise Harriet."

"You want to know if you should give her some of the money? I would say no."

"No that isn't it Nellie. I was wondering if you would sell the shop to me and I would give it to Harriet as a Christmas present. She is a good child."

"Did the lot of you win money at the Races on Saturday?"

"What you talking about?" asked Nora.

Clytie slipped by the two women in order to face Nellie. Then she put her finger to her lips and Nellie understood what she wanted to say. Although Toby was no longer considered Judes husband, and she was carrying Jonas' child, Nora was still legally her mother in law and she didn't want to make her feel uncomfortable.

Later that evening Nellie spoke to her husband regarding Clytie's offer and also Nora's for the house where Harriet worked as a dressmaker and hair stylist. Francois' advice to her was to sell the house to Clytie, but she should give the other house to Harriett. She was an industrious woman who really worked hard and he knew that in Nellie's will, the house was to be given to her anyway.

There wasn't a lot for Otty to do because most of the baking was a communal venture, and each family member would be bringing some kind of dish to the Christmas Day celebrations. There was the usual cleaning to be done, furniture to be polished, dishes to be washed and returned to the China cabinet and new curtains to be hung which she and Nellie did together while enjoying the songs of the season. Francois would occasionally look in from the verandah to see the progress that was being made. They could hear the music coming towards the house. The Tuk Band and Tiltman were making their rounds. Nellie was sure that by the time they reached her home, they would be drunk from alcohol consumption, and in the distance she could hear their familiar greeting.

*Christmas comes but once a year,*

*So open the larder and give me a beer.*

"Is there anything to give them to eat?" asked Nellie.

"I make some ham cutters 'cause I know they would come by," said Otty.

The leader of the group did not trust himself to open the gate and enter the premises, so Francois beckoned them to come in. They were very entertaining with their little verses and some of them were completely inebriated, especially The Tiltman. He had consumed too much alcohol but was doing a fantastic job on his stilts. Everyone wondered how he achieved such a feat in his state.

# 41

Christmas Eve night! Different odours and aromas wafted through Plum Tree Village. Varnish, paint, cake, pudding, ham, roast pork, garlic pork, fricassee chicken, pepperpot and assorted pies. Nora arrived at Nellie's with her specialty of Jug-jug. The pigeon peas and rice she would bring with her the following day. To please Francois, Ida made Seafood Gumbo and Clytie Christmas cake and baked ham.

"See all of you at church tomorrow morning," said Nellie.

*Christmas Day*

The church was packed to capacity although it was only four forty five in the morning. Francois, Nellie and the rest of the family sat in the fifth pew, enjoying the music which the organist had chosen for their enjoyment. Ahead in the first and second row, the pews were empty. Most of the worshippers were dressed in white as was the custom for a Christmas morning service. The altar was adorned with replicas of the Baby Jesus and Mary and Joseph and the Star which had guided the three wise men to the Baby Jesus.

The first hymn, 'While shepherds watched their flocks by

night,' was sung with much gusto with Ida Franklin singing to the top of her lungs. She was enjoying her first Christmas back in Barbados.

The Reverend stood at the door shaking hands as each member exited the church after an enjoyable service.

"I'm glad you could make it," he said to Francois.

"A very lovely service," Francois replied

"I believe the family is ready to enjoy this beautiful day. Lots of lovely things to eat and good company,"Reverend Willoughby said.

"As usual sir," replied Francois.

"And what's on the dinner table Miss Nellie?" he asked.

"The usual Christmas dishes!"

"Makes my mouth water just thinking about it," he replied.

"And how are you spending this beautiful day?" asked Francois.

"I'll be in the vicarage all day. Some kind soul will probably bring something by for my lunch."

"We can't have that," said Francois. "This is not a day that one should spend alone. I'm sure my wife wouldn't mind if you joined us at the dinner table."

"Don't go to any trouble sir."

"No trouble at all. My wife usually makes enough food to feed the whole village."

"I wish you hadn't invited him," whispered Nellie.

"It's Christmas. Where is your charity?" he joked.

"It isn't going to be the same with him sitting there. What happens if someone says something that he doesn't think is funny?"

"Then he can just get up and go home. But I don't think that will happen. I think the man has a sense of humour."

"Did I tell you he offered to sell me one of the pews at the front of the church?"

"What did you tell him?"

"I said I could see God from where I usually sit."

"That's my Nellie," he said laughing.

Around midday Otty was making the last minute preparations. An assortment of vegetables was boiling away on the stove. Carrots, beets and string beans and the macaroni and yam pie were put into the oven. And soon the family started to arrive. Jules and Jonas arrived and she handed a platter of strange looking pies to Otty. It looked as if the oven had been opened a bit too early and they had all fallen. She said it is called Yorkshire pudding.

"Then the people in Yorkshire don't know how to cook," mumbled Ida Franklin.

Otty could only laugh because she was thinking the same thing. Last to arrive was the Reverend still in his priestly attire and the first thing he requested was a shot of Bajan rum.

"Lord he can throw that back like a real rum drinker," said Ida. "In my time the man of the cloth used to set the example. Get one for me Clytie. If he can drink, I can do it too."

"But you don't drink Aunt Ida."

"It is a special occasion Clytie and I intend to enjoy myself."

The men sat on the verandah and Otty deposited a bucket of ice, ginger ale and a bottle of rum on the table, while the women set about to place the Christmas lunch on the table. On the side bar, there were an assortment of drinks; Sorrel, Mauby and Ginger Beer. Francois sat at the head of the table and Nellie on the other end. Father Willoughby sat next to Nellie, Percy next to Francois and the rest of the family were seated throughout.

After everyone was seated, a lengthy prayer was offered up by

Father Willoughby. When he was finished, Ida decided she would assist Otty and Nellie in bringing in the dishes. As a matter of fact all the women were now running back and forth with platters and piping hot dishes.

"Everything looks just delicious Miss Nellie," said the good man. "And those Yorkshire Puds? Who made them?"

"Judes did," replied Nellie.

"They were just delicious."

"Well Miss Nellie, I must say that I am really pleased to have been invited to your beautiful home. I had no idea that you lived so well. Wasn't this Gus Ridley's home?"

"Was!" said Nora.

"Nevertheless, it is a beautiful home and that was indeed a wonderful meal. Now tell me what you think of this man Brandon Harvey. You are a solicitor Mr. Bertrand. Do you think he committed the crime?"

"I can't really say Father Willoughby. I don't have all the evidence and as they said, nothing really pointed to his guilt."

"Then why did they arrest him again?"

"I think that had something to do with breaking and entering."

"Funny thing though," said the priest, "there is something about him which makes me rather uneasy. I just can't seem to put my finger on it."

"Well I'm sure he's getting a wonderful Christmas meal," said Francois changing the subject and getting up to place a record on the gramophone.

"What are you playing for us?" Father Willoughby asked

"I'm playing Nellie's favourite, 'O holy Night' by the Mormon Tabernacle Choir."

"Beautiful voices, but such a shame they don't believe in the same God as we."

"We all have to answer for ourselves," said Ida picking up his plate.

"I don't think I've met you," he said turning her.

"She is my aunt. This is my mother's sister," said Clytie. "She used to live in Carlina."

"That's interesting. I never knew that Una had a sister."

"I know you is a man of the cloth," said Ida, "but you can't know everything."

Clytie nudged her aunt with her elbow.

"That is true," the priest said laughing. "You are indeed Miss Prescott's sister. She never mixed her words. So Mr. Trotman, I haven't seen you in God's house recently."

Percy was silent. The priest had caught him off guard.

"We've got a little business we do on Sunday mornings," said Francois.

"You must always put aside a little time for God," he said.

Nellie came out from the bedroom with her box of presents. She handed the first gift to Harriet. An envelope! Her niece opened it and read the contents.

"Thank you Aunt Nellie," she said tears running down her face. "You have been very good to my family. I don't know what to say."

"Thanks would be more than enough," said Nellie.

"Aren't you going to tell your mother what you got?" asked Nora.

"Aunt Nellie has given me the house where I work."

"Nellie, you are a real good sister."

And so the presents were handed around with everyone oohing and aahing with the gifts they received. Most pleased were Harriet and Francois. Francois, because of the new fishing line Percy had bought for him. The last to receive a gift was the

Reverend Willoughby. Francois stared at the gift waiting to see what he would receive since he was invited at the very last minute. Nellie stared back to see his reaction. Inside the neatly wrapped gift was one of Francois' shirts he had bought in Ghana. The reverend seemed delighted.

"I don't know how often I will be able to wear it, but it is beautiful."

"Liar," whispered Ida forcing her niece to nudge her with her elbow. "Miss Nellie, that man got two faces."

"You think I don't know that Miss Ida?" whispered Nellie.

"And if you know that, why you invite him?"

"Aunt Ida, this is Nellie house and she can do whatever she wants."

"Well it is Christmas Miss Ida and I thought it would be good to be charitable."

Everyone was happy when he finally decided he had to go. He had eaten well and consumed nearly a bottle of Francois' rum, in addition to taking one of his shirts.

"Thank you again Miss Nellie and Mr. Bertrand. It was indeed a beautiful Christmas. One of the best I have had in a long time and I hope this wouldn't be my last invitation."


The following day which they referred to as Christmas Bank holiday, the Bertrands spent at Bottomsley with a few of their friends including Dr. Sims and his wife Annabelle. It was enjoyable and uneventful since Sarah Bottomsley decided she was going out for the day. Nellie found the couple to be indeed cheerful and easygoing people, not all like Sarah Bottomsley.

Later that evening when they arrived home, they were greeted with the news that Judes Peterkin had given birth to an eight pound baby girl and that mother and child were doing well.

# 42

With the Christmas season over, things were now back to normal and everyone was looking forward to the trial which was due to begin in two weeks. All efforts were made to find Jennifer Appleby but it seemed as if she had simply disappeared from the face of the earth. It had also been learnt that all the funds were taken from the account which had been opened for her in London. Since her departure, no one had heard anything from her or from the children. Nora suspected the latter were not allowed to get in contact with anyone, and that made her sad because she liked the two girls. Jennifer's only wish was a better and safer life for them. But why hadn't she gotten in touch with anyone? It was just a little strange but since they had no way of remedying the situation, they dismissed it from their minds. Even little John Chambers had now forgotten about her and Mary Sealy had taken her place in his heart.

The New Year seemed to have put Sarah Bottomsley in a good mood. She was more approachable and even found a little time to play with her younger grandchild, when she was not imbibing with Grandpa Bottomsley. He was still a very strong old man, but Emily had the feeling that Dementia was setting in because he constantly repeated himself; but he was a happy man.

"How is my favourite grandson?" he asked Douglas one day. "What did you do in school today?"

The little boy sat beside him and started to converse.

"We learnt about different lands and their people," the child replied.

"Ah Geography! That was my favourite subject. I used to dream that I was far away when the teacher was explaining the different cultures. I thought I was in India going Tiger Hunting, and in my head I killed Leopards and lions in Africa."

"Really Grandpa?"

"Oh yes," said the old man proudly.

"Is that where the savages live?" asked the little boy.

"No there are no savages there. Who told you that?"

"My teacher said there were lots of savages there and they brought some of them here to work."

Emily's smile turned to a frown when she heard what her son had said.

"What else did she say?" his mother asked.

"That was all. We went on to talk about big wild animals."

"Do you know what a savage is?" asked Old Bottomsley.

"Yes. They are people who live in Africa and India."

"Dear oh dear!" said the old man.

"I think I've got to pay a visit to the school," said Emily. "Run along Douglas and change your clothes. Mary has made something special just for you."

"Oh Grandpa! What are we going to do? How could they say such things to children?"

Old Bottomsley took his grand daughter's hand in his.

"Life can be cruel Emily. You know that. Take Sarah for instance. After living here for so many years, nothing has changed in her way of thinking. Sometimes she reminds me of Millie.

They have the natives at their beck and call. The natives raise their children, they wash and cook for them, but they will never consider them equal. My son God rest his soul, had a different outlook on life. He loved a woman but because of the shame it would have brought, he was forced to hide it until the day he died. I think if God had given him a couple years more, he would've eventually made Nellie his wife, but he died alone Emily because Nellie wasn't allowed to be with him. That was the time when he needed the comforting hand of someone who really loved him. Sarah wasn't and still isn't a warm human being. Don't allow the same thing to happen to you and the children."

"What are you trying to say Grandpa?"

"Deception is a terrible thing. I can't tell you what to do, but I think when the children are old enough, you should tell them the truth about themselves. Don't allow the same thing that happened to you to happen to them. You know the pain you suffered when you didn't know what was happening to your life. Spare them the indignity. You give them the information and let them handle it the way they see fit."

"It is such a difficult decision Grandpa."

"It is not difficult my child. Don't allow teachers and outsiders to poison the children's minds. They may not be able to see it right now, but the day will come when they will ask you why you hid it from them."

"I don't think the time is right Grandpa. They are much too young right now and wouldn't understand. Sometimes I look at Nellie and I can feel such love for her and I know she loves me too, but after all these years we are still holding onto a secret."

"That's what I was trying to tell you."

"What about Mother? I would like to discuss it with her, but I know what she's going to say. Where is she anyway?"

"I don't know. She drove away about an hour ago, but never said where she was going."

"We should go over and take a look at the house to see what the workmen have done so far," said Emily.

"That's a good idea. How I wish Millie was here to see it too."

"I'm sure she wouldn't agree with our removing all her clothing and changing everything."

"Of that I'm sure Emily. Of that I'm sure!"

"It was progressing well the last time I looked in on the workers Grandpa. I'm sure Grandma would be happy with the repairs we have made."

"Have you decided whether you want to sell it or rent it?" the old man asked.

"I've decided to keep it in the family a while longer, so selling it right now is out of the question."

<hr>

*The trial*

A jury of eight men and four women were chosen and Brandon Harvey's trial was set for the following week. Against Francois' wishes, Nellie decided she would attend. Emily also decided she would go on the first day and Sarah Bottomsley couldn't understand why her daughter would want to attend the trial of such a low life like Brandon Harvey.

The Prosecutor had taken his seat and glanced over at the solicitor Christopher Peacock who was busy scribbling notes on a pad. Mr. Peacock did not look up. The jury entered and finally a handcuffed Brandon Harvey was led into the courtroom and placed in the prisoner's dock. Next entered the judge in his black gown and powdered wig, and surveyed the courtroom before he took his seat.

"All rise," shouted the bailiff.

The spectators all scrambled to their feet, and Emily and Nellie made it through the door just before it was closed and sat in the last row of the courtroom. They strained their necks in order to see the accused, but their seats did not afford them a good view. All they could see of the accused was the back of his clean shaven head. The opening remarks which seemed to take the better part of the morning were made and the accused was called upon to make a plea. Then the first witness was called. The policeman who had arrested Brandon Harvey was the first to be questioned by Mr. Peacock. After half an hour of bantering back and forth, between the judge, the prosecutor and Mr. Peacock, it was now the prosecutor's turn for questioning.

"No questions My Lord," he replied.

"Are you sure?" asked the judge.

"Quite sure My Lord," he said with a smile.

Mr. Peacock seemed a little unnerved at the answer, and whispered something in Brandon Harvey's ear. He thought for a moment, and then shook his head.

"Well since there are no more questions at the moment, it's a good time to adjourn this case until nine o'clock tomorrow morning," said the judge pounding his gavel on the table.

"Are you coming back tomorrow?" asked Nellie.

"I had no plans to attend. He's only on trial for forced entry into Ursy's house."

"Maybe tomorrow they will question him about the murder and I want to be here to hear about it. I don't want to sit there alone. Please come back tomorrow."

"There's nothing to be afraid of Nellie. He won't be able to escape."

"It doesn't seem real Nellie. It is more like a story you would read in a crime a magazine. Anyway I'll meet you here again tomorrow morning around half past eight after I have taken Douglas to school. I promise you I won't be late again."

Nellie and Emily were seated in the fourth row of the courthouse awaiting the start of the proceedings. The courtroom was like a beehive. The onlookers were whispering and laughing. They were there to see the man they all thought had murdered the housekeeper from Bottomsley plantation. Although he was only on trial for breaking into the house, many of the local people had only murder on their minds. Suddenly there was absolute silence. The handcuffed man was led in and everyone tried to get a good look at him.

After calling a couple witnesses, Brandon Harvey was called upon to testify.

"State your name," said the prosecutor.

"Brandon Harvey."

"Mr. Harvey, remember you are under oath. Please state your name," the prosecutor repeated.

"My name is Brandon Harvey," he repeated loudly.

Mr. Peacock was annoyed and let it be known.

"My Lord, my client has already answered that question. I don't know where all this leading but I object to this kind of questioning."

"Mr. Beaton, "said the judge, "is this questioning leading somewhere?"

"My Lord, my questions are indeed leading somewhere and if the court will indulge me, I do intend to get to the point."

"Well hurry, we haven't all day," the judge replied.

"Mr. Harvey, that's what you say your name is, please tell the court what you were doing at the house where a certain murder had taken place."

"I object my Lord. This is not a murder case. My client is charged with breaking and entering," said Mr. Peacock.

"Please rephrase your question Mr. Beaton."

"Mr. Harvey, please tell the court the reason why you were at Ursy Smith's house on the night you were arrested."

"I was looking for any clues that would lead me to my girlfriend."

"And did you find any sir?"

"I didn't have the time. I was arrested as soon as I entered the house."

"You mean you were arrested as soon as you *broke* into the house."

"You can say that," said Brandon Harvey.

"You said you were looking for your girlfriend. And is her name Jennifer Appleby?"

"Yes sir."

"And where did you meet Miss Appleby?" Mr. Beaton asked.

Brandon Harvey paused before he answered the question.

"Remember you are still under oath Mr. Harvey. Shall I repeat the question for you?"

"No sir. About eight years ago, I met her at her home in St. Peter."

"And what were the circumstances surrounding this meeting?"

"I went to her home."

"Were you invited Mr. Harvey or did you just show up on her door step."

"I showed up on their doorstep."

"Their doorstep?" asked Mr. Beaton.

"Yes, she lived with her father and daughter."

"And what happened after you arrived there?"

"I don't understand the question sir."

"Well were you welcomed with open arms? Did they say come in and have dinner with us?"

"I don't remember sir."

"Tell me Mr. Harvey, when did you arrive on this island?"

"About eight years ago."

"So are you trying to tell the court that when you showed up at the home of Miss Appleby, it was the same day you had arrived on the island?"

"You could say that."

"Listening to you speak Mr. Harvey, I get the impression you are an educated man."

"Yes sir."

"So you know the laws of the land Mr. Harvey. When I travel home to England, I must be in possession of a passport and other travel documents. The officers scrutinize my documents and then I'm granted permission to enter the country. You know there is a certain protocol when one enters and leaves a country, don't you Mr. Harvey?"

Brandon Harvey knew where the questioning was leading and decided to cooperate.

"Yes sir."

"Then tell the court why no documents were found regarding your arrival onto this island."

"I have no idea sir."

"So you arrived here at the air base with your passport and travel documents and no one even bothered to look at them?"

"That's not what I'm saying."

"Then what are you saying Mr. Harvey?"

"All I'm saying is that I don't remember what happened. It was a long time ago."

"Remember you are under oath. Please tell the court your name," shouted Mr. Beaton.

Again Brandon Harvey paused and looked around.

"Your name sir!" commanded Mr. Beaton.

"Thomas Hurley," he replied.

At first everything was silent. Then it was as if all hell had broken loose, as people started to run in and out of the courtroom. The judge banged his gavel on the desk, but no one listened. Then he banged it once again and threatened to clear the courtroom. Thomas Hurley alias Brandon Harvey sat quietly staring ahead.

"Mr. Peacock, please approach the bench," said the judge. "Did you know anything about this?"

"I can assure you my Lord that I knew absolutely nothing about it."

Mr. Beaton was also called before the judge and the case was adjourned for two weeks to give the barristers a chance to prepare their cases. It was no longer just breaking and entering, but something much larger was hanging over Thomas Hurley's head. Nellie couldn't take it any longer and along with Emily, left the courtroom.

"What's the matter Nellie?" her daughter asked.

"It's just so strange to see a man who was supposed to be dead sitting in the dock and speaking."

"It was all a lie," said Emily. "One big lie! He'll get what's coming to him. You'll have to wait for Francois. He doesn't know that you are ready. I've got to go home and tell Sarah this bit of news."

"I'll walk to Francois' office and meet him there."

"Wish me luck Nellie. I've got to break the news to Grandpa and Sarah."

Grandpa Bottomsley was sitting on the verandah with his favourite drink in his hand when his granddaughter arrived home.

"How did it go this morning?" he asked.

"Where is Mother?"

"I think she went in to rest."

"The weirdest thing happened this morning. You are not going to believe what I'm about to tell you. I think you should call Mother. I want her to hear this."

A tired looking Sarah Bottomsley sat down next to her father in law.

"You woke me from my nap. There had better be a good reason."

"Thomas Hurley is alive," said Emily.

"What do you mean he's alive?" asked the old man.

Sarah sat as if in shock.

"Apparently the constable couldn't find any documents for Brandon Harvey and on a hunch decided to check the unsolved cases and Thomas' fingerprints matched Brandon Harvey's."

"Dear Lord," said the old man, "how did he get away with this for all these years?"

"I don't know. He must've had some help."

"I'm going back to my room," said Sarah getting up and walking away.

Emily and her grandfather stared at her. They couldn't believe she had nothing to say regarding this surprising piece of news.

"I think she knew he was still alive," said Old Bottomsley.

"Are you referring to the outbursts she has now and then?"

"Yes, I think he must've been the rogue who has been stealing things from the house."

"Jennifer Appleby!" said Emily. "She's the one who has been helping him. We could all have been murdered in our beds."

The old man made the sign of the cross. Sarah had alluded to the fact that she had seen Thomas Hurley but he had never believed a word. She was right. He had been walking in and out of Bottomsley whenever he wished. But how?

"Do you think she is alright?" asked Emily.

"Maybe I should check on her," said the old man.

"Just leave her alone. Maybe she needs time to absorb the reality of the situation."

"What will they charge him with Emily?"

"Murder! Impersonation! I don't know Grandpa. We must wait for the facts to come out. I think he is willing to talk. I wonder if his sister will ever find out."

# 43

## DEAD MAN TESTIFIES IN COURT

*Pandemonium broke out in the High court yesterday when a breaking and entry trial turned into somewhat of a three ring circus. The accused, Brandon Harvey who had been earlier accused of murder turned out to be none other than Thomas Hurley who had been reported missing for more than ten years. He had been arrested for breaking into the murdered woman's home. The judge adjourned the case for two weeks in order to give the barristers time to prepare their cases. Mr. Hurley who was married to Sarah Bottomsley of Bottomsley plantation seemed visibly shaken as he was handcuffed and led away from the courtroom.*

Sarah Bottomsley turned as white as a sheet. She dropped the newspaper onto the chair and went to her room. She knew that Thomas Hurley was still alive, but she knew she couldn't tell it to anyone for fear they would think she was mad. Now she would never be able to show her face in public again. In her mind all she could think of was the humiliation, and that the man who had made visits to her room demanding money and her body was indeed Thomas Hurley. She wished she had said something to Alastair. He was a solicitor and would have been able to help her, but because of her grandchildren, she had kept silent.

Sarah never showed her face again that day in spite of everyones' efforts to discuss the shocking bit of news. They thought of calling in Doctor Sims but she said she was fine.

"I don't like it," said Alastair. "She is just too quiet."

"That seems to be her way of coping," said Emily as she turned off the bedside lamp.

---

"What is wrong with you woman?" asked Percy. "You like a setting hen. Can't say a word to you unless you start snapping!"

"I behaving like a setting hen?"

"Yes and if you keep carrying on like this, I'll just move into next bedroom and leave you in here by yourself."

Thomas Hurley's reappearance was getting to her. She didn't know what to make of the whole thing, but Nora was waiting for the perfect opportunity to speak to her sister.

---

"What do you think is happening at Bottomsley?" asked Nellie.

"I don't know. It must be especially hard on Sarah since she was married to him."

"She is stronger than she looks," said Nellie. "She will handle it."

The Bertrands too turned the lights off and settled in for the night."

A chair was missing from the dining room table. Mary looked around but it was nowhere in sight, so she continued to set the table for breakfast. Soon Alastair came out followed by his wife and then Grandpa Bottomsley.

"Will you take Douglas to school this morning?" she asked her husband.

"I can drop him off on the way. Have you something planned for this morning?"

"After I take John to school, Grandpa and I are going around to the house. The workmen should be finished and the plumbers and electricians promised to be there today. But before I go, I must talk to Mother. She is just too quiet."

"Where is my chair Mary?" Alastair asked.

"I thought you had it in the bedroom sir."

"Did you take it into your room Grandpa?"

"Haven't touched it Emily."

"Maybe Mother took it. But why? She's got a chair in her room."

"Maybe you should look in on her. She hasn't shown her face since yesterday morning," said Alastair.

Emily knocked on the door but there was no answer. She turned the door knob and looked in. It was pitch black because the curtains were still drawn.

"Mother?"

There was no answer. Emily moved towards the window and bumped into something. It was the dining room chair lying on the floor. She opened the curtains and found Sarah Bottomsley hanging, a rope around her neck. Her eyes were open and staring. Emily could not scream nor could she speak. She walked backwards to the door and stepped out closing it behind her.

"What did she say?" asked Alastair.

"Please call Nellie and take the children to her. Mary will pack a bag for them. I know Nellie will be happy to have them for a couple of days."

"Emily, what is the matter?" asked her husband.

Everyone, including the children was now staring at her. Alastair went to Sarah's room and opened the door.

"Oh my God!" was all he could say. "I'll take the children to Nellie. Call her and let her know we are on our way."

"No school today!" shouted Douglas. "We are going to see Miss Nellie and Uncle Francois."

"You wouldn't give Miss Nellie any trouble, will you?" asked their mother.

Old Bottomsley sat there while everything spun around him in circles. He seemed to know what the problem was. No sooner had Alastair left with the children, than he too opened Sarah's door and saw her body dangling from a rafter in the bedroom.

"It was just too much for her," he said. "The human soul can take only so much."

"Is there something we should do?" asked Emily.

"Call the constable. You must report it. I can't believe that Sarah took her own life,"said the old man.

Emily, who was now in her room speaking with her grandfather, had forgotten to mention it to Mary. The housekeeper walked through the house with a broom and dustcloth in hand. She opened Sarah's bedroom door and a piercing scream rocked the foundation of the home. Emily and her grandfather hurried out to see what was wrong.

"Grandpa please bring her a glass of water," said Emily.

She drank the water but still wasn't able to talk.

"It's alright Mary," she said to her housekeeper. "We just found her and we forgot to tell you."

"But she is dead," the woman finally said.

"Yes. We have called the police and they should be here soon."

"Alastair just told me the news," said Nellie. "Are you and Grandpa alright?"

"We're waiting for the police to show up."

"If you're not comfortable sleeping there, you and Mr. Bottomsley can stay with us until this is over."

"I think we'll go to Grandpa's house Nellie. That way the children won't suspect anything."

"Douglas is smart Emily. He knows more than you think he does."

"Why? What did he say?"

"He hasn't said anything, but children just have a way of figuring things out."

"We'll tell them that their grandmother died in her sleep. Where is Alastair?"

"He's on his way back."

"Thank you Nellie. I don't know what we would've done without you."

"Does Francois know?"

"No he has already left for the office."

The coroner arrived along with the vehicle from the morgue, and a body bag. Fifteen minutes later, the Police also showed up on the scene. After spending a little more than an hour in Sarah's room, the constable came out and told Emily that her mother had committed suicide. The body was taken down and driven away leaving the household in shock.

"I won't burden you with questions," said the constable. "I think I understand why she did what she did."

"Thank you sir."

"I will leave you now, but I'll be back to ask a few more questions."

Alastair and Emily walked with him to the door. Sarah's book which she had left on the chair the previous evening was still fluttering in the wind. It almost broke Emily's heart.

"It is very sad," said Alastair hugging her.

"I can't believe Mother is gone."

"This one's for you Sarah," said the old man with a shot glass of rum in his hand. "You weren't the best of daughters in law, but you weren't the worst."

"When you feel better, we will plan the funeral,"said Alastair.

"I think we should have a private funeral. Mother wouldn't want the world to know she went this way."

"You're right. A simple burial with just family and close friends! I'll go to see the Reverend and explain the circumstances to him."

About an hour later, Alastair returned from his visit to the Reverend. He seemed annoyed.

"What did the Reverend say?" asked Emily.

"Her body cannot be placed in the church."

"Why not?" asked a teary eyed Emily.

"He is willing to say a prayer at the graveside, but since she committed suicide, her body cannot be taken into the church."

Emily sobbed and sometimes she wailed. She couldn't believe that her mother, who had given so willingly and had been so generous to the church she had attended, would now be laid to rest without a proper burial.

"I hate them all," she shouted.

"Who do you hate?" asked her grandfather.

"All of those self righteous bastards," she screamed. "Sarah was in pain. That's why she killed herself. Now they are refusing to lay her to rest without a proper burial."

"Come, come," said the old man. "I'm going down there to talk to him. He can't do that to Sarah."

"Those are the laws of the church," said Alastair. "I don't think he is doing it out of spite."

"He can make an exception for Sarah. He has been sitting at the Bottomsley table eating and drinking almost every Sunday. What does he mean that he won't let her into the church? I'll have a few words with him," the old man said.

The good man could not be persuaded in spite of Old Bottomsley's threats. Now they called upon Nellie and Francois to find out if Reverend Willoughby would commit Sarah's body to the earth. He did not need a lot of persuading. Nellie's Christmas dinner and her generosity towards the church were still lodged in the uppermost cavity of his mind. Although he couldn't perform the ceremony inside the church, his words raised the family's spirits and proved to be a great consolation to them. Only the immediate family, Francois and Clytie were in attendance. Nellie had remained behind with her two grandchildren. No one believed a secret could be kept on the island, but Sarah's interment had remained a secret. They knew she had taken her own life, but there were absolutely no spectators on the day of the funeral. The hearse with the casket quietly made its way into the cemetery and Sarah was laid to rest beside John Bottomsley and Millie Bottomsley. The children were told that their grandmother had died in her sleep, but it didn't seem to affect them too much.

Alastair and Emily had made a decision. They were going to put Bottomsley Great House up for rent, but would keep the rum production going. They were going to move into Grandpa's refurbished home where there was enough room for the whole family. Emily could not open Sarah's bedroom door because she did not want to be reminded of the horrible way her mother ended her life.

They decided to leave Bottomsley in two months. The plumbing, electricity and the telephone were still to be installed. Her mother's untimely death had put a stop to the renovations.

"I know that was going to happen," said Ida after her niece returned home from the funeral. "She wasn't a nice woman. That didn't mean she had to kill herself, but the good book say that what a man sow, he will reap."

"She was selfish, but she wasn't a bad woman," said Clytie with tears streaming down her face.

"Ain't a thing we can do about it now. She take herself out of her misery."

"She was real shame Aunt Ida. After they put her name in the newspaper connecting her with that Thomas Hurley, she didn't see a way out. She was real hurt Aunt Ida."

"That don't mean she had to take her life."

"Well she is with Master Bottomsley now. I hope he let bygones be bygones and welcome her," said Clytie.

"They didn't get along good?" asked Ida.

"Not so good."

"I was wondering something. Why the daughter so close to Nellie? Even when the yellow hair woman pass 'way, the daughter send the children to Nellie. Nellie was just a housemaid and she and that child isn't the same age. Strange that they got such a friendship. Now if she did send the children to you Clytie, I would understand. I just don't understand why she send them to to Miss Nellie."

"But Aunt Ida, Ma was a lot older than Nellie and they was real good friends."

"It isn't the same thing."

Clytie decided it was time to change the subject because she knew Ida was treading on treacherous ground.

# 44

The Trial

The two weeks given by the judge to get everything in order had gone by. It was time for the trial to start again. What were the charges? A renewed charge of murder and impersonating another! The seats in the courtroom were all taken, and the mother and daughter sat next to each other. The jury, eleven whites and one black man entered and took their places. Then a handcuffed Thomas Hurley was led into the room. He looked healthy but one could see worry written all over his face. The last to enter the courtroom was the officiating judge.

"All rise," said the bailiff. "The case of people against Thomas Hurley is due to begin."

The Crown prosecutor Mr. Beaton and Thomas Hurley's solicitor Mr. Peacock were called to the bench and the judge spoke quietly to them. Thomas Hurley took this opportunity to look around the courtroom. His eyes scanned the room and returned to the two men huddled in front of the judge.

"He is making me nervous," said Nellie.

"And his re-appearance is responsible for Sarah's death," said Emily.

Several witnesses were called including Nora Trotman and Percy Trotman who testified about what they knew about the murder of Ursy Smith. It was now Thomas Hurley's turn.

"The court calls Thomas Hurley back to the stand," said the bailiff.

"State your name for the court," said Christopher Peacock.

"Thomas Hurley."

"Mr. Hurley, did you on the night of the eleventh of September murder Ursuleith Smith?"

"No sir."

"Thank you. No more questions."

The prosecutor was surprised at the brief questioning, but he had made his list and it was certainly not going to be brief.

"Mr. Hurley, please tell the court when you arrived on this island."

"It was about seventeen years ago sir."

"And I take it you were one of those people who came here because you heard that the island offered a great lifestyle for someone who was educated."

"You can say that sir."

"I understand that you worked for the owner of Bottomsley plantatation and upon his death married his widow and moved in, shall I say, as Lord of the Manor?"

"If you put it that way, I must say yes."

"And did you have a happy marriage with the Lady of the manor?"

"Like all marriages, it had its ups and downs."

"Please tell the court what happened on the night you supposedly disappeared."

"I cannot remember the details sir."

Nellie stiffened in her seat.

"Tell the court what you can remember."

"We, that is my wife and I had an argument. I left the house and started driving. On the way I bought a bottle of rum and just kept driving."

"What was the argument about?"

"I don't remember."

"Where did you go?"

"I drove in the direction of St. Lucy until I found myself on a cliff overlooking the ocean. I opened the bottle of rum and I remember that I sat there drinking straight from the bottle staring out into ocean."

"How long were you there?"

"I don't remember sir."

"What happened after that Mr. Hurley?"

"I don't know. I must've consumed the entire bottle. I do remember thinking I had to relieve myself and so I got out of the car. I must've fallen over the cliff. I don't remember anything else until I showed up on the Appleby's doorstep."

Nellie sighed. She looked around and saw her husband standing at the back of the room. She was happy to see him there. Although he wasn't sitting next to her, his presence meant a lot. Their eyes met and he smiled.

"That's where you met the young woman Jennifer Appleby."

"Yes sir."

"Mr. Hurley, did you know you were still on the island of Barbados?"

"I thought I was."

"Were you suffering from amnesia sir? Did you know then that your name was Thomas Hurley?"

"Yes I knew who I was."

"You knew you were still on the island of Barbados. You were not suffering from amnesia. So please explain to the court why you didn't contact your wife. After all she thought you were dead. I think it would've been the decent thing to do to relieve her of her suffering."

Thomas Hurley put his head onto his arms. He then looked up and continued to speak.

"I do understand your point sir, but I have no explanation for what happened. I didn't know how long I was in the water and I had a horrid gash on my forehead. I guess I should've called later to say I was still alive."

"You still had an opportunity to contact your family. Days went into weeks and weeks into months, years, and yet you didn't let them know you were still alive. Instead you took on a new identity. Why Mr. Hurley?"

"Our marriage was not a happy one sir. I had no say at all in the matters of the plantation. I felt like a second class person living on that estate. Besides that sir, my wife had nothing. Everything belonged to her daughter. I guess I should've called. I just don't know," he said on the verge of tears.

"So did you set out to punish your wife?"

"I wouldn't say that sir."

"What else would you call it? Charades Mr. Hurley?"

He did not reply.

"Did the young woman Miss Appleby know that Brandon Harvey and Thomas Hurley were one and the same?" Mr. Beaton asked.

"No. I never told her."

"Yet you sent her to Bottomsley plantation to apply for a job in the household? Why Mr. Hurley? Why?"

"My Lord, he's badgering the witness," shouted Mr. Peacock.

Thomas Hurley was now quietly sobbing. It had become too much for him especially since he had found out that morning that Sarah Bottomsley had committed suicide. The judge adjourned the case until the following morning, giving Mr. Hurley time to pull himself together.

"I told you that you had nothing to worry about," said Francois.

"What would've happened if he had remembered what happened that night?"

"Perhaps he did remember, but he couldn't tell the Prosecutor what he had been up to. Maybe he is trying to keep his prison sentence down."

# 45

"Mr. Hurley, you are still under oath," said Mr. Beaton. "Please tell the court where you were on the night of September eleventh last year."

"I was at home."

"Did you see Jennifer Appleby that night?"

"Yes sir."

There was a bit of a commotion because Nora had already testified that Jennifer had spent the night in St. Lucy with her children.

"I will repeat the question Mr. Hurley. Did you see Jennifer Appleby on the night that Ursuleith Smith was murdered?"

"Yes sir."

"Mr. Hurley, didn't Jennifer Appleby sever the relationship with you and take her children to St. Lucy to be away from your clutches?"

"My Lord, I object," shouted Christopher Peacock. "That is hearsay."

"I'll rephrase my question Mr. Hurley. After you moved from your communal home, did your relationship with Jennifer Appleby end?"

"No sir."

Again there was a commotion in the court.

"If this happens again," said the judge banging his gavel, "I will be forced to clear the courtroom."

"Please tell the court Mr. Hurley, did you see Jennifer Appleby on the night of the eleventh of September?"

"I had made arrangements to pick her up in St. Lucy and bring her back here to spend the night."

Nellie's mouth dropped open as if she were in shock.

"And did you pick Miss Appleby up in St. Lucy?"

"Yes sir."

"And did you go back to the home you had shared together?"

"No sir."

"Where did you go? You said you had had made arrangements to bring her back so you could spend the night together."

"We had a secret meeting place where we spent time together."

"Where was that?"

He hesitated for a moment and then he spoke.

"We used to meet at the vacant home of John Bottomsley Senior."

Emily gasped. The pieces were now falling into place.

"And what time did you arrive there?"

"It was just after eleven sir."

"And once there, you did what people in relationships do. And after that what happened Mr. Hurley?"

"I fell asleep sir."

"You fell asleep. Ladies and gentlemen, he fell asleep!"

"It is the truth sir."

"And did Miss Appleby fall asleep also?"

"I think she did."

"How far away is the home where you had your secret rendezvous from the home Miss Appleby shared with the deceased?"

"I would say ten miles."

"What time did you wake up the following morning?"

"I think it was just before five."

"When you woke up, was Miss Appleby there?"

"Yes sir."

"That means neither of you left the house that night."

"I didn't!" said Thomas Hurley.

"Are you trying to tell the court that Jennifer Appleby left the home after you fell asleep?"

"That's possible."

"Please tell the court how this woman could walk ten miles to Miss Smith's home, murder her and walk another ten miles back and slip into bed beside you."

"Maybe she didn't walk sir."

"What do you mean?"

"Maybe she drove. Her father taught her to drive but she never did have a driver's licence."

"Have you ever seen her driving?"

"Yes sir. Sometimes when we were out in the country, I allowed her to drive my car."

"Did you notice anything strange about her the following morning?"

"No sir, Miss Appleby was a very complicated young woman. It was difficult sometimes to understand her. She had suffered at the hands of her father and had developed a very tough exterior."

"Suffered at the hands of her father?"

"Yes sir."

"She was an adult. What could he do to her?"

Nellie and Emily exchanged glances. The can of worms was about to be opened.

"Well sir, he wasn't very nice to her."

"Did he beat her? Did he treat her badly? What did he do?"

"He slept with her."

The court was once again buzzing. Even the judge seemed shocked by the last bit of evidence."

"Are you saying he had an incestuous relationship with his daughter?"

"Yes sir and fathered her two children."

It was too much to absorb all at once, so the judge again adjourned the case until the following morning. The people in courtroom left in silence. They had never heard anything like it before. It was exciting news, for there was never too much going on on the Rock.

# 46

"Mr. Hurley, I must remind you that you are still under oath."

"Yes sir."

"You told the court that it was possible that Miss Appleby drove your car to Miss Smith's house on that fateful Saturday night."

"Yes sir."

"Is there any reason why Miss Appleby would want to murder the woman who saved her from her daily beatings at your hands?"

"Objection My Lord," shouted the Mr. Peacock. "Again that is hearsay."

"Mr. Hurley, why did Miss Appleby move out of your home and move in with Miss Smith?"

"I didn't have an income and we used whatever money she had to live on."

"Would you say that was her reason for moving out of your communal residence?" asked the prosecutor.

"Just a part of it sir. Jennifer, I mean Miss Appleby was a very strong person and sometimes we did have disagreements. I guess she thought it wasn't good for her daughters to be confronted with that kind of behaviour, but I never laid a hand on her sir. She was quite complicated. She had masochistic tendencies especially when we were in bed together. That's what the children probably heard and thought I was beating their mother."

"Are you telling the court that Miss Appleby begged to be beaten?" asked Mr. Beaton.

"Not in so many words, but I knew her well and knew what she wanted."

Laughter came from the back of the court room.

"I'll ask you again Mr. Hurley. Why would Miss Appleby want to murder the very woman who befriended her?"

"Well Miss Smith found out something about Miss Appleby and that made her afraid."

"Which one of them was afraid Mr. Hurley? Miss Smith or Miss Appleby?"

"Miss Appleby sir."

"Is it a secret or would you like to tell the court what Miss Smith found out?"

Thomas Hurley paused for a moment, sipped a bit of water and replied.

"You see sir, we needed money. Her wages were not enough for all of us to live on, so we hatched a plot to extort money from someone."

"If I'm not mistaken Mr. Hurley, weren't you the one who encouraged Miss Appleby to apply for the position at Bottomsley?"

"Yes sir."

"Why?"

"Because they paid well and the Bottomsleys were known to be quite generous."

"But you said the wages at Bottomsley were not enough, so you turned to extortion."

At that moment, Francois and Nellie entered the courtroom and slipped into the last row.

"Whom did she try to extort money from Mr. Hurley?"

"From a Nellie Peterkin sir."

Shocked to hear her name, Nellie's knees became weak. She had no idea why her name was called, but she immediately expected the worst.

"Who is Nellie Peterkin?" asked the prosecutor.

"She worked at Bottomsley plantation but now lives in St. Lucy. She is no longer Peterkin. She got married but I don't know her new name."

"So when Miss Smith found out that Miss Appleby was extorting funds from Miss Peterkin, what did she do?"

"Nothing as far as I know."

"Are you telling the court that Miss Smith allowed Jennifer Appleby to continue extorting money from one of the island's citizens and did nothing about it?"

"Yes sir."

"If she did nothing about it, does that mean Miss Smith was also receiving some of the money from Miss Appleby?"

"I don't believe so sir. I believe Miss Smith had her eyes on Miss Appleby. Miss Smith preferred womens' company to mens' and encouraged Miss Appleby to move into her home. Shortly after that, they became lovers."

Onlookers glanced at each other.

"And where did you get your information Mr. Hurley?"

"From Miss Appleby sir.

"And where were her children?"

"They had been sent off to London sir."

This time Nellie and Francois turned to stare at each other.

"So Miss Appleby was free to carry on her relationship with her lover, and because of her allegiance to her lover, Miss Smith remained silent. The silence which in the end would cost her her life!"

"You can say that sir."

As if rehearsed, one loud gasp from the onlookers echoed through the walls of the courtroom. Francois and Nellie again turned to look at each other. They couldn't believe what they had just heard.

"And you were the jilted lover, so you killed Miss Smith."

"I didn't kill her. Miss Smith found out that Miss Appleby and I were still seeing each other and she became quite jealous. She had even threatened to throw Jennifer out of her home. Miss Appleby was afraid Miss Smith would go to the police with the extortion information and so she had to get her out of the way."

Another gasp! Even the judge was speechless.

"Mr. Hurley, where is Miss Appleby?"

"I don't know sir. When I was released I tried to find her, but found out she had left for England."

"You are under oath sir. Please tell the court where Miss Appleby is."

"In England I suppose. I don't really know sir."

"So the monster you created, who tricked everyone else, in the end also tricked you?"

"It looks that way sir."

"One more question Mr. Hurley. Did you happen to know the name of the perfume Miss Appleby used from time to time?"

"Yes sir. Last year I gave her a bottle of 'Lady of the Night' for her birthday."

"That was the same scent a witness identified, as the car drove by that fateful night when Miss Smith was murdered My Lord. One more thing Mr. Hurley," said the prosecutor pulling two pieces of paper from a folder. "Do you recognize the handwriting on these notes?"

"Yes sir."

"Whose handwriting is it?"

"It looks like my wife's sir."

"When you say my wife, are you referring to Sarah Bottomsley?"

"Yes sir."

"Please tell the court why Sarah Bottomsley would want to blackmail Nellie Peterkin."

"I don't know sir."

"Alright then. Please tell the court why Mrs. Bottomsley would write a note like this. *Mr. Alastair likes his eggs over easy etc. etc. The sanitary inspector come by the last Thursday of every month to spray the cesspools.* You lived in the Bottomsley household for quite a few years. Was Mrs. Bottomsley an educated woman?"

"Yes sir."

"So are you trying to tell me she wrote this note with so many grammatical errors? Wasn't it the servant's job to do the ordering of foodstuff and looking out for the sanitary inspector?"

"Yes sir."

"Didn't Miss Appleby practise day in and day out to emulate Sarah Bottomsley's handwriting? A woman who never once harmed her! Didn't the two of you set out to put the blame of extortion on Mrs. Bottomsley? You sent Miss Appleby to apply for the job at Bottomsley plantation so that she could spy on Sarah Bottomsley for you and draw her unsuspectingly into this drama you both created? Answer me!" shouted Mr. Beaton.

"Yes sir."

"And you both drove an innocent woman to her death. Isn't that right Mr. Hurley?"

"It looks that way sir."

"Thank you. No more questions My Lord!"

"The court is adjourned until Monday the fifth. I must remind the jury that nothing heard or said in this court is to be discussed among each other, nor with anyone else," said the judge banging his gavel. "I want to see you Mr. Beaton and Mr. Peacock in my chambers."

As Thomas Hurley was being led from the court room, his eyes fell upon Nellie and he stared at her until he was hustled out by the two guards. Did he recognize her or was his stare a way of saying to her...... I saved you from the same fate.

---

"I can't believe what I just heard," said Nellie.

"Jennifer Appleby! She seemed so innocent."

"Of all the people on this island, why did she choose to blackmail me?"

"I still think Hurley had something to do with it. He was probably the one who chose to blackmail you," said Francois.

"Why?"

"That we will never know for sure, but I think it was revenge."

"For trying to kill him? It was an accident."

"Somehow he had his suspicions about Emily and since you had money, you were the easiest target."

"I still don't understand why he didn't tell the court about the night he was in my home."

"Don't you realise that he placed the blame on Jennifer for everything? He couldn't blame her for entering into your home and trying to drive you insane. He didn't know her back then. Not that I don't think she was fully responsible for some of the things, but I'm sure they both planned everything down to the last detail."

"And Ursy never breathed a word about her blackmailing me. Why?"

"She chose love over allegiance," said Francois.

"I never knew that she liked women," said Nellie. "But then again, I have never heard Clytie talk about her and any man."

"Goes to show Nellie. You must be careful where you put your trust."

"Well I can breathe easier now. That part of my life is over," said Nellie. "Her silence seems to have cost her her life."

"By the way, the Constable said he would like to come by sometime early next week."

"What does he want?"

"Hurley's troubles aren't over yet. There is still extortion and this impersonating business. He said he also wanted to speak with Nora since she was the last person who had contact with Jennifer Appleby."

---

Emily and Mary Sealy were busy packing boxes. The family was moving into the Old Bottomsley home. A car drove up and a door slammed.

"Alastair is back," said Emily walking quickly to the verandah.

A sophisticated looking blonde woman had started to climb the steps.

"Good morning," said Emily.

"Good morning."

"May I help you?" Emily asked.

"Don't you recognize me?" she asked.

"I'm sorry, but I don't."

"I'm Ginger Hurley-Strathmore."

"Ginger? Thomas Hurley's sister?"

"Yes."

"What can I do for you?" asked Emily remembering how much she had destested the woman.

"I came by to offer my condolences. I heard about Sarah only last week."

"Thank you."

"I know you must hate me and I don't blame you, but I did like your mother."

"Then why did you and your brother treat her the way you did?"

"We had to take charge. Sarah was weak and the household staff stole everything from right under her nose."

"Don't lie to me Ginger. Clytie and Ursy would never have taken anything from this household."

"You were too young to remember. Your father had just died and you were heartbroken."

"And you and your brother connived to send a heartbroken and lonely child off to England alone?"

"You don't understand."

"Yes I do understand. Your brother is now reaping all the bad seed he had sown. I hope he spends the next hundred years in Glendairy prison."

"You don't mean that."

"Yes I do and one more thing Ginger, I thought I should tell you. My mother is alive and well."

The woman stared at Emily as if she had seen a ghost.

*My God, Emily is completely out of her mind, thought Ginger as she hurried down the steps.*

Mary Sealy stared at Emily. She thought that whatever her employer had said to the woman had scared her out of her wits.

"Why you looking at me so Mary?" Emily asked lapsing into Barbadian dialect. "I ain't crazy. I give that old thief something to think about. She probably think I heading for the mad house."

"You could never end up in the mad house Miss Chambers," said Mary laughing.

"I like it when you talk like that."

"You mean like a Bajan?"

"Yes ma'am."

"Mary I was born and raised in this briar patch."

# 47

After much haggling between the solicitors, and the inability to track Jennifer Appleby down, the case of Thomas Hurley came to an end. He sat in the prisoner's dock while the judge read the jury's decision. He was happy to see his sister there, for it gave him a bit of solace. He now looked like the old Thomas Hurley. Just a little older with thinning reddish orange hair. The charge of murder was dropped because circumstantial evidence pointed directly to Jennifer Appleby but he was charged as an accomplice to extortion. The crime of being an impostor was also dropped. However he was given a sentence of three years in Her Majesty's prison at Glendairy after such time he would be deported back to England. He seemed to breathe a sigh of relief for he had expected a stiffer jail sentence.

The local population was not happy. Perhaps he hadn't killed Ursy Smith, but he did have a hand in her untimely demise.

"If it was one of our men, he would be in Glendairy until the end of his days," said Nora.

"Look at the trouble he caused around here and only get three years in prison," Clytie replied.

"Remember what Miss Una used to say. If you white, you alright, but if you black, you have to stand back."

"She said a mouthful," said Ida.

"When I hear he was still living, I nearly went mental," said Nora. "The only person that ever come back from the dead was Lazarus."

"Amen to that," said Ida.

"Now I hope we can get some peace around here," Nora replied.

"It is real sad to see Emily move out of that house though," said Clytie. "After all it is her birthright."

"She isn't selling it. She is only renting it out. Anyway nobody don't want no more big house these days. Take too much money to keep them running," said Nora.

"Now that Sarah gone, she don't have to fuss with nobody. She doing what she want to do," said Clytie. "I wonder what Nels got to say about it."

"What can she say?" asked Ida. "It is hers to do with as she please. A young girl like her shouldn't have so many problems. If it ain't one thing, it is another."

"The Good Lord is going to make her way easy," said Nora.

"I don't know about that," said Clytie. "She isn't too pleased with the church no more. After they refuse to let them bring Sarah casket in the church, she say she is finished with all the self-righteous people of the world."

"She will find her way back to God," said Ida. "She got to. Anyway when is she coming by again? I want to see the old man Bottomsley."

"Why?" asked Nora.

"Because I want to talk to him. We don't have a lot of time left on this earth so we got to make the most of it."

"I didn't know you and Old Bottomsley was friends," said Nora.

"Child you can't know everything."

"Aunt Ida, they are real busy right now. They are moving to the Old Bottomsley house this weekend."

"We could go by and lend a hand. After all she is like family."

Sarah's death was hard on the old man. She was his drinking buddy and his companion during the day. Since she died, Emily found that her grandfather was sleeping more and more and was becoming even more forgetful. He tried to be his jolly old self, but it took too much effort. He hardly drank anymore and even the news that they were all moving to the house he had shared with Millie, didn't raise his spirits. It was now a chore to play with his great grandchildren. He was now settled back into his old bedroom and at night Emily could hear him talking to himself.

"Who are you talking to?" she asked one night.

"It's Millie. She is still as stubborn as she ever was."

Emily and Alastair looked at each other. It didn't look good. Maybe she was slowly losing her Grandpa. She decided to stop everything and take him up to the country for a visit. She left the children with Alastair and she and her Grandfather took a Saturday drive into the country. Needless to say, Ida was happy to see him. They sat on the porch and they talked and talked.

"My days are coming to an end Ida."

"You talking nonsense Bottomsley."

"We all have to go sometime, and Millie is lonely and wants me to come home."

"Lord have mercy," said Ida. "Millie can't call you home. Only God can do that."

"The bones are old and tired," he said. "Ida I just lost my sister."

"What sister?"

"I just lost Sarah."

"She wasn't your sister. She was your daughter in law."

"I could've sworn she was my sister. Anyway she took her own life Ida. What a shock it was to see her hanging there. I hope she and my friend Millie are getting along now because they didn't get along before."

Ida realized there were moments when he remembered the past and moments when he got everything confused.

"Clytie, I think I'm losing Grandpa," said Emily. "Just after Sarah's death, Grandpa seems to be going also."

"No Miss Emily. Mr. Bottomsley is strong. He isn't ready to go yet."

"He has become very forgetful and he seems to have no enthusiasm at all for life."

"That happens to everybody Miss Emily. You going to see Nellie?"

"Yes, she is expecting me. I should be going."

"Did Alastair tell you about our little chat?" asked Francois.

"Yes he did and I'm still thinking about it. The problem is that Grandpa isn't doing very well. I think Sarah's death has really taken the wind out of his sails. If she had been ill, it wouldn't be too bad, but the way she did it, has really cast a shadow on the family."

"He's asleep on the verandah," said Nellie.

"That's all he does now. I don't think he will be with us for too much longer."

"Death is a terrible thing," said Francois, "but it is something we have no control over."

"I know," she replied sadly.

Three weeks after his visit to Nellie, John Bottomsley Senior
passed away. Although she had expected it, Emily was grief-stricken
nonetheless. Douglas couldn't understand why his Grandma and
his Grandpa had to leave. He was at the age where he hadn't yet
understood death.

A quiet service with the Reverend Willoughby officiating at
the graveside was the final farewell for a man who had left England
and promised never to return. His wish had been granted. Emily
had requested the services of Reverend Willoughby since she
wanted nothing to do with the parish priest who lived close to
Bottomsley plantation. He hadn't allowed Sarah's body to be
brought into the church, so Emily promised she would never set
foot in the church and she didn't. When they would overnight in
St. Lucy, as they did from time to time, she and the family would
all go to the church that Nellie attended. The good Reverend had
lost a generous parishioner.

The Chambers had settled into her grandfather's home and
everything was going according to plan. The children were snug
in their beds and Alastair and Emily sat outside on the verandah
looking at the moon and listening to the BBC news. When the
news was over she spoke to her husband.

"Grandpa and I had a little chat a couple months before he
died. He said I should let the boys know about their background.
He reminded me of the shock and horror I went through when
Douglas was born and if I allowed the same thing to happen to
them, they may never forgive me."

"I think he was right. Keeping a secret like that can only lead
to one thing and that is hurt."

"Then do you think I should tell them."

"We should tell them," he said.

"When do we do that and what do you think will happen?"

"Douglas loves Nellie and Francois. John is a bit young but he loves them too. We shouldn't second guess our children."

"You're right."

"Francois told me he spoke to you about taking his place in the firm."

"Yes but back then I couldn't leave Grandpa alone."

"Does that mean you are considering it?"

"Yes. John is in school and one of us can leave at the end of the day to pick them up."

"Chambers and Chambers! That sounds good."

"I can't believe that Francois is giving it all up. He says he wants to spend more time with my mother?"

"What did you say?" asked Alastair.

"I said......"

"I heard what you said. That will make Nellie very happy."

The following morning at the breakfast table, Emily and Alastair spoke to the children regarding Nellie and Francois.

"Is it because our other Grandma died?" asked Douglas.

"No, it's because she is really your grandmother. You see Douglas, Nellie is my mother."

"She is?" asked the child with surprise all over his face. "Anyway I like her better than Grandma Sarah. She is nice to John and to me. Grandma Sarah didn't like children."

"That's not true Douglas. She showed her love in a different way."

"She always ran away from John and he is only a little boy."

"Do you remember when you lived with Grandma Nellie?"

"No," Douglas answered.

"You lived with her for almost a year."

"Why? Didn't you want me?"

"No Douglas, it was nothing like that. When you were born, Grandma Sarah …

"I'll explain it to him,"said his father.

After Alastair had explained it all, both parents waited with bated breath for his reply.

"I knew she didn't like me," said Douglas. "She threw me out when I was a little baby. But why didn't you come to get me?"

"Your father was away on business and I was alone. I had no one to turn to and no idea what I should do."

"Didn't you look for me?"

"Yes but I couldn't find you until one day I spoke to Miss Una, Clytie's mother. Do you remember her?"

"Yes I do. She liked me too."

"She told me where I could find you."

"And is that when you brought me here to live?"

"Yes. Grandma Nellie was very sad when we took you away from her. She didn't want you to move back into the house with Grandma Sarah, but your father promised to protect you with his life."

"And what did Grandma Sarah do when I came back?"

"She tried to be nice, but she wasn't used to children."

"When can we visit Grandma Nellie and Grandpa Francois?" he asked.

"When would you like to visit them?"

"Can we go today?"

"Of course! Do you know why we have told you this story?"

"Yes, because like you, when I get married, I don't want anyone to send my babies away."

Emily looked at her husband and tears filled her eyes. He was far wiser than his years. That's the way she had brought him up.

# 48

"This is a surprise," said Nellie. "Why didn't you let us know you were coming? We would've prepared something special."

"Aren't you boys going to say hello?" Alastair asked.

"Hello Grandma, hello Grandpa," said Douglas.

John tried to do the same which made everyone laugh, everyone except Nellie.

"We thought it was time to tell them the truth," said Emily. "I didn't want the same thing that happened to me to happen to them."

Nellie shed lots of tears. Tears of joy and tears of relief. She had never expected that day to arrive when she would hear her grandchildren call her Grandma. And more tears were shed, when Emily called her Mother. Francois and Alastair watched the two women. Francois was happy for his wife and Alastair, great relief that everything had turned out so well.

"I can't find Otty," said Douglas.

"She is not working today, but you can knock on her door. She would be happy to see you."

The two children went in search of Otty and returned holding her hands. So happy was she that she decided to forget about her day off and make lunch for the family.

"Grandma said I could visit you in the kitchen. Do you have any apples for me?" asked Douglas.

"You mean Miss Nellie."

"No, her name is Grandma, not Miss Nellie," said the child. "She is my Mama's mother. Grandma Sarah wasn't really my grandmother."

Otty believed the child was confused until she heard Emily call Nellie Mother.

*It is true, she thought. Nellie is Miss Chamber's mother.*

"And another thing," said Emily, "we wanted to let you know that I will take you up on your offer to enter into partnership with Alastair."

"What a blessed day!" said Nellie.

"Now we can go on that trip to Paris," said Francois.

"Are we going to Paris?" asked Nellie.

"Most definitely!"

"But I have no clothes to wear. I'll have to get a new wardrobe for the trip."

"I'm sure your wardrobe is full of beautiful things," said Emily.

"I have nothing. Come and I'll show you."

The two women went to Nellie's bedroom. Nellie looked at her daughter and tears flowed again.

"I never thought this would ever happen," she said.

"I'm happy that it is all out in the open."

"There's something I should tell you Emily."

"What is it? Are you going to tell me you're really not my mother?"

Nellie laughed.

"Nothing of the sort. It has to do with Thomas Hurley."

"What about him?"

Nellie narrated the story about Thomas Hurley and how he had tried to blackmail her by entering her home and pretending to be John Bottomsley's ghost. She told her that Miss Una had been sceptical and told her to get a witness to the happenings.

"Nora decided to stay with me that night, and your father did come by. Do you remember the smell of his tobacco Emily?"

"Of course!"

"I could smell that beautiful aroma of his pipe tobacco and I tried to talk to him, but he never replied. Nora and I decided to go to bed when suddenly there was the smell again. Just a little stronger. He had never visited me twice in the same night. Suddenly he called out my name. I was frightened and so was Nora, but she had come to the house prepared. She had brought a stick with her. The voice started to question me, but Nora told me to be quiet. When we opened the door and came face to face with someone, Nora struck him with the stick. The intruder fell to floor and when we got the lamp and looked at the face, we realized it was Thomas Hurley. Frightened! Lord we were both very frightened! After wrapping him in a sheet, we carried him to the cliff and threw him over. That's when we saw that he had parked his car there too. It was one of the worst things that has ever happened to me."

"Have you told this to anyone else?"

"Only Francois. Nora said it was a secret we should take to our graves. If Hurley hadn't shown up, I would never have told you about it."

"I guess he got what he deserved. But it was a strange thing. That was the only thing he didn't seem to remember when he was giving testimony."

"Do you think he really didn't remember about that night?"

"I don't know. It's difficult to say."

"Did you notice the way he stared at me when he was being taken away?"

"I didn't notice," said Emily.

"But thinking back, there's one thing one thing I do remember. Back then, Clytie told me she thought Hurley was having an affair. When I asked her why, she said that he leaves the house around six o'clock two or three evenings during the week and never made it back until late. She thought the woman was married because he had never slept out. He and his sister Ginger were always laughing about something the next morning. Little did I know they were laughing because of the trick they were playing on me."

"I forgot to tell you she showed up at Bottomsley."

"Ginger?"

"What did she want?"

"To tell me how sorry she was about Sarah. Anyway what I told her scared her out of her wits and I haven't seen her again."

"Are you still looking through the wardrobe?" asked Francois sticking his head inside the door.

"Yes and I was right. She does have enough clothes for Paris," said Emily with a wink.

———

"Clytie, I couldn't believe it."

"Me neither Nels, but I am real glad for you."

"You tell Nora yet?"

"No, but I know she will be happy."

"The two of you always whispering," said Ida.

"Aunt Ida, we are friends and friends always whisper to one another."

"You can tell her," said Nellie, as she started out for Nora's home.

"Well Aunt Ida, you should sit down because I have some real good news for you."

"What you have to tell me?"

"Lord I wish Ma was here for this."

"She isn't here Clytie, so tell me what the good news is."

"You know that Nellie has a daughter?"

"Well I don't know for sure, but it could only be that Miss Emily."

"Why you say that?"

"Because I see how they look at one another. I know that something wasn't quite right, but I never thought that they was mother and daughter. That mean that Nellie and Old Bottomsley son............. Oh!" said the old woman. "What a thing that is."

"It wasn't easy Aunt Ida. There was a lot of crying and a lot o' pain. Lord how I remember those awful days."

"When you look at Nellie and then that young woman, you could see the resemblance in the faces."

"Hallelujah," said Clytie. "At last the truth come to light."

"But Clytie, tell me something," said Ida, "when ................"

They were interrupted by a couple of customers who had walked into the shop.

"We can talk later."

"Nora, what did you do with the money Jennifer Appleby gave to you?"

"Well hidden dear sister."

"Well get it out because you will be using it."

"On what?"

"We're going to Paris. You, me, Francois and Percy."

"Paris? Me? Percy? How this come about?"

"Girl it is time to celebrate."

"What we celebrating Nellie?"

"Emily told the children that I am their grandmother and that I am also her mother."

"Say that again Nellie."

"You heard me. It is true."

Nora sat down and cried and cried.

"All these years it was such a struggle and now everything is alright. Yes Lord, everything is alright."

"Are you happy for me?"

"Of course Nellie. You was the only family I had and the only person in this world I could count on."

"And I could always count on you too."

"Francois got o' lot o' vacation time," said Nora.

"He decided to give up the business and Emily is taking his place in the firm. My daughter will be taking my husband's place," she said proudly.

"I thank you Lord," shouted Nora. "It is about time."

Percy walked in with his fishing rod and his afternoon catch.

"Percy we going to Paris."

"How we getting there Nora? We swimming?"

"We are going to Paris with Nellie and Francois."

"Hello sister in law," said Percy. "You tell Nora we going to Paris?"

"Yes we are Percy. Anyway I must be getting back home. I promised Otty that I would help her hang the new curtains. You can tell Percy the rest of the news."

"What news?" asked Percy as he watched Nellie disappear from sight.

"Sit down Percy. I never tell you any of this, but today you will hear everything."

Percy was a little concerned because Nora hardly ever kept anything from him.

"You remember when we lived in the tenement at Bottomsley?"

"How could I forget?"

"Well that was when Emily was born. News went around the village that Nellie's little baby Emily had died. That wasn't true."
"What?" shouted Percy.

"Nellie's baby and Sarah Bottomsley's baby were born around the same time. You know Sarah couldn't bring one living child into this world."

"What you trying to tell me Nora?"

"Well Sarah baby was born dead and Bottomsley take away Nellie's baby and give it to Sarah. Emily come along thinking she was white until the day Douglas was born."

"Yes Douglas. I had always found that real strange," said Percy. "I always wondered where Nellie got that baby, but you know I don't ask anybody about their business. But why Emily give away that child?"

"She didn't give it away. Sarah throw that baby off the plantation the minute it was born. You see Percy, he didn't look like he look today. He didn't have blonde hair and blue eyes. He looked like a red skin black child."

"Lord have mercy!" said Percy.

"You mean that didn't make any difference to that Sarah? It was only a poor little child."

"That woman was selfish and she thought the people here on

this Rock would look down on her if her daughter had a black child."

"So where was the father when all this was going on?"

"He was out of the island with Francois."

"So what is the good news now?" asked Percy.

"Well it is all now in the open. Emily tell her children that Nellie is her mother and also their grandmother."

"How they take it?"

"That little boy Douglas is real smart. Know what he say Percy? He tell his mother that he know Sarah didn't like him nor his brother. He tell her that he know that Grandma Nellie and Grandpa Francois love them."

"All o' this went on and I didn't know a thing. You hide that from me for more than thirty years."

"That isn't all Percy. I got something else to tell you."

"You better see Reverend Willoughby if you got all this confessing to do."

"Stop it Percy. This is serious business."

"I'm listening," he said as he puffed on his pipe.

"It got to do with Thomas Hurley. He was blackmailing Nellie. You know that already, but you don't know how he was doing it. He was pretending to be John Bottomsley and would come to Nellie house at night smoking a pipe and asking a lot o' questions."

"But John Bottomsley was dead."

"He was pretending to be John Bottomsley ghost."

Percy put his pipe down and concentrated on what his wife was saying.

"John Bottomsley really used to visit Nellie, but he just used to smoke his pipe. We think that Nellie tell that to Clytie when she was still working at Bottomsley and Hurley overhear it.

He wasn't sure about the relationship between Nellie and John Bottomsley and decide he had to find out, so he pretend he was John Bottomsley ghost. Nellie tell Miss Una that she and John Bottomsley used to talk at night, but Miss Una didn't believe a word, so she say I should sleep by Nellie to see if it was true. Sure enough John Bottomsley come by smoking but never say a word. About one hour later, he come back, but this time he was talking. When we open the bedroom door, somebody was standing at the door and I hit him with a stick. We thought he was dead, so we wrap him up in a sheet and throw him over the cliff."

"That was when Hurley disappear?"

"Yes and Nellie and me decide to keep it a secret till the day we die."

"So why you telling me now?" asked her husband. "A secret is a secret."

"Because Hurley show up again. He wasn't really dead."

"Well I think we should forget about it and don't mention it again."

"Glad you understand Percy. Toby don't know nothing about Nellie and Emily," said Nora.

"He will find out soon enough," said his father.

"Seeing that is out of the way what we doing now about Paris?"asked Nora.

"If my dear friend Francois say I should go, then I am going with him."

"Don't forget I am paying for the ticket Percy."

"Half o' that money belong to me Nora," he said smiling and picking up his pipe.

# 49

The latest bit of gossip was not in the newspaper, but it found its way on the tongues of the gossipmongers throughout the island. It didn't matter to the Chambers or the Bertrand family. They were happy to be united and happy that they no longer had to keep things a secret.

Judes decided to get a divorce. She had no intention of returning to England because she wanted to marry Jonas. In him she had found a great father and provider.

"We should put Bottomsley great house up for sale and advertise it in a British newspaper," said Emily.

"That's very sensible. It has been on the market for over three months and no one wants to rent it. It is either too expensive or people are superstitious because Sarah hanged herself in there."

After advertising for a month and half in a London newspaper, a buyer was found for the property. He however wanted the whole plantation. Land, factory and rum production. They were going to make a very handsome profit. There was one stipulation before the deal was signed. Alastair wanted Clyde to be kept on as overseer and the field hands employed for at least one year to give them a chance to find other employment. And so Bottomsley would be no more although most people still referred to it as Bottomsley plantation.

The sign outside the Solicitor firm now read 'Chambers & Chambers.' Francois had sold his share of the company he had founded more than thirty years earlier to Emily Chambers. He was still called upon in times of need but most of his time was spent with Nellie.

"Nellie," he whispered one day, "I've got something for you."

"I know. The tickets to Paris!"

"Even better," he replied.

"What is it?"

"Come Long John," he said to the puppy. "Come and meet your new mother."

He had found a little terrier which looked exactly like Long John. The little dog wagged its tail and jumped all over Nellie.

"I don't want to call him Long John," said Nellie.

"But I thought you liked the name," said her husband.

"I don't want him to go the same way Long John went."

"What should we call him then?"

"We'll call him Max. I like that name," she said.

"Then that's what we will call him."

"Max, Douglas and John will be happy to see you," she said.


"Are you excited Nellie or should I say Mother?"

"You can do it at your own pace Emily. It doesn't matter. You know I'm your mother and I'm proud to call you my daughter."

"Are your bags packed?"

"Oh yes. Paris, Nellie is on the way to see you again! Nora is so excited that she keeps packing and unpacking while Percy just sits there smoking his pipe and watching her."

BENEATH THE FLOWERING FLAMBOYANTS

"I wish we could go also, but that's not possible right now."

"Are you coming to the airbase on Sunday morning to say goodbye?"

"Of course. We can't let you and Francois leave like that."

"Don't forget that Otty has the keys to the Vacation house in St. Lucia. You can go there and take the grandchildren for a little change of scenery."

"We'll see," said Emily.


A call was made to Clytie and Ida. They were very excited but said they were going to miss them.

"Six weeks is a long time," said Clytie close to tears. "Bring that nice perfume for me. I don't have too much left in the bottle."

"Clytie, after all these years you still have some of that perfume left?"

"I only use it on special occasions," she said. "Christmas, funerals and things like that."

"How is Miss Ida?"

"All she is talking about is how Francois bring her back here in a plane, and she wants to know if it is the same plane you are leaving on today."

The two women talked and laughed a little more until Francois told his wife it was time to go.

"Well Otty, this is it. Take good care of Max and you can take the grandchildren for a weekend, but you've got to let Emily know ahead of time. When they come up, you can sleep in the extra bedroom. Keep the doors locked and if anything should happen, call Emily and Alastair right away."

"Nellie, this is the third time you've given Otty those instructions. Come on. Let's go. The taxi is waiting and we've still got to pick up Nora and Percy."

"Goodbye Mr. Bertrand. Have a good trip."

"Thank you Otty," he said, then turning around and winking at her. "What would you like from Paris?"

"Some of that nice smelling perfume sir," she said with a shy smile.

"I'll see what I can do."

"Have a good time Miss Bertrand," she said as she lifted up the little puppy.


Percy looked dapper. He was wearing a brown pin striped suit and a brown cloth cap with a peak and his wife was dressed in one of her daughter's creations.

"I look alright Nellie?"

"You look wonderful," her sister replied. "And Percy, you will fit in right there in Paris. Right?" she asked Francois.

"He already looks like a Parisian."

Emily, Alastair and the two children were already there when they arrived.

"You look beautiful Grandma," said Douglas.

"What about Grandpa?" Francois asked.

"You look beautiful too," he replied.

"How about handsome?" asked his father. "Men look handsome, women look beautiful."

"Hello Nora, hello Percy," said Emily. "Do you know my husband Alastair?"

"Pleased to make your acquaintance," said Percy puffing on his pipe and looking the part.

"Do you remember Nora?" Nellie asked the children. "This is your aunt Nora and her husband Percy."

"I remember her, but I don't know him," said Douglas.

It was time to go. A final announcement was made for all

passengers on the flight to Paris with a stop in London. Percy's knees grew weak. Getting on board an aircraft seemed very exciting but now that it was time to go on board, he wasn't sure, so he grabbed onto Nora's arm.

"You think it is safe to go up in that thing?" he asked.

"Come Percy. Play the part. Don't let nobody know you never been on a plane."

"We'll miss you mother," said Emily.

"Yes Grandma, we will miss you and Grandpa," said Douglas as he started to cry.

John too started to cry and soon tears were running down the faces of the parents.

"Take care of yourself and the children," said Nellie hugging her daughter.

"Say goodbye," said Emily as they all started to wave.

The Boeing 707 rolled down the runway and was soon out of sight.

"What a lovely lady that Nellie is!" said Alastair.

"That lady is my flesh and blood." said Emily. "My mother!"

# 50

A car stopped in front of the shop and Clytie saw her son and another man step out. A man she had never met.

"Ma, this is Mr. Wickham. He's the new headmaster of the school."

"Pleased to meet you Mr. Wickham," she said wiping her hands on her apron before shaking his.

"Mr. Wickham is new to the neighbourhood and I told him that you owned this grocery store. He has a list of things he would like to buy."

"Give it to me sir," said Clytie holding out her hand.

"Mrs. Prescott, you've got quite a young man here," he said.

"What you mean by that?" she asked.

"I'm just complimenting you on the good job you've done with him. You should be very proud."

"Thank you sir," she said grinning from ear to ear.

"We were having a discussion this morning about his future and I think he should go to Teachers' college."

"That's what my friend Nellie was saying to him for a real long time."

"Without that piece of paper, one never knows what will

happen in the future, especially since they are still bringing in teachers from the Mother country."

"Maybe you're right. I think he should go sir. You never know."

"Mr. Wickham," he said correcting her.

"Yes Mr. Wickham, I will see to it that my son get only the best."

"Well I must be going," said the headmaster shaking Clytie's hand again.

"Thank you sir."

"Mr. Wickham. Remember?"

He collected the items which Clytie had placed on the counter, paid her and she watched as they descended the steps and spoke for a little while before Mr. Wickham got into his car and drove off.

"What do you think Ma?" asked Jonas returning to the shop.

"Well you now have a baby to support, so you have to look out for yourself and that child."

"What about Judes Ma?"

"What about Judes?"

"I would like to marry her Ma."

"She is a married woman son."

"I went to Bridgetown to talk to Toby. He said he wouldn't stand in my way if that is what Judes wanted. He is set up with someone else and really doesn't care."

"Who he set up with?" asked his prying mother.

"A woman who owns an establishment called "The Trixie club."

"I think I hear 'bout that club before. What kind of establishment it is?"

"You don't want to know Ma."

"Look I am a lot older than you. Nothing can't shock me son."

"Well when the sailors come in, she provides companionship for them."

"You mean she got a whorehouse?"

"I prefer to say a house of ill-repute, but since you put it that way Ma, I must say yes."

"Lord I wonder if Nora know?"

"I don't think so. Neither does Judes. I wouldn't tell them anything."

"Well if the way is clear, then you should marry Judes and give my grand daughter a name."

"You're the nicest mother," he said kissing her on the cheek. "And Ma I think Judes and I should get a home of our own."

"You get married first, then go to the Teachers' college and leave Judes where she is safe, with me and Ida. After college, we could talk 'bout a house for the family. After all it will only be me and Ida there. There is more than enough room for her and the baby."

"How long is this Teachers' College thing Jonas?"

"About three years and I understand that the pay is very meagre. It is a good thing I saved up what I made before."

"You make me real proud son," said Clytie.

"Ma you like Mr. Wickham?"

"He seem alright."

"He lives by himself in a big house by Austin corner and I think he is looking for a wife. I bring him by because he is a real nice man. His wife died about six years ago and like I told you, he bought that big house close to Austin corner and lives alone in it."

"Boy you trying to marry off your old mother?"

"I want you to be happy Ma. He just asked me if I thought you would go for a drive with him."

"Lord have mercy! My son trying to marry me off. Wait 'til Nellie come back and I tell her 'bout this."

"Miss Nellie would be happy for you Ma. And I would like Miss Nellie and Mr. Francois to be Abigail's godparents. Do you think she would like that Ma?"

"Abigail? What 'bout Clytie or Nellie?"

"Ma those names are real old fashioned. Judes like that name and we are still thinking of a second name for her."

"Well I can't really speak for Nellie and Francois, but I think they would be happy to be the godparents. You know Nellie think the world of you. Anyway, she going to be real proud that you going off to Teachers' college and that you are making a lady out of Judes."

"Who was that man with Jonas?" asked Ida coming out of the backroom of the shop.

"He is the new headmaster at Jonas school."

"Clytie, I think you soon going to be leaving us," she said.

"What you mean Aunt Ida?"

"I got this feeling that he was real interested in you. I was peeping from behind the door. He was looking at you with real sweet eyes and I hear what Jonas say."

"You just like Ma Aunt Ida. You don't miss a trick."

"Well now I know that you soon going to leave me by myself."

"I would never do that to you Aunt Ida. Wherever I go, I taking you with me."

"That mean you going somewhere Clytie?"

"No Aunt Ida. I can't see in the future."

"Well I see somebody coming along and making you a happy woman," said the old woman bursting into raucous laughter.

"How I look Aunt Ida," asked Clytie after she had changed her dress for the third time.

"You real nervous. You ain't got to make no fuss. This ain't the first time you going out with Wickham."

"I still want to look good."

"Trust me Clytie. You look good. He isn't going to find another woman 'round here who could fill your shoes."

"He like he real interested in me Aunt Ida."

"Well take your time. You too old to have children, so there ain't no rush."

"I can't wait for Nellie and the rest to come back. I getting real nervous."

"It ain't nervousness Clytie. It is what they call love. We used to say that taking your time ain't laziness and Clytie, I can say that you take your time and I am real happy for you. You wait and the good Lord send somebody who respect you and is good to you."

"You listening Ma?" asked Clytie looking upwards.

# ACKNOWLEDGEMENTS

Special thanks to the following persons for their support and assistance.

My husband Wolfgang Braun

Bruce Wallace

Kevin Goodridge

Leila Inniss

Virgil Broodhagen

My mother Gervaise Holder

Annette Holder and Lorna Holder

Marvyn Goodridge